The truth <u>will</u> kill...

"TAUT."
Seattle Times

"TRULY COMPELLING."
Deseret Morning News

"TERRIFYING."
Baltimore Sun

"TERRIFICALLY EXCITING."
Pittsburgh Post-Gazette

"TO DIE FOR."
The Oklahoman

"CHILLING . . . RIVETING."
Biloxi Sun Herald

"TIMELY AND SCARY."
Washington Times

P9-DNO-509

Resounding acclaim for
New York Times bestselling author
STEVE MARTINI and
GUARDIAN OF LIES

"The writer has shifted gears in a big way, moving his wry hero out of the courtroom and into the center of a breathless high-stakes thriller in the Lee Child vein. . . . [It] gets scarier with each page that is turned. . . . A wonderful protagonist, a terrifying villain, lots of unexpected humor, and an author who clearly knows how things work in the world of politics and law. . . . A thriller with broad implications and a very high entertainment quotient."

Connecticut Post

"Martini is a crafty pro."
Washington Post

"Steve Martini, the master of suspense thrillers, delivers an action-packed tale of murder and deceit. . . . A thrilling roller-coaster ride . . . Explosive! . . . Absolutely riveting. His characters are interesting, the story flows well from one situation to the next without confusing the reader, and you don't know how it all will end." *Wichita Falls Times Record News* (TX)

"Martini is an expert at good, old-fashioned, gimmick-free storytelling. . . . Paul Madriani has aged like a fine wine. He's a wary, battle-scarred hero with a decency that rings true. . . . A terrific series." Steve Berry

"*Guardian of Lies* [is] to die for. . . . It's action-packed fun." *The Oklahoman* (Oklahoma City)

By Steve Martini

STEVE MARTINI

GUARDIAN OF LIES

A PAUL MADRIANI NOVEL

HARPER

An Imprint of HarperCollinsPublishers

This book was originally published in hardcover and trade paperback July 2009 by William Morrow, an Imprint of HarperCollins Publishers.

This is a work of fiction. The events described are imaginary, and the characters are fictitious and not intended to represent specific living persons. Even when settings are referred to by their true names, the incidents that take place there are entirely fictitious.

HARPER

An Imprint of HarperCollins*Publishers*
10 East 53rd Street
New York, New York 10022-5299

Copyright © 2009 by Paul Madriani, Inc.
Excerpt from *The Rule of Nine* copyright © 2010 by Paul Madriani, Inc.
ISBN 978-0-06-123091-2

First Harper Premium printing: May 2010
First William Morrow trade paperback international printing: July 2009
First William Morrow hardcover printing: July 2009

HarperCollins® and Harper® are registered trademarks of Harper-Collins Publishers.

Printed in the United States of America

Visit Harper paperbacks on the World Wide Web at www.harpercollins.com

10 9 8 7 6 5 4 3 2 1

In wartime, truth is so precious that she should always be attended by a bodyguard of lies.

WINSTON CHURCHILL

ONE

To the drug lords of the Tijuana cartel, the man was an urban myth—and the cops were singing off the same page. According to the Mexican Federal Judicial Police, the assassin referred to in scattered press reports as the "Mexecutioner" did not exist.

To hear them tell it, the killer was a figment of the "button boys'" imaginations, the teenage hoodlums who fueled the violence in the rampaging narco zone near the border, where rumors of his five-figure contracts were threatening to raise the city's minimum wage for death.

It is true, these kids were illiterate and violent. They came from the barren Baja and the meager villages of Sinaloa, out of the mountains of Chihuahua, all looking for the same things: opportunity if they could get it, survival if they could not. They lived in banged-up sea containers and the tar paper barrios that dotted the hillsides around the city, and eked out an existence by offering their lethal services to the narco trade.

Get crosswise with this commerce and for a few

thousand pesos and your car's license number for identification, these kids would find you. They'd speed through the city on motorbikes with the silenced muzzle of a Mac-10 poking them in the ass down the back of their pants. They would twist the bike's throttle with one hand and use the other to blow your brains all over the inside of your nice new Lexus.

To these concrete cowboys, the Mexecutioner was not only real, they knew him by a different name for the soundless way he took his victims, and always at night. He was like the mountain of water rising from the darkness, washing his victim from a tranquil beach, a kind of unexpected, rough wave—*muerte líquida,* "liquid death."

The fact was, he liked it. It was a name that appealed to his dark sense of humor, so much so that at times he even used it on hotel registries—"M. Liquida," though always with discretion. He played variations on the theme when abroad. For travel in the U.S. he possessed a credit card in the name of J. Waters.

The house was located on a tree-lined lane in a neighborhood of large, expensive homes. Many of these could only properly be called estates. The one in question was the black swan of the area, run-down and in need of repair. Or so it looked. It sat back from the road, perhaps sixty yards, behind a wrought-iron gate. The house overlooked the Pacific Coast Highway and the town of Del Mar, California. It had an unobstructed view of the ocean in the distance, and in daylight you could see the beach, perhaps a mile away.

A seven-foot fence, made up of hundreds of black anodized metal stakes, each topped by a sharp spearlike finial, surrounded the entire property. This seemed out of place. It was too much fence and far too expensive for the dilapidated structure that sat behind it.

The only opening in the fence was the main gate out to the street. It was remotely controlled. He had seen the owner's car come and go. The gate automatically opened and closed behind him each time. There were no guards and no dogs and very few visitors. In fact, during all the hours he had watched the house, he had not seen one, only a few Federal Express and UPS delivery vans.

The fence itself was not electrified. There were none of the small yellow signs showing black bolts of electricity that warned people not to touch it. Only in America would you spend thousands of dollars installing an expensive electrical security system and then warn intruders not to harm themselves.

Liquida scurried along the ground just outside the fence, moving through the darkness, a vaporous, fleeting image that seemed not to leave a shadow.

A broken wooden balustrade across the back deck of the house leaned out, as if it was about to topple into the garden below. A shutter on one of the tall side windows hung askew. It seemed to dangle from a single hinge. Some of the wooden shingles were missing from the roof, and the exterior was in need of fresh paint.

He smiled at the ingenuity of it. Anyone cruising the neighborhood looking for a place to rob would certainly not pick this one. But the people who hired him had sent photographs, interior and exterior, close-ups, along with a diagram of the floor plan inside. Where they had gotten these he did not know, nor did he care, as long as they were accurate.

He slipped seamlessly through the line of bushes

outside the fence, careful not to make contact with any of the iron bars.

He checked the fence one last time for signs of contact sensors. He looked for the small gray plastic conduit that might contain wires. These could carry signals to the house and an alarm system. This was the third time he had checked the fence and the ground under it. By now he was certain there were no wires and no conduit to carry them.

The security system for the grounds relied entirely on the motion sensors deployed in the yard, nearer the house. He had discovered the location of two of these on his first visit ten days earlier. In the middle of the night, he threw several large clods of compacted dirt over the fence. Each time he waited to see what would happen. Finally, after several tosses, lights went on in the house. Ten minutes later a small sedan with a security company logo on the door showed up. They checked the yard but found nothing. The motion sensors had been adjusted to levels of low tolerance. A small bird landing near one of the sensors in the yard might not set it off. A crow flapping its wings and bouncing around on the ground probably would.

Over the next week he set about taking down the motion sensors. For this he used more than a dozen cats, strays he collected during the day from streets and alleys downtown. He transported them in cardboard boxes in the back of his car at night. He baited the cats with nip and then threw small weighted bags of catnip as far as he could toward the house. Then he released a cat through the fence.

Each time the lights in the house went on, followed a few minutes later by the arrival of the small white security sedan. When the guard saw the cat he laughed, turned, and headed back to the gate and his car. A minute or two later the lights in the house went out.

He did this for five nights running, each time in the wee hours, until finally one night the lights in the house did not go on. And security never showed up. The motion sensors had been turned off, at least until they could be adjusted for bigger game. It was a funny thing about human nature; it almost always operated to the detriment of the flawed creatures possessing it.

Three nights earlier, working from the back side of the fence and using gloved hands, he propped a large leaf from a magnolia tree in front of the lens of the single security camera that covered this side of the house. He carefully wedged the leaf into the hinged camera mounting so that it looked as if gravity or the wind might have stuck it there.

After three days, the fact that no one had removed it told him what he needed to know. There was no active monitoring of the cameras. The system was probably a continuous feed, analog or digital, it didn't matter. It would be reviewed only if there was an incident, at which time all they would see was a close-up of a leaf.

TWO

The upstairs study was a large room with a vaulted ceiling and heavy beams, two stories high. An antique iron spiral staircase led to the catwalk on the second level. Dark wood paneling and custom wood cabinets with little drawers lined the walls on both levels. Each drawer was locked and labeled with a neat printed card slipped into a brass holder and listing the contents. There were hundreds of them. It was from this room that Emerson Pike ran his business, Pike's Peak, investments in rare coins and precious metals. He had turned a small fortune in the last several years, especially as the stock market fell and wealthy people looked for tangible ways to invest their money.

Tonight he sat behind his desk with a certain look of exasperation on his face.

"Katia, please. You can't wind yourself into the drapes. Sit down and relax or do something else."

"Do what?" She shot an annoyed glance at him and refused to budge from the alcove in the window twenty feet away.

Katia was bored. Lately the only thing she wanted to

talk about was going home, back to Costa Rica. This was the one subject he tried to avoid at all costs. He had hoped that with the meal tonight, and her joy in cooking a typical Costa Rican meal for a few friends, her mind would have been off the subject at least for a few hours. Unfortunately, this was not to be.

All the guests had left and Katia now toyed with the five-thousand-dollar cashmere curtains, pulling and wrapping them around her body, like a sumptuous evening gown, over the dress she was wearing. She seemed in full Latin pout.

To anyone keeping tabs, Katia Solaz was Emerson Pike's latest flame. And she was gorgeous, five foot two, with a body to stop a clock, shimmering black hair, and a smile topped by smoldering eyes that could cause a man's knees to buckle. She was also twenty-six, young enough to be his granddaughter.

This invariably invited glares of disapproval in restaurants whenever he and Katia dined out. Emerson enjoyed sticking his thumb in the eye of convention. So eating out with Katia became the high point of his day.

He would sit in the restaurant next to her with a brazen smile, swallowing up, like a galactic black hole, all the censuring furtive glances. Occasionally, he would set off a social panic, striking up a conversation with some lady's husband and sending a nuclear shot of adrenaline through her heart by introducing him to Katia.

But as they say, for every silver lining there is a black cloud, and for Katia it was her moods. Mercurial did not begin to cover them.

Emerson had seen this often enough during the last five weeks that by now he thought he knew and understood her motivations well. In fact, he had no clue.

Emerson thought that in Katia's perfect universe, the woman always had both hands in the guy's pockets, frog-marching him down the street like a human debit card toward the nearest ATM.

In fact, Katia had little or no interest in his money as long as she had enough to survive. Katia had never known her father. There had never been an older male figure in her life. For this reason she enjoyed being with Emerson and caring for him. But she had come to California with a different agenda—education. Katia was interested in the colleges and universities in the area, if not for undergraduate studies then in hopes of one day pursuing a graduate degree in the States. And if Emerson was willing to help her financially, Katia would not say no.

Emerson had his own reasons for bringing her here to his house, and none of them had to do with sex or some latter-day search for the fountain of youth. Katia had become the cheese in the trap. It was as simple as that.

Perhaps "simple" was not the right term. Because lately she was asking a lot more questions, most of them arriving at the same point—when would they be going back to Costa Rica?

He kept putting her off, trying to distract her with various forms of entertainment. As long as she was smiling and having fun, he thought, she wouldn't ask to leave. To Emerson it was a test of his skills. If he was compelled to resort to force, it would be a clear indication that he was slipping, a warning that he had lost his mastery of the dark arts, the darkest of which was always deception.

"What are you working on?" She twisted herself into

the drapes and leaned so that her weight, petite as she was, hung from the rod overhead.

Emerson was certain she would rip the curtain from under the valance. "Those are very expensive," he told her.

"What?"

"The drapes."

"So? I am worth it, no?"

He glanced at her, not exactly angry, but with paternal charm.

Katia gave him one of those mischievous, dimpled smiles. She was playing it to the hilt tonight.

Inside, Emerson was sure she was laughing at him. She had used the same line and twinkle in her eyes two days earlier when watching a movie in the media room as she removed polish from her toenails along with the finish from an eight-thousand-dollar ebony-lacquered antique table. Katia could be endearing when she wanted to be, and a hundred-pound wrecking ball when she didn't.

"I can't remember, did you call home today?" he asked.

"Yes, I called home today." She mocked him in a singsong tone. "You already asked me. I told you, yes."

"Senior moment," he told her.

"What?"

"Nothing." Emerson was engrossed in the photographs spread out in front of him on the desk.

"Why do you care whether I call home every day? Es not important. They don't expect me to call."

"I thought maybe your mother might worry."

Her expression was something between irritation and suspicion. "I don't have to check in with my mother. I'm an adult. What is this thing with you about my mother anyway? You keep asking me where she is, when she is going back home to Costa Rica. Maybe you should live with her."

"Now there's an idea," said Emerson. "Is she as pretty as you?"

Katia ignored the question.

"I just don't want her to worry about you, that's all."

"Nobody's going to worry. And besides, I told you, my mother's not there."

"So you did. That means she's still down in Colombia?" This was what Emerson wanted to know.

"I don't know. I guess so."

"That's where you said she was."

"So?"

"So you don't care where your mother is? That's not very nice." Emerson was trying to appear casual, drawing her out as he studied one of the photographs through a magnifying glass.

To Katia, the constant questions about her mother, and Emerson's obsession with the photographs, were becoming a major annoyance.

At first she'd been excited to come to the United States. Getting a visa to the U.S. usually took months, that is, if you could get one at all, but not for Emerson. He invited her to visit his house in San Diego on a Monday. Tuesday, he filled out some papers and had her sign them. By Thursday, he had gone to the U.S. embassy in San José and returned with the visa. To Katia, anyone who could do this could probably spin gold from straw. If he had those kinds of connections, perhaps he could help her get into an American college or university.

Her only initial concern was that her name on the

visa was not complete. Pike had filled out the application in the American style, first and last names only. He had omitted her mother's paternal name. Katia was concerned that because the visa did not conform precisely to the name on her passport, it might be a problem. But it wasn't.

Thinking back now, she should have been much more worried about other things. Coming here with him was a mistake.

She watched him as he sat behind his desk looking like a miser counting his money. There were coins spread across the desktop, some in clear plastic envelopes, others lying naked, the yellow gold glinting under the light of the lamp. Emerson had a meeting in the morning with an investor. He was supposed to be assembling a selection of coins to show the man. Instead he was looking at the pictures again, this time with a magnifying glass.

The pictures did not belong to him. They belonged to her, or, more correctly, to her mother, who had borrowed Katia's camera for one of her recent trips to Colombia. The photographs showed her mother's relatives or friends, Katia wasn't exactly sure. They were people Katia had never met. She had long realized, since childhood, that her mother had some family skeletons in the Colombian closet, people she never talked about but visited on occasion. When Katia met Emerson her mother had been in Colombia again. The pictures had been left on the camera's digital chip. Emerson had asked Katia about her family and where her mother was, in innocent conversation, or so she thought. She saw no harm in showing him the pictures.

She never realized that the family skeletons might be

more serious until Emerson printed the photos and started obsessing about them, asking her questions and constantly pushing for details. He knew something she did not.

"You look tired. You should go to bed," she said.

He was yawning at the desk every few minutes now.

"I have work to finish."

"You could do it in the morning." She lay out, nearly horizontal in the grip of the drapes wrapped around her body, and bounced a little, testing the elasticity of the cashmere and the strength of the rod. This little act, à la Cirque du Soleil, was intended to annoy Emerson and catch his attention, getting him to think about things other than work.

It didn't. He ignored her, his focus directed through the magnifying glass at the photographs.

She fumed. Her mind began to work. They had been living together now for nearly three months, first in Costa Rica and now here. Each night they slept together in the same bed, but he never touched her. By the end of the first week in the States, she began to suspect that the only reason she was in the same room with him at night was so he could watch her. The old man was a light sleeper. Every time she stirred or went to the bathroom, she noticed he was instantly awake.

There were also other little things she noticed. Whenever they were out in public and he saw police in a car or walking, it seemed that he would always steer Katia in the other direction. She wasn't sure about this. So she tested him. In the mall one afternoon, she saw two cops patrolling on foot. She decided to approach them for directions to a shop in the mall. Before she had gone three steps, Emerson had grabbed her by the arm with such force that it left pressure marks on her skin.

Then ten days ago something had happened that told her she must leave—and soon. Periodically Emerson gave her money to send home to deposit for the support of her mother. Katia had left her part-time job when she came to the States. It was a kind of unstated understanding when they left Costa Rica. They would send it by Western Union online to a friend of Katia's in San José who would deposit it for her in Katia's bank account. Emerson would use one of his credit cards for the transaction.

But though cash went south, Emerson never gave Katia money to spend while she was here. The most she ever had in her purse was twenty dollars, this in case of an emergency or to buy incidentals. Emerson knew she didn't have a local bank account or a credit card, so he had to know she had no money. Perhaps he didn't think she needed much cash; after all, they were always together.

Emerson had bought her some jewelry and without telling him, Katia had sold it. She did her best to conceal this from him. She had pawned it downtown while he was seeing a client. He always left her to sit in the car or go window-shopping by herself for an hour. But she used the time to pawn the jewelry. A couple of days later Pike saw the pawn tickets in her purse.

At first she was afraid he would be furious. But he wasn't. He didn't seem to mind at all. In fact, it was almost as if he'd expected it.

It was what happened next that unnerved her. He took the cash she had gotten from the pawnshop. Then he allowed her to send an equal amount by Western

Union on his credit card to her family back home. She was, of course, grateful, but extremely puzzled. Why wasn't he angry? He certainly didn't need the cash. He would always spend lavishly on her whenever they went shopping, in some cases paying thousands of dollars in an afternoon. She had netted just a little over six hundred dollars for the jewelry. So why had he taken it away from her?

The more she thought about this the more uneasy she became. The only reason she could think of was that Emerson thought she might use the money to run, to fly back to Costa Rica. It planted the seed, the gnawing notion that grew and now blossomed, fully formed, in her mind. She did not dare raise it with him, not directly, for fear of what he might do. At the moment she had the run of the house. He would take her to town whenever he went. He allowed her to call home. In fact, he insisted on it. If she confronted him, all of that might end. Her growing suspicion could suddenly become fact, that she was no longer Emerson's guest, if she ever had been. For all intents and purposes she was now a captive. Katia had heard stories of young women who traveled to Asia and the Middle East with wealthy men, women whose families never heard from them again. It happened. She knew it.

After Emerson took the money from her, that night she gathered her passport and visa, and put them in a small overnight bag with some clothes and other personal items. She hid the bag under the bed in one of the guest rooms just down the hall from the master bedroom. This way, if he searched her luggage, he wouldn't find the travel documents. Without these she knew she could never get home.

"You're awfully quiet tonight. What's going on behind those beautiful eyes?"

His question startled her. Perhaps he could read her mind. "Nothing," she said. "I'm just relaxing."

"I know you're bored. Sometimes I'm not a very good host. Tomorrow I'll make it up to you." He yawned again. "Excuse me. I don't know what's going on with me tonight. Tomorrow we'll go somewhere, have some fun. After my meeting in the morning."

"If you like." For a man his age Katia marveled at his stamina. On the other hand, he'd had two cups of black coffee. She had been hoping that by now he would be headed to bed. She pulled herself back up and adjusted the bodice of the black evening dress.

As she did this, Emerson's sleepy fingers slid one of the photographs from the stack in front of him under a magazine on his desk.

Katia didn't notice.

"Why don't you watch one of your movies?" he asked.

"I'm tired of movies."

"Then try on some of your new clothes. Let me see what they look like on you."

"It sounds like you want to get rid of me? Maybe it is you who is bored—with me."

He looked at her from under sleepy lids. "How can you say that? Come over here and keep me company." He rolled the chair away from the desk and patted his lap.

Emerson could always turn on the charm. Now it seemed he used it less and less, as if it was no longer required and he wanted to conserve the energy that it consumed. As Katia had come to know him better, it seemed that Emerson was calculating in almost everything he did.

His gray hair was still full, thick and wavy. To look at him you would never guess he was seventy-two. The first time he'd told her his age she wouldn't believe him, not until he showed her his driver's license. His body was lean, and for a man his age he was powerfully built, and just under six feet in height. He exercised each morning for an hour on the elliptical machine and with the weights downstairs. He had pale blue eyes, a ruddy complexion, and thin lips, and he wore a kind of wry, wary expression, like a Kabuki mask.

To Katia, ever since arriving in the States he seemed to operate increasingly from behind this, as if there were small demons racing around inside pulling levers and turning wheels.

If he expected her to run across the room and fly into his lap, he was sorely mistaken.

She sauntered toward the desk. Her short evening dress clung to the curves of her body. Her five-inch heels clicked like slow castanets across the hardwood floor. She dropped into one of the upholstered wingback chairs across from him, and sat there all dark eyed and leggy, staring at him.

Emerson rolled his chair back toward the desk. He knew the only thing that would pull her out of this mood was another full-court press on one of his credit cards. It was beginning to drive him crazy.

"Why are you looking at the pictures again?" she asked.

"Just curious."

"About what?"

"I'm interested in your family."

"Why?"

"Because I love you, and I want to know everything there is to know about you." He almost said it with conviction.

"Uh-huh. You keep looking at the pictures and wanting to know who the people are. You ask me about my mother and her family. How she came from Cuba and what she's doing in Colombia. You have a lot of questions for someone who is just curious," said Katia.

"If it bothers you, I'll stop."

"I don't know. Sometimes I begin to think that maybe the way we met was no accident."

"What are you saying?"

She thought about it quickly and decided this was not wise.

"It's just that I don't understand. What are you looking for in the pictures?"

"Nothing," he said.

"You're looking for nothing? Then you're wasting a lot of time. If you tell me what you're looking for, maybe I can help you."

She fixed him with her piercing dark brown eyes.

"You said you didn't know any of the people in the photographs," he said.

"That's true."

"It's not important. There's no reason for us to argue about it."

He'd believed her when she told him she knew none of the people in the photographs, or where the pictures had been taken. According to Katia she had never been to Colombia. This seemed strange since her mother claimed to have relatives there and she visited them at least once a year. But she never took her daughter, nor, according to Katia, did she take any of the rest of her family from Costa Rica. Why? Emerson thought he knew the reason. It was in the pictures.

"Tell me the truth. You are looking for something or someone in those photographs. Tell me what it is. Maybe if you tell me, it will make sense to me. And then maybe I can help you." Katia was determined to find out what it was. Increasingly she felt that Emerson was a threat, to her, and perhaps to her family.

"I told you. I'm just curious."

"Yes, because you love me. You want to know everything about my family. I know, you told me."

He shrugged his shoulders. "It's okay, don't worry about it. Listen, why don't we go watch a movie in the video room?"

"I don't want to watch a movie." She sat there in a slow burn. "I want to know why you're always looking at those pictures. And don't change the subject."

"I told you the reason. Tell you what. Why don't I put the photographs away if it upsets you? I won't look at them anymore. The pictures are none of my business. I'm sorry I ever looked at them. If it upsets you, then I will not look at them again."

What was he hiding?

"You're right. It's none of your business," she told him. The Latin temper was starting to kick in. Emerson could feel the heat rising in the room.

"You looked in my camera." It was a sore point with Katia because Pike had taken it and uploaded the pictures without asking her. Then, by mistake, he'd put the camera someplace where she couldn't find it when they left for the States.

"I never told you you could go through my stuff and mess with my camera."

"I bought you a new camera when we got here, didn't I?"

"Yes. But you had no business going through my things without asking me."

"I was trying to surprise you," said Emerson. This has been the line since she caught him with the pictures in his computer. That he was planning on surprising her with glossy pictures of her family members as a gift.

Katia wasn't buying it. True, her mother took the pictures and there were supposed to be some family members in them, but Katia didn't know a single one of them. She had never been to Colombia, and she told Emerson that. These people meant nothing to her and he knew it. "You had them printed out without even asking." The more she thought about it, the angrier she became. He was nosing around her family. He may have been sending them money, but he was still an outsider.

"Don't get angry, Katia."

"And don't tell me what to do. Those are not your photographs. They belong to my mother. You had no right to take them."

"Fine, here. They're yours. Take them." Emerson leaned back in his chair, both hands up as if to surrender.

Katia didn't hesitate. She scooped the photos up and turned her back as she assembled them.

Pike didn't care. If retrieving the glossy printouts kept her quiet, fine. As long as she didn't tell him to erase the downloaded photo files from his laptop, what difference did it make? And by now there were digital copies in several places. Pike's laptop was configured for global travel. Once connected to the Internet, his home e-mail opened from anywhere in the world. Before they had even flown north, Pike had forwarded the digital images from Katia's camera to a laboratory in Virginia for enhancement and analysis. If all went well, the results should be back any day.

The only picture Katia didn't get when she grabbed them from the desk was the one Emerson had slid under the magazine. This was a shot he had enlarged and cropped to better see something in the background. He thought he knew what it was, but he wasn't sure. He tried to enhance it using consumer software. He could make out only a few details—lines and part of a circle. But because of the angle at which the original picture was taken it was impossible to make out anything else. None of the lettering or dimensions on the diagram in the photo could even be seen, much less read. But Emerson had a hunch as to what it was, and who the old man was too. They were the reason he kept going back to the photos.

Katia stood with her back to him, on the other side of the desk. He could tell by the way she stood, stiff, that she was still riding a wave of anger.

Unless he could patch this up, she would not be sleeping with him tonight. This would raise logistical problems: how to keep an eye on her without locking her up so she wouldn't rabbit. Once the lab report on the photos came back, if what he suspected was true, she would be someone else's problem. But until then, he wanted to keep her close. She was part of the genetic chain, and blood is thicker than water.

He waited a few seconds, then got up out of the chair and walked slowly around the desk until he stood behind her. He put his hand on her shoulder. Katia jerked and pulled away.

"Katia, please. Don't be angry with me. I didn't realize that I was upsetting you. Please forgive me."

"I forgive you," she said. "When are we going home?"

"A few more days."

Why? she thought. What was he waiting for?

She studied his face for a moment. It was impossible to read what was going on behind those eyes. He would tell her in a few days or a week now, but he would tell her anything to keep her here, to keep her quiet. He was lying and she knew it.

A single tear shimmered slowly down her cheek, like mercury running down a piece of silk.

THREE

Once over the fence, "Muerte Liquida" moved swiftly across the grass and slipped between the bushes at the side of the house. A thick row of camellias now shielded him from anyone who might be wandering in the yard or near the wrought-iron fence behind him.

He moved through the shadows toward the back of the house and climbed the steps two at a time. Halfway up he stopped. He reached out with a gloved hand and felt the deep, almost rutted, grain of the smooth fiberglass surface on what appeared to be the wooden handrail of the stairs. The entire exterior of the house, from the siding to the railings, every detail, was made of exquisitely fashioned fiberglass, all of it molded and shaped by artists who knew their craft. Whoever had done the finish probably worked at one of the Hollywood studios. It was all designed for illusion.

He climbed to the top of the steps. Once on the deck at the back of the house, he could see the broken balustrade. It completed the false impression of disrepair. The gap in the railing at the edge of the deck was covered by a clear sheet of acrylic, forming a solid barrier for safety. Unless the acrylic caught the glint of the sun or you were within a few feet, you would never see it.

It took him less than thirty seconds using a set of picks from his pocket to work the pins in the cylinder of the dead bolt at the back door. Using a tiny tension wrench and a pick, he aligned the pins along the sheer point inside the lock, and turned the cylinder until the dead bolt snapped open. In less than a minute he was inside and into the darkened pantry.

Liquida knew the routine. The owner was a bachelor. The maid and the cook came and went, neither of them lived in. The maid came three days a week and always left by four in the afternoon. The cook was there each day, from just before breakfast until just after dinner. Without exception she was always gone by seven thirty in the evening.

It was now just after ten at night, which meant that only the owner and his single houseguest were at home. The woman was part of his contract, but only because she was at the house with the old man. He knew about her from the photographs taken with a telephoto lens.

The presence of the woman complicated things, but only slightly. They had to be taken separately, without a sound and in different rooms. Otherwise, he ran the risk that one of them might get to a phone or a door, or worse, a loaded gun. No one had told him to expect firearms, but he had to assume there might be one, perhaps more. It went with the turf, the nature of the old man's business.

He stood stone still, listening for sounds, the hum of a motor in the kitchen, and something else, maybe a fan, an exhaust vent somewhere. In the distance he could hear voices, faint, almost muted. He couldn't be sure, but they sounded as if they were coming from somewhere upstairs.

He glanced around the corner of the door into the kitchen. There was no one there, but there were two dirty dishes on the counter, small dessert plates, forks, and coffee cups. They must have had a late-night snack. The motor he'd heard from the pantry was the dishwasher. It was chugging away.

Even though the nearest house was a hundred yards away, Liquida moved in a crouch, low, beneath the line of windows over the sink. He saw what he needed on the countertop of the island in the center of the kitchen. It was a hard wooden block with slots and the handles of eight knives were sticking out of it. He had his own, a folding survival knife with a razor-sharp blade. But he loved to use what was at hand, to make it look as if the murders were the result of a botched burglary.

Down on one knee he reached up over the top of the counter and with a gloved hand sampled the cutlery. He pulled one out and then another until he finally settled on a ten-inch chef's knife. It had a needle-sharp point and a solid wooden handle that matched all the others. When the cops found it they would know where it came from. He could tell by the swirls in the metal that the blade was high-carbon steel. He tested it with his gloved finger. The cook, no doubt, kept the edge honed to a sharp finish.

He moved away from the bright lights of the kitchen and down the dark hallway toward the living room and the front of the house. He knew from the floor plan that the stairs were to his left. The voices upstairs were now growing louder. He could make out a few words. They were arguing over something. The woman wasn't shouting, but there was a definite edge of anger in her tone.

Liquida strained to listen, trying to pick up the threads of the conversation on the second floor. Perhaps it was for this reason that he didn't see the maid until he rounded the corner and faced the foot of the stairs. At first sighting, his eyes opened like saucers. She wasn't supposed to be here. She had her back to him and was walking the other way, down the hall toward the dining room. Liquida froze in place, then tried to lean back into the shadows of the hall. At the last second, before he could retreat, the maid turned and saw him. She must have sensed the motion behind her.

For a split second she stood there, a quizzical expression on her face, wondering who he was, or, perhaps more to the point, what he was.

Liquida's appearance often had this effect, for he wore a hooded lightweight neoprene wet suit to easily rinse the blood off. He closed the distance in an instant, and before breath could carry sound from her body, his gloved left hand was over her mouth.

A stream of warm blood ran like a river from her abdomen down over the handle of the knife and the neoprene diving glove on his right hand. From the vigorous pulsing he knew it had severed a main artery. He kept his hand to her mouth until her knees buckled, her body convulsing.

"Woman, what are you doing here at this hour?" he whispered in her ear. Liquida did not kill from wanton disregard. It was his business. He harvested people in the way a farmer harvests crops, because he was paid to do it. When fate placed a life under his knife because of the vagaries of chance, there was always regret. The fate of being in the wrong place at the wrong time. The maid had stumbled into death in a cosmic collision between time and space.

She went limp in his arms. He looked straight into her eyes, her pupils open like the lens of a camera. Her full weight was now completely supported by the handle of the knife wedged in her body. He eased her to the floor and slid out the knife.

FOUR

At this moment Katia had but a single thought as she looked at Emerson across the green felt inlay of his desk. It was strewn with more than two dozen gold coins of different sizes and shapes. Some of them were clearly hammered and stamped by hand. There were gold escudos from the old Inca mines of Peru and double eagles from the SS *Central America* that had sunk off the East Coast of the U.S. in 1857. They glinted in the muted light of the large study.

In the morning he would go a few miles away to La Jolla to see his client. He would take Katia with him and make her sit in the car and wait. He had done this before. If she was lucky he might give her a few dollars and tell her to go shopping. But the cash he gave her was never enough to go far.

He had already loaded most of the coins he would take tomorrow into a small sample case on the floor near the desk. They were valuable just for their gold content. They were worth much more to collectors. She had heard Emerson talk about this. Other coins encased in two plastic sheets lay scattered, off to the side of the desk, near the phone and the needle-sharp letter opener that some might have mistaken for a replica of a Byzantine dagger. Katia knew better, because he had told her. The dagger was real, fashioned from the finest Damascus steel and dating to the fall of Constantinople in the fifteenth century. Emerson Pike had paid more than forty thousand dollars for the piece at a Christie's auction three years ago. This was supposed to mean something to her, but it didn't, other than the fact that Emerson Pike had more money than he could use.

"I'm sorry I was so angry," she said. "I don't know why. I think I am just tired."

With the very suggestion he yawned. "Of course you are. Listen, I'm going to take a shower, try to wake myself up so that I can finish up here. Then I'm going to come to bed. Why don't you go on ahead of me? I'll be there in just a few minutes."

He put his hands on Katia's shoulders once more. This time she did not pull away. Now was not the time to provoke him. Let him continue to believe.

He leaned down and kissed her on the forehead, called her "sweetie."

She hated it when he called her that. It reminded her of Tweety, the stupid yellow bird in a cage in the cartoons. Still she gave him a smile, the full twinkle job. Two could play this game.

"You're right," she said. "I am tired. But first I want to get a glass of milk. Do you want anything more?"

"After that meal? You have to be kidding. I'm stuffed. Why, I'm falling asleep. But it was delicious. Don't ever let anyone tell you you're not a good cook," said Emerson.

"I won't."

He yawned once more, stood there, and smiled at her.

She could tell by the satisfied look on his face that Emerson believed she was back in the fold, at least for now. He would be fondling his ego in the shower, having won another battle. Emerson thought that at least there would be no need for separate bedrooms and the locked doors that could follow.

Katia turned and headed out of the study, her heels clicking on the hardwood floor until she reached the plush carpet of the hallway outside. Emerson followed her. Katia turned toward the top of the stairs that descended to the first floor. Emerson headed the other way, toward the master bedroom and the shower. "See you in a few minutes, sweetie."

"Yes." She could tell that the jaunty bounce was gone from his stride. Still, Katia was afraid that with the coffee and the shower Emerson would revive himself. It would be a long, uncertain night wondering if he was asleep, afraid each time she moved that he would wake. And by then the coins on his desk might be locked away.

She took two steps down the stairs, then suddenly stopped and turned. She waited as she watched Emerson disappear down the long hallway and into the master bedroom.

For a few seconds Liquida stood over the maid's body, ten feet from the foot of the stairs. Straddling her, he carefully avoided the spreading pool of blood as he studied the situation. It presented complications, but nothing insurmountable, matters of adjustment to the original plan, little details. Still, they were important if the authorities were to believe what he wanted them to. He worked it out quickly in his head.

Then he heard footsteps coming from upstairs, a woman's heels on wood and then silence. Only at the last second did he realize she had traversed from the wood to a carpeted surface and was still moving this way and at speed. She was above him, directly behind him in the hallway at the top of the stairs.

He slipped toward the shadows of the dining room, away from the foot of the stairs, and watched. If she saw the maid's body before he could get to her on the stairs, everything would change. If he had to chase her up the stairs with the bloody knife, he could throw the plan out the window. He would have to torch the house, burn it to the ground to cover the physical evidence. If she screamed and the old man grabbed a gun, the coroner might be rolling his body and not theirs out to the hearse in the morning.

She came into view on the landing above, started down two steps, and then suddenly stopped, as if she'd remembered something. The adrenaline pulsed through his veins. He was sure she saw the body. He gripped the knife. In his mind he was already flying up the stairs to take her until he realized—she wasn't looking this way. Her attention was drawn to something behind her in the hallway upstairs. She stood there for two or three seconds and then, as suddenly as she'd appeared, she was gone, back up the steps and down the hall.

He waited almost twenty seconds, certain that whatever fleeting distraction caught her attention would soon be dealt with and that she would be likely to return. But she didn't.

He listened intently. There was nothing but silence. Then he heard the sound of running water drumming on a hard surface somewhere toward the back of the house, a bathtub or a shower. Maybe they were settling in for the night. That would make it much easier.

He retreated silently back down the hall, toward the kitchen. He was dripping blood from the knife on the hall carpet, but it didn't matter. As long as he didn't step in it on the way back and track it upstairs everything would be fine.

Katia paused on the stairs, then turned around, headed back up, and entered one of the guest rooms along the hall. Working in the dark, she fished under the bed for the overnight bag, the one with her passport and visa. She ditched her heels, dropped them into the bag, changed her dress for a pair of hip-huggers and a blouse, and then put on a pair of running shoes and a jacket. It broke her heart to leave behind all of the clothes and some of the other things Emerson had bought for her, but there was no way to carry all of it. As it was, the small overnight bag was full.

By the time she was finished, the water from Emerson's shower had been running full bore for almost five minutes. Without a sound, she crept into the master bedroom. She had carefully thought it all through. This had to be her first stop. He had gone to the ATM that afternoon. She had watched him count the bills before he put them away in his hip pocket. He had left his pants on the bed. She pulled his wallet from the back pocket and quickly counted the cash, two hundred and sixty dollars in twenties along with a few smaller bills. She breathed a sigh of relief. She knew from her search on the Internet that this would be enough, at least for the first part of her journey. She took it all and tossed the empty wallet back onto the bed.

She grabbed Emerson's cell phone from his belt and, with the overnight bag over her shoulder, headed back down the hall, this time almost at a run. She ducked into the study and went directly to his desk. There she scooped into her bag every loose coin she could reach from the top of the desk. She took both of the plastic sheets with coins and stuffed them into the bag as well.

Then she grabbed a piece of paper, one of Emerson's embossed letterhead. Her eyes scoured the top of the desk for a pen but there wasn't one. Typical of Emerson, he had every trinket and toy imaginable on his antique desk except something to write with. She fished in her purse and found a pen and scrawled a quick note in Spanish. She knew that he would be able to read it. Whether he would comply was doubtful.

I am going back home to Costa Rica. I took some coins but only for airfare. Please do not try to follow me. I do not want to see you again. If you come near me, I will call the police.

She signed it with a large letter "K," dropped the pen on top of the paper, and then grabbed the letter opener, the Byzantine dagger, off the desk and laid it across the top of the note as a paperweight.

He looked at the window over the sink, then checked his watch. He had no choice. He had to move and move quickly. He could not stay below the level of the windows and complete what he had to do. The way he was clad would cause anyone outside who happened to be looking to take immediate notice. He reached around the corner of the door and flipped off the lights in the kitchen. He quickly stepped up to the sink, washed the blood from the knife carefully, making sure that he got it all. Then without taking it off he rinsed the blood from the neoprene diving glove on his right hand as well as from the suit covering his forearm. The instant he was done he stepped away from the windows and back into the hall. He used a small dish towel to dry the gloves, the surface of the suit, and then the knife.

He started down the hall, headed for the unfinished business upstairs.

Zipping up the overnight bag, Katia ran out of the study and back down the long hallway toward the master bedroom and the back of the house. As she passed the door to the master bedroom, she realized suddenly that Emerson had turned off the water in the shower. He would be coming out any second.

She dashed toward the end of the hall, toward the door that led to the back stairs and to the garage below. There was only one more thing she needed. She held the door behind her so that it closed with a gentle click. Then she moved down the steps as quickly and silently as the rubber-soled tennis shoes would carry her.

Emerson would be donning his robe, running a brush through his hair and heading back into the bedroom any moment. Katia knew the routine. She had maybe two minutes, if that. By now she knew every move she had to make. She had thought it out carefully. This was her last chance.

FIVE

He was halfway up the stairs when the steady sound of running water somewhere at the rear of the house stopped. In the abrupt stillness, Liquida froze in place. In the momentary silence he thought he heard something.

It was a distant and muted whisper of sound, faint, almost imperceptible. Perhaps the brush of a shoe across the deep pile of the carpeted floor somewhere at the other end of the hallway overhead.

He readied the chef's knife, now clean and bright in his hand, and crouched on the stairs, ready to spring the instant anyone appeared on the landing above. Liquida strained to hear and for several seconds listened motionless on the stairwell. There was a slight creak and then a click. It could have been a switch snapping on or off somewhere at the other end of the hall. Or maybe it was just the house settling, causing it to creak. He listened for several seconds, his gaze trained like a laser on the landing above. There was nothing, no one, no movement. In the silence after the constant sound of the running water, his hearing was playing tricks on him.

He edged toward the top of the stairs and peeked over. He could see all the way to the end of the hall. The long corridor was clear, no one was there. Quickly he ascended to the top of the landing, then moved silently toward what he knew from the floor plan was the old man's study. This was the nerve center of the house, the place of business. He assumed it was where the voices he'd heard earlier had come from. The lights were still on inside the study. Unless they left the lights on all night, and he had never seen this before, they had not gone to bed.

He approached the study door nearest the stairs. At a distance, perhaps ten feet, he silently darted across the opening. As he did this he gained a quick visual scan inside the study. There was no one at the desk at the far end. Of that he was certain. It was only a fleeting glimpse, but he saw neither the old man nor the woman. If the angel of death was with him, the two would now be in different rooms and he would be able to take them separately and in virtual silence. He made his way to the study door and stole a quick glance inside. The room appeared to be empty, at least from this angle. There were portions of the study's interior he could not see.

He scanned the catwalk above, the part he could see from the open doorway. Again, there was no one there. He ventured down the hall toward the other study door, the one closer to the bedrooms farther down the corridor. From here he could see the rest of the study and the remaining section of catwalk on the study's second level.

Katia had long since opted to use the bath near one of the guest rooms down the hall as her private sanctuary for preparation before sleep. So Emerson wasn't surprised when he stepped from the shower and found himself alone in the master bath. He toweled himself dry and put on his robe, then stood in front of the mirror over the vanity while he ran a comb through his still damp hair. He couldn't believe how tired he was this evening; the guests for dinner, the tension of dealing with Katia, and the heavy meal, none of which he was used to, had taken their toll.

He examined his face and an ingrown hair in his beard, then turned off the light and headed for the bedroom.

He was half-expecting to see Katia already curled up under the covers. So when he didn't, it took a second before the image that confronted him registered. She was taking longer than usual to get ready. The room didn't look any different than it had ten minutes earlier, except for his pants at the bottom of the bed.

Emerson turned and opened the top dresser drawer. He pulled out a pair of boxer shorts while glancing in the mirror over the dresser.

His pants were still there on the end of the bed but were now crumpled in a heap. None of this alarmed him. He seemed groggy until he saw the other item in the mirror, his empty wallet lying open on the bed next to the pants. It was like a shot of adrenaline. Instantly he was awake.

SIX

Once in the garage, Katia quietly opened the driver's side door of Emerson's big Suburban. She had to stand on the running board to reach the visor over the steering wheel so that she could pull one of the remote controls from where it was clipped. It was the control for the gate out in front. She had seen Emerson use it many times, coming and going.

Suddenly she heard creaking footsteps on the floor overhead. Emerson was in the master bedroom. She reached up and grabbed the remote from the visor. She glanced quickly at the other remote. She didn't dare use it. If she opened the overhead garage door, Emerson would hear it upstairs. She climbed down from the running board. Katia left the driver's side door open to avoid the noise of closing it.

She exited the garage by the side door. Suddenly she was out in the crisp night air, running as fast as her legs could carry her. There was a vapor of low fog over the ground. Now for the first time fear gripped her. In less than a minute, Katia was beyond the gate and out on the street, closing the mechanical barricade behind her, praying that this would not be heard back down the driveway in the big house.

She ran headlong up the street and tossed the remote into the brush in a deep ravine off to the side of the road. She ran, not down the hill toward the lights of Del Mar, but up the hill, in the other direction, into the darkness. Katia was scared, driven by fear, but her mind was clear. She knew exactly what she was doing.

When Emerson came out of the shower and saw the note in the study, he would get into his car immediately and start looking for her. The missing remote would only slow him down for a few seconds, just long enough for him to punch in the code on the keypad at the gate.

What she was counting on was that he would then turn in the wrong direction, to the right, toward Del Mar and the old coast highway, the obvious avenue of escape.

By then Katia would be standing in front of one of the other houses up the hill, using that address to call a taxi on Emerson's cell phone. Before he could sort it out, she would be in San Diego, and he would be looking in all the wrong places, trying to find her.

It registered immediately. Emerson didn't have to pick up the wallet and look. He knew. The way it lay limp, pitched up like a collapsed tent; the cash that had fattened his wallet that afternoon was gone.

He didn't bother to put on his slippers. Instead he ran barefoot out of the room, down the hall toward the study.

"Katia! Katia!" There was an ugly, angry edge to his voice. There was nothing paternal in it. Emerson was mad, mostly at himself for being so stupid. He should have locked her up, and now he knew it. He slammed through the door into the guest room next to the master bedroom. This was the place Katia used to get ready at night, but the lights were out, the room was empty.

He rocketed back out into the hallway. He raced down the corridor toward the study and the stairs in the direction of the front door. He called out her name, glanced into the study as he ran by the first door. He didn't see her, but something else, out of the corner of one eye, a shadow moving quickly toward the other door, near the head of the stairs. Instantly it dawned on him. Katia would need more than the cash in his wallet to get back to Costa Rica.

In less than two strides, he slowed to a walk and then came to an abrupt stop, planting himself between the stairwell and the study. The confident, thin smile spread across Emerson's face. He took a deep breath, regained some composure, drew the bathrobe around himself, retying it with the belt, and walked calmly into the study. "Where's the money from my wallet?"

The last syllable had barely rattled from his larynx as the mind-numbing agony fired the cells of Emerson's brain. The needle-sharp point of the chef's knife penetrated half of its length, into Emerson's left kidney. With a quick twist the blade sliced the organ open, paralyzing him in a paroxysm of pain. An arm came around at the level of his throat, too tall for Katia. But by then his brain was filled with other things.

The shock enflamed every nerve in his body. The involuntary contraction of his own muscles arched his back as he heard the sound of his own snapped vertebrae. More excruciating than any pain the human brain could imagine, it made it impossible for Emerson Pike to suck in a thimbleful of air, enough to emit even a single sound. It seemed to last forever. He stood suspended in that place where the tortured mind pleads for death. Relief from the agony came only as the darkening empty void of death rolled over and enveloped him.

SEVEN

Sometimes it's how you back into things in life that is most unsettling. It was how I met her, over the bananas in the produce section of a small market on the main drag up in Del Mar, not far from the racetrack. It was a Saturday morning and I was headed to the races to hook up with some friends. A cup of coffee in one hand and a bag with a muffin trapped under my arm, I was busy trying to separate a single banana from three others when she caught me in the act.

"Could you help me, *señor*? *Por favor?*" She stood there looking at me, maybe five foot six in heels, shimmering dark hair past her shoulders, dimples, and a smile that could start a war.

"Ahhh ..." She looked down for a moment, collecting her thoughts, translating in her head. "Do you know ... umm ... do they have plantains? You know plantains?"

I must have given her a kind of dull look. It wasn't because I didn't understand the question.

"Plantains." The way she emphasized the word with the fingers of each hand at the corners of her mouth, full lips, a dark-eyed beauty, visions of Catherine Zeta-Jones descending from the big screen to haggle with me over bunches of bananas. She could read the stupidity of it all in my face, and she laughed.

"Ahh. I don't know."

I wasn't sure if I had a clue as to what a plantain was, but if I could have invented one in that moment I would have done it.

She had that shiny, well-scrubbed look, the girl you dreamed about when you were twenty, the one you didn't even try and date because you knew it was all a vaporous wet dream. The only place you could truly hold her was in your delusions. She would vanish the moment you touched her, tapped to go to Hollywood or hustled off on a modeling contract somewhere. Why bother to break your own heart?

She picked up one of the bananas and held it up. "Similar but larger." She spread her hands about eighteen inches apart.

"*¿Habla español?*"

"*Un poco.* Only enough to get in trouble," I told her.

She laughed. There was something magical in it. I sensed by the way she smiled and instantly sized me up that it was not the first time she had seen this kind of confusion from men. It was in the air, surrounding her, atoms of volatile ether. It should have been a warning. To her, it was nothing unique, just part of nature, another fly in the trap.

"I need plantains to practice some recipes for a dinner party in two weeks. I am cooking for friends," she said.

"Am I invited?"

She looked at me, a kind of twinkle in her eyes. "Nooo. Well, maybe. But only if you can help me find plantains."

We talked about what she was cooking.

She called it a typical Costa Rican dinner. She asked me if I understood, but I didn't.

"You know, I don't know if I've ever seen any of those—plantains—here in such a small market. You might find them in one of the larger grocery stores in San Diego."

"Oh, no, es too far." Her face fell but only for an instant, a momentary and put-on pout, until her facile mind seized on another thought. She sniffed a little toward the large paper cup in my hand. "Café? Umm, smells good. What is your name?"

"Paul. Paul Madriani."

"Ah, very nice name. Madriani." The *d* and the *r* tripped off her Latin tongue with a musical quality I had not heard in a while. *"¿Italiano, no?"*

"Sí. And this Italian is about to have breakfast." I held up the banana and grabbed the bag from under my arm. "Would you like to join me?"

She looked over her shoulder, toward the door. "My friend is doing business at an office down the street. He will be a while. And your coffee smells very good. I suppose it would be okay."

"If you're sure he won't mind." Looking at her, I was suddenly getting visions of a jealous guy holding a loaded pistol to my face.

"Who cares?" She gave me a kind of indifferent smile and grabbed a banana.

Breakfast it was. She picked out a muffin and we headed for the checkout. Outside at the kiosk, I bought her coffee and we planted ourselves at one of the umbrella-shaded tables.

"You know es difficult to find good coffee here. My

friend. Sometimes I think he is loco. He has only instant coffee in his house. Es poison." The seriousness with which she said this made me laugh.

"Es true. I tell him. No good. He has *casa grande,* a big house, and a cook. Mexican." She glanced over and rolled her eyes a little. "And instant coffee. I tol him it's going to make me sick. I ask the cook about plantains. She looked at me like I'm crazy. She says 'bananas on steroids.' She will not cook them. Doesn't know how, she says. Very stubborn woman. I doan think she likes me."

I gave her the name of two or three larger grocery stores in the area and told her she might not have to go all the way to San Diego to find them. She didn't have anything to write on.

I found one of my business cards in my wallet.

Then she couldn't find a pen in her purse.

I reached into the inside pocket of my sports coat and pulled out a pen. I handed it to her and she wrote the names of the markets in tiny script on the back of the card.

"So you're not from Mexico?" I'm making small talk. The answer is obvious if she's making a typical Costa Rican meal.

"Oh, no. Costa Rica. San José. Before that, Puriscal. In the mountains. Have you ever been to Costa Rica?" She took her eyes off her writing for a second to look at me.

"No, but I've heard good things. It's supposed to be very beautiful."

"Oh, *sí.* Es beautiful. I love my country," she said. "I cannot wait to go back."

"How long are you here?"

"I don't know. I thought thirty days. But now it looks like it's going to be longer."

She finished writing, picked the business card up, and turned it over. "What is this Madriani and Heens?"

"Hinds. Madriani and Hinds is a law firm."

"You?" she said.

"I'm Paul Madriani," I told her.

"You're *abogado*?"

"If *abogado* is a lawyer the answer is yes. I'm one of the partners."

"I am impressed. Very good." She looked at the card and thanked me for it. "Ah, and I see your name is on the pen as well."

"We have the pens printed with the firm name and address for clients."

"Very nice. You don't mind if I keep it?"

"Of course not."

She clicked the point of the pen closed, dropped it in her purse and continued to look at the business card as she felt the embossed letters with the tip of her finger.

We talked for a while. She told me about her friend and his business selling rare coins, that he often took her shopping. While she enjoyed this, she was getting tired of it now and missed her family. Then she turned the tables and started her own inquisition.

In ten minutes' time she learned more about me than some of my friends who have known me for years. She was a Latin litany of questions, where I lived, what I was doing in Del Mar, whether I was married. This as she checked my finger for a ring. When I told her I was widowed, she said she was sorry, and before she could take a breath asked if I had any children.

She was not shy. Still, there was a kind of charm in the innocence of it, as all these questions seemed to come naturally to her, like water from a fountain.

"I have one daughter," I told her.

"How old?"

"She's in college, and if I had to guess, I'd say maybe just a few years younger than you."

"So you think I am young?"

"Like most things in life, age is relative. You are certainly younger than me."

"Why are American men all like this?" She cradled the coffee in both hands and shrugged her shoulders. "I don't understand. Why do they say I am young and they are old?"

"Maybe because it's true."

"Who cares? Makes no difference," she said. "How old do you think I am?"

"No. No. I don't play that game."

"What game?" she said. She looked at me as if she didn't understand.

"In this country, guessing a woman's age is a good way to get in trouble," I told her.

She laughed. "Nooo. I won't be angry. Please." Before I realize, she's reached across the table and brushed the back of my hand with the long nails of two fingers. "Tell me."

Like a man who has lost a leg, the sensation of her fingernails on the back of my hand seemed to linger long after she had withdrawn her hand from mine.

"Tell meee." She smiled and gave me a sideways glance, the full two-dimple show, coquette.

"How would I know?"

"Make a guess."

"I don't know."

"Come on." She put the cup down and grabbed my hand with both of hers. She wasn't taking no for an answer.

"Let me see. Twelve."

She gave me a look as if she might slap me. So I looked at her closely. She turned her face, first one side and then the other.

"Hmm. If I have to guess, maybe twenty-two."

"Aw, you are not serious." She pouted a bit.

"Am I close?"

"I'm not telling."

"No, now you have to tell me."

"No." She looked at me with her big, oval dark eyes. The way she sipped her coffee and looked at me over the top of her cup, the calculating gaze, told me that I had probably underestimated by a few years, but not much.

"They must have found the fountain of youth in Costa Rica," I told her.

She gave me a puzzled look. "Esscuse me?"

"Never mind."

"I know some lawyers in Costa Rica. In San José there are many." She looked at my business card. "Coronado, where is that?"

"Down the coast, just a little south of here. It's across the bay from San Diego."

"Ah. And what type of legal work do you do?"

"Mostly criminal trial work."

"Really? That must be interesting. You must be very intelligent to do that."

"It has its moments. Sometimes it's interesting, sometimes it's stressful, and there are times when it can be boring."

"So if I get in trouble, I could call you," she said.

"Well, you have my phone number now."

"Yes, I do." She slipped my business card into her purse with the pen.

We finished our coffee. I had to run to catch my friends. We said good-bye. That was nearly two weeks ago.

EIGHT

This morning Katia does not look nearly as young or as innocent. The smile is gone, as is the twinkle in her eyes. But even without makeup, and missing a solid night's sleep in the women's lockup of the county jail for the better part of three days, she is still strikingly beautiful.

Harry Hinds, my partner, has insisted on coming along this morning, whether to confirm this fact or to save me from myself, I am not sure. But it seems that Harry now has a stake in all of this. Without realizing what they were doing, the cops have rung Harry's bell. As a result we may be in this for the duration.

Strange as it sounds, it was the police who came knocking at our door yesterday morning, not Katia who called. Among the items the cops found in her purse when they arrested her was my business card. This piqued their curiosity. Following the murders and the suspect's arrest, authorities wanted to know what I knew, in short, how my card had gotten into her purse before the events, if, in fact, that was the order in which things had happened.

They asked specifically whether she had ever been to my office on a legal matter regarding business. I told them no. They asked if I'd ever been to the house where she was living with Emerson Pike in Del Mar. Again I told them no. So there was no lawyer-client relationship? No. That opened the floodgates. What did we talk about? They wanted to know every detail. When I explained the quixotic manner of my meeting Katia, in the market that morning two weeks ago, and our conversation over coffee immediately afterward, they seemed to back off.

And that was the only time you met or talked with her? Yes.

Of course, by then it didn't matter. It was too late. Someone, somewhere leaked to the media that a lawyer's business card identifying me by name was found in the suspect's purse. It has been all over the local news for twenty-four hours, the breathless nonstory of the lawyer who may be involved. So now Harry wants to know what the cops know. It has become a game of lawyers' tag, and for the moment it seems that I am It.

So this morning we are busy pulling together the details, the few things that we think we know, how the police caught up with Katia in Arizona on a bus halfway to Houston, where she was headed. According to the newspapers, because the police have not officially confirmed it, they tracked Katia from a cell phone signal, a phone she had stolen from the man she was living with, her friend, the coin dealer who now is dead, along with his household maid. This is the basis for all this unpleasantness and one more reason why you might want to think twice before shopping for bananas on a Saturday morning in Del Mar.

I must admit that I never connected Katia by name with the crime until the police knocked on my office door. There is enough crime in this part of the state that one more murder, more or less, doesn't always catch your attention, even if it's blaring from the evening news. But after the cops left, I went diving for the papers, everything I could find in print since the night Emerson Pike was killed.

Using the public defender, Katia is to be arraigned on two counts of first-degree murder tomorrow morning. At the moment, I'm not sure that we can help her. The mountain of incriminating evidence seems almost overwhelming. Harry and I have consulted the public defender to ensure that we are not stepping on toes. We have established an attorney-client relationship for the purpose of evaluating whether we might take the case. For one of those nefarious reasons that lawyers sometimes seize upon, the public defender was quite happy to have us do this. Why? Because, if nothing else, it will keep me off the stand as a witness.

Katia's lawyer can't be sure what his client may have said to me the day we met or how such an innocuous and innocent episode might be dressed up or drawn out to look incriminating if I were forced onto the stand; the specter of another older man being hustled by the young, alluring suspect. The best way to inoculate Katia from this is to draw me into the case. Once I talk to her, even tangentially, as lawyer to client, my testimony is verboten. The prosecution probably couldn't even get my business card into evidence.

Katia seems happy, even if surprised, to see me. Why she didn't think to use my business card to call, I'm not sure. And I don't ask.

"I guess we should start at the beginning, why you took the bus?" says Harry.

This isn't exactly the beginning I might have started with, wondering instead how she met Emerson Pike and how their relationship developed. But I leave it to Harry for the moment.

"If you wanted to return to Costa Rica, why not fly?" says Harry. "There are direct flights to points south out of San Diego."

"I couldn't," she says. "The first place Emerson would have looked for me was the airport."

"Emerson Pike was dead," says Harry.

"I did not know that. All I know is that he was alive when I left the house." She looks at me on this. "You must believe me. I knew he would follow me. And the first place he would go would be the airport in San Diego. Besides, I didn't have enough money to take a plane."

"Let's talk about that, the money," says Harry. "Pike's wallet, the one the cops found on the bed, had your fingerprints on it. Did you know that?"

She shakes her head no, and then says, "Of course. I am not surprised. I took the money from his wallet. I already told the police that. I needed the money for the, how do you say? The *boleto*."

"The ticket," I say.

"For the boose." She is talking about the bus. "It was the only way I could get away from Emerson. He wouldn't give me money. And he wouldn't let me go."

Harry is standing less than two feet from her, one foot on a chair, looking down at her. This is one of his favorite postures when he's visiting someone in jail and wants answers. "Why wouldn't he let you go?"

"I don't know." She looks at him, shaking her head. "He wouldn't tell me. I asked him, over and over again. But he refused to tell me. He said he loved me. But I know that wasn't true."

My partner shoots me a cynical glance. Harry is thinking, older man, younger woman, the oldest reason on earth.

Katia's darting eyes vacuum up Harry's thoughts. "No. Es not that," she says. "It's something else. It's something to do with the pictures. I'm sure."

"What pictures?" I ask.

She spends several minutes telling us about the photographs taken by her mother in Colombia the year before and the fact that Emerson Pike seemed to be obsessed with these the moment he found them in her camera. She tells us that it was then that Pike first suggested they take a trip north to the States to stay at his house near San Diego, and about Emerson's wizardry in obtaining a short-order visa for her, as if on demand.

Harry has a puzzled look. "How long did you say the visa took?"

"Three days."

Harry makes a note. "Easy enough to check it out," he says.

Katia tells us about her mother who, as far as she knows, is still down in Colombia, visiting relatives. Emerson was having Katia call home every day, checking to see if her mother had gotten home yet, back to Costa Rica. According to Katia, although she can't prove it, she is certain that Emerson was not going to take her back to Costa Rica until Katia's mother was back there, and maybe not even then. Emerson Pike's captive. This may be the best defense she has, perhaps the only one.

"Why didn't you go to the police, or the Costa Rican consulate?" I ask. "If you'd gone to them, you wouldn't be in this mess now. They would have provided assistance. You know that."

She looks at me sheepishly. "I couldn't be sure of that. Emerson was a powerful man. He had a great deal of money. He would have friends in the police. Look at how quickly he was able to get the visa for me to come here." She has every explanation in the book for not making two simple phone calls.

"Did he ever hit you?" Harry plumbs the depths and comes up empty.

"No."

"Did he ever lock you up, confine you anywhere?"

"No. But I think he was going to. If he knew I was trying to leave."

"But he never did it?"

"No. He would not let me have cash. He took money away from me whenever he found it. And then he would send money to my family in Costa Rica. It made no sense unless he was trying to keep them quiet and keep me here against my will."

"Did you tell him you wanted to leave, to go back to Costa Rica?"

"Almost every day. Sometimes several times a day."

"And what did he say?"

"He made excuses. Next week. Next month. Two weeks from now, and then he would change the subject."

"Did you think of going to the police?" Harry knows this is the first question the prosecutor will ask if they get Katia on the stand.

"No. But if I had to, I would have. He knew it."

"These pictures," I ask, "the ones your mother took, why would they be of concern to Emerson?"

"That's what I wanted to know. He wouldn't tell me," she says.

"Where are the pictures now?"

According to Katia, the police have them. They were in her bag the day they arrested her. She and Emerson had argued over the photographs the night she left. He had finally given them back to her and she had stashed them in her overnight bag before she left the house.

"That brings us to the bag," says Harry. "What else was in there?" Harry already knows, but he wants to hear what Katia has to say.

"You mean the gold coins and the stubs from the pawnshop dealer? I already told them all about it." Katia is talking about the police and her earlier statements to them.

Her plan was simple. When she flew into the country with Pike coming north, they landed and changed planes in Houston. She knew she could get back home from there. She also knew she had enough money from the cash in Pike's wallet the night he was killed for a one-way bus ticket from San Diego to Houston. She had gathered the bus fare information off the Internet when Pike wasn't looking.

According to Katia, the gold coins she took from Pike's study were to cover the cost of an airline ticket from Houston home to Costa Rica. The exact cost of the airfare was less certain. She couldn't be sure. But she knew one thing. She needed time to cash out the coins. According to Katia, the bus ride would give her that time, all the while putting distance between herself and Emerson Pike. While he was searching the airport for her, she would be gone. She fenced some of the coins at a pawnshop in a small town in western Arizona just hours before the police caught up with her. The pawn tickets were still in her purse, along with the cash. When they stopped her, Katia thought she was being arrested for theft.

One thing was clear, if anyone should be in jail it was the pawnshop owner. Katia had no idea of the value of what she was selling. According to expert appraisals, she had pawned more than thirty thousand dollars in rare coins and had received just over fourteen hundred dollars in cash, far less than the gold content of the coins she'd sold.

"What happened to the rest of the coins?" says Harry.

"They were in my bag," she says.

"No. No, I mean the other two hundred and eighty-six coins. That's what the police are estimating is gone, the ones from the drawers. The ones you broke into."

Katia gives me a puzzled look, then back to Harry. "I didn't go near any of the drawers. I didn't need to. I took only what was on the desk. There were nineteen coins and twelve others in two plastic sheets. I counted them carefully on the bus when no one else was looking, down inside my bag. I am sure. This is not a question. I took no other coins," she says.

According to the police there was almost half a million dollars in coins missing from Emerson Pike's study the night he was murdered. "You're sure you don't want to think about this?" says Harry. "Where you might have put them?"

"I am sure." Katia looks at him, indignant. "I know what I took and what I didn't take." She looks at me, imploring. "That proves it, don't you see? Someone else was there. Besides, I didn't have time to take anything more even if I'd wanted to."

"Why not?" I ask.

"Emerson was in the shower. I could hear the water running. I knew he would be coming out any moment. I didn't have time to take anything else. It was all I could do to grab the coins on the desk and write the note. I barely got out the door as it was."

"What note?" I ask.

She looks at me, puzzled. "I already told the police about it. The note I left for Emerson, the one on his desk. I told him I was taking some coins, but only enough to get back home to Costa Rica, and please not to follow me. I told him that if he did I would go to the police."

This leaves Harry and me looking at each other. We have a list of items found by investigators at the scene, supplied by the police to the public defender's office, part of early discovery. Harry flips through the list, running his finger down each page. When he finishes the last page, he looks up at me and shakes his head.

"There was no note, Katia. The police didn't find any note," I tell her.

"I don't understand," she says.

"Has anyone explained to you what the investigators found at the scene?"

She shakes her head. Katia is in the dark. Even the public defender hasn't told her everything.

"They found Emerson Pike's body on the floor in the study. The maid, did you know her?"

Katia nods.

"She was stabbed to death downstairs. They found her body at the foot of the stairs, near the dining room."

"Poor lady. Emerson called her to come to work that

evening," she says, "to clean up after I cooked. It was late. She didn't want to be there. You remember?" She looks at me. "The plantains."

"Yes."

"I prepared the meal that afternoon. The guests came and left. Only two couples. Emerson wanted her to clean up." Katia's talking about the maid. "I told him it could wait until morning. But he refused, said no, and he called her." She slumps back into the hard metal chair, realizing for the first time the enormity of what has happened.

The police have questioned the guests, but according to the reports, they know nothing.

"There were fourteen drawers of coins." Harry eases off the subject. "The locks on the drawers were broken, and according to the police all of those coins are missing."

"I didn't take them," she says.

"I know." Harry is starting to believe her. It's the problem of there being almost too much evidence, when all the ducks line up too neatly.

"Both Pike and the maid were stabbed with a knife from the kitchen downstairs," he says. "The police found it. There were no fingerprints on the weapon. Whoever used it washed and dried it, then left it on the sink. There was just a single tiny spot of blood near the handle. What they call a trace. The blood matched that of the maid."

"I don't understand," she says.

"The police are assuming that whoever killed Emerson fled down the stairs and ran into the maid. They may not have wanted to kill her, but they panicked. They had to kill her in order to escape."

"What does this have to do with me? I didn't go out that way. I went out through the garage, down the back stairs. I had to use the remote control from Emerson's car to open the gate."

"And how do we prove that?" says Harry.

"My fingerprints. They must be on the door to the garage," she says.

"Unfortunately, your prints are all over the house," says Harry. "You lived there for several weeks. Even if we found your prints on the back door, there's no way to prove when they were placed there. It could have been that night, or it could have been two weeks earlier."

You can see the hope as it dies in Katia's eyes. Then another spark: "The remote," she says. "The one for the gate out in front. I threw it into some bushes off the road. We can find it," she says. "It will prove that I went to the garage, into the car."

"Even if we could find it, all that proves is that you left by the gate," says Harry. Harry knows, as I do, that the state's theory of events following the murders will be highly malleable, sufficiently pliable to embrace a number of different avenues of escape. They will have already identified several problems with the evidence. Not only was the murder weapon, the knife from the kitchen, cleaned and lying on the counter for the world to find, but no fingerprints were found on the front door, just smears of blood around the doorknob. This is in fact not uncommon at bloody crime scenes. In a frantic headlong escape a clear, readable print is more often the exception rather than the rule.

And it gets worse. Emerson Pike's body was found with two major wounds, one in the back that was by all accounts fatal, causing shock and massive bleeding. The second wound is the problem. Harry tries to explain this to Katia, who seems dazed by the details, all of which seem to drift in a vicious circle ultimately coming back to point at her.

"The second wound," says Harry, "was postmortem, inflicted, done after Pike was already dead. The police are saying this second wound was the result of anger on the part of the killer."

"I don't understand," she says.

"They have to explain to the jury why anyone would bother to stab a person who is already dead," I tell her.

"It's sick," she says. "A person who would do that es loco, crazy."

"We can hope but I don't think the DA will go quite that far," says Harry. "They might go as far as angry, maybe mad as hell, but crazy is one we'd have to prove ourselves. What is more likely is that their shrink is going to say the killer was trying to send a message to the dead by leaving one of Pike's expensive toys sticking out of his chest."

Harry gives her a moment. He stands there watching her, waiting to see, if given this mental image, she might suddenly crack and come clean.

She shakes her head, shrugs a shoulder. "*¿Cómo se dice* 'shrink'?" she says.

"A psychiatrist," I tell her.

"Ah."

"Head doctor," says Harry. "You understand that the police will put one on the stand to testify?"

"I see. Yes."

"Well. He may tell the jury that in his opinion the second wound was intended as an angry message to Emerson Pike after he was dead that he had too much money. That perhaps he wasn't sharing enough of it with his killer."

She sits there, eyebrows furrowed and a puzzled expression. If Harry is touching any sensitive nerves, you wouldn't know it.

"There is nothing you want to tell us?" says Harry.

She shakes her head, looks at me.

"Okay." Harry expels a big sigh. "The weapon the police found sticking out of Emerson Pike's chest was a very expensive dagger," says Harry. "Word is, he used it as a letter opener."

With this Katia's face lights up like a lantern. "Yes, I remember it," she says. "It was on his desk."

"Is that where it was the last time you saw it?" I ask. "On the desk?"

"Yes." But as she says this, a dark expression crosses her face.

"The police found a set of latent fingerprints on the dagger's handle," says Harry. "Guess who they belong to?"

"No. No. No—no." Frantic eyes, Katia looking first at Harry, then back to me. "No." As if by saying it enough times she can make the dagger and the prints vanish. For several seconds she seems to struggle for breath. One hand to her stomach, as if Harry's words have squeezed every ounce of air from her lungs, like a bellows.

"Are you all right?" I ask.

"Please. I can esplain." She reaches out and touches Harry's arm. He steps back, away from the chair. "You misunderstand. Listen to me, please."

In thirty years of practicing law, Harry has heard it all, so why not? "Go ahead."

"Es true, I picked it up. I would have told you. I forgot."

"The dagger?" says Harry.

"Yes. But it's not what you think. I picked it up to put it on top of the note. I told you about it, remember? I wrote to Emerson that night, a short note, telling him I took the coins and not to follow me."

"Yes."

"I left the note on Emerson's desk, in the study. I picked up the dagger. It was on the desk. I put it on top of the note to hold it there. So he would find the note, that's all."

"A paperweight."

"Yes." She nearly jumps out of her skin, pointing at me as I say the words.

"Essactly," she says. "I used it to make a paperweight. Do you understand? That's how my fingerprints got on it. Don't you see?" She looks at me and then back to Harry with pleading eyes. "You do believe me, don't you?"

Harry thinks about it for a moment. He fixes her with a long and uncomfortable stare, and then glances over the top of his glasses at me. "What do you think?" He's asking me.

Before I can answer, Harry does it himself. "A paperweight for a nonexistent note, one you say you left at the scene, but the cops never found." He gives her one of his sardonic smiles. "Do you have any idea what the police would have done if you told them that the day they arrested you?"

Katia swallows hard. "No." From her expression, if Harry told her "summary execution" she would believe it.

"They'd still be laughing," he says. "Do you know what that means?"

She shakes her head. "No."

"That the police sometimes don't know the truth when they hear it."

NINE

Alim Afundi longed for the arid Zagros Mountains of his homeland and for the village of his father. He wondered if he would ever see his home again. He knew he would never see his parents. Both had been killed two years earlier in an errant attack by American warplanes while visiting relatives near the border with Iraq. The mighty Satan called the accident "collateral damage" and dismissed it as part of the unfortunate cost of peacekeeping.

And for now Afundi and his comrades remained on another continent half a world away.

It was nearly a year since their escape from America's fenced fortress at Guantanamo Bay. This word, "Guantanamo," was one they had never heard or known of until they achieved their freedom. In the months that he and his men had been held, there had been no visits from international groups or others representing the prisoners. Afundi's American captors had seeded rumors within the prison that they were on the American mainland in a place called Florida, surrounded by swamps and shark-infested seas, and from which there was no way home.

There had been a few attempts at escape, but as far as Afundi knew, he and his comrades, six of them, were the only freedom fighters thus far to succeed. They cut through wire, tunneled under fences, and waded through swamps until, exhausted and lost, they stumbled into a group of armed military men.

Despondent, believing they had been recaptured, Afundi tried to kill himself by cutting his wrist with a small blade from a razor. But he was saved by two of the men in green fatigues. It wasn't until later, when Afundi's own counsel general visited him in the hospital, that he realized that the men who saved him were Cuban soldiers, and that the American prison fortress was itself an island in the middle of a Cuban sea. Had his freedom fighters known it, Afundi believed they would have stormed the fences in the American compound even in the face of machine-gun fire.

For weeks Afundi and his men remained as guests of the Cuban government, feted and entertained, waiting for the propaganda coup of their escape to be unveiled to the world. But this never came. The Americans, it seemed, were too embarrassed to admit their own incompetence, and therefore disclosed nothing regarding the escape to their own press. Afundi was then certain that the Cubans would disclose it in concert with his own government. But strangely they did not.

Instead, six weeks after their escape from Guantanamo, Afundi and his men, along with an interpreter, boarded a Cuban military plane and flew west, away from the island and farther from their homeland, toward a rendezvous with armed allies in the mountains of Colombia. They carried twenty million dollars in cash from their own government and were told that they would receive their orders for their next mission as well as the training necessary to carry it out from the people in Colombia. The small area of that country, tucked up against the Pacific Ocean on the western approach to the Isthmus of Panama, had been controlled since the 1960s by the Revolutionary Armed Forces of Colombia, better known as FARC.

Alim had learned much from his FARC hosts in the months he and his men had been with them. The organization operated within Colombia as a kind of government in exile. The FARC possessed an informal alliance with his own country as well as other nations. They participated in a complex web of international connections and subnational associations. These included people's governments on nearly every continent, freedom fighters such as the Taliban in Afghanistan, and drug cartels that, along with kidnapping for ransom, the FARC used to derive most of its funding.

The relationships were complicated, but for Alim and his men it reduced down to a single common goal shared by all: the desire to annihilate the Great Satan, to eliminate the power of the American regime so as to shake its grip once and for all on the rest of the world.

To Alim, that the devil should die because of its warfare and interference in the affairs of others should come as no surprise. The irony was in the fact that after launching successive wars over oil in the Middle East, it should meet its fate because of a war on drugs launched in its own backyard, a war that most had already forgotten about.

In the 1980s and early '90s the Americans had linked arms with the Colombian government in a decade-long war to drive drug traffickers from Colombian soil. The Americans succeeded, only to have the cartels reappear in an equally violent form in Mexico, directly across its own border in places with names that Afundi could barely pronounce, Tijuana and Ciudad Juárez.

The proximity of these forces to the huge amounts of money and armies of violence at their command had now caused Satan to try to wall himself in.

The Americans had planted new listening posts abroad in an effort to revive their human intelligence networks. They used technology to listen in on telephones and to read e-mail. But with all of this they were now more vulnerable than ever before. They had done nothing to alleviate the anger of millions, which carried on its wings the threat that soon Satan would face something he could not even begin to comprehend.

Elements of the plan were already under way. Money had been delivered to the cartel to begin work. They were not told the precise nature of the cargo to be delivered. They were told that the product of their labors would be theirs to use as they wished once it was completed and the delivery was made. The Mexican cartel was now a critical element in the plan.

And for the moment the cartel had saved both Afundi and his mission. For how long he couldn't be sure. The problem arose because Alim had allowed the woman to come here into FARC territory in the first place. Because the old man was sick, he needed her. FARC had provided doctors, but the old man wanted his daughter. Alim was desperate. He would do anything to keep him alive.

The difficulty arose because the man he had assigned

to watch her had not done his job, that and the fact that she should never have been allowed to leave. That was the blunder.

It had all started with an argument. When the old man told them how long it might take, Afundi knew they couldn't wait that long. The doctors had already given him their estimate that the old man might have six months left, eight at the outside. That was four months ago. If he died, it was over. They all knew it. Afundi's government had sent over technicians to look at the problem. They determined that the Russian possessed both information and techniques without which the entire project was hopeless. Safety devices incorporated in the original assembly could not be overcome except by those with specific knowledge of its design.

In the quarrel that followed, Alim and his men, including the one who was supposed to be watching the woman, became so bound up with the interpreter in arguments with the Russian, insisting that they could do much of the work for him if only he showed them how, that no one even noticed the woman and her camera.

Alim had no idea there was even a problem until months later. Fortunately, the FARC had sources in Costa Rica. An American tourist had started asking questions, and even brought up the name Nitikin. Some judicious probing and the fact that the tourist had somehow found photographs, and Alim jumped on it immediately.

The cartel in Mexico possessed what Afundi did not: access across the border by way of travel documents for daily business and people with the skills to solve the problem.

True, the man was a mercenary being paid, but he

acted swiftly and, for the moment at least, the project was still alive. But he had left a loose end and now it was threatening to come unraveled. It was a sensitive issue, one that Afundi was anxious should not be allowed to disturb the old man or, for that matter, his daughter. She was in permanent residence now, though as far as Afundi knew, she had not yet come to realize this. There would be no more phone calls home or trips to Medellín. At this point the opportunity for harmful information to flow in either direction was far too great.

The cartel's man would have to deal with the loose end. This morning Afundi was busy with the interpreter, writing riddles to make sure that this happened and that it happened quickly.

Liquida sat at a table at an outdoor café on Orange Avenue in Coronado, two blocks from the lawyer's office. He considered his options as he sipped a cappuccino and dipped the pointed end of a biscotti into the frothy brew.

The lawyer's name, Paul Madriani, and his firm, Madriani and Hinds, had popped up in the news the day before. This morning Liquida was scanning more details as he sipped his coffee. According to the news accounts, it was now confirmed, they were representing the woman.

The local papers and the San Diego television stations were full of it. The double murder in a high-end neighborhood up in Del Mar, the gory scene and the arrest of the young woman, was hot news. So far it was confined to the local press. If he was lucky and if he worked quickly, it would stay that way, a San Diego story with a sad ending and no more questions.

So far the press and media reports were limited to a few details about how authorities had caught up with her in Arizona, trying to flee; some veiled conjecture as to her live-in relationship with the old man; and speculation that she might have been in the country illegally.

The press pounded the illegal-alien angle with relentless sidebars to the murder story, another violent criminal from over the border and more innocent victimized gringos. Of course, they failed to note that one of the victims, the maid, was herself Mexican, and for all Liquida knew, she might have been undocumented as well. This morning's paper said the female suspect was believed to be from either Mexico or Colombia. Sooner or later they would get it right and start nosing around in Costa Rica. Liquida's employers made it clear; they were counting on him to deal with the problem before that happened.

He read on. Halfway down the page, the maid's brother was interviewed. He told reporters that his sister was not supposed to work that night but that she had been called in at the last moment. The brother had dropped her off at the murder house at nine thirty. Liquida must have just missed them. It bothered him, but not enough to stop nibbling on his biscotti.

He hadn't arrived outside the fence at Pike's house until a quarter to ten. Had he been there earlier and seen the maid and her brother drive up, he would have postponed the entire event.

According to the reports in the press, the maid's brother returned to pick her up just before midnight, when she didn't call home and efforts to reach her on her cell phone failed. He rang the bell at the front gate, but nobody answered. What he did after that wasn't clear. The police had instructed him to say nothing more.

Some of the details, including what little the news reporters picked up regarding the crime scene, were at variance with the facts as Liquida knew them. As usual, the authorities withheld all of the critical forensics, any trace evidence, the trail of blood inside the house, the wounds, and how and where they were inflicted. The only specifics about the weapons came by way of the vague information that the victims died of stab wounds and the disclosure that one of the victims was found upstairs and the other on the first floor.

Having taken down the old man, Liquida had figured that he was home free. How hard could it be to rouse the woman and draw her into the study? After dispatching Pike he made some noise, stomped on the floor a few times, and waited.

When that didn't work, he pushed over a small display case in the study. This smashed the glass in the case and dumped various cups, other awards, and mementos across the hardwood.

When the woman didn't come running, he began to wonder if she was deaf. He started a search of the rooms on the second floor, but he couldn't find her. Liquida came as close to panic in that moment as he could ever recall.

His first thought was that she had seen him and fled, perhaps from the top of the landing when he first saw her. If so, the police could be arriving at any minute. Liquida began to sweat. He moved frantically from room to room, searching every place he could think of. He went down the stairs into the garage and found a car door open. He checked inside for the ignition key. It wasn't there. He thought maybe she had tried to take the car and couldn't.

Then he noticed that the side door leading from the garage into the yard was open. She must have gone out that way, but he didn't follow her. If she had reached a phone, the police would be on their way.

He raced back upstairs. If he couldn't get the woman, he would make a quick effort to find the documents and beat a hasty retreat. He started looking for the documents in the most likely place, the study.

It was then that he found it, the note the woman had left for Pike. It was toward the front of the desk, under the pen and the ornate letter opener. He read it without picking it up. His pulse dropped forty beats. She hadn't seen him. She was on the run from the old man, and she had taken some coins. Liquida dropped into the chair behind the desk to catch his breath.

He couldn't be certain how long she'd been gone. He estimated that at least ten minutes had passed since he'd seen her up on the landing from down below. He pieced it together in his head. The noise of the running water had to be the old man taking a bath or a shower.

He guessed that when she heard this, the woman made her move. She hadn't lingered for long or he would have caught up with her.

Things were not going well. First the maid and now this. He was trying to figure out how he could track her down and wondering when the next flight to Costa Rica was. He was staring across the desk at her note on the other side when it occurred to him that the problem of the missing woman and the abrupt way in which she'd left might actually present its own solution.

Once the two bodies were discovered and the police were called in, it wouldn't take them long to start counting heads and realize she was gone. Neighbors probably knew she was living in the house with Pike. The cook certainly knew it. Pike's friends knew it. Process of elimination: two dead bodies and she is gone; either whoever killed the others took her hostage, or she did the deed herself. When they caught up with her, and they would, the fact that she was running free, they would arrest her in a heartbeat.

He considered his options. There weren't any. The only thing serving to confirm her denials would be the note, and the police would probably claim she wrote that just to cover her tracks. The authorities would arrive at the obvious conclusion: either there was an argument and a violent struggle or she simply wanted money. Either way, she killed Pike, and ran into the maid on her way out; that's what the evidence would show.

He got out of the chair and went around the desk. He was reaching for the note when something instinctual stopped him. It was Pike's letter opener, the oversize dagger on top of the paper.

Even now, sitting here on the street drinking coffee and watching as the traffic coursed down the broad avenue, past the lawyer's office, Liquida had to smile.

He realized immediately that she had to finger the dagger to put it on top of the note. He looked at the blade. It was very sharp, both edges. A woman, dainty hands, would not pick such a thing up by the blade. She would take it by the smooth bronze handle.

It was so simple, made to order. He picked it up by the blade between gloved fingers and used a heavy hardbound book to pound the end of the handle. He drove the dagger between the old man's ribs in the upper chest area. Two good strokes and the blade was embedded almost to the hilt. He grabbed the note off the desk, flinging the light plastic pen onto the floor where it hit his foot and went under the desk. He didn't care. He had what he wanted. He folded the note and slipped it into his pocket.

Then he searched for the documents. He found what he thought might be one of them, but he wasn't sure. It was the right size, a glossy print. It appeared to be hidden under a magazine on the desk. But it didn't conform to what he remembered from the description of the photos he had been given. All the same, he unzipped the front of his suit and stuffed the single photograph into a quart-size ziplock bag. He placed the bag back against his chest and zipped up the suit. He would let them decide if it was part of the deal.

He searched the desk drawers and two antique wooden filing cabinets that stood against the wall behind it. He went through every file. There was no sign of any of the other documents. He looked around the study. All of the coin drawers would have been too small to contain the photos, eight by ten inches from what he had been told.

He spent several minutes looking in the master bedroom, the only other place he could think of where the old man might have kept them. But he had no luck. He looked in the bedroom where the woman kept her clothes, some in the closet and others folded in the bureau drawers. He combed through them. He didn't find the documents, but he did find her camera. This was on the short list of items they wanted. It was in a case with one additional storage chip and an extra battery. He took the whole thing.

He gave up the search for the documents and went back to the study. The only other item he was specifically instructed to look for was Pike's laptop computer and any storage devices that might be hooked up to it. The laptop was on the desk with a single thumb drive plugged into it. He bagged the computer and the thumb drive. Then he went to work with his survival knife, the one strapped to his leg. He jimmied more than twenty locked drawers in the study and swept everything that looked like gold from each drawer into a large folding canvas bag that he'd brought for this purpose. By the time the bag was full, between the gold, the laptop, its cord with the power box, the thumb drive, and the woman's small camera, he was afraid the bottom would fall out of the canvas bag. He could barely lift it.

The gold was an added perk, the freedom to take whatever he wanted from the collection of coins as long as he disposed of them in a manner that could never be traced. There would be no way for the police to know how many coins the woman took or who broke into the drawers. Now, instead of a random burglary, they would solve the crime quickly and in the process take care of the woman for him.

Down in the kitchen he washed up the chef's knife one more time and left it on the sink. As a finishing touch, he added just a tiny trace of blood from the maid. This he picked off her body with the point of his own knife and carefully transferred to a crevice near the handle. He knew that the evidence technicians would find this and that police would conclude that the maid was killed last. He transferred smears of blood from Pike onto the maid's clothing, this to further reinforce the order of death. A little blood smeared on the front door near the handle, with the door left partially open, and Liquida made his escape. He went out the way he had come in, out the back door, locking it behind him.

Eighteen hours later police in Arizona picked up the woman. One enterprising reporter for an Arizona paper got wind of some of the coins taken by the female suspect and interviewed the pawnshop owner where she'd peddled them. Everything was working perfectly, or so he thought.

Liquida had never been in this much trouble before on any job. The people who hired him were not happy. It is the problem when you are hired to kill people but you are not told why, which is often the case.

He had been led to believe that the woman was not critical to the job. They had told him that if she was away from the house at the time Pike was killed, that that would be acceptable. In which case he was to use his best efforts to find and retrieve the documents, the photographs if he could, and to forget about the woman. He was told that killing Pike was critical in order to separate the old man from the documents. If he could find the photographs, he was to get a bonus.

The problem was that the man and the woman seemed inseparable. One never left the house without the other. It was for this reason he concluded that he would have to take them both.

But according to his employers, allowing her to escape death was one thing, setting her up for murder was another. His plan to have her arrested had blown up in his face.

In Liquida's business, clients were never interested in excuses, or in how difficult a job was. You commanded a high fee because you could do the work. Once you failed on a major contract, word got out. If your failure jeopardized people in high places, you could lose more than just your career.

This morning as he sat drinking his coffee he was waiting for a message. All of the machines inside the Internet café were busy. He would have to wait.

Liquida never used cell phones. They were far too dangerous. Even dynastic drug lords thought to be immortal were visited by death from the sky, found charred and frozen, their ears gone, but with one of the tiny plastic phones melted to the side of their head.

Instead Liquida maintained no less than twenty different e-mail addresses, each under a separate alias and all of them free—Hotmail, Yahoo, and a dozen more. The best, the most protected, were operated by overseas providers, in places where the reach of the U.S. government was limited or, better yet, nonexistent. He would contact employers on a regular basis and they would reply.

He used each address only once, and discarded each daily, like underwear. He alternated among providers to make it difficult for the government to set him up, to track his movements, or to read his mail.

To mask the messages he used encryption, not the stuff for e-mail that came loaded on your home computer, but custom made. In Liquida's world, paranoia was an acquired discipline. This meant that the keys to almost all commercial encryption software were already in the possession of the American government.

He hired a gentleman in Guadalajara who fashioned the encoding software from complex algorithms. After that the man destroyed the master key to prevent anyone else from getting at it. Liquida knew this because he'd watched him do it, thirty seconds before he killed the man, cutting his throat and torching every inch of his office with gasoline.

After Pike's murder and the disappearance of the woman, there was relative silence for a time. This changed abruptly with the news of the woman's arrest. According to Liquida's contact, the go-between who had acted on behalf of higher-ups to commission the job, the inefficiency with which it was done was now threatening ominous results.

While Liquida was not told why this was a problem, he was told that people would soon be asking questions about Pike and his background. He knew very little about the old man.

Pike's documents were still unaccounted for. The one he produced was on its way to them by DHL along with the old man's computer.

But the most ominous problem, the one that caused him to stay up nights wondering if they might soon be issuing another commission, this time on his own life, was their unbridled anger over the woman's arrest. Either she was important or she wasn't. If she was critical to their plan, they should have told him this, in which case he would have arranged it so that she could not escape.

The answer came in an encrypted e-mail message five minutes later. He took the message from one of the computers inside the café and downloaded the encoded machine language onto a tiny thumb drive plugged into the computer's USB port. Then he erased the message from the in-box, removing it from the most obvious location inside the computer. He knew there would be copies of it in other places, both inside the computer and with the various providers along the ether chain. But this could not be helped and all of the copies were scrambled. And even if someone could read it, unless they knew what they were looking for, they might not understand it.

He removed the thumb drive and retreated to the table outside and his coffee.

From his backpack he removed a small antiquated notebook computer. It was the size of a thin hardcover novel. Somewhat beaten up and worn, it had never once been connected to the Internet or any other computer network. It contained no data of any kind, only the basic operating system and a single user program.

Liquida booted up the computer and punched up the program. He slipped the thumb drive into the single USB port on the back of the machine and pulled up the message. After several clicks on the keyboard the words appeared, not encrypted, but in plain Spanish. As usual, it was brief and, except to the most discerning reader, it would have been completely obscure.

> The following is a riddle. See if you can find the solution:
> You have released the serpent of coiled and twisting justice. The head is female but with scaled eyes. She does not see, and therefore cannot strike. But beware the thrashing tail. It may turn over rocks not comprehending what is there and snag vines not knowing to what they are attached. It may crawl into places it should not go. Solution: how do you dispatch a serpent?

It was not what Liquida expected. They were not worried because the woman had information she might reveal. She knew nothing. Her eyes were scaled.

He studied the message, and from the lines of the riddle he quickly deduced the problem.

He had driven the woman to the one place he should not have, into the glare of a trial in an American courtroom. It was not what she might say, but what they might discover as a consequence that worried his employers. The serpent's thrashing tail was the probing investigators and inquisitive American lawyers who would attach themselves to the woman before and during her trial.

Unlike other places it was a process that could not be sedated, put to sleep with bribes. Kill the judge here and it was instant national news. Shoot one of the lawyers and another would take his place before they could remove the body. If you became too obvious, the hammer of the American federal government, with all of the dark forces at its command, would fall on you. Liquida knew that his own employers would kill him long before they allowed that to happen.

He took a deep breath. He had no idea what they were up to, but whatever it was, they now believed it to be in jeopardy because of what he had done. The serpent "may crawl into places it should not go" in the words of the riddle. He had set in motion something neither he nor they could control.

It was by far the largest contract he had ever received. People didn't pay that kind of money unless what they were doing was substantial and with a high degree of risk. What revelations might be uncovered he had no idea; what's more, he didn't care. He didn't want to know. It was not his business.

What was his business, and the only thing that occupied his mind at the moment, was how to achieve the ultimate message of the e-mail, the answer to the riddle. The way you kill a serpent is by cutting off its head.

TEN

The fact that Katia told us about the note first, about writing it and leaving it on Pike's desk, but never mentioned the dagger is, according to Harry, part of the deeper equation of truth.

"Think about it," he says.

This morning Harry, I, and Herman Diggs, the investigator we have used for some years now, are inside the yellow police tape that surrounds Emerson Pike's house on the hill above Del Mar. Herman is inside the house with one of the homicide detectives going over details of the crime scene.

The other homicide detective and a small cadre of uniformed cops stand huddled out near the front gate. Harry has the public defender's file, including copies of the police and investigative reports from that night and for several days afterward as they processed the scene. Everything has now been transferred to us.

"If she plunged that dagger into Pike's chest, then I'm a sword swallower and I'll eat it whole," says Harry. He is talking softly, under his breath, even though the officers are too far away to hear anything.

"You saw the look on her face. She didn't know a thing about it. Nothing clicked until I mentioned her fingerprints and then only because she realized she moved the damned thing when she put it on top of the note."

Harry is preaching to the choir. The entire chain of events leading up to and surrounding the murders reeks of contrivance. I had decided to take the case long before that point. Katia reminded me of my daughter. I could see Sarah caught up in circumstances in a foreign country, and I wondered if anyone would put out a helping hand. Katia had felt trapped and I knew it, though Harry did not.

"None of it makes sense," he says.

"I know."

"Then why don't you say something?"

"Why, do you need convincing?"

He gives me one of those patented Harry looks. "Strangest damn house I've ever seen," he says. "Looks like it's falling apart until you get up close. Place gives me the willies."

"It's what Katia said, remember, when she asked Emerson about it. He just passed it off, told her he had a strange sense of curb appeal and that she'd get used to it in time. She didn't understand what he was saying."

What is clear is that Pike designed the house to avoid attention. It wasn't what you would call an eyesore, just enough so that you wouldn't look twice. It was all he had, that and the security system, to protect the place when he was away, which was most of the time.

"Weird," says Harry.

"Maybe."

"There's so much, I don't know where to start. Nothing we've heard, read, or seen so far makes any sense," says Harry. "So I guess the house fits right in. We're supposed to believe that Katia stuck the dagger into Pike in a rage, then stumbled into the maid downstairs and killed her, but then had the presence of mind to wash off the knife only to leave it on the sink…"

"With a trace of blood on it," I remind him.

"Yeah, pure as a transfusion, no cross contamination," says Harry. "She stabbed Pike and then the maid with the same knife and all we get on the knife is a trace of the maid's blood, none of Pike's."

"And you would think she'd have rinsed her hands at the same time she washed off the knife," I tell him.

Harry gives me a quizzical glance as we cross the grass near the side of the house.

"Begs the question, how did the blood get on the front door?" I ask. "According to the lab report, again, all of it belongs to the maid, no cross contamination, though they found evidence of Pike's blood on the maid's clothing."

He thinks about this for a second. "The cops will probably say she touched the door before she realized it, then went back to the kitchen to ditch the knife."

"I see, so she caught herself, but then forgot about the dagger upstairs, the one in Pike's body with her prints all over it, and no blood at all on the handle, just her fingerprints. So why didn't she wash them off?"

"Because she didn't plant the dagger to begin with," says Harry. "Some other dude did it. It's the only thing we've heard so far that makes any sense."

"To us, maybe."

In the early going it can often look like a slam dunk,

all the little inconsistencies in the state's case, the things a prosecutor won't be able to explain. In most cases, you can be sure that before they get to trial the state will find a way to wrap them all neatly into their case.

"We both know what the DA is going to say, through his experts, of course," says Harry. "That your average killer is scared witless. That after the crime Katia panicked. And because of this she made stupid mistakes, blood on the door, dagger in the body. Three cheers for panic and stupidity."

Harry makes all of this sound sufficiently plausible to worry me. Jurors might just believe it.

Harry is looking at his notes. "Seems for a while the cops thought they might have had evidence of drugs, but it turned out negative."

I look at him.

"They found three or four little muslin bags, the tops tied off with string. They tested the substance. It came up catnip."

"Three or four of these, you say?"

Harry pages through the report, finds it with his finger. "Actually five. One of them was ripped open. Some traces of dander on it, so they assume a cat must have gotten it."

"Did Pike own a cat?"

Harry shakes his head. "Not as far as I know. No animals. Police would have brought in animal control. And there's no indication in the report. According to the people who knew Pike, he was out of the country more than half the year, traveling. Mostly in Latin America, I assume for business. He would have to board an animal if he had one."

"Let's check it out. See if there's any record of Pike having owned or boarded a cat."

Harry makes a note.

We cease our aimless prowling along the grass at the side of the house and look for the motion sensors, part of the security system that was down the night of the murders.

"Do we know where the motion sensors are located?"

"In this area somewhere," says Harry. He looks through the file. There is a diagram of the outside of the house, but it is not to scale. Harry can't be certain where the nearest sensor is located. "Let me check with one of the homicide detectives," he says. "Gimme a second."

Harry heads off toward the gate, where the cops are all clustered.

In the meantime I wander toward the house. A breeze hits the line of camellias as I approach them and something catches my eye. The wind keeps the bush open for a second. It could be a piece of trash, perhaps a small paper wrapper. In the fluttering leaves I see it dangling inside the foliage, off white and oval shaped. As I peer closer, it appears to be streaked by a tea-colored stain.

For a moment I weigh whether I should have the cops come over and tag it. If it's what I think it is, forensics already has five of them. One, more or less, isn't going to make much difference.

I turn to look. I can hear the sound of Harry's voice in the distance. He has not yet reached the clutch of cops at the gate. He is waving with his arm in the air and talking as he approaches them. I position myself between the gathering at the gate and the bush. Using my back to block their view I reach into the bush and pluck the little bag from where it is hanging. The muslin is damp, probably from dew, and tied with string. As I handle it I realize it is heavier than it looks. There is something hard inside, two or three items that feel like small pebbles cushioned by something softer.

Suddenly I hear Harry talking with someone as they approach from behind. Casually I slip my hand into the side pocket of my trousers and allow the tiny bag to slide down and join my change before removing my hand.

Harry introduces the detective. I shake his hand and a couple of seconds later he shows us where two of the sensors are located. One near the base of a tree, the other in a planter bed twenty yards away.

"But they were off that night?" I ask.

"That's what it says. I didn't write the report," says the detective.

"According to your investigating officers, the security company was forced to shut them down because of malfunctions."

"If that's what it says."

"Do you know when the system was shut down?" I ask.

"If it doesn't say in the report, you'd have to talk to the security company."

I thank him and he goes back to join the small cabal of blue at the front gate.

"Mister helpful," says Harry.

"Did forensics find anything else outside?"

"Not as far as we know. No blood. No footprints, though I doubt they were looking very hard. No evidence of forced entry, nothing suspicious…"

"Except for a security system that didn't work," I say. I stand looking toward the fence and the two motion sensors that are positioned less than a hundred feet apart. "We know one thing. The killer came this way, over that fence, probably right where we're standing. He didn't knock on the front door, so if I had to guess, I'd say he took those stairs." I nod toward the back deck.

"Because of the security camera," says Harry.

"Yep."

"That was my guess too," he says.

Pike's house had two levels of security, the motion sensors and the cameras. All the other cameras were working that night. They showed nothing unusual until approximately ten thirty, when the cameras out in front caught a figure running down the driveway toward the gate. It was Katia on her way out. It showed her using the remote device to open the gate and then tracked her for only a few more seconds until she disappeared. This was in one of the reports. The only camera that wasn't functioning properly was the one on this side of the house. It was blocked by a large magnolia leaf that the wind had blown and that somehow had lodged in front of the lens. At least that's the theory the police are operating under.

Harry looks toward the camera mounted on a pole near the fence behind us. "That's a big lens. First thing I noticed."

"What's that?"

"No magnolia leaves on the ground around it."

"Maybe Pike has a good gardener," I tell him.

Harry nibbles on his upper lip for a second, then shades his eyes with one hand. "No, that's not it. You have to have a tree before you get leaves," says Harry. "You see any magnolia trees out there?"

Harry is a bit of an amateur arborist. He knows more about trees than I do, which may not be saying much.

"Take my word for it, you don't," he says. "If the wind blew that magnolia leaf over that lens, it flew in on the jet stream from another county."

"You're sure about that?"

"As sure as I am that that leaf came by car. I'm getting a bad feeling," says Harry, "the kind that sends little tingling pulses through what's left of the hair on the back of my neck."

"Why is that?"

"Our friend who jumped the fence and came this way, he seems abnormally inclined toward rearranging the things of nature," says Harry. "And for some reason that scares the hell out of me."

ELEVEN

The request for services came from across the country, about as far from Virginia as you could get without going to Hawaii or Alaska. But it wasn't this that made it peculiar. Herrington Labs fielded work on a daily basis from customers all over the globe.

The company had been in business doing special photo development, enhancement, and analysis, for more than sixty years. It had facilities in three states, all of them on the eastern seaboard.

For the first thirty years of its existence, the company's bread and butter were government contracts, mostly with the military, the Department of Defense, space, and various intelligence agencies. Aerial and early space photography and their development and analysis were among Herrington's specialties. Much of its work was classified. It hired large numbers of former military photo analysts and darkroom technicians in its labs. Company executives wined, dined, and maintained tight rapport with officials in the Pentagon.

At the time the name Herrington Labs, to those who recognized it, was nearly synonymous with the federal government. There were people, including some in the press, who believed that Herrington was owned by the government in the same way that Air America was owned by the CIA.

In the early seventies things began to change. The secrets of digital photographic enhancement, the kind that allowed pictures from other planets to be shot back to Earth and clarified in brilliant colors and sharp contrasts, was like the discovery of fire. It had potential for highly classified military applications. Powerful forces in government did not believe this was something to be shared with commercial vendors. The thought that much of this technology would find its way onto store shelves around the world in little more than a decade never entered their minds. They were too busy building government computer labs and other facilities in a futile effort to corral it.

As a result Herrington found itself under pressure to market its services to corporations, businesses, and the few well-heeled individuals who could afford them. By the mid-nineties, the swing away from Uncle Sam to the private sector was complete, so that rarely did the company see an RFP, a request for proposal, from any government agency. Herrington was doing fine, but its orientation had changed.

It was for this reason that the request that arrived by e-mail from California stood out. An analyst named Orville Honeycutt recognized the manner in which the request was fashioned. It was something he had not seen in decades, not since before the end of the Vietnam War. He guessed that this was the reason the assignment had finally been sent to him for processing, that and the fact that it was crap. It rattled around in one of the company's servers for nearly three weeks while other staffers dodged it. In-house e-mail threads showed that four other analysts had sidestepped the job, saying they were too busy.

Honeycutt was one of the last company dinosaurs, sixty-two and a former military orphan hired out of army photo intelligence in the late sixties. He was now literally counting his days until retirement. As a short-timer, he got all the crap.

To top it off, the odious smell of paint was driving them all crazy. The painting contractor had been at it for two weeks. He was doing all of the offices and common areas. He may have been painting at night, but the smell lingered all day.

Some of the staff were getting outwardly hostile because of the mess, plastic drop cloths and sheeting over their desks in the morning, and paint dust everywhere. But mostly it was the smell. They were even leaving windows open to air the place out at night, in violation of company security.

Honeycutt tried to put it out of his mind and checked the directory of customer accounts on his computer, looking for Emerson Pike's name or the name of his company, Pike's Peak, which was on the signature of his e-mail along with his address. He needed to find an account number for billing before he could start the job. There was none. Emerson Pike was not a regular customer.

Honeycutt shot him a quick e-mail telling him to go on the company's website and either fill out the form setting up an account, or else provide credit card information for the billing. The job would not be started until one or the other was completed.

But Honeycutt's curiosity was piqued by some of the

terminology used in Pike's original e-mail that accompanied the digital images. These referred to techniques of enhancement that were applicable to older film technology. They were largely obsolete, but in their day were commonly used for intelligence work, most of it highly classified. This caused Honeycutt to wonder who Emerson Pike was, so he included a two-line postscript asking if Pike was associated with military or civilian intelligence and if so, what agency, as this might expedite the matter.

After hitting the Send button, he snapped open the attached images and assembled them into the company's holding software for processing. This way he could examine all of the images simultaneously on the large flat monitor on his desk. There were seven photographs in all, one of which was a botched attempt at enlargement that was disclosed in the original e-mail. The shots looked to be ordinary, outdoor pictures of a small group on some kind of outing.

The pictures did not have the secret look of photos taken by a body-worn or hidden camera, no long angles or a single stationary viewpoint. Whoever took them was moving around and appeared to be mingling with the group. But the men in the shots weren't smiling for the camera or posing. In fact, they didn't seem to notice at all that the pictures were being taken. From the various gestures, hand and arm movements, and changes in body attitude captured in the still shots, Honeycutt guessed they were engaged in animated conversation.

The group consisted of six men in all, though only four of them appeared in focus in two of the shots. They were standing in a clearing, and what appeared to be a small structure, probably a house, was in the background of one of the pictures. There was a heavy wooden table with a few chairs around it in the distance, closer to the structure. The setting was forested. In two of the pictures, Honeycutt could see that in the background there was a deep valley with mountainous terrain on the other side, off in the distance. The wispy vapor of clouds rose from the canopy across the valley.

Only one of the figures appeared in all seven shots. It was an old man. Honeycutt couldn't tell how old, but definitely up in years. The fact that each frame seemed to be centered on the old man led Honeycutt to conclude that whoever took the pictures had some special interest in him.

He punched up the magnification on one of the images. The old man's skinny body and spindly legs, the wiry cords in his neck, and the texture of his leathered face consumed the screen. Honeycutt adjusted the contrast, softening the stark lines between sunlight and shadow. The old guy was wearing camo-cargo pants cut off at the knees and left to fray. He looked ragged and unkempt. Except for the intense expression in his eyes, you might judge him to be forlorn. There was several days' worth of beard growth on his face and he was wearing a pair of scuffed black leather boots, the kind you might find in an army surplus store. There were no socks showing above the leather tops. His feet were probably bare inside the boots and the shoes looked too large and clunky for such frail and skinny legs.

Wherever the pictures were taken, it must have been chilly. The old man was zipped up almost to his chin in a faded weather-worn military fatigue jacket. One of the others was tarped in a blanket, Indian style, that hung around his shoulders. They all had on sweaters or jackets. Looking at the terrain, Honeycutt suspected that the temperature might be the result of altitude.

He was wondering why anyone would be willing to spend so much money processing what appeared to be ordinary photographs of six men in ragged clothes somewhere in the wilderness. Enhancing their resolution and enlarging them to near poster size with the clarity requested in Emerson Pike's e-mail would cost him several thousand dollars. He was just about to log off and return the images to the server when something caught his eye. It was only a few letters in the dappled sunlight, faded print over the breast pocket on the old man's jacket in one of the pictures, but the letters were Cyrillic.

Honeycutt sat back in the chair for a moment. He studied the complexion of the old man's face. It was weathered, like tanned leather, but underneath you could tell he was fair skinned. The lack of excess flesh on his face, its sharp angles, gave him almost a Nordic look. What hair was left appeared to have been blond at one time, and might be again if he washed it. Now that he noticed, the old man was different from the other figures in the photographs, all of whom appeared dark complected, perhaps Latin, southern European, or Middle Eastern, he couldn't be sure.

Honeycutt leaned forward, took the mouse, and drew a flickering box around the area of the lettering on the old man's chest. He punched up the program, blowing the boxed image to nearly full-screen size. The resolution dipped to a fuzzy haze. The light was not good, but the letters he could see were definitely Cyrillic.

He punched out and reduced back to the original image as he danced the computer's cursor over the figure, searching for another target. He didn't find one. He selected one of the other photos and pulled it onto the larger screen. This time the old man was farther away, maybe twenty feet from the camera lens, his body was turned sideways, and his left arm was raised in a gesture, as if making a point.

Honeycutt found what he wanted. He enlarged the view of a shoulder patch. Its colors were muted for combat; frayed at the edges and faded by the sun, it showed an oval wreath of leaves surrounding a central circle. In the center was a round shield. A perpendicular sword behind it pointed upward, with two crossed arrows bisecting the center. A smaller patch below it bore the numeral 79.

He hit the keyboard and printed the item, then swung around in his chair and scanned the bookcase behind him looking for an old blue denim three-ring binder. Honeycutt was hoping that he hadn't tossed it in the trash during one of his exuberant getting-ready-to-retire office cleanup parties.

TWELVE

Liquida picked up one of the gold coins, what collectors called a cob, an irregular hand-stamped Spanish escudo. He flipped it over and noticed the numbers and letters stamped on the other side. From a small book he had taken from Pike's house the night of the murder, he knew that the coin had been poured and stamped in Lima, Peru, probably three hundred years ago.

He dropped it into the bubbling crucible knowing that he had just dissolved several thousand dollars of its value. The risk of fencing the coins was too great. The authorities would be looking for them in every pawnshop in the country. For this reason he had decided that he could save only one of them, a single coin worth more than a hundred thousand dollars, so rare and valuable that he could not bring himself to destroy it. He set it aside on the table as he continued to work.

Liquida was huddled all alone inside a dingy autobody shop a few miles north of the Tijuana border station at San Ysidro. It was a front for a "chop shop" owned by an acquaintance, a place where they cut up and sold parts of stolen cars, or changed out VIN numbers if it was a high-end boost destined for some rich mogul in Asia.

For a few dollars, the owner gave Liquida the keys and let him use the chop shop at night when the place was closed.

Liquida stood next to the steel table of a forge, holding the torch in one hand as he fired the bottom of the small crucible with oxygen. He used only an occasional spurt of acetylene to speed things up. He wanted to avoid cutting up the crucible in the process.

Every couple of minutes he dropped a few more coins into the brew. Six shiny small ingots lay steaming in their little molds, cooling on a table a few feet away.

He looked at them admiringly, as if they were freshly baked pies on a windowsill. At the same time he was beginning to understand the saying that being rich doesn't mean you're happy.

He goosed the acetylene one more time and tried to digest the latest veiled e-mail from his masters down south. He'd decoded it on the small computer earlier that day. They were beginning to drive him crazy. The latest was another frantic message, this time with another job, more pressing than the last. Of course there would be more money. They gave him a name and an address and again instructions on things to look for after the wet work was done. They had found something on Pike's laptop, the one Liquida had grabbed that night and sent south in a box filled with plastic packing peanuts, along with the photo from the desk and the woman's camera.

Liquida informed them that he had not yet had time to cut the head off the serpent. He wished they would make up their minds. They told him the serpent could wait and sent him scurrying to Travelocity for an airplane ticket.

As if this wasn't enough, Liquida was discovering that killing the woman now locked away inside the female section of the county jail was like dealing with affirmative action, ladies only. If you were a man trying to do the deed, you had to go to the back of the line and wait.

If she were in the men's side of the jail, she would have been dead four times by now. A single phone call to a number in Tijuana by nine in the morning and she would have been suicided all alone in her cell before noon.

But the women's jail was something else. This would require him to make his own arrangements directly with some angel of suicides at the jail, and Liquida drew the line at this. It was one thing to kill people for a living; it was another to talk directly with some idiot inside a jail about having it done, especially a woman.

If she was facing serious time, she might give Liquida up just to get a little slack on her term. And if she tried to choke the snake and screwed it up, she would roll over on him in a Mexican minute. Liquida would go down for something that he didn't even dirty his own hands on. This was against his religion.

No, it would have to be done outside the jail, between there and the courthouse.

Fortunately, there was only one jail that took women in San Diego County and it was located almost twenty miles from the courthouse. She could die of old age just getting there on the sheriff's bus, unless the bus was hit by a train or a spaceship on the way.

Liquida was beginning to wish that he hadn't stopped to wash the knife that night. If he had followed her directly up the stairs right after seeing her, the woman would be feasting with her ancestors by now. And instead of sweating in some security line at TSA and doing the morning cattle call on the Jetway, he would be down in Cancun with a calculator and a scale trying to time the next spike in the price of gold.

Liquida remembered something. He walked a couple of steps to his jacket, hanging from a nail on the wall. Liquida reached into the inside pocket and pulled out a folded piece of paper.

Using just the forefinger and thumb of his right hand, he slid the pieces of the folded paper against each other until it opened up. He looked at it, slowly weighing all the options, whether at some point in the future he might have a use for it, an opportunity to turn it to his own advantage. But he could think of none.

He held the paper up by the bottom corner and set the torch to the top, then held it as it burned down past the letterhead with the name on it. The flame had raced almost to his fingertips before he released it. The final glowing ember consumed the last trace of Katia's note to Emerson Pike as it lifted tiny specks of hot ash into the air. Liquida watched as the last of these cooled and fell like dust to the cold concrete floor.

THIRTEEN

Y ou say that Pike's first meeting with you was no accident. You believe he was looking for you. Why?" This morning I am out at Las Colinas in Santee, the women's detention facility in the county, meeting once more with Katia.

"It was a feeling," she says. She sits at a table in the small conference room, running her hands through her hair, which now looks knotted and stringy. The jail comb and the harsh shampoo are taking their toll. She tells me some of the other women are giving her trouble. The Latinas inside are mostly Mexican. Many of them know each other from street gangs. One of them in particular, a big Mexican woman with a scar on her face, is friends with one of Katia's cell mates. The two of them are giving Katia trouble. Katia's youth and good looks, the fact that she is from a different culture and has tried to distance herself, have made her the object of the usual jailhouse frictions and jealousies.

I ask if any of them have threatened her.

She says, "Only a little."

I try to explain to her how it works, the jail pecking order.

"I don't know what to do. I am afraid," she says.

"I'll see what I can do. Talk to someone in the sheriff's jail unit." This will have to be done carefully, with an eye toward a housing change. Otherwise, the wrong kind of intervention will only make it worse. "But for right now, let's talk about how you and Emerson Pike met, down in Costa Rica?"

"I was going to school. I am a student at the university in San José. I did some modeling on the side to make extra money, mostly clothing and makeup. My photographs, a set of them with my name, were on the modeling agency's website, in their gallery of models. Emerson telephoned the agency. He said he wanted to hire me to do a photo shoot. He said he wanted to do some local advertising for his coin company. That's what he said."

"Did you do it?"

"Of course. He was willing to pay a lot of money, so I was happy to do it. The ads with my pictures were to appear in newspapers and magazines. But I remember thinking it was a little strange."

"Why was that?"

"Emerson had no idea what he wanted, so the agency set up the pictures. They had me wear a bikini and smile at the camera while I was holding a small stack of gold coins in each hand. I thought it was a funny way to sell to investors. But Emerson didn't seem to mind, and who was I to judge?" says Katia. "Still, that was the first clue. I should have realized."

"Realized what?"

"Men," she says. "Sometimes they come to the modeling agencies, mostly Americans…" Then she looks at me. "Sorry."

"That's all right, go on."

"They…they hire models after they look at the pictures on the website. They pay for photo shoots they never use, just to meet the women."

"Pike never used the photographs?"

"No. And he never did any advertising in Costa Rica. I didn't know that until later. He seemed very nice. He invited me to dinner. We went out. He was fun to be with and he entertained well."

I asked her what she meant by this.

"The best restaurants and nightclubs," she says. "This went on for several weeks. I got to know him, at least I thought I did."

Katia was comfortable with him. She introduced him to her friends and a cousin who was visiting from Limón at the time, all except her mother, who was away down in Colombia visiting other relatives.

"Does your mother know you've been arrested?"

"I haven't been able to talk to her. Your friend Harry, that is his name, correct?"

"That's right."

"Harry was going to telephone one of my friends and ask her to leave a message at my mother's house. He tried to call my mother's cell phone, but there was no answer. She usually leaves the phone behind, turned off, when she goes to Colombia. I assume she has not returned."

"Harry mentioned it."

"She will want to know what's happening."

"So you think Pike sought you out because he liked your photographs on the modeling agency's website?"

"It's what I thought at first," she says. "But later I realized that was not it. After he met my family, he kept asking questions. Mostly he wanted to know where my mother was."

"Why?"

"I don't know. It was as if he wanted to meet her. I told him she was away in Colombia. He asked what she was doing down there. I told him she was visiting relatives. He was very interested in this."

"Did he say why?"

"No. Just that he wanted to get to know my family. Whenever I asked him why, this is what he would say— 'Because I want to know your family.'"

"And you didn't believe him?"

"No. All he wanted to know was who the relatives in Colombia were. Strange, no?"

"Yes. Go on."

"I told him I didn't know them. It's true. They are relatives of my mother but I have never met them. She mentions them once in a while but she tells me that they are distant relatives, that I wouldn't really like them."

"Did she say why you wouldn't like them?"

"Not really."

"And you never asked?"

"I assumed there was some problem."

"You mean trouble with the law?"

"Es possible, I suppose. My mother never said anything."

"But that's what you're thinking?"

"I don't know. One of them is old, at least that's what she says, and she goes down mostly, I think, to take care of him."

"So your mother is from Colombia?"

"No. She was born in Costa Rica, same as me."

"And your father?"

"He's dead. He died when I was a baby. He was Tico, born in Costa Rica."

"How did your mother's relatives get to Colombia?"

"I don't know. As I said, she would never talk about it."

"But Emerson kept asking you?"

"Yes, all the time. And then one night we talked about it and I remembered I had some pictures in my camera that my mother had brought back with her from her trip a few months earlier. He was all excited."

"Pike?"

"Yes. I thought it was funny. I laughed at him. He wanted to see them. I told him it was late. We had just come back from a movie. He said no, no, he wanted to see them, right now. So I got the camera and showed them to him."

"Go on."

"He kept asking me who they were. We looked at them in the little window in the back of the camera. I told him I didn't know. I assumed they were my mother's relatives. She borrowed my camera. She never told me the pictures were there. I found them when I went to use it. But it must be her relatives, no? Who else would it be?"

"What did Pike do then?"

"A few days later he told me he was going back to the United States and he wanted me to come with him for a visit. He invited me to come stay at his house near San Diego."

"And you wanted to go?"

"Sure. Why not? But I told him I couldn't. I had no visa for the United States. He told me no problem. And as I told you before, he got the visa."

"Harry is looking into that, how Pike obtained it so quickly," I tell her.

"Yes, and there was another problem too. Emerson must have been in a rush," she says.

"What do you mean?"

"Well, he insisted on completing the application for me, the application for the visa. He said I would sign it but he would fill it out because it would go faster. I didn't like that. What, he thinks he's smarter than I am?"

"So what happened?"

"I gave him my passport because he needed information from it to fill out the form, but he got my name wrong. I didn't see it. He just had me sign the form. I wanted to look at it, but he said he was in a hurry. He had to go someplace and he took the form with him. Next thing I know he comes back with the visa and my name is not right."

"Wait, wait, wait...you mean you didn't go to the U.S. consulate with him when he delivered the application?"

"No. He said it wasn't necessary, that he could take care of it. He took my passport and the application and the next thing I know he has the visa."

"But the name is wrong. Did he misspell it?"

"No. He didn't put down the last part of my name—Nitikin. I always used it, Katia Solaz-Nitikin. Solaz is my father's name. My mother's family name is Nitikin. It was on my passport. Emerson knew I used it. It was the name on the modeling agency website. It made me angry because if he'd let me fill out the application, I would have done it correctly. It's the way he was. He always had to do things, even if it wasn't his business."

"A control freak," I say.

"Yeah." She snaps a finger and points at me. "That's it."

"But in the end the name on the visa wasn't a problem. I mean, you got into the country all right?"

"It would have been better if I had not." She looks around at the dismal surroundings, the concrete floor and the dingy walls of the small room we are in, with a female sheriff's deputy outside the door.

"What happened next, between you and Pike?"

"When we got to his house, everything changed," she says.

"Changed how?"

"Emerson seemed different. Nervous, as if he was watching me all the time. I told you about the money, how he took it away from me. He told me we were going to take trips to see things, but we didn't. He would buy me clothes, take me to clubs. But I could tell he wasn't doing this because he liked it. He was doing it to keep me quiet, so I wouldn't ask to go back to Costa Rica. Then I found out that before we left to come up here, he had copied the pictures from my camera to his computer without telling me. It's why I forgot to bring my camera. Emerson took it out of my bag where I kept it and he didn't put it back. So when I took the bag it wasn't in it."

"Where's the camera now?"

"At my mother's house in Costa Rica."

"And the pictures from Colombia, they're still in it?"

"As far as I know. I asked him that."

"Pike?"

"Yes. I asked if he erased them when he copied them to his computer. He didn't ask me. He just did it."

"What did he say? Did he erase them?"

"He said no, they were still there."

"And you believed him?"

She shrugs her shoulders. "I don't know."

"Is there a telephone at your mother's house, any way that we could call down there?"

"No. She has a cellular, but she turns it off when she goes to Colombia."

I give her a slip of paper and a pen and Katia writes the address of her mother's house on it. In fact, it is a description of how to get there.

"Is there anyone in Costa Rica who could retrieve the camera for us, a friend or relative who could get it from the house and ship it to us?"

She thinks for a moment and shakes her head. "Lorenzo, perhaps."

"Who is Lorenzo?"

"Lorenzo Goudaz. He is a friend of my family, but he has no key to my mother's house. Besides, he will be angry when he finds out what has happened to me. I introduced him to Emerson in San José but Lorenzo didn't like him. He told me not to trust him."

"Did he say why?"

"He said Emerson was too nosy, asking too many questions. He told me to be careful. I should have listened to him."

I take his name and telephone number to put on Harry's short list of contacts in Costa Rica in hopes that perhaps this Lorenzo can contact Katia's mother.

"You say Pike had a computer with him in Costa Rica and he used it to copy the pictures."

"Yes, a laptop."

"I assume he brought it back to the States with him when he came home?"

"Of course. That's how he printed the pictures in his study. The ones the police took from my bag."

A cop's best friend, your own computer, the first thing they seize at any crime scene. Only in this case, it's gone.

"Do you know what happened to it?"

"What do you mean?"

"Pike's computer is missing. The police didn't find it at his house."

"It was on the desk in the study. It's where he kept it. It was there when I left that night."

"You're sure?"

"Yes. I saw it when I put the note on the desk."

According to one of the homicide investigative reports, Pike had a website for his business. A wireless antenna for the Internet and a printer, all in the study. But there was no computer.

Ordinarily this would be a problem for them, limiting leads. More often than not, the answer to what happened is in the computer, e-mails and the things people research on the Internet, all of which leave tracks. But the police don't seem to be concerned at all in this case, probably because they have Katia and a seeming mountain of evidence against her. But like the missing cache of coins, they didn't find Pike's computer on Katia when they arrested her, and they can't explain why. All the little unanswered questions.

According to Katia, it all comes back to the pictures.

I ask her about her mother and whether she has ever had any problems with the law.

"I know what you are thinking," says Katia. "My mother goes to Colombia, so she must be involved in drugs."

It's obvious from the way she gripped this that the same thought has crossed Katia's mind. "No. It's not true. She has never had any problems of that kind, and she would never do that. I would know. None of my family has ever had anything to do with drugs. You can check, but you will find nothing. Besides, I don't think Emerson was looking for drugs. It was something else."

"How do you know?"

"I don't. It's just a feeling. But I don't think so. He was looking for someone or something in those pictures. You should talk to my mother," she says. "Maybe she knows something."

"How do I get in touch with her? Do you have a phone number in Colombia?"

Katia shakes her head. "She has no cell phone with her. I don't even know where she stays. Usually she calls home every week or so from a phone in the city."

"Where does she call from?"

"Medellín."

FOURTEEN

For three days after finding the binder and identifying the insignia, Orville Honeycutt nibbled at the edges of the Pike photo assignment. He burned a day of sick leave playing hooky. He had more than a month of leave, and what he didn't use he would lose when he retired.

To see what was in Pike's photos he needed to get at the lab in the basement when no one was there. The opportunity would come tonight. The painter was working downstairs. Nobody was going to stick around with the fumes trapped down below.

It was late afternoon, four thirty. He went online one more time, checking to see if Pike had responded to his e-mail to provide a method of payment. There was no reply. Honeycutt could send him one more notice and if he didn't hear back simply close the file, but he didn't want to.

He thought for a moment and then picked up the phone. He called a cell number across the river in the District of Columbia.

Freddy Younger answered.

"You got a minute?" said Orville.

Younger recognized the voice immediately. Freddy and Orville had worked together in army intelligence decades earlier when they were both young and stupid. They used to carouse at night before Freddy got married and had kids and Orville got old. They did the same type of work and it kept them in touch over the years, only Freddy's pension was much better than Orville's. He worked doing photo forensics at the FBI's crime lab.

"What's up?" said Freddy.

"Something I want to run past you."

"Shoot." Freddy listened but sounded distracted.

Orville told him about Emerson Pike and his pictures, about the old man in the military fatigue jacket, and about the insignia on the shoulder patch, the Seventy-ninth Regiment, what Orville had discovered about its history. It wasn't much, just a few lines on a page in the old denim binder. This was filled with loose-leaf pages, periodically updated by U.S. intelligence agencies and given to their private contractors doing photo work. This was before computers and the digital age. The updates would come periodically by regular mail.

Intelligence, and particularly the military, always wanted to keep tabs on foreign troops around the world, their numbers and where they were deployed. The material in the binder was decades out of date. This may have been the only reason he found what he was looking for. Inside was a page with a picture of a shoulder patch identical to the one Honeycutt had found on the fatigue jacket.

"Are you near your computer?" asked Orville.

"Yeah."

"I'm shooting you an e-mail. It's blank, but check out the two attachments."

Honeycutt sent him a copy of the enlarged shoulder patch and a second image showing part of the name over the breast pocket on the old fatigue jacket with the Cyrillic letters, only the first two of which were decipherable, *Н И.*

"It just went out. You should have it in a minute." Orville had Googled the Russian Cyrillic alphabet and knew that the first two letters on the name patch translated to *N I* in English.

"Why so important?" said Freddy.

Orville explained that, according to the information in the binder, the Russians had reorganized all of their rocket brigades in the early 1960s. At that time the Seventy-ninth had only been up and running for a few years. It ceased to exist shortly after the reorganization, sometime between '63 and '64.

"So, somebody's got an old Russian army jacket," said Freddy.

Freddy sounded indifferent until Orville told him about the unit's last overseas assignment. Then there was a long silence.

"How old did you say these pictures were?" asked Freddy.

"I didn't," said Orville, "but the same thought crossed my mind. That maybe somebody scanned some old photos into a computer. No, the files are too small and they aren't TIFFs." He was talking about Tagged Image File Format, the usual form of a digital image generated by a scanner. "They were all taken four months ago, on the same date," said Honeycutt. "The man who sent them to me sent the original digital data files, complete, and they don't lie."

"What did you say this guy's name was?"

"Emerson Pike." Honeycutt took a deep breath and edged toward what he really wanted. "Can you do me a favor?"

"What's that?"

"Write down the name Emerson Pike."

"Pike, I assume, is spelled just like it sounds?"

"Correct. Obviously, I don't have his date of birth or a social security number. I'm guessing he's probably up in years based on the information in his e-mail and the way it was written. He lives in California, according to the electronic signature on his e-mail, a city called Del Mar. With the address and name, I'm sure you can find driver's license records that'll give you his date of birth. With that you could run a background check on him for me."

"What?"

Orville was over the line and he knew it. Doing an unauthorized background check using Justice Department databases could land Freddy in big trouble. It could cut off his pension before he even got it.

"If you can't do it, just say no."

"No," said Freddy.

"Listen, just do me this one favor. Just think about it before you say no."

"I already said no, and I did think about it. If I got caught nosing around FBI background records, driver's license data, and did an unauthorized disclosure, you know what would happen?"

"Don't get caught," said Orville.

"They'd fire my ass, then they'd arrest me, and I'd

spend the next year and a half trying to explain to a federal judge how I was just doing a little favor for a friend. No thanks. And you know you should be very careful even asking me to do that."

"That's why I'm talking to you on your cell phone," said Orville.

"Tell me what you're looking for. You think the man's got a criminal history?"

"No. I think you're going to find big blanks, long periods of time with no entries, and probably files you won't be able to access."

"You think he's a spook."

"Retired spook," said Orville.

"Then the answer is hell no," said Freddy.

"Listen. I can tell you there's a good chance I'll find more information in the images. I'm still working on them."

"How did you get this stuff?"

"Over the transom," said Orville. "He sent them by e-mail. I don't know if he took the pictures or if somebody else did. But whatever I find I'll share with you if you help me. It may be nothing, then again, your people may want to know."

"And if it's nothing and I do a background check on this guy and somebody finds out, then what? Even if it is something, how do I go to them and tell them how we got the information? NO!"

"Thanks," said Orville.

"Anytime."

"Listen, if you change your mind and find anything on this guy, give me a call and I'll show you whatever I've got at this end."

"Let's get together for a drink sometime," said Freddy.

"Sure thing. Just think about it," said Orville. "That's all I'm asking."

"You're crazy," said Freddy. "Take care."

Honeycutt heard the line go dead. He hung up the phone and checked his watch. Another few minutes and the lab staff downstairs would be gone for the day.

The smell of paint made it difficult to work. But it was the price that Honeycutt had to pay if he wanted to use the photo-editing lab after hours. The painter was still at it.

Tonight he was busy finishing some of the smaller offices and work areas in the basement. He had been at it since five, and if his schedule held he would knock off just before midnight to clean up and start again the following evening.

Now that Honeycutt was in the lab, he could see the images that Pike had sent him on the oversize high-definition screen, the figures enlarged to almost half their actual size.

In all, there were seven separate digital images, six original exposures that had been shot on the same date four months ago. The only exception was the attempted enlargement, the image that was so badly mangled by poor focus, resolution, and glare that it was worthless. From the digital data he couldn't be certain when the enlargement was originally made, but it had last been opened and edited two days prior to Pike's e-mail. That was probably when Pike realized it wasn't going to get any better, gave up, and sent it in to be professionally processed.

Honeycutt knew from Pike's e-mail that the attempted enlargement was something in the background of one of the other pictures. What he didn't know was which one. Take his pick. There were six.

Pike probably assumed that the lab would work off his own failed enlargement, cleaning it up.

Honeycutt wanted to work from the original rather than Pike's degraded copy so that he could use the lab's software to render the enhancements and get the best image possible.

Worse, Pike's enlargement failed to copy sufficient file data from the original shot so that the original could be easily identified.

To Honeycutt, Pike's enlargement was nothing but a white fuzzy blur with a few dark lines on it. With nothing else to orient him, finding the original picture and then locating the tiny speck in the background that represented Pike's target took the better part of an hour. It was like finding a single piece to a jigsaw puzzle in one of six different puzzle boxes.

He looked for color, the shade of white in the enlargement, and then tried to imagine how small it might be in the original digital frame.

There was a piece of white cloth on a flat boulder off to one side in one of the pictures. Not it.

One of the men was holding a sheet of paper. He appeared in four of the shots, holding the paper in a different position with differing shadows and shades of light in each one. Honeycutt was able to eliminate two of them just by looking, and then used the magnification of the software to eliminate the other two.

When he finally found what he was looking for, Honeycutt suddenly realized what was happening in the pictures, the arm gestures and all the frenetic movement. The item in question provided the missing context for the photographs because the old man kept pointing at it. Only the stop-action of the camera's shutter kept his outstretched finger from getting there.

The men in the pictures weren't just talking, they were arguing. If Honeycutt had to guess, what they were arguing about had to do with the square white speck in the distance, the one on the table behind them, near the house. It was this document that Pike was trying to read.

Honeycutt went to work quickly. Resolution and glare reduction were easy. Computerized algorithms had to be applied to provide proper focus. The camera's auto focus had seized on the moving figures in the foreground, so the item in the distant background was beyond the focal point of the camera's lens. The digital software effectively re-created the enlarged image of the document by using computerized numerical probabilities and refocused the enhanced image. The sharp edges of paper came into clear view.

Honeycutt could now see more than a single page, a stack of pages, maybe ten, maybe twenty, he couldn't tell. They were large sheets if the size of the table was any measure. The pages covered the width of the table from one side to the other; he guessed maybe three feet top to bottom and not quite as wide. The white speck looked much smaller in the original photograph because of the oblique angle from which it had been photographed, with the paper lying flat on the table.

Enhanced and enlarged on the big screen he could see that the pages were bound together, with what looked like tape all along the far edge at the top. But the angle made it impossible to make out details on the page, only a mirage of lines and curves, as if their shadow seemed to float just off the surface of the paper. There was some kind of detailed drawing on the top page. That was clear.

Using the software it was possible to attempt to re-create the image from a less oblique, even perpendicular angle, as if the item had levitated up off the table to face the camera. The problem was that the accuracy and reliability of such a computer-generated "veritable" photograph, given the distance involved in the original shot, was sketchy at best. The algorithms of the software could reproduce the *Mona Lisa*, but they needed at least a minimal amount of basic information from the original before they could do it. Honeycutt could be left with large pixilated blanks if the data was not sufficient in the original image for the magic of the algorithms to fill in the missing information. But he had gone too far to quit now. He checked his watch. It was after eight o'clock.

It took him forty minutes and three separate attempts tweaking and adjusting the parameters of the program before he was able to come up with something that even looked as if it might work. It came back not as an image, but as a list of numbers several pages in length on the screen. Honeycutt sent the coded instructions to the wide-format printer in the other room. He then leaned back in the chair, took off his glasses, and rubbed his eyes. He was getting hungry, it was late, time to go home.

It took nearly a minute before the printer's motor kicked on in the other room.

Honeycutt got up out of the chair, sauntered across the hall, and turned on the light just in time to catch the point of the needle-sharp stiletto full force in the center of his stomach, two inches beneath the hard bone of his

sternum. The eight-inch blade sliced through the diaphragm, its pointed tip penetrating well into the lower
chamber of his heart.

Liquida held him for no more than four or five seconds before Honeycutt's knees buckled and his body
collapsed onto the heavy-mill plastic of the drop cloth.
Orville tried to stay on his knees, holding his stomach,
but Liquida toppled him with his foot into the fetal position.

"I thought you were never going to get around to printing that. Thought I might have to chase you down." Liquida talked to him as he moved to the other side, picking
up two of the corners of the drop cloth and getting ready
to close it up like a bag.

Honcycutt's eyelids flickered. He lay there, his pupils
following his killer as Liquida moved around him.
Blood spurted from the wound in his stomach in a pulsing arc, out onto the plastic. Honeycutt tried to stop it
with his hands but he couldn't. It continued for thirty
seconds, maybe less, as Liquida moved around adjusting the plastic as needed to contain the blood. In a single
sputtering pulse it stopped. When he looked at Orville's
eyes, they were glazed, the lids half shut.

Liquida had arrived at three that afternoon. He went
immediately to the front desk at Herrington Labs with
an envelope addressed to "Orville Honeycutt," the
name given to him by the people who employed him in
Colombia. Apparently, they had gotten it from an e-mail
they received on Emerson Pike's computer. The envelope to Honeycutt was marked URGENT—PERSONAL AND
CONFIDENTIAL. Inside was a blank piece of paper. Liquida then went out to his rented car in the parking lot
and with a pair of field glasses he watched through the

windows as Honeycutt was called and came out to the front of the office to retrieve the envelope. He got a good look at him, and another a couple of minutes later when he came back and angrily confronted the receptionist, who pointed to the door and shrugged her shoulders.

At the end of the day, Liquida waited for Honeycutt to come out. When he didn't, the Mexicutioner figured he was working late. After borrowing a pair of paint-splattered overalls from the painter's van, he bagged the painter just after seven in one of the rooms downstairs. He wrapped the man in plastic and rolled him out to the van in a large wheeled trash cart he found in the basement. The Herrington parking lot was virtually empty. Dressed in the overalls, no one on the street paid the slightest attention as Liquida loaded the large plastic bundle into the back of the van and closed the doors. Taking advantage of opportunities and using what was at hand was part of his trade.

He rolled and wrapped Honeycutt in the same way he had the painter. He used two more sheets and plenty of duct tape to make sure nothing leaked and then hefted the body into the cart.

The last item was the man's computer. Most of the large screen was covered by numbers, but across the top were smaller boxes with pictures in them. The man had courteously left the items Liquida was looking for on the screen. Except for one thing—there were not six photographs as he had been told by his contact, but seven. He thought about this for a second, then looked at the image of the extra picture. He couldn't tell what it was. No problem, he would delete them all.

The system was an Apple, a little different from the

PC, but Liquida had used one in his travels several times before. It was what you say, user friendly. He wrote down the name of the file so that if he hit the wrong key and the pictures disappeared from the screen, he could call them up again. The special program was a little tricky, but he quickly figured out how to find the pathway to the files. Within a couple of minutes he had tracked the images back to the server where they were stored. He deleted everything, including the covering e-mail from Emerson Pike and the billing inquiry sent in reply by Honeycutt. If there was anything more, it would take a computer expert to find it.

According to the people down south, as long as it didn't look as if anything violent had occurred in the office, and the bodies simply disappeared, by the time the authorities sorted out the missing person's reports it would no longer matter. They were merely buying time. This only made Liquida more curious. Whatever they were doing had a time frame, and apparently it wasn't terribly long.

He would dispose of the bodies along with the van in a lake he had already mapped out. There was only one more item of business. He went back to the printer room and pulled the large sheet of paper from the top chute of the wide-format printer, then laid it out on a table in the room to look at it.

Liquida leaned over the table as his eyes wandered across the large sheet. It was a drawing, something like the pictures you see pasted to the inside of a washing machine when you take out the screws and lift off the metal panel. There were letters that looked as if they were printed backward, with blank spaces, as if some-one had dropped little pieces of paper over part of them and that part had not gotten printed on the page. The only things Liquida could decipher in the text were some numbers, and even those had gaping blanks. They offered nothing by way of understanding.

His expression was one of puzzlement. This was not among the photographs he was looking for, so it had to be the extra picture he had seen on the screen. The people down south did not know about this picture, but Liquida smiled, because he was sure they would want to look at it. He picked up the large sheet of paper, folded it, and put it in his pocket. He would probably send it to them, but not just yet.

FIFTEEN

nless I am wrong, the killer tied the knot. I pluck at it with the sharp point of a penknife from my desk drawer for a minute or more before I get it loose.

Slicing into the small muslin bag or cutting the string is not something I want to do, just in case there is something important inside, something beyond the simple cumulative evidence that the police already have. I'm pretty sure I already know what it is, but I want to see it for myself.

If Harry knew about this, he would tell me that it's curiosity that killed the cat. So far he has come up with a blank as far as Pike owning any of the felines. According to the gardener and Pike's cook, there were no animals, at least none that Pike owned. But the gardener admits to having rolled over several of the small white muslin bags while mowing the lawn in the week or so leading up to the murders. He remembers because it sounded like rocks when he hit them.

Having positioned a clean sheet of paper on the blotter

of my desk, I pour out the contents of the muslin bag, the one I purloined from the bush at Pike's house.

Inside is a mash of tiny shredded leaves, what looks like tea, and in fact is. The things we don't know, but can learn online. Catnip is a variety of tea sometimes taken as a medicinal for ailments by humans, that is, when it's not being used to drive the feline set crazy.

For me at the moment, however, what is of more interest is what is buried inside. I open the matted mashed ball with the point of my penknife. What I find are five metal hex-head nuts, the kind you would use to screw on bolts. I would guess them to have a three-eighths-inch inside diameter. I have no idea of their individual weight, but you can be sure that I will have someone put them on a scale before we go to trial.

Whoever made up the bag put the metal nuts inside for heft, to give it weight so that the bag would have distance when he threw it. By doing this he could get the bag inside the motion sensors before he released the cat to set off the alarm.

According to the report that Harry read, the police have five of the small bags. I have one. God only knows how many the gardener rolled over and chewed up on his mower before the night of the murders, or how many more might still be lying around the property. Whoever used them was inventive and persistent. He kept throwing the tiny bags until he got what he wanted, a security system so annoying that the owner would have it turned off.

I scoop the contents back into the bag, including the five metal nuts, and retie the top of the bag with the string. I deposit the bag, along with my penknife, in the center drawer of my desk. One more piece in the puzzle. From the beginning this has been a case of puzzles inside puzzles.

Something Katia said to me during our meeting at the jail earlier in the week has been needling me but I can't figure out why.

I wander down the hall to Harry's office.

As I break the plane of the open doorway, I see that Harry is behind the desk, busy working, pencil in his hand. He looks up at me. "Did you see my note?"

"About Templeton, yes. Any other bad news?"

"Not at the moment," says Harry, "but with the Dwarf on the case, I'd stay tuned if I were you."

Larry Templeton, aka "the Death Dwarf," has been assigned to prosecute Katia's case. He is, without question, the most deft death-penalty prosecutor in the DA's office, perhaps in the state. I have lost track of the number of capital cases he has won, lacking enough fingers and toes to count them all. That a wing of the death house at San Quentin has not yet been named for him is itself a measure of injustice.

"Word is, he's looking to settle up with us over the double-tap thing," says Harry.

We haven't been up against Templeton since *People v. Ruiz*, the murder of Madelyn Chapman, the software mogul shot twice in the head in a tight bullet pattern you could cover with a quarter. The case was coined by the press "the Double-Tap Trial."

"That he didn't take Ruiz down wasn't for want of trying," I say.

"Tell him that. I think the columns for 'best effort' and 'runner-up' are missing from Larry's scorecard. I suspect it might have something to do with compensation for lack of physical stature," says Harry.

Templeton suffers from a condition known as hypochondroplasia, a form of short-limbed dwarfism. He stands just over four feet tall, but you wouldn't know it when he gets loose in front of a jury. All the mental power in that bald head comes tripping off the tongue. He has learned to turn a deficit in stature to an advantage. Jurors become riveted, and if you're not careful, you can find yourself getting spritzed with seltzer and having your ass kicked in Larry's circus act.

"What do we have by way of discovery in Katia's case, besides the police reports, I mean?"

"Not much, just what we got from the public defender. Our blanket discovery request went out Friday. It'll be a week, maybe ten days before we start seeing much."

"I'm looking for the copy of Katia's Costa Rican passport and the visa for her U.S. entry. I thought we had those."

"We do," says Harry. "The ring binder behind you on the shelf, third one down."

I grab it, open the cover, and unlock the mechanism that allows the pages and the plastic envelopes to slide free around the two large rings.

"Actually," says Harry, "I think I've got copies of those here somewhere."

When I turn around again, Harry is reaching into the stacked letter basket at the edge of his desk, holding a fistful of papers three inches thick, stuff he's working on.

"I contacted the State Department, trying to find out how Pike got the visa expedited. Of course, they referred me to Consular Services, visa section." Harry is licking his thumb and picking through the top corner of the stack of papers, looking for the right ones.

"I called Consular Services, they won't answer questions over the phone. Has to be in writing. So I sent out a letter. Federal government, we're gonna cool our heels," says Harry. "Here it is." He pulls out one, two, three documents. "Copy of my letter, the visa, and the Costa Rican passport." Harry hands them to me. "What are you looking for?"

"I'm just checking on something." I look at the copy of the visa first. The original of the document is protected from forgery by holograms. On the photocopy these show up as ghostly shadows of Lincoln and the Capitol dome. No doubt there are also security threads in the original paper that don't show up on the copy at all. Katia's photo, a head-and-shoulders passport shot, is on the left. Next to it at the top is the location of the "issuing post," in this case San José, Costa Rica. Below this is her name, surname first, given name underneath it.

I check the copy of her passport next. It's the thing Katia told me at the jail, what's been rattling around in my head, that the names on the two documents didn't jibe. They don't. The surname on her passport is listed as "Solaz-Nitikin." On the visa it's "Solaz." This latter is the name on the charging documents in the criminal case as well, the criminal information filed by the prosecutor's office, though the other, "Katia Solaz-Nitikin," is listed as an alias, "aka." I'd paid no attention to it before.

"What do you know about passports and visas?" I ask Harry.

"Ask me, I'm becoming an expert," he says.

"Look at this." I lay the copies down on the desk side by side, facing Harry.

"Look at the surname on each document."

"Yeah, that's typical in Latin countries, Hispanic composite names. See?" Harry points to the copy of the passport. "Here, you see the first surnames on the top line, 'Solaz-Nitikin,' and then here, next to it, it goes back what, looks like three, no four generations. It starts with her father's name, mother's maiden name, grandfather's paternal name, grandmother's maternal name, so on and so on, so what's your point?" says Harry.

"Why wasn't the last name 'Nitikin' included on the visa?"

"She probably dropped it when she filled out the application. Sometimes they do that, especially in the States."

"That's the point. Katia didn't fill out the application. Pike did. And she called him on it. He knew that she used the surname 'Solaz-Nitikin' because that's the name he found her under."

"So what's your point?" says Harry.

"Pike found Katia by way of a website for a modeling agency. She was listed on the website as 'Katia Solaz-Nitikin.' What she told me is correct. I found the site online. Pike told the agency he wanted to do some advertising in Costa Rica for his company and paid for a photo shoot with Katia. But he never used any of the shots or followed through on any advertising."

"Maybe he changed his mind," says Harry.

"Or maybe he already had what he wanted, a way to meet Katia."

"You think he used the modeling thing as a con to hit on her?"

"No. I think Pike was searching for something on the Internet, but it wasn't Katia's picture. It was her name, and if I had to guess, I'd say it was the one he dropped from her visa application.

"Think about it. You're trying to bring this woman into the country. You're filling out her visa application and you're working from her passport. Look at it." I point to the passport copy on Harry's desk. "There it is. She uses the hyphenated form of 'Solaz-Nitikin' as her surname, but Pike drops the last name. It seems to me you would use at least the hyphenated portion of the name, the one that's on her passport, so that the two documents would conform when you checked in at U.S. immigration; that is, unless you had some reason not to include the name."

"But if you're right and he dropped the name intentionally and immigration flagged the difference when he came in, then they've got problems," says Harry.

"Not necessarily. Pike probably figured he could finesse the passport at immigration, first because of all the other names on her passport, none of which were included on the visa. And if that didn't work, then he'd use whatever it was he had that got her the expedited visa in the first place."

"So you're thinking he didn't just pay somebody for that?" says Harry.

"I don't know. But I don't think he'd whip out his wallet in an immigration line at the airport with all of those cameras watching, an army of immigration officers there, and a long line of people behind him."

"Got a point," says Harry. "But why would he want to drop the last part of the hyphenated name?"

"That has been bothering me for two days. It kept

banging around in my head, until I dropped the name 'Solaz' out of the middle. If you never met the woman and I told you I was going to introduce you to someone named Katia Nitikin, what would you think?"

"Russian," says Harry.

"Look." I take a piece of paper and a pencil from his desk. "There are several ways you might write the name 'Kathy' in Spanish. You could use 'Kathia,' or 'Kathy,' or 'Katia.'" I turn the paper around for Harry to read. "But in Russian there is only one way it is generally written, and that's 'Katia.'"

"Okay, so her mother's dad is Russian?" says Harry.

"And Katia's mother was sufficiently sensitive to this that when she named her daughter, she used the Russian spelling. What does that tell you about Mom?"

"That she probably had a close relationship with her dad?"

"Bingo. Put it all together. Mom hangs out in Colombia visiting relatives that Katia has never met. A relative or relatives who, according to Katia, no one else in the family except her mother has ever met."

"The old man's on the lam," says Harry.

"Uh-huh. Pike sees the photographs of the mother's last trip, gets all excited, and immediately hustles Katia off to the States where he has her calling home every day—asking where Mama is and when's she coming back."

"So Pike was looking for Mr. Nitikin, assuming Grandpa's still alive," says Harry. "And you think Pike was killed because of that?"

"Two murders made to look like a badly botched larceny, gold coins and pawn tickets on Katia when they catch her, but none of the rest of the missing coins. The computer, the one the cops didn't find at Pike's house, it was a laptop," I tell Harry. "Katia saw it. He had it with him in Costa Rica. He used it to download the Colombian photographs from her camera without her knowledge. Katia saw it on his desk the night she left, and unless she killed him, and I don't think she did, she was right as rain to run, because she got out of that house half a beat ahead of whoever did."

"Hand me that binder," says Harry.

He wants the document binder from the shelf, the one I had just opened. I hand it to him and Harry riffles through it. He finds what he wants.

"'Six photographic prints, eight by ten,'" Harry is reading this to me. "It's the property inventory sheet from when they took her into custody in Arizona," he says. "The prints she took back from Pike that night. They were in her bag when they arrested her."

"We need to get copies of those photographs yesterday," I tell him.

SIXTEEN

Ten after seven in the morning and Zeb Thorpe was already sweating. "Make it fast. I've got a full day, starting with the director, in twenty minutes. That means you got ten."

In his sixties, craggy faced, a retired marine colonel, this morning Thorpe was pumping enough adrenaline he could have gone toe-to-toe with George Patton and chewed the stars off his helmet.

As the FBI's executive assistant director for the National Security Branch, he headed up four separate divisions: Counterterrorism, Counterintelligence, the Directorate of Intelligence, and the WMD Directorate. All of these had either been created or drastically reorganized as a result of the move toward homeland security.

Today he had a complete dance card, first a full-dress briefing with his boss, the latest and momentary head of the FBI. Then the two of them would spend their afternoon dodging bullets and bricks from the political drive-by mob on the Senate Judiciary Committee. Most of the members of the panel had one thing on their minds—making the bureau and, in particular, the new acting director, look like crap. It was the second day of Senate confirmation hearings on his boss's nomination and Thorpe already knew the man wasn't going to survive.

Yesterday, before the midafternoon break, the committee had knocked most of the snot, blood, and brains out of him. And these were people from the president's own party. They kneed him in the groin before asking him why he wasn't back in his office phoning the ACLU for recommendations on how to fight crime and end terrorism. Today they would try to get him on his back on top of the green-felt-covered witness table where they could properly gut him before calling the White House to send over the next victim.

Why not, they had done it twice in the last six months with other candidates and nobody lifted a finger. It was politics as blood sport. The job of director was becoming a revolving door and it was spinning like a tumbler in a washing machine.

As far as Thorpe was concerned, the political parties that occupied the House and the Senate reminded him of two retarded Siamese gorillas sharing the same brain. Together with their feeders and handlers on Wall Street, they'd spent a decade toying with the national economy, trying to get everybody in the country into houses they couldn't afford. When this set fire to the national economy, crashing markets, destroying whole industries, and generally torching the entire circus, they tripled the national debt in order to smother the flames with money.

Having solved that problem, the beasts had spent the last seven months lowering the chain on Homeland Security to see what would happen next.

Thorpe's own staff had an office pool going, taking bets on how long it would be before some group dropped sarin gas in a crowded subway, or lit up an American city with a mushroom cloud and gamma rays. In his more sanguine moments, Thorpe was beginning to wonder why there wasn't a hunting season on members of Congress.

This morning he was in a particularly foul mood, jowls down to his drawers. Part of the reason was this meeting dropped into his schedule at the last minute by his assistant, Raymond Zink. They were in the small conference room off Thorpe's office, Zink, the heads of two of the four divisions, and Thorpe.

"We think we may have a problem," said Zink. "It's information that came from one of our photo analysts in the lab."

"What are we talking, surveillance shots?"

"No, sir. A contact outside government sent our analyst some pictures, digital images."

Thorpe opened the file in front of him on the table.

"What we have are two enlargements received by our man. All the names are in the file. He says that, according to his source, there are six photos in all. The original pictures were sent to a private laboratory for processing by a gentleman in California. An employee at the private lab sent the two enlargements to our man, asking if he could access information from secure bureau databanks, confidential information on personal backgrounds and whatever else he could find."

"Stop! You're not gonna tell me the man in our lab did this?" Thorpe couldn't even conjure up the sea of blood on the floor if Senate Judiciary got a handle on this.

"No," said Zink.

Thorpe took a deep breath. "Thank God for little favors."

"Our employee was actually quite discreet. But he was curious," said Zink, "he took a shot and went on the Internet. He didn't think he'd find anything because he assumed that the fellow who sent him the stuff, the other lab technician, had probably already checked. But when he pumped in the name of the gentleman from California, the fellow who sent the pictures to the private lab, his computer screen lit up like a pinball machine. The man's name was Emerson Pike."

"Was?" said Thorpe.

Zink nodded. "The Internet printouts are in the folder. Why the technician at the private lab didn't Google the name, we don't know, but apparently he didn't, or if he did, he omitted to mention that Emerson Pike was murdered in his home in California, apparently just a few days after he sent the photographs in for processing and analysis."

Bill Britain, head of the bureau's Directorate of Intelligence, handed Thorpe a short half page with printed information. "Take a look. It's a summary of Emerson Pike's background. We printed out only the headings and high points, but it gives you the picture."

Thorpe devoured the words on the half-page sheet, then looked up. "All right."

"It gets more curious," said Zink. "Our lab man tried to contact his friend at the private lab to give him the news that Pike was dead. When he did he was told that his buddy hadn't shown up at work for two days and hadn't called in. What was more disturbing was that his car was in the parking lot, but nobody knew where he was. They told our guy that if the employee didn't show up by the end of the day or phone in, they were going to call the police and have them check into it. Our man didn't wait. He turned over what he had to one of our agents."

"So yesterday," said Zink, "the agent went over to the private lab, a place called Herrington's—"

"I'm familiar with it," said Thorpe. "It's across the river, in Virginia. We did contract work there years ago."

"Right," said Zink. "The missing lab analyst still hadn't shown up for work. The police came by and got information on contacts and next of kin, getting ready to do a missing person's, I guess. Our agent asked if they could take a look at the photo images sent in by Emerson Pike. They had to finagle a bit, but finally they got one of the supervisors to let them take a peek. The only problem was, the photos were gone."

"What?"

"The supervisor looked, checked their system up one side and down the other, and couldn't find them. After an hour and some disc diving by their IT people, they concluded that somebody had removed them from the system. They did find references to Pike and the photos on their website e-mail system, but the system was set up to strip attached images from incoming client mail in order to save space on the company's servers. As a consequence, there are no copies of Pike's digital images in their system."

Thorpe turned his attention to the file in front of him. "Aren't these the pictures?"

"No," said Zink. "That's what was sent to our man. Those are only two enlargements of what he was told is a single digital frame. There were additional photos, according to his source, either six or seven, he couldn't remember."

"And unfortunately, the two enlargements don't show facial features or any clue as to location," said Britain. "The first one is a shoulder patch from a field tunic for a Russian missile brigade. We received background on it from military intelligence at the Pentagon. It's old."

"The picture?"

"No. The tunic," said Britain. "Our man in the lab says his source, who is also a photo analyst with experience and skill, assured him that the digital images were shot about four months ago. He's not sure if he was given a specific date. If he was, he couldn't remember."

"Go on."

"The Russian missile unit dates to the early sixties and ceased to exist sometime around 1965, after the Cuban Missile Crisis.

"The next enlargement," said Britain, "the name patch over the pocket, is from the same jacket, according to the source. The only portion of it we can read are the first two letters of the soldier's name. They're Russian Cyrillic. The English translation is *NI*.

"Next is a series of documents," said Britain. "The first set, marked 'Top Secret—Classified,' are from the executive committee of the National Security Council, most of them dating to the late fall, early winter of 1963. The last one, I believe, is dated just sixteen days before President Kennedy was assassinated. Behind those are a series of translations from Soviet military and intelligence files obtained by the CIA in the early nineties, just after the collapse of the Soviet Union. The original documents date back to the period between October and the end of December 1962. To save time we've summarized the critical items on a single page, yeah, I think you have it there."

Thorpe read the summary through once, very quickly. "Wait…wait…wait," he said. "I remember hearing about this guy from some of the old fossils at CIA, musta been what, thirty years ago now, the legend of Yakov Nitikin. He's a bag of smoke. Soviets floated the name after the Cuban missile mess so we'd chase ghosts. I can't remember, what it was that they called him?"

"The Guardian of Lies," said Llewellyn.

"That's it." Thorpe snapped his fingers and pointed at Llewellyn. "Always count on Herb for a good memory."

"It was a takeoff on Churchill's famous quote," said Llewellyn, "that in time of war the truth is so precious that it must always be attended by a bodyguard of lies."

"That's what we thought at the time," said Britain. "But it appears we may have been wrong. The old Soviet intelligence documents behind the summary, those were obtained from KGB files after the Soviet Union collapsed. According to those, Nitikin was real, and so was his secret."

"So what you're telling me is, this guy Nitikin is the one wearing the jacket in the two enhanced photos?" said Thorpe.

"It would seem to fit with the two first letters of the last name over the pocket," said Britain.

"Okay, let's assume I buy into this. It's all very interesting, but it's ancient history. We're talking 1962, almost fifty years. I mean, I guess it's possible that the man could still be alive, maybe. But the item sure as hell isn't. There's no way."

Thorpe looked at Herb Llewellyn, seated across the table from him. "Tell me I'm right, Herb!"

"I'd like to. In any other circumstance I wouldn't hesitate, but in this case I'm afraid I can't."

"You're kidding."

"No."

Thorpe looked at his watch. He didn't have time for a physics lesson. "Ray, do me a favor, go out and tell my secretary to call the director's office and tell him I'll be there in a couple of minutes. I'm running a little late."

Zink headed out of the conference room with the message.

"Herb, for the moment I'll assume there's some basis in fact for your belief in perpetual shelf life, and we can talk about that. But I suspect that if this guy's even alive, and he has anything at all, he's probably in a wheelchair somewhere sitting on a pile of corroded metal."

"I don't think so," said Llewellyn.

"We'll talk about it when I have more time," said Thorpe. "For the moment I think we're chasing rainbows here. The stuff in the old Soviet files could be disinformation for all we know. Back during the Cold War, both sides were big on that. Put a fairy tale in your file and let the other side find it. In the meantime you're spending a billion dollars looking for Goldilocks."

"What about Pike's murder and the missing photo analyst?" said Britain.

Zink came back into the room and closed the door behind him. He was carrying a sheet of paper in his hand.

"I don't know," said Thorpe. "The whole thing just doesn't smell right. The only thing we have linking the Russian's name with Pike's murder is a lot of hearsay from a photo analyst who's missing. And even that's tenuous. We're reaching into fifty-year-old Soviet documents to make the connection."

"Not exactly," said Zink. "Not anymore. Take a look at this." He handed the sheet of paper to Thorpe.

"What's this?"

"It's the booking sheet on the suspect in Pike's murder. I had my secretary pull up what she could find off the law enforcement database on the state's case while we were meeting. That was on my desk.

"The suspect is a foreign national by the name of Katia Solaz. She's in the country on a Costa Rican passport. According to my secretary's note, the woman was living with Pike at the time he was killed. But check out the alias; one of the names she used was Katia Solaz-Nitikin."

Thorpe took a deep breath as he looked at the name on the sheet. "You're sure about this?"

"I have to assume that if the police picked it up on the booking sheet, they must have gotten it from somewhere, either a passport or a driver's license."

"Get a couple of agents out of the San Diego field office to go over to the courthouse and comb the police file on this thing. And don't wait. Do it today. Tell them anything with the name Nitikin on it, we want to take a look. Also see if they can get additional background on the suspect, particularly as regards family, also where she's from in Costa Rica."

Both Zink and Britain were scrawling notes on legal pads as Thorpe spit out instructions.

"Tell the agents to look through everything, all documents and physical evidence, whatever the police have. Also anything they seized at the time of this woman's arrest and anything they found at the scene, or anywhere else, that belonged to her. Oh, and see if the police found any computers at Pike's house."

"Good point," said Britain. "Why didn't we think of that one earlier? Maybe we can find the digital images Pike sent to the lab. Who knows what else."

"Tell the agents to keep their eyes peeled for pictures, and be sure and tell them what they're looking for, an older man in an olive drab fatigue jacket," said Thorpe. "If they find photos fitting that description, tell them to sit on them and to call here immediately. I don't want those pictures disappearing again unless we're the ones doing the vanishing act."

Thorpe looked at his watch. "Damn it, I got to run, go prop up the human punching bag so he can get the crap kicked out of him again." Thorpe was packing up his notes, grabbing the file. "Ray, check my calendar, let's meet again, first opportunity, as soon as we find out what's in the crime file. And, Herb, you and I still have to talk about the gadget."

SEVENTEEN

Alim waited in the trees at the edge of the forest for one of his men to return with the information that he wanted. The man in question had been assigned a simple task, to watch Nitikin's daughter whenever she wandered free in the camp. The man had failed. Because of this, the woman's photographs of her father, along with Alim and his men, had found their way into the American's laptop computer and from there to a laboratory for processing in the United States.

Afundi's first thought was that Nitikin's daughter was working with the Americans. Together with the interpreter he cornered the Russian and braced him with questions.

Nitikin assured him that his daughter knew nothing, and he wanted it to stay that way. The Russian knew only too well the perils of knowledge. He told Afundi that all she knew was that her father had deserted from the Soviet army many years before. She believed that to be the reason he was in hiding.

To Afundi this made no sense. If desertion from the Soviets was his only reason for hiding, why had Nitikin not gone back to his family in Costa Rica when the Soviet Union ceased to exist? Surely she must have asked her father that same question many times.

By then Afundi realized he himself had asked one too many questions. He could read in Nitikin's eyes his fear for his daughter. Alim dismissed it all as a misunderstanding. He slapped the old man on the back and told him not to worry, that everything was now fine. But it wasn't.

Alim and his small troop of escapees from Guantanamo had been selected for the job not because they were trained fighters or because they had any special skills for completing the operation. They were picked because it was Alim who'd delivered the information to his country's Cuban consul, and from there directly to Alim's government.

The message that came back was verbal and remained unwritten, but it was clear. Secrecy was vital not only for completion of the operation. It was critical to the republic's continued existence once the mission was over. The information was to be confined to those who already knew and no one else; this meant Alim and his colleagues with whom he had already shared it. All further contact with Alim's own government was, under any circumstance, forbidden.

Alim first learned the secret from another old man who was still fighting another war. He was Cuban, and like the old Russian, he was also dying.

Fidel Castro had been curious about the man who'd led the escape from the American compound at Guantanamo. And when Fidel was curious about something he always got answers, or rather others got them for him. As one of the great charismatic leaders of his time,

Castro knew that the key to human conduct was motivation, and he wanted to know what motivated Alim Afundi.

He learned that Afundi's parents, his father a farmer and his mother a peasant, had perished under American bombs. The U.S. government claimed it was an accident. Ordnance dropped from planes flown off the decks of an American aircraft carrier sailing in the Persian Gulf had somehow found its way beyond the Iraqi border, a few hundred yards and onto buildings mistakenly identified as an Al-Qaeda outpost.

Fidel learned that it was this single act of unrequited violence that had transformed the otherwise quiet son of a cattle herder into a fire-breathing freedom fighter, and a mortal enemy of the Great Satan.

He invited Alim to dinner in his private quarters a few days later. The Cuban government had treated Afundi and his men as heroes. Now Alim was told that Castro wanted to honor him personally.

Fidel was no longer the head of the Cuban government. He had long since stepped down because of illness. His graying beard looked thin and a bit withered but his eyes burned with a zeal that Alim had seen only in the fiery gaze of ardent mullahs.

Over food, cigars, and Cuban rum, the last two of which Alim respectfully declined because of his religion, Castro spent the evening regaling his guest with recollections of the revolution, all of this through an interpreter.

Afundi was not wealthy, and in terms of world history he was not well educated. He knew almost nothing of the Cuban revolution. To Castro, who had stood before legions of captive audiences, people ordered to bake in the hot Cuban sun for hours and who had heard it all before, the young, eager face at his dinner table was a clean slate upon which to write.

Castro started where it all began, with the failed assault on the Moncada barracks in his youth, before he knew what it was to be a revolutionary. He told Alim about his capture along with his brother Rául and their imprisonment and of their later journey to Mexico to train for the coming revolution. He talked about the return to the island with a force of fewer than a hundred men and the ambush by Batista's militia that had nearly wiped them out.

"It is why you never leave an adversary breathing and aboveground when you fight a war. They had two opportunities to kill me, one in prison, which they passed up, and the second in the ambush, when they missed," Castro told him.

To Alim, the man may have been old and in ill health, but you would not have known it from the stamina he exhibited that night. The gathering lasted nearly twelve hours. It did not end until long after a rooster sounded in the yard outside and sun streamed through the windows of the dining room where they sat.

Castro conversed all night in what was largely a one-way monologue. Alim sat nodding politely, grinning appropriately when he needed to and listening as the interpreter conveyed in Farsi Fidel's recollections and, to the degree possible, his passion for the subject. He talked of Che and the capture of the government munitions train at Santa Clara that sealed Batista's fate, and of how he, Fidel, had swept into Havana at the head of an army. He spoke of going to New York to speak to the United Nations, of plucking chickens in the presidential suite of the hotel, of the U.S. invasion at the Bay of Pigs, and the many failed attempts by the Americans to assassinate him over the years.

He talked about the American CIA on whose direction his friend Che had been executed in Bolivia. He talked about American efforts to crush the revolution and to impoverish the Cuban people through forty years of economic embargoes, actions that Fidel said were similar to those America had imposed on Alim's own homeland.

As the night went on, Alim realized that even with the rum Fidel had consumed, he was going to outdistance his guest. By three in the morning, Afundi was dying. He had experienced sleep deprivation as torture, but Castro's form was more potent because of Alim's need to show continued respect toward his host. By six he could no longer make even the pretense. Alim fell asleep.

At some point, he didn't know how much time had passed, he was startled from his slumber by Castro's shouting. He lifted his sleepy head just in time to miss the next blow landed by Fidel's closed fist on the table's surface. Through the interpreter, Castro's words came streaming in: "...betrayal by a trusted ally in the face of imperialist aggression."

Fidel's voice climbed to a roar and bristled with anger as he chomped on his cigar. Then he turned to look angrily at Alim.

Afundi was mortified. He was certain he had offended his host by falling asleep.

It took him a few seconds and a few discreet questions to the interpreter before he realized he was wrong. Alim came to grips with the snippets of Fidel's message he had missed while dozing. It was something to do with Castro's alliance with the Soviets and Russian missiles placed on Cuban soil for defense. Apparently, Castro's fury had not been quelled by the passage of more than forty years.

"In the end," said Fidel, "the only Russian who remained true to the revolution has spent his life hiding from his own government in the mountains of Colombia." Then he turned his blazing eyes on his guest. "In the event that you are wondering, it is the reason I have invited you here this evening.

"By the way, before I forget, I have for you and your men a present. It isn't much, perhaps just a small taste of home." Castro reached over to the shelf under a table alongside his chair and pulled out a newspaper. Immediately, Alim saw the stirring banner on the front page, the large cursive letters in Farsi. He recognized the newspaper. It was the provincial sheet published by his own government and circulated in the mountains near his home. Afundi hadn't seen news from home in nearly two years.

"I had it delivered in one of our diplomatic pouches," said Fidel. He tossed it to Afundi across the table. "Share it with your men. They need to hear from home."

Alim took the newspaper and a drink of water in an effort to wake himself, and tried to glance at the newspaper as he listened.

After spending the entire night reliving his life, it took Fidel less than five minutes to come to the point.

There was a stark contrast between the sentimental old man who lived in the past, the one who had talked Alim to sleep, and the operational warlord Afundi had woken up to in the morning. Alim recognized the difference immediately.

Fidel told him about Nitikin, how they'd met and

about the secret they shared. It was Fidel's sense that fate had delivered Alim and his men to him at a critical moment, when all the stars were aligned, while he still had breath to deliver the message, and his old Russian friend still had the strength to act upon it.

As Castro spoke, Afundi held the newspaper on his lap and glanced at it occasionally with one eye. When Fidel turned to grab the decanter of rum once more, Alim quickly flipped the newspaper over to see the back side. There he saw the photograph of a large American warship. The moment he read the caption printed beneath the photograph, his eyes seemed fixed on the four-column photograph.

According to the paper: "The American warship *Ronald Reagan* plies the waters of the Persian Gulf on its most recent tour. Its warplanes routinely kill innocent women and children in cities and villages throughout the region. It delivers without mercy the infidel's poisonous bite on other nations where the Great Satan seeks to impose his will on true believers and the faithful throughout the Islamic world."

By the time Fidel finished pouring his drink, Afundi's eyes were back on him, though his mind was not.

"I am certain," said Fidel, "that given enough diplomacy and time, your own government will see the wisdom of my plan. And that you yourself will come to understand its opportunities. Of course, it must be handled with a good deal of care and discretion. But I'm sure you already know that. You see," said Fidel, "it is a grand opportunity delivered to you and to me, by destiny."

Destiny or not, for the moment Afundi had problems. The old Russian was sick once more. He was resting in the three-room hut with his daughter. One of the doctors had looked in on him that morning. The physician told Alim that it was not serious, just that the old man was tired. They were working him too hard. He needed more rest. If they were lucky he might be down only for the day, perhaps two. But without him they could make no further progress.

If this were not enough, now there was something else, one more problem to worry about.

Alim saw his man rushing back toward him from the hut. The man had exited from a back window. The fact that he had nothing in either hand told Afundi that the search had been unsuccessful.

"You didn't find it?"

"No." The man was breathless.

"You went through everything?"

"All of her bags and her clothing. Besides, I haven't seen her with it. And I have been watching her closely this time. I don't think she has it."

"Then where is it?" said Afundi.

"I don't know. Maybe she took it with her when she went home. If so, it could still be there, in Costa Rica."

Afundi thought for a moment. It was a delicate subject, and not one that he wanted to raise either directly or indirectly with the Russian or his daughter.

The man from the Mexican cartel had sent three items to them after killing the American at his home in California and trying to kill Nitikin's granddaughter. He sent the dead man's laptop, a printed photograph that none of them recognized, and a small digital camera in a pink leather case.

Afundi had directed the killer to look for a camera because Nitikin's daughter had told them she borrowed her daughter's camera to use during her last trip to Colombia. It was the camera that had taken the photos of Nitikin, Alim, and his men.

When Alim checked the camera sent to them from California, he found nothing except photographs apparently taken there, in California. Initially Afundi was relieved. He assumed that the original photographs from Colombia had been erased.

But the reprieve was short lived. That morning, through the interpreter, he had gone out of his way to ask Nitikin's daughter if she could help him with a new camera he had purchased. He showed her the camera from California without its pink case and with none of the photographs of the Russian's granddaughter still in it. The mother didn't recognize it. She told him she had never seen one like it. It was much nicer, newer, and smaller than the one she had used. It was all Alim needed to know. The camera and perhaps the Colombian photographs were still out there.

It was possible that no one would find them, at least not before it was too late, but then again, given his luck so far...

EIGHTEEN

Harry and I are wearing a rut in the road, twenty miles each way every time we need to meet with Katia at the women's lockup in Santee. But today Harry doesn't seem to mind. "I think we found one of the coins taken from Emerson's study," he tells me. "And this one wasn't in Arizona."

According to Harry it showed up in a probate estate, an old man who'd succumbed to a heart attack a couple of weeks ago. His executor found the coin in his safe along with a printed card showing its provenance. The police now have the card and the coin.

"Please don't tell me they identified Katia as the seller," I tell him.

"No, according to the records the seller was a man named John Waters. We don't know if there's any identification on him yet. I'm told Templeton's people are checking it out."

"Stay on top of it."

"You bet," says Harry.

This morning when we get to the jail Katia knows by

the expression on our faces that there is a problem. We are closeted in one of the lawyer-client cubicles.

"What's wrong?" she says.

"I want you to think very carefully before you answer the next few questions," I tell her.

She looks to Harry, then to me. "Tell me what's wrong."

"Did you ever have any difficulty sleeping at night when you were living with Emerson Pike at his house?"

"Sometimes. Sure. I was in a strange house. Especially at the end, I was scared."

"Did you ever take anything for it, any medication to help you sleep while you were there?"

"No." She shakes her head.

"Did you ever borrow any medication from Mr. Pike?" I ask.

When she turns to look at me, her eyes are alight with the sudden realization of where this is going. "You're talking about Emerson's sleeping medicine."

"Then you knew about it?" says Harry.

"You want to know if I gave Emerson medicine to sleep the night I left."

"Did you?" says Harry.

"Yes."

"Damn it." Harry turns away from her, looks at the opposite wall, and swears under his breath, several choice words.

"Why didn't you tell us?" I ask.

"I don't know. Aye, aye . . . I didn't think it was important."

"Not important!" Harry's voice goes up a full octave as he turns to look at her again.

"Let's keep it to a mild roar," I tell him.

When Harry looks at me, I nod toward the door and the guard stationed outside. "We don't want them calling the Dwarf's office with a blow-by-blow and color commentary when we leave."

"How the hell could this not be important?" This time Harry whispers, but the venom is still in his eyes.

"But Emerson didn't die of drugs. You told me he was stabbed to death," says Katia.

"That's not the point," I tell her. "The problem is, you didn't tell us and you didn't tell the police about the medication you gave him. Now they have a toxicology report showing that Pike had an elevated level of sleeping medication in his system when he died."

"And they have your fingerprints on the bottle from the medicine cabinet in his bathroom," says Harry.

The look on her face says it all. "No. No. I didn't try to poison him, if that's what you're thinking. I only gave him the medicine so that he would sleep, so that I could get away. When everything happened, when they arrested me and I found out that he had been stabbed to death, I didn't think about the medicine. I would have told you if I had remembered, if I thought it was important, but it wasn't."

"We can all take bets, but I doubt that the police are going to see it that way," says Harry.

"When he didn't fall asleep, when Emerson refused to go to bed and instead took a shower, I realized that the medicine was not going to work. I thought I must not have given him enough, so when he went into the shower I ran. I can tell, you don't believe me."

"The question is not whether we believe you," I tell her. "It's what the prosecutor will do with the toxicology report and your fingerprints on the pill bottle."

"He has the dagger with your prints, now the medication," says Harry. "Tell us everything. No more surprises. I want to know everything and I want to know it now."

"It's what I told you. Emerson would not let me out of his sight."

"He allowed you to go to the grocery store alone, where we met," I remind her.

"True, but it was only because he had a meeting a few blocks away with a customer. He gave me a few dollars and told me to buy food for a practice dinner I was going to cook. He knew where I was, and that I couldn't go far. Every time I moved during the night, he would wake up. That's why I gave him the medicine."

"Had you ever given him any medication or other drugs before that night?" says Harry.

"No, never, but that night I knew it had started to work. I could tell he was sleepy. I told him to go to bed but he wouldn't do it. He kept shaking his head and rubbing his eyes. He said he was going to take a shower and that it would wake him up, because he had work to do. He always had work to do. That's when I realized he wasn't going to fall asleep. I knew if I didn't leave that night, I would never get away."

"So what did you do, put it in his food?" says Harry.

"I put it in his coffee when we had dessert. I crushed up two pills and mixed the powder into his coffee. I gave him decaf hoping he would sleep. You remember when we first met?" She looks at me and smiles. "I told you the man I was living with never had any good coffee in his house. He always drank bad coffee."

"I remember."

"Emerson didn't know the difference. I knew the coffee was so bitter he would never taste the medicine. But

I gave him just two pills. If I had wanted to kill him, I could have given him the whole bottle. I knew two pills would not harm him."

"What about the maid, she was there?" says Harry.

"I didn't know she was going to be there until later. That's when Emerson told me he had called her. I told him it wasn't necessary, that I could clean up, do the dishes. But he said no. He wanted the maid to do it and he didn't want to wait."

"So you'd already given Emerson the pills when you found out the maid was coming," I say.

"That's right. I figured it was not a problem. She would be working downstairs in the dining room and the kitchen. When Emerson got sleepy I would help him to bed, then get my bag with the passport, money from his wallet, some coins from the study, enough just for an airline ticket, and go out through the garage. The maid would never know I'd left. And if I was lucky, Emerson would not wake up until morning. That's what I thought. But he refused to go to sleep." She gives Harry a kind of plaintive expression. "I know now it was probably not the right thing to do. It must look very bad, but at the time it was all I could think of."

Given the low dose, the cops would never have given the sleep meds a second thought. It's a common enough prescription. The natural assumption would be that Pike had taken the stronger dose himself, especially if he'd built up a tolerance to the medication over time. But all the assumptions went out the window when they found Katia's fingerprints on the prescription bottle.

Alone, by itself, and given the sum of other conflicting evidence in the state's case, this might not be cataclysmic.

What worries me is the wild card, the prosecutor Larry Templeton and the artful ways he might try to use this. We may get a peek at the Dwarf's crystal ball tomorrow when Harry and I meet with him on another issue.

It's a courtesy call. Why Templeton has asked for this meeting we're not sure. It happens all the time. A clerk puts something in the wrong box in the evidence lockup, and it takes them a few days to find it. It seems the evidence clerks have misplaced the six photos taken by Katia's mother in Colombia, the photographic prints made by Emerson Pike, reclaimed by Katia the night he was murdered and seized from her by the police the day she was arrested.

NINETEEN

We have to assume that as long as the man in question is alive, the item is viable," said Llewellyn.

Herb Llewellyn was in his early forties. He had a shock of tousled salt-and-pepper hair over horn-rimmed glasses. His dress shirts, the sleeves of which were always rolled above his thin, bony elbows, seemed to bear a perennial spot of ink, either fresh or faded, from a pen that leaked in his breast pocket. This morning he was meeting with Thorpe in Thorpe's corner office at FBI headquarters.

"Explain to me how that works," said Thorpe. "I'm still not convinced on the issue of shelf life. Everything I've ever read says ten, maybe twelve years tops, after that it may be dirty but that's it, and even that's minimal."

Thorpe wanted to be sure he knew what he was dealing with before he went up the chain and got his head handed to him by someone who didn't like the message he was delivering, especially if there was any chance he was wrong. The acting director had now fallen on his own sword. Thorpe wasn't even sure if he knew what higher authority looked like anymore.

"In this case, you can forget everything you've read," said Llewellyn. "And I don't say that lightly. It's a special case."

"In what way?"

"The Soviet Seventy-ninth Brigade, according to the accounts in the Russian documents, possessed a highly skilled field-level maintenance unit. The FKRs were designed to be completely field maintained.

"More to the point, each transport van contained multiple replacements for every critical part. We're talking about a gun type here, simplicity itself, exceedingly reliable and easy to maintain. The entire device could fit into a fair-size steamer trunk. The gun barrel would be no more than perhaps three feet long and between three and four inches in diameter, with a smooth bore. According to the information in the documents, the man we're looking for was one of the brigade's top armorers. He was trained and experienced in maintenance on the system in question. He would know how to store it, how to keep it alive, and if necessary, how to bring it back to life."

"That's possible? He could do that?"

"With an ample supply of replacement parts, yes."

"What about the Russians? Can they help us at all?" said Thorpe.

"State Department has been in contact with them. Relations, as you know, are not good. On the international front, to deflect heat, in the event that something happens, they're taking the position that it's an old-empire problem, a holdover from the Soviets for which they are not responsible. Unofficially, they're trying to obtain design details, drawings if they can find them. But it's an old system. It's been obsolete for decades, not even remotely close to anything in their current arsenal. Their thermonuclear stockpile, fifty megatons or more, enough to take out twenty square miles, would be implosion-type bombs, a core of plutonium surrounded by conventional explosives and triggered by highly complex detonation systems. What we're hearing is that a lot of the documentation on the older-type weapons, the stuff we're dealing with here, was trashed after the collapse of the Soviets. So finding information may be next to impossible."

"So correct me if I'm wrong. You're telling me our cause for concern turns on two contingencies: that the man is still alive and that he has the necessary spare parts to keep the weapon alive."

"Correct."

"We may know more about the man in a day or so. For now, let's talk about the parts," said Thorpe.

Thorpe and Llewellyn were about as different as two people could be. Llewellyn was an intellectual from MIT, a scientist who headed up an office of nerds all packing scientific calculators that could perform three hundred functions and carry out equations to a dozen decimal points. For this reason it seemed strange that the two men always gravitated toward each other whenever there was a crisis, as if each compensated for some deficiency in the other.

"Let's assume for the moment that he doesn't have the parts. Could he fabricate them?"

"It's possible, but it becomes much more problematic. The tolerances required for fabricated parts would be critical. He would require access to tools and dies that would be difficult to obtain. Even with the proper equipment, it's questionable. Without skilled help I would say his chances of success drop dramatically. The man's an armorer, not a machinist."

"Good," said Thorpe. "Now how do we know he has the spare parts?"

"The KGB reports," said Llewellyn. "We know that the Russian, Nitikin, arrived on Castro's doorstep at Punto Uno the afternoon of October twenty-eighth."

"Excuse me. What's Punto Uno?" said Thorpe.

"It was central command, military headquarters for the Cuban government during the missile crisis. Castro always hung out there whenever there was a national calamity."

"So Castro was involved personally?"

"We don't know, but we have to assume so. According to the KGB reports that were compiled from Soviet military accounts, Castro was present at Punto Uno when the Russian arrived. Apparently the Russian was invited inside the compound. He was there for a little over an hour. What happened inside, who he met, who he may have talked to, the Soviets couldn't be certain."

"Castro would have wanted to cover his ass," said Thorpe. "He wouldn't want to get crosswise with the Soviets."

"Nor they with him," said Llewellyn.

"So we have no idea whether the Cubans might be involved now?"

"No," said Llewellyn.

"Go on, let's get back to the parts."

"The Russian was seen again later that night, October twenty-eighth, this time at the port at Mariel. Both times, at Punto Uno in the afternoon and at Mariel that night, he was driving a large Soviet transport van. According to the Soviet military and the later KGB reports when he arrived at Mariel, he was under the protection of a good-size contingent of Cuban troops. They estimated more than two hundred armed soldiers and at least two armored vehicles. It's clear he wouldn't have gotten off the island without the Cubans."

"So what you're saying is that to get it back, the Russians would have had to engage in a shooting war with their allies," said Thorpe.

"Correct. And according to all the reports," said Llewellyn, "Moscow wasn't willing to do it. At that moment they had a full plate trying to stare us down."

"The van the Russian was driving," said Thorpe, "I assume this is the key piece of evidence?"

"Correct. It was a fully equipped Soviet mobile-weapons van. According to the KGB it had the weapon and a full complement of replacement parts."

Llewellyn handed Thorpe a photograph. It was an enhanced enlargement showing a line of military vehicles, what looked like heavy-duty trucks parked side by side near a sizable Quonset building with a corrugated arched roof.

"That was taken by a U.S. Navy Crusader on an aerial recon flight on October twenty-fifth, three days before the Russian disappeared. The building is located at Bejucal. It was the central storage site. We didn't realize it at the time because of the single security fence and the absence of any real military presence around it. Apparently the Soviets believed the best defense was deception," said Llewellyn. "It may also have compromised their internal security.

"The vans, here and here." Llewellyn directed

Thorpe's attention to the photograph with the point of his pen. "Those are mobile-weapon movers. That's what our Russian friend was driving when he showed up at Punto Uno and again at Mariel. The limited security around the facility probably explains how he was able to drive it away. We know that the weapon type in question had already been deployed, because three of them were aimed at Guantanamo. Of course, we didn't know that until the 1990s. The delivery system would have been on a truck and trailer. It would have flown off a ramp—"

"He doesn't have one of those?" said Thorpe.

"No. The original delivery system would have been more cumbersome than it was worth. It would have been too large and too visible. He certainly wouldn't want to use it today. It would be much easier to deliver it on a ship, or better yet, the bed of a truck."

"So what you're saying is that if he had the van, he had the weapon and the parts, and with that he doesn't need anything else to maintain it."

"Essentially, yes. With a gun type there are no tricky detonators. My people are working on it but from what we can see, the only thing he might need other than the parts he already has is a little fresh cordite to fire the projectile down the barrel, and that he could probably get almost anywhere."

Thorpe issued a deep sigh, then leaned back in his chair.

"Okay, so the Soviets tracked him to Mariel. What happened then?"

"Soviet intelligence reports that the Cubans helped him load the van into the hold of a registered Liberian vessel. The ship sailed that night, the twenty-eighth. The Russians thought about sinking it with a sub but they had nothing in position because of the U.S. block-ade around the island. They had recalled all their subs out to the mid-Atlantic in an effort to reduce tensions and avoid an accident with the U.S. Bottom line is, the ship, the van, and the man all disappeared."

"The Liberian vessel," said Thorpe, "do we have a name? With a name we get shipping records. Even after forty-five years we might see where the vessel landed."

"I thought about that," said Llewellyn. "Our intelligence people checked our copies of the old Soviet documents. It looks as if the vessel's name was in the KGB reports, but for some reason it was inked out, redacted by the Soviets, we don't know why."

"And of course without the original document we can't look behind the ink."

"Correct," said Llewellyn.

"So we don't have a clue as to where this guy went or whether he might still be there today?"

"Until we had access to the KGB reports, he was just an urban legend, one that Emerson Pike was apparently obsessed with. We talked with people Pike worked with before he retired and they all said that he believed the legend to be true. Even after he retired, whenever he traveled, friends said he was always on the lookout. It looks as if perhaps he found him. The Soviet apparatus searched for Nitikin for almost thirty years, until the empire collapsed, and they never found him. So you have to assume the Russian is fairly resourceful," said Llewellyn.

"And old," said Thorpe.

"Yes, but that may not be an advantage," said Llewellyn.

"What do you mean?"

"Well, I mean if he sat on it all these years, why would he use it now? Unless, of course . . ."

"Unless what?"

"Unless he's dying and he knows it, in which case it's either use it or lose it."

"So he has to restore it before he dies," said Thorpe.

"My guess is that he's found help. He would need it. It's possible but not likely that he'd be able to move it himself."

"You're thinking subnational terrorists," said Thorpe.

"If the plan is to use it, that would be my guess," said Llewellyn. "No nation I can think of is going to want to have their fingerprints on an event like that. And while a nation-state could take it and put it in their arsenal, without the capacity to maintain it, what good is it? In ten years they've got a corroded hunk of junk. No. Unfortunately, there's only one purpose to be served by a dinosaur like this, and that's to turn it loose and let it roar—to make a statement that the world will understand."

Both men knew that when it came to potential helpers, there was no shortage of candidates.

"So you're pretty sure there's no chance he goes to use this thing and gets a fizzle?" said Thorpe.

"There's always the exception in the physical universe," said Llewellyn, "but I wouldn't place too much reliance on it in this case. You have to remember, the first one of these we made, gun type, we didn't even bother to test it. We just shipped it across the Pacific and dropped it. That's how certain we were that it would work."

"You've convinced me," said Thorpe. "What are we talking about in terms of size?"

"Are you asking mass, the size of the weapon, or yield?" said Llewellyn.

"All three."

"The warhead would be bigger than a bread basket. Unfortunately, we don't have a picture. The only one we know of is a photograph of one of the missiles itself on a ramp aimed at Guantanamo. We know the warhead was situated in the midpart of the fuselage. How large or heavy we can't be sure," said Llewellyn. "You'd want to use a truck to move it. I'm guessing a small box truck would be more than adequate."

"In other words, the kind you can rent anywhere," said Thorpe.

"Right."

"And yield?"

"That we do know. Think in terms of Little Boy," said Llewellyn.

"You're kidding. I thought you said this thing was field tactical for battlefield use."

"It is. Back then I guess they thought bigger was better," said Llewellyn. "No. It's almost precisely the same. A smaller package no doubt, but it's the same type, and the same yield as Little Boy, fourteen kilotons, and it would be very reliable. That's what I was saying. We tested Fat Man, the implosion device, in the New Mexico desert to make sure it would work. But Little Boy, that was a gun type, a sure thing. The first test was the live performance over Hiroshima."

TWENTY

arry Templeton's facial features have always reminded me of those statues of Lenin pulled down by the mobs at the close of the Soviet Union. His bald head and goatee, the forceful jaw and the deep-set eyes, make for a powerful image.

Seated behind his desk, as he is this morning when Harry and I are ushered into his office, we get only a slight sense of Templeton's diminutive physical stature. This comes from his abbreviated upper body hidden partially behind stacks of case books and files on his desk. He lays down his pen on top of the papers he is working on and beckons us to enter.

"Gentlemen, gentlemen, please come in, have a seat." He gestures with a broad sweep of his right arm toward the two client chairs opposite his desk. His other arm appears to be trapped under the desk.

"Looks like a den of iniquity." Harry is not moving, blocking the way, taking it all in.

There is a thick Persian runner, leading from the door, under our feet. It matches the larger Persian carpet under the desk, which is oak, antique, and massive, behind which Templeton sits on a specially built raised chair, like a rajah holding court. All that is missing is the turban.

In the corner near the windows, Larry has erected a carved wooden panel, teak, I would imagine, and very ornate. The framed prints on the walls have the definite exotic influence of the East, sheiks with large head-dresses and sickle-shaped Sumerian swords.

Larry's digs in the DA's headquarters have never held the appearance of a government office. He has deco-rated them out of his own pocket since the beginning and has done so lavishly.

"Mr. Hinds, always good to see you. Mr. Madriani. How are you? Linda, you can go. Close the door on your way out." Templeton dismisses the secretary who has ushered us in.

"Only thing wrong is it smells like Tammany Hall in here," says Harry.

Templeton brings a finger to his lips to shush him until the door closes. With his secretary outside, Larry smiles, then lifts the smoking offender from under the desk and gives us one of his characteristic looks: devil with a stogie, arched eyebrows, and a polished head. "One in the morning, one in the afternoon, the doctor prescribes them," he says.

"So that's what did it," says Harry.

"I know, don't say it, stunted my growth. Hinds, you gotta get up earlier in the day if you're going to try to spring that one on me."

"How about we go one-on-one, a little basketball?" says Harry. "I'll give you an edge. Put you on roller skates."

"I see you're as sensitive as ever to the plight of the

disabled." Templeton leans back in his chair and smiles at him from behind a veil of cigar smoke. "You haven't changed."

"Show me someone who's disabled and I'll show you a tear," says Harry. "But let's not change the subject. I thought this was a no-smoking zone, county building and all."

"They don't ask and I don't tell. Hope you don't mind." Larry doesn't wait for an answer. He flicks a little ash into an open desk drawer on the other side. "I'd offer you one, but they're too expensive."

"What is it, administrative or criminal," Harry says, turning toward me, "a violation of the no-smoking ordinance?"

"I'm not getting into this one," I tell him.

"Smart man. Besides, it's only an infraction. Insulting a midget, now that's federal," says Templeton.

"Which title is that?" asks Harry.

"When I find it, I'll send you the citation." Templeton reaches out and shakes my hand. "How come you were so blessed as to get this dipshit as a partner?" he asks.

"Luck of the draw." I settle into one of the chairs across from him. "You look as if you're prospering," I tell him.

"No lack of offenders to prosecute, if that's what you mean. It's a bumper crop." He gestures toward the files stacked on the floor; off to one side of his desk, they climb the wall a good two feet.

Harry turns slowly in place, taking in the Dwarf's new surroundings, his freshly decorated office. If you can get past the cigar, you can still catch a whiff of the paint. Templeton has moved up in the world since we last met. The office is twice as large and has a corner set of windows to boot.

Harry is busy checking out the Persian runner on the floor, lifting the corner and reading the label.

"Are you a collector?" says Templeton.

"No, but I've seen a few of these fenced for fees. This one looks expensive enough to fly," he says.

"I'd be happy to put you out the window for a test drive," says Templeton.

"Later," says Harry. "After you bring in the belly dancers and we see the seven veils."

"I'll give you the name of my decorator," says Larry.

"Don't bother. I couldn't afford it," says Harry. "Just tell me where you keep the magic lamp. I may need to rub it to spring a client one of these days."

"I hope it's not this one," says Templeton. "Because if it is, the genie's gonna need a new battery. He's definitely not going to have enough juice."

"That bad?" I say.

Templeton takes a drag, looks at me, nods slowly and blows a smoke ring in my direction.

"You called the meeting," I tell him.

"So I guess we should get down to cases."

Harry picks up on the serious tone and waltzes over to take a seat.

Templeton leans forward, braces his hands, short armed on the surface of the desk, the cigar still between his teeth. "Before I go any further, I have to have your word that nothing said here will be repeated outside this room. Do I have your word?"

Harry and I look at each other. "What are you talking about?" I ask.

"I have to have your word." He takes the cigar from his mouth.

"That would depend on what you have to say," I tell

him. "If you tell us you have hard evidence that somebody other than our client did the deed, you can be sure that before they strap her to the gurney and insert the needle I'm gonna mention it to somebody."

"No, no. I don't want you to misunderstand. You're not going to be hearing that your client didn't do the crime. Based on all the evidence we have so far, which is, in a word, 'overwhelming'…"

"Please try not to scare us," says Harry. "I break down easily."

"I've noticed. No, everything we have points to your client. You've seen the prints on the dagger, the toxicology report, and the fingerprint evidence on the medication bottle. And there's more, the coins she took, the pawn tickets in her purse."

"What about the coin from the probate estate?" says Harry. "The seller on that one was a man. What do you have on this guy John Waters?"

"No doubt an alias," says Templeton. "A dead end."

"What do you mean a dead end? Have you checked it out?" I ask.

"We're still looking at it. But I wouldn't hold your breath. She could have passed the coin off to somebody else. Or had help at the house with the murders. The fact is that the only person who had any contact with this guy Waters was the purchaser of the coin and he's dead. According to the executor the buy was made in cash, so there's no check or account that we can trace. Like I say, a dead end. So let's get back to the toxicology report," says Templeton.

"What, now you're going to show that she tried to poison him?" I say.

"I'll concede the point; given the amount of the drugs

in his system she merely tried to put him to sleep. Under different circumstances, given the evidence, we might even be talking today about reduced charges, dropping the special circumstances, something less than a capital offense.

"That would be pretty generous," says Templeton, "considering that Pike's murder took place during the commission of another crime, the robbery. If that was all there was, I might have entertained a pitch for something less. But we can't forget the maid. We have multiple murders here. And that one is very hard to swallow."

"How could we forget?" says Harry.

Templeton looks at both of us. "No, either Pike woke up after she medicated him or the medication didn't work. At the moment we're not sure. But either way, it's clear. Pike stumbled in on them in the midst of the burglary, probably while they were in the process of stealing the coins. They killed him, took his computer and perhaps other items of personal property. At this point we can't be entirely sure of what's missing. We're still looking, but you can be sure we'll find it."

"You keep saying 'they.'" I tell him.

"Excuse me?" Templeton looks up at me.

"You said, 'They killed him.'"

"Well, yeah," says Templeton, "we haven't caught up with the codefendant yet. But we will."

"You're telling us there was a second perpetrator?" says Harry.

"Well, yeah. You didn't know that?"

Harry shakes his head.

"At first we thought she might have done it alone, but then a couple of weeks ago we figured it out."

"Figured what out?" I ask.

"Whoever it was entered by way of the back door," says Templeton. "It appears your client tried to unlock it for him, but the maid must have locked it again. Both sets of fingerprints were found on the knob. The lock was picked for entry, so her helper appears to have come prepared and had some skills. We found scratches on the tumblers, both the dead bolt and the door lock.

"And we've talked to some of the hired help and others who knew your client. It seems she was seen all over town, Del Mar as well as other places, almost always in the presence of other men, talking to them. Sooner or later we'll find the right one."

"What are you saying?" I ask.

"Well, you've seen the woman," he says. "She's gorgeous. Catch me at a weak moment and who knows, maybe even I would have helped her out."

"She may be petite, but you'd need a ladder," says Harry.

"Let's not get personal," says Templeton. "You can dress her like a nun when you bring her to court, but there's no denying she's knock-dead gorgeous. And if I can't get at least half the judges in the county, the male half, to take judicial notice of her good looks I'll quit."

"Okay. So she's pretty," I tell him.

"Pretty!" Templeton's voice goes up a full octave. "Your partner must be quite the lady's man." He looks at Harry. "If all he can say about Katia Solaz is that she's 'pretty,' his date card must be full every night."

He waits for me to say something, but I don't.

"As I was saying, according to all the witnesses we've spoken to, she never had a problem finding men to talk to. Fact is, unless I'm mistaken, isn't that how you met her? The first time, I mean." When I look up, Templeton's glowing face is boring in on me.

"What?"

"I was informed from one of the police reports that that's how you and Ms. Solaz first met. What was it, she approached you in a grocery store and started talking, is that right?"

"Yes." What else can I say?

"How did she do it, just walk up to you?" he says.

"She was looking for something. I don't remember," I lie.

"I'll bet she was," says Templeton.

"It was nothing like that," I tell him.

"Right," he says. "And your heart didn't go pitty-pat either, I'll bet. Well, if she met her lawyer that way you can figure she may have found men to do other things for her in the same way. Spread a little honey around and bees will come."

The blood drains from my head as I filter all the details. The cops showed up at our office door with my business card, the one they found in Katia's purse when they arrested her. I had given it to her that morning at the grocery store in Del Mar. The police asked me if I was her lawyer, and if not, how she came by my card. I explained it to them, and they left.

If the cops have been busy looking for a co-conspirator, it begs the question. Why have they never returned to ask me if I had an alibi for the night of the murders? My mind starts to race. Where the hell was I? I have a sudden compulsion to tear through the pages of my calendar. I can't remember.

Harry and I sit stone faced, staring at the Dwarf from across the desk.

"You look surprised." Although this is not directed at one of us in particular, Templeton seems to be looking at me as he says it.

"Do I?"

"Surely you didn't think she did it alone?"

"I don't think she did it at all," I tell him.

Templeton ignores me. "She would have needed help to blank out the camera at the side of the house and to take down the motion sensors. You didn't think we bought into the concept of coincidence, did you? Hell, she couldn't possibly have carried all those coins herself. We got an estimate from a coin expert, just on the stuff we know is missing, and the weight would have been more than a hundred and forty pounds. That's more than she weighs, and it doesn't include the stuff she took, the coins she hocked along the way on her bus trip. No, there's no question, somebody entered the house from that side, and they left the same way when they were finished."

This would, of course, explain what happened to the large cache of missing coins and Pike's computer. According to the police, Katia's co-conspirator has them.

"And there's a good chance that whoever it was set her up," says Templeton.

"What do you mean?" I say.

"Well, think about it. He left with the lion's share of the coins, and he avoided having his picture taken on the security cameras coming and going. You notice he sent her out through the front gate, right into one of the security cameras that was still working. Guess he figured somebody had to take the rap. So now he's got most of the gold, and she's left facing the death penalty, twisting in the wind, as you might say."

He allows this to settle on us like mustard gas.

"Bullshit," says Harry. "If what you're saying is true, she'd be mad as hell. You don't think she would have told us by now?"

"Maybe there's a reason for that," says Templeton.

"What?" says Harry.

"I don't know. Mr. Hinds, maybe you should talk to your client. You are, of course, free to make of this evidence whatever you can in her defense. Personally, I don't think it will make a difference," says Templeton.

"Spare us your heartfelt assessment of our case," says Harry.

"Of course, but there is one more item, the reason I asked you to come over here today. A bit of a wrinkle that's developed."

"What wrinkle?" I say.

"Do I have your word that what I'm about to say doesn't leave this room?"

I look at Harry. He nods. "Go ahead."

"It better be good," says Harry.

"Ordinarily I'd let you flounder for a few weeks, push and shove over the items in dispute. I could leave you with the illusion that they've simply been misplaced. But that would be deceptive."

"And, of course, you'd never do that," says Harry.

"Never," says Templeton.

"You're talking about the missing photographs?" says Harry.

"Six of them, I believe. They were taken from your client and inventoried when she was arrested."

"Where are they?" I ask.

"That's the problem."

"Don't tell me they've been destroyed," I say.

"No, at least not as far as we know."

"What do you mean as far as you know? Listen," says Harry, "either deliver them up or tell us where they are."

"That's the problem. I can't."

"Why not?" I say.

"I can't tell you that either. What I can tell you is that you would be wise to take the matter into court at your earliest opportunity. File a Brady motion. I won't oppose it. Give you my word. Get a ruling from the court if you can."

Brady v. Maryland is the seminal case in criminal discovery. Under the U.S. Supreme Court ruling, the government is required to deliver to the defense any and all exculpatory evidence. Even if the evidence by itself may not prove innocence, if it tends in that direction the state must turn it over.

"Personally, I think the photos are probably irrelevant and immaterial," says Templeton. "It's hard to see how you could fashion a defense around six photographs. Of course, I don't know what the photos represent. Maybe you could enlighten me," he says.

"Last time I looked, Brady is a one-way street," says Harry. "We don't have to truck information in your direction."

"I just thought as long as we were sharing things," says Templeton. "And, of course, as far as I'm concerned you're entitled to look at the photographs."

"But you can't just give them to us?"

"Sorry," he says.

"I don't get it," I tell him. "If you think the photos are immaterial, why wouldn't you oppose a Brady motion?"

"File it and find out," says Templeton. "That's all I can tell you. You won't get the photographs any other way."

TWENTY-ONE

Anyone familiar with such things might have been skeptical, but Nitikin knew that regardless of the passage of time, more than forty years, the device itself was virtually pristine.

The reason for this was the manner in which it was stored. Soviet physicists had long known that the greatest threat of deterioration to a gun-type nuclear device would be from oxidation and corrosion of the metal parts, and degradation of weapons-grade uranium if it were subjected to oxygen and hydrogen in the atmosphere for long periods.

Corrosion resulted from the close proximity of highly enriched uranium and ferrous metals, in this case tungsten carbide steel. Separate the uranium from the steel, and store each of them properly, in the case of uranium in a vacuum-sealed container, avoiding moisture and humidity, and the shelf life for a weapon of this kind would be extended geometrically, almost indefinitely.

The two subcritical elements of uranium, the projectile and the four concentric rings of the target, had been machined to precision and stored in their separate sealed lead-contained vaults while the weapon was still in the Soviet Union, before it had ever been shipped to Cuba. They had never been removed.

Nitikin had never even seen them, but he knew they were there from the periodic Geiger readings he took through the test vents in each of the lead cases. From these readings he knew that the two separated elements of weapons-grade uranium, the target and the projectile, neither of which alone possessed critical mass sufficient to cause a chain reaction, would, when combined under pressure at the proper velocity down the gun barrel, result in a massive chain-reaction detonation.

If it worked properly, the entire sequence, from detonation of the cordite initiator launching the uranium bullet down the barrel, to the flash of light hotter and more brilliant than the core of the sun, would take but the barest fraction of a second.

The parts were relatively easy to assemble as long as you had the proper tools, protective gear, and, most important, a deft touch with the tongs needed to position each of the elements while they were bolted or fitted into place.

For Nitikin it was this last part that had become the problem. He had developed a slight palsy in his hands. Over the past few years it had worsened. He knew that he could no longer manipulate the metal tongs either to load the gun with the subcritical uranium projectile or to fasten the uranium target rings to the tungsten carbide tamper at the muzzle end of the barrel.

Nitikin had told no one about this, least of all Alim or any of his cadre. He was afraid of what they might do if they knew, not for himself, but for Maricela, his daughter.

Nitikin, at least in his mind if not his heart, remained the staunch warrior. But he knew that Maricela was afraid, fearful of what was happening. He kept the details from her for her own safety. But she was not stupid. How much she knew, he couldn't be sure. He told her not to ask any questions and to remain out of sight as much as possible.

She had asked him to leave with her on her last trip, to go back to Costa Rica and to live with her and her children there. For Nitikin it was strange. For the first time in recent memory, he actually wanted to go. But by then it was too late. Alim and his men had arrived with money for the FARC rebels and funds for the cartel in Mexico. Alim knew about the device. Nitikin was trapped.

For himself he did not care. Living and hiding with the bomb had been the purpose of his life for so many years that it no longer mattered. But he loved Maricela and did not want her harmed.

He had stalled for time, hoping Alim would allow her to leave, to go back home to her family. Twice he had asked Alim to permit men from the FARC whom he trusted to see her home safely and twice Alim had put him off. Nitikin had already told Maricela that if they permitted her to go, she was never to return to visit him again, under any circumstance. Though the thought crushed his heart, he would say good-bye to his daughter and never lay eyes on her again in this life. Yakov Nitikin knew he was a dead man. If age did not take him soon, Alim would, the moment his usefulness ended and his knowledge became a burden.

TWENTY-TWO

I f the study of crime is a science, its first rule of physics is the law of opportunity. Every cop on the beat will do two things first: nail down the time frame for the crime, and then cast his net over the universe of possible suspects and start trolling for calendars.

If you kept your appointments, and your social agenda for the evening didn't include sticking knives in Emerson Pike, they would cross your name off the list.

When they are done, the police will zero in on the names that are left, concentrating on people like me who don't have an alibi for the night in question. It may not be rocket science, but it works.

I have scoured my calendars, the one at work as well as my personal Outlook file from my smartphone, the cellular I carry on my belt. There are no entries on either for the night that Pike was killed, nothing but blank space. I have gone so far as to check my phone records to see if I might have made calls from the house or my cell phone during the period that the police believe the crimes were committed, a rough ninety-minute time frame between nine and ten thirty. I am left to conclude that after hours I lead a dull life. I could find nothing.

Some people would at least slap their computers around, send an e-mail to a friend. Generally I don't even do that. If I'm not prepping for a case, I'm reading or watching a movie on cable. With my daughter, Sarah, away at college, widowed and living alone as I do, unless a nosy neighbor peeked at me through a window, I have no way of proving where I was that night.

"You worry too much," Harry tells me.

This afternoon I am driving over the bay, on the bridge from Coronado to the courthouse downtown, Harry in the passenger seat. We have an order-shortening time, allowing us an early hearing on a Brady motion. We are going after Katia's photographs. True to his word, Templeton has filed no objection.

"You don't think it's strange the cops never came back and asked me what I was doing that night, where I was at the time of the murders?"

"Cops screw up," he says. "It's the order of the universe." According to Harry, "They probably just forgot. They talked to you once. Maybe they just didn't go back and look at their notes, figured they had everything they needed. Don't go kicking a sleeping dog," he tells me.

"This particular dog is four feet tall and the last time I looked he wasn't sleeping. Templeton didn't forget. If homicide didn't come back and ask me for an alibi, it's because the Dwarf told them not to."

"And why would he do that?"

"You tell me."

"You're getting paranoid," says Harry.

"Then what was all that chatter from Templeton

about the stream of men following Katia around, the fact that she was a man magnet, and oh, by the way, isn't that how you met her?"

"That's just the Dwarf jerking you around. He's trying to get under your skin," says Harry.

"Then you can tell him he's succeeded."

"If you're that worried, check your credit card statements, your ATM card. Chances are, if you went anywhere that night you might have used plastic to buy something. That'll put you someplace other than Del Mar. We can send a copy of the receipt to Templeton and you can start sleeping again at night."

I have already done this and come up empty. I don't tell Harry because I have a bigger problem.

"Forget about it," he says. "I mean, there's no reason to worry, right?"

I look over at Harry in the passenger seat. "Are you trying to convince me or yourself?"

"What I mean to say is, you know you didn't do anything."

"Is that a question or a statement?"

"Don't put words in my mouth. You tell me you didn't do anything. You say you talked to her once in the grocery store, and I believe you. That's the end of it. Let's just get this thing done. Get the photos, see what's in them, and maybe we can make this whole mess go away. Besides, if you ask me, Templeton's whole theory of a co-conspirator is screwy. You can take every one of his facts, turn them around, and explain them away based on the killer coming in through the back door as Katia went out through the garage."

"I'd agree with you except for one thing. Juries don't like scenarios that hang on good fortune and serendipity.

Templeton's theory that two people did it would be much easier to sell."

Harry says nothing. Silence in the car for a moment. "And so you're thinking this is especially true if the second person is Katia's own lawyer."

"We've been working together for too long. You're now doing mind melds," I tell him. "Let me ask you a question?"

"Shoot."

"What would you say if I told you I met up with Katia more than one time before the murders?" I am concentrating on the road, but as I say it I can tell that Harry gets whiplash turning his head to look at me.

"What are you saying?"

"That I saw her one other time before Pike was murdered."

"Aw, shit," says Harry.

"I know. Don't say it. I didn't tell the cops. One of the stupider things I've ever done."

"This is like a bad dream," he says.

I glance over and Harry is bug-eyed, staring out at the road as if in a trance.

"Nothing happened," I say. "It was in the afternoon, about a week before the murders. She called me at the office, said she was going to be in Coronado later that day. She said her friend had some business to conduct and she was going to be window-shopping. She wanted to know if I could get together with her for a drink. I checked my calendar. I had nothing up, so I told her sure, why not? We met at the Brigantine, out in front of the office, had two drinks. The conversation lasted maybe forty minutes, that was it. She left and I went home."

"Why didn't you tell the police?"

"They didn't ask for an alibi, so I figured they weren't looking for an accomplice, they were just trolling for information. They wanted to know if I was representing her, and if there was no lawyer-client relationship to get in the way, they wanted to know how I met her and what we talked about. What could I say? There was no lawyer-client relationship when we met. You can be sure they'd already talked to Katia and they knew that. I told them about the first meeting, how she got my card, and that was it. They asked me if I'd talked to her or seen her since, and I said no."

Harry gives me one of his stern looks.

"You don't have to say it, I was stupid. I felt sorry for her, in the country all alone. I knew she wasn't happy. When we had drinks at the Brigantine, she told me she wanted to go back to Costa Rica but the guy she was living with wouldn't let her go. I told her to call the Costa Rican consulate or the police and they'd find a way to get her home. I told her if she had problems with them to call me and I'd wade in. If I told the homicide detectives this, it would have been all they needed to hang her. They would immediately assume she'd found another way to get free and that she willingly turned her back on the simple legal recourse that was available to her. So I didn't tell them. So go ahead and shoot me," I tell Harry.

"Find me a gun," he says.

"I figured it was none of their business. If they were looking for evidence to bury her, they'd have to find it someplace else."

We rumble over the freeway for a couple of minutes in silence as Harry absorbs all of this, his head in his hand as his elbow rests against the lower sill of the window on the passenger side.

"Katia didn't have a cell phone," says Harry. "She had to take Pike's to call the taxi when she escaped from the house. That means there's a good chance that when she called you to set up drinks that afternoon, it was from the landline at Pike's house."

"And Templeton would have the phone records," I say. "I know that now. It's why he's breathing down my neck. He knows somebody at the house called the law office just a few days before the murders. He knows you didn't know her. We'd never done any legal work for Pike, so he wouldn't be calling us. So it had to be Katia who was calling and it had to be me on the other end, because he knew we'd already met."

"How did you pay for the drinks at the Brigantine?" says Harry.

"Three guesses. First two don't count," I tell him.

"Credit card."

"Yep. You can bet that Templeton's had his investigators visiting every place I've spent money since I met her, flashing photographs of Katia and me and asking the help if they ever saw us together."

"So the cops would have already been to the Brigantine talking to the bartender and the waitresses," says Harry.

"Do you want to go over and ask them?" I say.

"No."

It entered my mind like an icicle two nights ago as I lay in bed and thought about everything Templeton had said during our meeting. He believes I have taken Katia's case for one reason, so that I can control her, keep the police away, and keep her quiet. Once she is convicted, who is going to believe her? His invitation across the desk to Harry to talk to his client was Templeton's effort to save her. He's not sure about Harry, but he has reason to believe that I'm the devil.

He has no doubt already seen my credit card statements and phone records. He could do that without my knowledge. Unless I'm wrong, he won't wait long to get his hands on my calendar. Why he is waiting, I'm not sure.

TWENTY-THREE

A s Harry and I enter the courtroom this afternoon, Templeton is in his special chair that he uses only in court, perched up high at the prosecution-counsel table. He doesn't need the chair for mobility, but for height. Huddled around him are four other people, one of the homicide detectives, a woman, and two gentlemen with their backs to us. They're all wearing blue power suits, the men in pinstripes. There is a heavy satchel briefcase on the floor next to one of them. Unless they are carrying this for exercise, it appears to be locked and loaded, ready for action.

"The Dwarf's brought the entire office," says Harry. "I thought he said he wasn't going to oppose this."

The seats on this side of the railing, for the public, are empty except for two journalists. Arguments over a motion on evidence, even in a notorious murder case, never draw much of an audience. They know the defendant won't be here. Katia's presence is not required. I told her I would call her at the jail the moment we're finished.

Communication with Katia is becoming a problem,

especially since eruption of telephone-gate at the county jails. A few weeks ago the sheriff's department was caught recording lawyer-client conversations on the jailhouse telephone system. Copies of these found their way to the DA's office on discs. Ordinarily this would be a felony under state law, but to do this you have to prove intent. The sheriff claims the lawyer-client stuff was mixed in with other telephone conversations that the department was allowed to record, a glitch in the computer-operated recording system. Except for lawyer-client communications, jail inmates have no right of privacy. Bugging cells and "accidentally" installing snitches to sleep in the bunk above a target inmate has always been part of the game.

Regardless of what law enforcement does to gloss over this, communicating with Katia is now a problem. Unless Harry or I hop in the car and drive twenty miles, all the way out to Santee, there is no safe method for talking to her.

Harry and I approach, up the center aisle toward the swinging gate at the bar in front of the judge's bench. The woman at the table turns and suddenly I recognize her. She is Kim Howard, the United States attorney for the Southern District of California.

Harry and I become walking ventriloquists, put on our best smiles and try to suck it up.

"What is she doing here?" whispers Harry.

"I don't know."

Apparently one of the reporters is wondering the same thing. Now that she has turned toward him, he's leaning over the railing trying to engage her in conversation.

She smiles politely and waves him off by shaking her

head. If I'm reading her lips correctly, she can't discuss it right now.

"Maybe it's the visa," says Harry.

For weeks now, Harry has been bounced back and forth like a Ping-Pong ball between the State Department and their Consular Services office, trying to get information on Katia's visa, on how Pike managed to get her into the country so quickly.

With the hushed announcement by Howard that we've arrived, the papers spread out on the counsel table in front of them vanish into a manila folder and from there into the single briefcase on the floor. By the time we get inside the bar railing, everything is clean and we are confronted with only smiling faces.

Templeton looks like the bird that swallowed the cat. "I think the judge wants to do this in chambers today." Having sprung an entire army on us, he does amazingly quick introductions. "I think you know Kim Howard."

"I do." We shake hands.

She gives me a smile, then quickly frisks me up and down with her eyes, the kind of appraisal you might expect if you were dead but had somehow misplaced your grave. Templeton has been talking.

He does the honors with the two men. The younger one is the bellboy, a deputy U.S. attorney from Howard's office in San Diego, brought along to carry the bag.

The older one is gray haired and sober, with heavy-lidded eyes over thin lips, one corner of which turns up the slightest millimeter as he shakes my hand. Templeton introduces him as James Rhytag, deputy assistant attorney general. Howard should take lessons from him. You can't tell what he's thinking. Everybody's dead to him.

"Deputy assistant AG, that's pretty high up," I say. "Then I take it you're not from these parts?"

"Washington." The lips barely move as he says it.

"What division?"

"We can talk inside." He means the judge's chambers. He gestures with his head toward the two reporters who are now leaning over the railing trying to collect business cards, like trained seals slapping for fish.

It seems no one is carrying cards today, so the reporters open their notepads and shoot for full names and correct spellings. They keep pointing to Rhytag, asking for his title, and what he's doing here. With all the federal firepower, they know they've stumbled into something. The only two people in the room who seem to be less informed are Harry and me.

Templeton climbs down off the wheelchair, gets behind it, and starts pushing. He leads the assemblage past the bench, toward the hallway that leads to the judge's chambers.

Harry and I fall back to the rear. He leans over and says into my ear, "Why don't you excuse yourself to the men's room. Let me go in with the judge and find out what this is about." Harry is worried.

"If Templeton wanted to arrest me, he wouldn't need the federal government to do it. Besides, we have the luck of the draw." I nod toward the plaque on the wall outside the door, the one that says HON. PLATO QUINN.

Once through the door and into the judge's chambers, Templeton pushes his wheelchair right up to the front lip of Quinn's desk, climbs aboard, and then invites the U.S. attorney and Rhytag to take the two client chairs on either side of him. This leaves Harry and me to share the couch against the back wall with the federal baggage boy.

Templeton tries to chat him up, but Quinn sits there, imperiously waiting until everybody is inside and seated and the door is closed. The judge is tall and angular. He sits bolt upright in his chair behind the desk, sharp-angled beak nose, narrow face, and bald head. Quinn has always reminded me of the eagle on the great seal.

Templeton edges in with the introductions. He starts with the U.S. attorney, but before he can get her name out, Quinn steps all over it. "Mr. Madriani, Mr. Hinds." He looks at Harry and me seated on the end of his couch like orphan afterthoughts. "Good to see you both again. I hope everything's going well."

"Your Honor, what can I say? We're back in your courtroom again, so it can't be too bad."

He laughs.

A trial judge has not been assigned to Katia's case as of yet, but criminal pretrial and law-and-motion matters are dished up to only two judges in the courthouse. One of them is Plato Quinn. Harry and I have tried cases before him. Toy with him and Quinn can exhibit the abrasive qualities of a drill sergeant. Do a trial in front of him and survive the experience and a kind of affinity is formed that you see in combat. If, for some reason, the federal government is about to crawl up our back, there is nobody I'd rather hand the scratcher to than Quinn. He is not likely to be pushed around.

Templeton manages to get through the introductions before Quinn cuts him off again. "I guess I'm a little confused. And don't misunderstand me, it's not that I'm not happy to see you all, but why are all these people here?" He puts this to the Dwarf. "What I show in the file is a motion to produce under Brady filed by the defendant with no response or opposition, no points and authorities from the prosecutor's office."

"That's correct," says Templeton. "The district attorney's office offers no opposition, Your Honor."

"Your Honor, if I may." With the sound of Kim Howard's voice, the guy at the other end of the couch has the briefcase open and a thick file out of it.

"I think we can cut through this very quickly," says Howard. She reaches behind her without looking. Her assistant puts the file in her hand, like a relay runner passing the baton. Howard pulls a sheaf of stapled papers from it, maybe three or four pages, and hands it to the judge.

"I have here a federal court order issued by the federal district court for the District of Colombia removing jurisdiction over this matter, to wit, the motion to produce six identified photographs seized from the defendant in the present case of *People of the State of California versus Katia Solaz*. Federal removal is grounded on federal question jurisdiction, under statute conferred on the United States Foreign Intelligence Surveillance Court in Washington, D.C.

"As you can see, the order was signed and filed by the district court three days ago."

"Mr. Madriani, have you seen this?" says Quinn.

"No, Your Honor. This is the first we've heard of it."

Howard snaps her fingers and her assistant produces two copies from the briefcase, one for me and another for Harry.

"Excuse my ignorance," says Quinn. "But what exactly is the Foreign Intelligence Surveillance Court?"

"Perhaps a little background is in order." This comes from Rhytag.

"Yeah, Jim, I think you're best to handle that," says Howard.

"I don't care who handles it. I just want to know what's going on." Quinn doesn't like being stepped on, even by another judge wearing federal robes.

"The Foreign Intelligence Surveillance Act of 1978 established a special federal court entitled the United States Foreign Intelligence Surveillance Court. It also established a special court of review for appeals from the FISC, FISC being shorthand for the court. Since that time the law has been amended under the Patriot Act to change the size and composition of the court, but its purpose remains the same."

"Which is what?" says Quinn.

"To oversee and adjudicate requests from federal law enforcement agencies for surveillance warrants against suspected foreign intelligence agents operating within the United States. They're called FISA warrants."

"Excuse me," says Quinn, "I know Mr. Templeton just introduced us, but exactly who are you?"

"I'm James Rhytag, deputy assistant attorney general in charge of the Justice Department's National Security Intelligence Division."

"That's quite a title," says Quinn. "In light of the federal district court's order, I'm not exactly sure what my role is in this matter any longer. I assume I still have jurisdiction over the criminal case."

"As far as I know," says Rhytag.

"That's big of you," says Quinn. "So you're telling us that these photographs, the ones Mr. Madriani and his client want access to, are off limits, under some kind of federal seal, is that it?"

"In a word, yes," says Rhytag.

"You have anything you'd like to say, Mr. Madriani?" Quinn looks at me.

"Yes, I'd like to know where the photographs are."

"I'm not at liberty to say," says Rhytag.

"Maybe I missed something," I say. "What you're telling us is that the jurisdiction of this special federal court is limited to the issuance of these surveillance warrants, for spies operating in the United States, is that correct?"

"That's right," says Rhytag.

"What do the six photographs have to do with surveillance warrants?" I ask.

"That's classified. You're not entitled to know," says Rhytag.

"Your Honor, what we have here are two murders with a truckload of unanswered questions. We have questions concerning one of the victims, Emerson Pike, and what his background was, how he managed to expedite obtaining a visa to bring the defendant into the country, a U.S. visa that would ordinarily take months but which he was able to obtain from the United States consulate in Costa Rica in three days. You wouldn't know anything about that?" I put the question to Rhytag.

"Sorry," he says, and just shakes his head.

"We know that Emerson Pike was obsessed with the photographs in question," I tell Quinn, "and that the pictures were taken by the defendant's mother..."

"Where? Where were they taken?" says Rhytag.

I look at him. "If you want to share information, give me copies of the photographs and tell me what you know, and I'll give you all the information I have, on one condition, that it doesn't place my client in legal jeopardy."

"Why don't you just tell me where the photographs were taken," says Rhytag. "Costa Rica? It was Costa Rica, wasn't it? Why don't you just tell us what your client has told you and we can get past this very quickly."

"I assume you're looking for Mr. Nitikin." It's a gamble, but it pays off. Rhytag's eyeballs nearly come out of his head as he turns to look at me.

"What has she told you?"

What is even more interesting is the confused look on Templeton's face as he sits there turned around in his chair, looking first at me, and then at Rhytag. Whatever the feds know, they haven't shared the details with their friendly prosecutor.

"Let us talk to her," says Rhytag. "We'll give her use immunity."

"On what, on the murders?" I ask.

"Not a chance," says Templeton.

Rhytag leans over toward Templeton, while Kim Howard occupies the Dwarf's other ear. Howard's assistant quickly gets up off the end of the couch and stands directly behind the wheelchair to block Harry's and my view. They huddle in front of the judge's desk.

"If you want to borrow my chambers to talk for a few minutes, you can have it," says Quinn. "By the way, who's Mr. Nitikin?"

Templeton raises a hand to hold off the judge. They confer for a few more seconds before Templeton says, "Okay, all right. Your Honor, I'm not entirely sure what's happening here, but maybe there is a solution that meets all of our needs. This is what I'm prepared to offer, and I should preface it by saying that I'll have to clear it with my boss, but I think he'll go along. Two issues," he says.

Templeton turns in the chair to look at me as Howard's assistant steps out of the way.

"If she cooperates"—Templeton is talking about Katia—"if she talks to the government and the information she provides is useful and, and this is a big point," says Templeton, "if she gives up the co-conspirator, whoever helped her at Pike's house, I'll entertain an LWOP, reduction to a life term without the possibility of parole."

"In your dreams," I tell him.

"That assumes there is a co-conspirator," says Harry. "How the hell can she give you something that doesn't exist?"

"We won't know that until she tells us, will we?" says Templeton. "But I've made the offer. Your Honor," he says, turning back toward the judge, "since the state has now made the offer, and I'll put it in writing, the offer must be conveyed to the defendant. It's not within the province of her lawyers to reject it. That decision belongs exclusively to the defendant. They can advise her, but they can't make the decision for her. And I would ask, so that there is no misunderstanding or confusion as to the terms, that both Mr. Madriani and Mr. Hinds be present when the offer is explained to her." Templeton looks directly at Harry as he says this. "And I'll have it translated into Spanish so that she can read it as well. To avoid the death penalty is no trivial matter."

"No, it's not," says Quinn. "You'll convey the offer, Mr. Madriani, Mr. Hinds."

"We'll be happy to convey it," I tell him. "But I can assure you she'll turn it down."

"How can you be so sure?" Templeton turns around and looks at me.

"Because I know my client, and if you pulled your head out of your ass, you'd be able to see the light of day."

"Mr. Madriani!" says Quinn.

"Sorry, Your Honor, but two people have been murdered. Someone broke into Emerson Pike's house that night. We know that because the police found pick marks on the lock at the back door. The only reason the killer didn't get the photographs in question is because they belonged to the defendant's mother. Katia Solaz convinced Emerson Pike to give the photographs back to her the night she left, the night he was killed. Katia Solaz got out of the house a heartbeat ahead of whoever killed him. Otherwise she would be dead and the photographs would be gone."

"Yeah, and we have your word for this, is that it?" says Templeton. "Your Honor, we think she killed Emerson Pike with the help of an accomplice." He turns back toward Quinn. "And together they cleaned out the house, took the coins and the defendant's computer."

"If robbery was the motive, why did they take only the computer and some of the coins?" I ask.

"Because they couldn't carry anything more," says Templeton. "It's called physics, the law of gravity."

"Wrong," I tell him. "The computer was taken because it contained the original downloads of the digital form of the photographs. You didn't know that, did you?"

Harry gives me a shot in the ribs with his elbow, as if to say shut up.

"Your Honor, it wasn't a burglary in the conventional

sense. Whoever came to kill came because of those pictures. That's what they wanted. That's why those photographs are at the heart of our case."

"What's in the pictures?" says Quinn.

"Ask them." I point to Rhytag.

"Can you give us even a clue?" says Quinn.

"No, sir," says Rhytag.

"I have an obligation to assure that the defendant gets a fair trial," says Quinn.

"And I have an obligation to protect national security," says Rhytag.

"Find Pike's computer and you'll find the killer," I tell them. "And it's not my client."

"Then tell me where to start looking," says Rhytag.

"Seems we're back where we started," says Harry. "I have one suggestion."

Rhytag looks at him. "What's that?"

"The federal government has regulatory powers over most banks, correct?"

"What's that got to do with anything?" says Rhytag.

"We have a name—John Waters. According to information, Mr. Waters received a cash payment in the amount of a hundred thousand dollars for the sale of one of the gold coins belonging to the victim, Emerson Pike. It may be a long shot, but it's possible this Mr. Waters may have deposited that sum in a bank account in this country. You could check your computers for the name John Waters and see what you find. I mean, he'd have to use a social security number or taxpayer ID number to open an account, right?"

Rhytag thinks about it for a moment, then makes a note. "I don't suppose you have a date of birth?" he says.

"It's an alias." Templeton says it with scorn.

"So what?" says Harry. "If someone opened an account under that name, we should find out. In the interests of national security." He looks at Rhytag.

"Mr. Madriani and I agree on one thing, Your Honor," says Templeton. "Find Emerson Pike's computer and you'll find one of the killers. Because the other one's already locked up in the county jail. Convey the offer to your client." He turns to look at me. "Tell her she has a chance to live. It's the last one she's going to get. Let's see what she says."

He gives me a sinister smile.

TWENTY-FOUR

Yesterday afternoon after she hung up the receiver in the telephone booth at the jail, Katia realized she had forgotten to thank Paul. It was clear that either he or Harry had talked to the authorities at the jail, because things had become much better.

Paul called to tell her about what had happened at the courthouse, the argument over the motion and the missing photographs. He told her they would meet at the courthouse in a few days. He had many important things to discuss with her, none of which could be talked about over the telephone. Katia was to be taken to the courthouse, where some of this was to be discussed in the presence of the judge, in the judge's office, and with the prosecutor available outside in the courtroom. Katia asked him what was happening. Paul told her he could not talk about the details over the phone and the conversation ended. She would have to remember to thank him when they met at the courthouse.

It was amazing how quickly things had improved. For the last several days, ever since the fight in the shower, all of her problems at the jail had vanished. The Mexican

Chicas who had been badgering Katia since the day she arrived, particularly the big one with the pockmarked face and the scar on her cheek, were now leaving her alone and licking their wounds.

Katia thought about this and smiled as she strode across the yard, back toward the unit where her cell was located.

The big Mexican still glanced at her occasionally with angry eyes. But the moment Katia looked back at her, the Mexican would look away. And her nose still did not look quite right. She and her friends now kept their distance. Even in the dayroom, which Katia had avoided for so long, she was now free to roam and watch television and no longer had to hide.

She knew that either Paul or Harry had made this possible. They had talked to someone at the jail, because one of Katia's three cell mates, the Chica who ran with the big Mexican and was causing her problems, had suddenly been transferred to another cell. In her place a new Latina, Daniela Perez, was moved to the top bunk, above Katia.

Daniela was not Mexican. She was Colombiana, originally from Bogotá, and like Katia, she was alone, without friends in the jail. Ordinarily Ticas would be leery of Colombianas. People from Costa Rica have long feared the drug violence of Colombia. But somehow Daniela seemed different.

She was quiet. She kept to herself. But she would smile and say hello whenever they passed. This was not done in the jail. To smile or to say anything that might be seen as courteous was a sign of weakness. It would make you a victim, someone to push around.

She wondered how long Daniela would last if she was

acting in this friendly way with others. Sooner or later she would smile and say hello to the big Mexican and the Chica gang would start in on her.

For two days Katia watched Daniela from a distance. The Colombiana was older and taller than Katia and seemed quite fit. She lifted weights every day in the exercise area. And while Daniela was pretty, Katia could tell she had lived a hard life. It was difficult to guess her age. Katia estimated maybe mid-thirties.

She had a large tattoo on her back that ran almost to the elbow on her left arm, a web like Spiderman's that bulged and flexed whenever she lifted weights. Katia was amazed by how much Daniela could lift. She did not look that strong. It was in the technique, how she moved her body. Even some of the other women, the regulars who seemed to own the weights, were impressed. Katia saw two of them talking to Daniela, who said a few words, shook the hand of one of the other women, and then left to walk out to the yard.

It was that afternoon that everything changed. Katia had gone to take a shower. She often did this earlier in the day to avoid the other women. With the water running and facing the spray, she didn't see or hear them. The big Mexican and two of her friends came into the large communal shower bay behind her. They were wearing sweats and running shoes. Even though the Mexican was large and outweighed Katia by at least fifty pounds, she always traveled with at least two others.

One of them groped Katia from behind. When she turned around, startled, and tried to cover herself with her hands, they all laughed.

"Relax, we're not going to hurt you. We're just going to have a little fun," said the big one. When she reached out and tried to touch her, Katia pulled away. Then they started with the insults. They told her how worthless Ticas were, how the Costa Rican women preened like peacocks, showing their bodies in order to kowtow to the gringos. Katia turned and tried to finish her shower.

"Don't you turn your back on me, bitch." The big Mexican grabbed Katia, spun her around, pulled her out of the spray, and pushed her against the tiled wall where the Mexicans could get at her without getting wet. The big Mexican's two friends grabbed Katia's arms and held them to the wall. The big Mexican pumped some soap into her hand from the dispenser on the wall and rubbed it on Katia's face and into her eyes.

"Leave her alone!"

Katia's eyes burned. She couldn't see a thing, but she heard the voice. It came from somewhere outside the shower bay.

Suddenly the two women released Katia's arms. She slid along the wall, away from them, toward the running shower. While they had their backs turned, Katia was able to quickly rinse some of the stinging soap from her eyes. In the yellow haze she saw Daniela standing in the entrance to the shower bay. She was wearing shorts, a jail top, and running shoes. There was a sheen of sweat on her body, as if she might have been out in the yard running.

"Why don't you just leave her alone?" said Daniela.

"Why don't you mind your own business?" said the big Mexican. "Unless maybe you would like some of this too."

"I don't think there's enough of you to go around," said Daniela.

"Oh, you think so?"

"I know so."

It happened so quickly that Katia wasn't even sure what she saw. Through the lingering sting and blur of soap she remembered a flash of slick, muscled body as Daniela closed the distance. She came at them so fast and with so much aggression that the first instinct of the Mexican's was to back up. This forced one of them, the one closest to Katia, into the spray of the shower.

They braced themselves with their hands out, ready to take her. But Daniela was no longer there. She had dipped down onto her hands on the tile floor and spun her body. With a single powerful sweep of her muscled leg, she reached out and swept the feet from under all three of them.

Katia remembered the sound. It reminded her of coconuts on concrete as their heads hit the hard tile floor. The next thing Katia knew, the three women were on their backs, sliding across the soap-covered tile as if in slow motion. They lay there for several seconds with their mouths open, dazed.

Only one of them tried to get up. It was the big Mexican, and it was a mistake. She held on to the wall to steady herself, got to her feet, and with a look of fury in her eyes, she got a bead on Daniela, lowered her shoulder, and charged.

The sleek Colombiana stepped to one side, like a toreador in a bullring. She grabbed the Mexican by the hair as she passed and redirected her head, faceup, right into the tile wall.

Katia remembered the dull thud, the vibration against the wall, and the red river of the Mexican's blood that was flushed by the running water down the drain.

The woman lay there on the floor for more than a

minute before her wide-eyed friends even stirred to help her, and when they did, they gave Daniela a wide berth in order to get there.

Katia thought the Mexican might be dead. But it didn't even seem to faze Daniela. To her it was simply the natural order of things, the law of the jungle in jail.

Katia and Daniela had spent most of the time since the shower altercation hanging together and talking.

Daniela told Katia that she had been arrested three days earlier in San Diego on charges related to drugs. But, of course, like everyone else in the jail, she was not guilty.

Paul had told Katia not to talk about her case with anyone, and so she did not. Even when Daniela asked Katia what she was in for, Katia told her flatly that her lawyers had told her it was best not to discuss the matter. It was difficult. Katia knew that she owed her safety and her newfound sense of independence to her friend.

After lockdown in the evenings they played cards, as they did tonight on top of the small table in the cell. Daniela had taught her several new games. Tonight they were into the third hand of gin rummy and Katia was having difficulty trying to decide whether to discard a three or a five when the cart rolled up in the hallway, outside their door. Katia turned her head to look. It was clean towels for the next day.

"I'll get it, you play," said Daniela. She got up, walked over, and watched through the thick glass in the door as the laundry inmate outside stacked two towels. The inmate was about to put the towels on the pass-through, the metal device like a large mail slot next to the door. Then one of the male guards came down the hall. Starched uniform, sergeant's stripes on his sleeve, hair in a crew cut, he stopped at the cart and talked to the inmate. Daniela couldn't hear what they said, but her heart nearly stopped when the guard looked at the towels, then reached into them for a quick frisk while he looked into the laundrywoman's eyes. Guards often found drugs and other contraband this way.

He went on and the laundrywoman gave him a contemptuous sneer. Then she placed the two stacked towels into the pass-through. Daniela took them on the other side.

"Okay, I laid down the five," said Katia.

"Just a sec." Daniela put one towel on Katia's bottom bunk. The other she put on her own mattress. As she did so, she slipped her hand into the inner fold of the towel to feel for the tiny raised points of the checkered plastic handle. It was not much bigger than the box the playing cards came in, but the Walther PPK .308 carried a deadly punch. It was all she would need.

Yakov Nitikin could stall no longer. Alim was growing restless. Increasingly he conferred with the technician his own government had sent. The man was not familiar with the Russian device, but he knew enough about weapons design to realize that the time for assembly had arrived.

The barrel was clean. There was no corrosion, and the few tiny traces of oxidation that appeared on the metal parts had been meticulously cleaned and removed by careful handwork using strips of emery cloth. This was followed by a bath in light machine oil to remove any residue of abrasives left by the cloth.

Nitikin supervised all of it. First he instructed Alim's men and then he watched them as they worked. He paid particular attention to the inside bore of the gun's smooth barrel. Yakov was looking for any signs of pitting in the metal surface, anything that might cause drag or slow the speed of the projectile as it was fired down the barrel. The muzzle velocity required was a thousand feet per second, roughly the speed of an American .45-caliber bullet.

Even though the projectile was not designed or intended to clear the muzzle, and the barrel was less than three feet long, any significant reduction in velocity would result in a premature detonation. As the two subcritical elements of uranium came in close proximity, but before they could properly be assembled under pressure to initiate a chain reaction, a small nuclear explosion would tear the device apart, what physicists had long called a fizzle. Radiation would spill out, but it would be largely confined and easily cleaned up. The device and the entire mission would be a failure.

Alim's technician knew this. What he didn't know was the proper order of assembly to make the weapon field ready. He had tried on several occasions to coax this information from Nitikin. But Yakov had given him sufficiently vague and confusing responses, further muddled by the need for translation between Russian, Spanish, and Farsi, that the man finally threw up his hands and said something to Alim. They gave up. Nitikin had, for the moment at least, remained indispensable. He decided that the time had come to play his hand.

Through the interpreter he told Alim that he had two demands. They were not requests. If Alim wanted his bomb, he would have to comply with both.

As the words were translated into Farsi, Yakov watched as Alim's eyes transformed to two tiny slits and the cords in his neck protruded like steel cable.

First, for the final assembly of the device he, Yakov, would use none of Alim's men, or his technician. In fact, they were barred from the hut where the work would take place.

Alim didn't like it. He was furious, arguing with the translator. At one point he reached for a pistol, seemingly ready to kill the messenger.

Before Alim could calm down, Yakov delivered the second demand. Maricela, Nitikin's daughter, was to be delivered home to her house in Costa Rica by men of the FARC whom Nitikin trusted, with assurances guaranteed by the FARC that neither she nor her family would be harmed in any way.

Alim's face flushed with anger.

But for Nitikin, both points were nonnegotiable. The reason for not using Alim's men was the language barrier. At least that's what he told Alim. It was a dangerous process. One mistake, if the two portions of subcritical uranium came in contact or even close proximity, they could get a full-yield nuclear explosion, or at a minimum irradiate a good piece of the jungle. Yakov didn't want any confusion in the room and no bystanders to get in the way.

He would do the assembly alone, with the assistance of a single FARC rebel.

Without Alim's knowledge, Nitikin had already selected the man. He was in his early twenties and seemed to have the best hands in the camp, long, nimble fingers and what appeared to be excellent hand-to-eye coordination. Both Nitikin and the rebel spoke Spanish, the common tongue. If Alim wanted his bomb, this was the price. He left little for the Persian to bargain with.

As Alim talked furiously with his technician, Yakov slipped in a few final choice words to the translator. He told the man that he and his FARC assistant would be "tickling the tail of the dragon."

Then he watched as the translator conveyed the message. He wasn't looking at Alim. He was checking the expression on the technician's face as the man's shifting eyeballs suddenly shot in the direction of the Russian.

Yakov was not a good gambler, but if he had to take odds, he would have been willing to bet that the day they assembled the bomb, Alim's technician would find some good reason to be in Medellín, a few hundred miles away.

TWENTY-FIVE

arry and I had to wonder why, if the Foreign Intelligence Surveillance Court is so secret, the minions who pull its levers would want to show up in a state court judge's chambers to tell us about it. The answer is that levels of government often like to piss on one another. It's a bureaucratic pastime.

The first thing we did when we got back to the office was to have it swept for electronic devices. When the detection equipment was turned on, it lit up like a Christmas tree. When they were finished, we stepped outside and they asked Harry and me if we wanted it removed. We conferred for a moment and agreed that the answer was no. Better the devil you know than the one you don't. Remove it, and they'd just find another better way.

So this morning Harry pitches one of the heavy volumes from our code books in the library. It lands with a thud on the table in front of me.

"Check it out," he says. "Fifty, U.S.C. 1803. It's the Foreign Intelligence Surveillance Act. According to this it was passed in 1978, and amended under the

Patriot Act a few years ago." Harry is reading from a stapled sheet of papers, something he printed off the Internet.

"The most recent figures that are public are four years old. There were more than eighteen thousand warrants granted in that year alone and only four or five applications that were denied. Who could have guessed there were that many spies?" says Harry. "Or that many rubber stamps, for that matter.

"Listen to this. 'Because of the sensitive nature of its business, the Foreign Intelligence Surveillance Court is a secret court: its hearings are closed to the public, and, while records of the proceedings are kept, those records are also not available to the public. Due to the classified nature of its proceedings, only government attorneys are usually permitted to appear before the FISC.' What does that sound like to you?" says Harry.

"I don't know. A star chamber?" I say.

"A federal grand jury," says Harry. "It's the same thing."

"In the meantime they have the photographs, and we can't see them. They know two people have been murdered, probably over these same photos, but they don't care because this is outside the purview of their law enforcement union card."

"At least you have the satisfaction of knowing that if the look on his face means anything," says Harry, "Templeton knows less than we do about what's happening."

"You mean with the feds?"

"Exactly," says Harry. "When you dropped Nitikin's name, Rhytag went supernova. He damn near melted the Dwarf, but Templeton didn't have a clue. Which makes you wonder, if all this stuff is so secret, why did

Rhytag and company show up in Quinn's chambers to tell us anything at all?"

"The reason's obvious," I tell him. "Once we filed the Brady motion, they didn't have much choice. It was either that or have Templeton tell the judge that the federal government had seized the photos from the evidence files. Either way, Rhytag's operation would have been smoked out. This way at least they got to talk to us, fish for information, like where the pictures were taken."

"True. They could have sent the FBI here to the office to ask questions but they know that's a dead end. Privileged information," says Harry. "Anything Katia's told us is covered by the attorney-client privilege, and there's no way they can get around it."

"Right. They could drag you and me behind closed doors in front of a federal grand jury, but they know they'd get the same answer."

"That's true. No federal judge is going to issue a contempt citation and jail two lawyers in a capital case because they refuse to violate privileged communications with their client."

"That's why Rhytag mentioned use immunity for Katia," I say. "He was testing the waters."

"If they gave her use immunity and agreed that nothing she said before the grand jury could be used against her in any criminal proceedings, she couldn't take the Fifth and remain silent," says Harry.

"And if they built a Chinese wall around the state murder charges and declined to share anything with Templeton, the immunity wouldn't apply there. So for that she'd still be on the hook," I say.

"Of course, if they tried to take Katia before a federal

grand jury, they'd have to allow her access to her attorneys before they did it," says Harry. "We can't go inside with her, but she's certainly entitled to legal advice and the right to confer with her lawyers."

"And that, of course, is their problem," I say. "If their only sanction is to have her held in contempt and jailed if she refuses to talk, since she's already in jail they have to know we're going to tell her to sit tight and say nothing."

If they didn't know it before, they know it now.

"And besides," says Harry, "that way she gets the upgrade to the five-star room at the federal detention facility."

Harry looks at me, shrugs a shoulder, and glances at the ceiling as if to say, Can you think of anything else?

I raise a finger. One more point.

"What's troubling to me is why Templeton invited us to file the Brady motion immediately. Why not wait? He knew the feds would be forced to come out of the shadows, to show their hand the minute it was filed. You have to wonder why."

Unless I'm wrong, this little tidbit will have Rhytag and his underlings looking for a stick to tie the Dwarf to so they can burn him at the stake. The quick Brady motion was Templeton's idea. The feds had taken the photos from his files, but they wouldn't tell him why. The curiosity must have been killing him, so he stirred the pot to see what would happen.

"We need to talk to Katia about everything, go over it all one more time, everything she told us, and we need to do it soon."

"It's already been arranged," says Harry. "She'll be on the morning bus day after tomorrow with the early arraignments. We don't meet with Quinn until one in the afternoon. That gives us all morning to huddle with her and pick her brain."

And it gives Rhytag two days to wire the courthouse holding cell where we will talk to her. He's going to be very disappointed when Nitikin's name never comes up. But we can convey Templeton's offer to her, the LWOP, and make sure the judge is satisfied she understands all the terms before she turns it down. Harry is convinced it's the only way we're going to get Templeton off my back.

"We can't get her in any sooner? Why not tomorrow?" I say.

"I already tried. Quinn's not available," says Harry. "That's as soon as we can do it. So what's next? Where do we go from here?"

"We go back to where we started. Pike was killed for the photographs. They're still the key to our case. We go after the pictures."

"And just how do you propose doing that?"

I check my watch. It's just after ten thirty in the morning and our script has run dry. But it's always best to leave them with an unanswered question. "How about an early lunch?" I say. "For some reason I'm hungry this morning." I give Harry a wink.

"Sure, why not?"

As we head out of the conference room, Harry turns toward his office. I grab his arm.

"I need to get my jacket," he says.

"Let's take a walk." We go out through the front door of the office in shirtsleeves. Instead of turning left toward Miguel's Cocina, through the little plaza and out under the arch onto Orange Avenue, we turn right and go out the back way, past the trash cans, to a small gate that leads to the parking area behind the buildings.

"What's going on?" says Harry.

"You asked me how I was going to get the photographs. Rhytag thinks he has the only copies. It's possible that he doesn't."

"If you're gonna tell me you got Pike's laptop," says Harry, "I'm going to start thinking the Dwarf may be onto something after all."

"No, it's not the laptop. But the day I met with Katia alone out at the jail, I think you were busy with something else. She told me something and I let it slide, because at the time I didn't think it was important. She told me that her camera, the one her mother used to take the shots down in Colombia, is at her mother's house in San José. She told me that as far as she knows, the original images that her mother took are still in the camera. Pike told her that he didn't erase them from the media in the camera when he copied them to his laptop."

"That's assuming we believe him," says Harry.

"If we're going to get the photos, it's the only shot we've got."

TWENTY-SIX

I f he ever got drunk and unruly in a bar, Herman Diggs would be the bouncer's worst nightmare, though you wouldn't know it from his smiling face and glistening bald head as it pops around the corner of my office door this morning.

"Understand you got something for me," he says.

I have never actually put a tape measure on Herman, but as he comes through the door he fills it with only a few inches to spare at the top and nothing on the sides. Herman is our investigator. African-American, in his thirties, he is a human brick. A blown knee in college crushed Herman's dreams of a football career and left him with a slight limp, though if you ever saw him run someone down and bury him from behind, you might question this.

"Let's go grab a cup of coffee," I say.

Herman and I stroll out to Miguel's Cocina, under the palm fronds over the patio. We sit at one of the small tables.

"I don't think they're open yet," says Herman.

"Harry and I have decided that certain things shouldn't be discussed in the office," I tell him.

Herman gives me a sideways glance.

"The walls have ears," I say.

"Who would do a thing like that?" he says.

"You don't want to know. But be careful using your phone or talking in your office concerning the matter we're about to discuss. Harry and I are using nothing but notepads and carrier pigeons for the moment," I tell him. "Don't send any e-mails or leave any voice mail on any of our office systems, or for that matter, our residential phones or e-mail. We'll have to find other ways to keep in touch. And forget the cell phones because they're now party lines."

"Federal government," says Herman.

I nod.

"What did you do, forget to pay your taxes?"

"How's your calendar?" I ask.

"I'm booked tomorrow afternoon. I got a court appearance for another client. After that I'm open for a few days. How much time do you need?"

"It depends on how fast you can work and whether you can find what we're looking for. It's the Solaz case."

I pull my wallet out of my hip pocket. I open it and fish out a tiny folded slip of paper. It's the one I gave to Katia that day at the jail so she could write down her mother's address. I folded it up and put it in my wallet. I kept forgetting to put it in the file. It is part of the reason the camera had slipped my mind.

"It's not a street number. They don't use street numbers the way we do. It's in Spanish. It's a written description of how to get to the house. She wrote it on this slip of paper."

"Costa Rica," says Herman.

"How did you know that?"

"Only place in the western hemisphere doesn't have mail service," he says. "Been there, know it well. What city?"

"San José."

"No problem."

It's the thing about Herman. He knows the central and southern part of the western hemisphere like the back of his hand. He and I first met in Mexico on a case that turned violent. When we finally popped up our heads, we realized we were the only two people in sight who could trust each other.

"What is it you're looking for?"

"A camera. I don't know what it looks like or where it's located in the house."

"Still or video?"

"Still—point-and-shoot, probably something small."

"Can you talk to your client and get a description?"

"I'll see her tomorrow in the lockup at the courthouse. I'm sure I can get a description, the problem is how to do it without having the world listening in."

"You think they're gonna wire the lawyers' conference cubicle in the courthouse?"

"Yes."

Herman gives a long, slow whistle. "What's this lady involved in? Besides murder, I mean."

"That's the problem. We don't know. And I'm not sure she does."

"Use notes," says Herman.

"I doubt if she can read English all that well, and I haven't written any Spanish since high school."

"Get somebody to write the questions down ahead of

time, this afternoon, in Spanish. Have her write the answers and you can have 'em translated when you're done."

"Good thought."

"Don't get me wrong, I don't mind taking a trip to Costa Rica, but why don't you just have her call somebody down there to look for the camera?" says Herman.

"I thought about it. If I have her call from the jail, the feds are going to know about the camera immediately. The FBI always has a resident agent at the embassies. If they get there ahead of us, we lose the camera and the pictures. Second, if we're correct in our assumptions, the camera contains some photographs we believe are central to our case. We don't know if we can trust the family. If we ask them for the camera, the pictures may disappear. We think the pictures are the reason Emerson Pike was killed. So be aware that there may be some risk involved here."

"You're telling me I'm gonna get hazardous-duty pay?"

"Be careful. You may earn it. The house in San José belongs to the defendant's mother. She's the one who took the pictures. Other than that we don't know anything about her. She may be a player. She may be an innocent bystander. She may not even be there. We don't know. According to Katia, there are no other family members who hang out at the house, just her and her mother, though she has friends who apparently have access, enough to leave a note at the house. Harry called one of them, a girlfriend of Katia's, and asked her to leave a message at the house for Katia's mother in case she came home. The mother was supposed to call the law office, but so far we've received no word. So we have to assume she's still gone. What I'm saying is that I'm not giving out any character references, so be on your guard."

"Got it."

"One other thing; when you're down there, keep your ear to the ground. In addition to the camera, we're looking for a lead on a man named Nitikin. He's the defendant's grandfather."

"Do you have a first name?"

"No. I'll put it on the list of Spanish questions. Given what we don't know," I tell him, "that's going to turn out to be a very long list."

TWENTY-SEVEN

Kim Howard entered the room, followed by Zeb Thorpe, head of the FBI's National Security Branch. They were meeting in the conference room at the FBI field office in San Diego, out on Aero Drive and not far from the Marine Corps Air Station at Miramar.

"How was your flight?" Jim Rhytag was already set up at the table, going over reports from the FBI transcripts.

"Don't ask," said Thorpe.

"What have we got so far?" Thorpe dropped his briefcase on the table and shed his suit coat.

"Has anybody briefed the White House yet?" said Rhytag.

"I'm told the national security advisor included it in his briefing to the president yesterday morning," said Thorpe. "The president wants an update every morning."

"I just started going over the summaries of the transcripts from the recordings, the office and phones," said Rhytag. "According to the analysts, there's not a lot.

Unfortunately, we got a late start. If we could have gotten the warrants a few days earlier, and surveillance in place faster, it would have made a big difference."

"We did the best we could," said Thorpe. "You forget, we had to shop for the judge."

Thorpe had a point. There were eleven judges appointed by the Chief Justice of the United States to serve on the Foreign Intelligence Surveillance Court. In any close case the FBI and the Justice Department had a pretty good idea which members of the court would give them a warrant and which judges might give them a hard time.

Rhytag's lawyers and Thorpe's agents had to wait nearly two weeks until the judge they wanted was on call. Then last weekend, when most of the judges on the special court were gone, they filed their application and snagged the judge they wanted.

It was a tough sell convincing a federal judge to allow them to electronically record conversations between lawyers, as well as between those lawyers and their client, who was already behind bars on state homicide charges.

The pitch they made was that the defendant, Katia Solaz-Nitikin, was believed to be a foreign agent working at the behest of an as-yet-unidentified foreign power. She had entered the United States in the company of a retired operative of the U.S. Central Intelligence Agency, Emerson Pike. She was then believed to have murdered Pike at his home in San Diego County. They then used the old Soviet intelligence documents linking Nitikin to the missing nuclear device. They used the photographs taken by Katia's mother, along with the information they had concerning the disappearance and possible homicide of the photo analyst in Virginia, which they claimed identified Nitikin as being alive. They established the family relationship between Katia and her grandfather. They then summed it all up. It was the government's belief that Emerson Pike had stumbled onto a plot involving Yakov Nitikin and a nuclear device in his possession, possibly involving the transport of that device to an unknown destination within the United States for the purpose of committing an act of terrorism.

They told the judge that it was the government's belief that Katia Solaz had murdered Emerson Pike to silence him and had taken the photographs in order to ensure that they did not fall into the hands of the United States government. In so doing she was engaged in assisting Nitikin in furtherance of a plot to plant a nuclear device on U.S. soil for purposes of terrorism.

They told the judge that the government did not wish to arrest Katia Solaz on these charges as of yet. Since she was already in jail, she was no longer at risk of furthering the conspiracy. But she was a valuable asset in the government's surveillance. The government lawyers told the court they understood that none of the information conveyed by Ms. Solaz to her lawyers could be used in a later prosecution on charges of espionage or terrorism. But given the risk of a loose nuclear device finding its way onto U.S. soil, the government had little choice but to lose the evidence against Ms. Solaz and gain the necessary intelligence to find the device. They would build a wall around the state murder case. None of the information obtained under the federal surveillance warrants would be shared with the state prosecutor or the local police, thereby avoiding any problems in the state's prosecution for the murder of Emerson Pike.

To these conditions, the court added one more. The government could record conversations between the defense lawyers or between the lawyers and their employees or agents, but only those conversations involving the Solaz case. Recording of conversations in the office involving any other matter were prohibited, and all such information coming into the possession of federal agents was to be treated as confidential. On these conditions the warrants were signed by the judge, allowing audio surveillance and telephone taps.

The problem for Rhytag and Thorpe was that because of the delay in obtaining the warrants, none of the electronic surveillance had been in place at the jail until after the last meeting between her lawyers and Katia Solaz.

"We know that Solaz's mother took the photographs. That much they let slip during the meeting at the courthouse," said Rhytag. "And if they're to be believed, Madriani and his partner know where the photographs were taken."

"Kim told me in the car on the way in," said Thorpe. "But they wouldn't tell you."

"They wanted to trade it for concessions in the state's case."

Rhytag couldn't share what he knew with the two criminal defense lawyers for fear that they would use it to go public. The information that there was a loose nuclear device somewhere in the hemisphere, probably in the hands of terrorists, and that this was the reason Emerson Pike was murdered, might shift the focus of suspicion away from their client. It could also result in a national panic, and cause whoever had the device to expedite their timetable. Even if Rhytag suspected that this was the reason behind Pike's murder, there was no hard evidence to support it. Templeton had a solid case against the woman, and she had a motive, money.

"Do you think Solaz is involved with the device?" said Thorpe.

"I don't know," said Rhytag.

"If so, she may have told her lawyers what Nitikin has," said Thorpe.

"To listen to the lawyers in the judge's chambers, they know a lot. Whether or not they really do, only the phone taps and wire transcripts will tell us."

"So far the only conversation we have between the lawyer, Madriani, and Solaz is one telephone conversation…" Rhytag finds the sheaf of pages. "Here it is." He passes it over to Thorpe. "It was recorded off the lawyer's cell phone. He called her at the jail. She called him back. It was right after the meeting at the courthouse. Very brief, nothing in it. He's holding everything until he meets with her at the courthouse tomorrow morning. He told her he didn't want to discuss things over the phone."

"You think he knows?" said Thorpe.

"I was hoping to have everything in place for a while so we could be listening in before they filed anything formal to obtain the photographs. That way we wouldn't have to mention the federal courts and surveillance right away. Unfortunately, it didn't work out."

"Well, taking her before a grand jury is not going to do any good." Kim Howard, the U.S. attorney, is looking at one of the transcripts. "This was yesterday. It's a conversation in the office between the two lawyers. If we hit her with a grand jury subpoena and offer immunity on any federal charges, apparently they're prepared to tell her to take the heat, sit tight, and let a federal judge issue a contempt citation."

"That's what I was afraid of," said Rhytag. "Unless we can talk the prosecutor into offering something on the murder charge, her lawyers aren't willing to bargain."

"What about the prosecutor?" said Thorpe. "Can't you get him to budge?"

"He made an offer, but it's not much. Here's the problem. He thinks one of the lawyers, this guy Madriani, is involved with Solaz. He suspects that the lawyer may be a co-conspirator in the murder."

"You're kidding me," said Thorpe.

"No, I'm not."

"If that's the case, how do we know the lawyer's not involved with Nitikin? What kind of evidence has your prosecutor got?"

"We don't know. We're not sharing with him, so he's not sharing with us," said Rhytag. "It's not just the national security angle. We've had to keep the state prosecutor in the dark to protect his case. If we let him partake of our information, we end up contaminating his entire prosecution, especially now with the surveillance warrants, listening in on the lawyers."

"What's he like?" Thorpe wants to know about the prosecutor.

Rhytag tells him about Templeton's disability. "Seems bright, a decent enough guy. Given the fact that we've told him next to nothing, I suppose we're lucky that he's cooperating with us at all."

"You may change your mind after you read this," said Howard.

The telephone on the side table behind Howard rings.

"Here, take a look." She hands Rhytag some pages of the surveillance transcript as she swivels in her chair to get the phone.

He reads for a few seconds. "Son of a bitch!"

"What is it?" said Thorpe.

"That little sucker, that moral pygmy, sold us out."

"What do you mean?"

"He's angry because we won't talk to him. It was Templeton who invited the defense to file the motion to get the photographs. He told them to do it now. Guess he figures that's going to smoke us out and give him some information. That little prick! He forced us into court before we could get the surveillance up and running. Damn it to hell," said Rhytag.

"Maybe we should tell him everything we've got," said Thorpe. "Stink up his case and let the state court dismiss it."

"Serve him right," said Rhytag. "If it wasn't such an abuse of justice, I'd call him on the phone right now and read him the transcript and record the telephone conversation."

Howard hung up the phone and turned back to the table. "She's here. I told them to send her in."

"Good," said Rhytag.

A couple of seconds later one of the secretaries opened the door to the conference room. In walked a young woman in running shoes, shorts, and a T-shirt. Her hair was disheveled, and she looked somewhat sweaty.

"Please excuse my appearance," said Daniela Perez. "I thought it might look suspicious if I changed my routine at the jail to shower and clean up this early in the day."

Thorpe made the introductions since he was the one who'd made the assignment.

Daniela's true name was Carla Mederios. She was born in Panama in the old Canal Zone to a Colombian mother and an American father. Her dad was an officer in the Army Corps of Engineers. He was killed before her eyes when Carla was fifteen years old. They had been shopping in Panama City when her father was taken by rampaging Panamanian thugs, one of the so-called dignity brigades. He was hacked to pieces by machetes, and his body dragged through the streets. It was a month before the U.S. invasion of Panama and the capture of Manuel Noriega.

Carla moved with her mother to Colombia and remained there until she returned to the United States for college.

It was no surprise that she spoke fluent Spanish. She was also an honors graduate of Pepperdine University, in Los Angeles. After college she spent four years as a lieutenant in the U.S. Army, two of them in combat in Afghanistan. It was there that she gained the artwork on her body and learned how to deal with unruly people in showers.

She returned from the military and studied law at the University of Virginia, where she graduated second in her class.

Mederios turned down four six-figure job offers from major law firms in New York, Chicago, and Los Angeles and instead went to Quantico, Virginia, where she trained to become an FBI agent. For the last three years she'd worked undercover, both in the United States and abroad. She was now considered one of the foremost female agents in the bureau, the reason she'd been picked for this assignment.

"Agent Mederios, have a seat, please." Rhytag offered her the chair next to him.

"I don't have much time," she said.

"Where does she think you are right now?" said Thorpe.

"I told her I had a meeting with my lawyer. After all, I didn't want to lie to her," said Mederios. "She thinks I'm at the jail, in one of the conference rooms. Tomorrow we're going to court together. I'd take her shopping and out to lunch, but we don't have enough time." Even Rhytag laughs at this. "She thinks I have a court appearance. I figured I'd put myself on the bus with her and we could talk."

"Have you gotten anything out of her so far?" said Rhytag.

"I've built up some goodwill," said Carla. "I let her beat me at gin rummy three days running. If you saw us together you'd swear I was her Doberman, on a leash, growling at the gangbangers. But she's reluctant to talk about her case. Her lawyer has filled her head with anxieties about trusting people in jail."

"She told you this?" said Thorpe.

"Right out of her lawyer's handbook," said Carla. "He told her not to discuss it with anyone, and she listens to him. To hear her tell it, the man walks on water."

"This would be Mr. Madriani?" says Howard.

"I don't know his last name. There are two of them. She calls them Paul and Harry."

"When you say he walks on water, does it look like

the normal lawyer-client relationship or do you think there might be something going on on the side?" said Howard.

"You mean a threesome with her lawyers? Now that would be kinky," said Carla.

"I'm talking about Madriani. That would be the Paul half of the partnership. Do you think she and the lawyer might have been having an affair?"

"There hasn't been any heavy breathing that I've heard."

"Keep your ear to the ground," said Rhytag.

"One thing is certain, she's scared. I don't think she's ever been in jail before. She's a little naive. If I were doing an evil deed, she's not someone I'd pick to do covert work."

"That may not be how it went down," said Thorpe. "She may have been enticed up here by the victim without knowing the reason."

"You mean Pike."

"Correct," said Thorpe. "When she realized what was happening with the photographs, she knew enough about Nitikin to know she was in trouble. So she had to get the photographs back."

"And to do that she ended up having to kill Pike, is that it?"

"It's possible," said Thorpe.

"The prosecutor seems to think she had some help," said Howard.

"We know she drugged Pike," said Thorpe. "One of our agents got a glance at a toxicology report. So she's not as innocent as she looks. Keep one eye open when you sleep."

"I'll try to get her to talk about the case, but—"

"Forget the case," said Thorpe. "Get her to talk about her life down in Costa Rica, her family. About her parents, particularly her mother. Share some intimate details with her about your own family. Nothing real. Make it up. Get her reminiscing about life on the outside."

"We know now that it was her mother who took the photographs," said Howard. "We need to know where the pictures were taken and where her maternal grandfather is."

"Yakov Nitikin. I read the file," said Carla. "If she's involved in the way you think she is, she's not going to tell me anything about Nitikin."

"She may give you a clue. It depends on who she thinks you are," said Thorpe. "If she gets in trouble again and she has nobody to lean on but you, and she trusts you, she may."

"Just an idea," said Rhytag. "I take it that after the fight in the shower there are hard feelings on the part of some of the other women."

"That's an understatement." Carla laughed. "It's why I needed the weapon. I wasn't excited about the idea of fending off eight or ten of them if they got me cornered somewhere out of sight of the guards. But if I have to pull the Walther, I'm going to be out of there. It'll blow my cover. It's one thing to have a zip gun. It's another to have a three-eighty with a full magazine."

"Given your attire I'm curious as to where it is right now," said Thorpe.

"You don't want to know," said Carla.

"The sheriff wasn't keen on a loaded handgun in his jail. I was advised that it's against state law," said Thorpe. "He told me that if you got caught with it, my ass was grass, because neither he nor any of his people knew anything about it, including the guard who slipped it into the towels for you. So if I lose my pension, you owe me."

"'Semper fi,'" said Carla. "I knew you'd been in the marines too long to let one of your troops go tits up in a county jail."

Howard looked at her, wide-eyed.

"Excuse my language," said Carla. "I've been undercover too long."

Thorpe laughed.

"So here's the deal." Rhytag was ignoring them. "Solaz is bottled up in jail on a murder charge with gangbangers who, after the brawl in the shower, would stick a shiv in her in a heartbeat. So if you aren't around to protect her, she's got problems, right?"

"I hope you've thought about that," said Carla.

"We have," said Rhytag. "She's not in any danger. We're keeping a close eye on her. Father Protector, the guard who slipped you the gun, has her on a special assignment in the jail dispensary while you're here. We're not going to let anything happen to her.

"But in the meantime," said Rhytag, "there's no reason we can't put all that fear to work for us. Here's how we do it. Tell Solaz that your lawyer pulled some strings with somebody he knows at the jail. They're thinking about transferring you someplace else. Tell her it's the honor farm. If you're right about her, and she hasn't been inside before, she's not going to know the difference. Tell her it's a place where they let inmates go when they think they can trust them, and it's much better than the jail. Tell her you already talked to your lawyer and there's a chance he might be able to have Solaz transferred with you. The problem is, to do this your lawyer needs a lot of personal and family background information to make sure she qualifies, so that when your lawyer goes to pull all the levers, it's not going to blow up in his face. He needs to know all the places she's lived, where her family is from, all the places they've lived, go back at least three generations. Take notes. You need to know whether any of her family members going back that far have ever been in any trouble with the law in any of the countries where they lived."

"This honor farm has high standards," said Thorpe.

"Platinum Diners Club only," said Rhytag. "You need to have any information her family has ever given her in this regard. Tell her that in most other countries, the government in the United States is able to check records, so she has to be sure to tell you everything she knows. If your lawyer finds something in the records that she hasn't told you about, he's going to think she's hiding something and she's going to be off the invitation list at the honor farm. In which case, when you leave she's going to be left behind all alone to entertain the angry women you pissed off in the shower."

"What if she wants to discuss it with her lawyer?" said Carla.

"Tell her she can't. Because if she does, her lawyer is going to want to talk to the people at the jail. If he does it's going to result in both you and your lawyer getting in a lot of trouble. You put her in the pit of divided loyalties," said Rhytag. "You came to her rescue; she's not going to want to get you in trouble. Besides, all she has to do is give you the family background and you'll take care of the rest. Otherwise you won't be able to play cards with each other much longer. If she doesn't deliver up the family tree immediately, let her look around at all the angry faces for a day or two and then tell her time is running out, you need the information or she may wake up one morning soon and you'll be gone."

"You're cold," said Carla.

"That's how you survive in an ugly world," he told her. "Think of it this way. The minute she mentions Grandpa Nitikin's name as a survivor, you take her by the hand, call the guard, go out to the front of the jail. We'll have agents from the bureau pick both of you up in a nanosecond and we'll put her in a private suite in the federal tower downtown so we can talk to her."

"Yeah, right, with the lights on day and night and the room temperature moving from the Arctic to the Sahara every half hour," said Carla.

"What can I say? The world is a dangerous place," said Rhytag.

TWENTY-EIGHT

Liquida was tired. He had spent nearly a week on the Mexican side of the border assembling the arms and munitions and observing war games in the desert east of Tijuana. He was still picking sand out of his teeth. While the men practiced, Liquida watched from a distance with a pair of field glasses.

There were seven trigger men, the oldest twenty-two, plus an expert with explosives who was in his mid-thirties. They were all handpicked and in good shape.

Only one of them, the demolition guy, knew that Liquida was involved. He and Liquida met each day to discuss how the training and preparations were going. As far as the others knew, it was the explosives man who was hiring them all. In fact, the money for everything, the men, the munitions, and the guns, had come from Liquida's employer down in Colombia.

The first day of training went fast. Teaching the seven button boys to use the inexpensive Chinese AK-47 knockoffs took less than half a day. The high-velocity Russian rounds of the AK would pass right through anything without ceramic plates behind it. The two, or possibly three, key targets might be wearing Kevlar vests, but they would not have combat armor.

Two days were spent on explosives training. This involved the shaping and placement of small charges, the use of detonators and high-yield detonation cord if it was needed to take off locks or cut through steel hinges. Liquida's explosives expert would do most of this work, but some familiarity with it by the others was essential in case he was wounded or killed in the early going.

The last day was spent on what high-tech American police called dynamic entry. In the law enforcement world, this type of training took far more time, but Liquida's small army had a big advantage. Unlike the police, they didn't have to worry about collateral damage. If they killed a dozen people getting in, it didn't matter as long as they got the right one before they left.

For training they used an old school bus that Liquida had purchased from a junkyard in Tijuana and had towed out into the desert.

For cover, each man in the assault group was given a photograph. It was a mug shot from the Mexican Judicial Police of one of the female mules who carried drugs across the border for the Tijuana cartel. From all appearances she was small fry, not of sufficient importance or risk to be transported to court in one of the sheriff's small vans. She was forty-one years old. She had been arrested in San Diego, housed at Las Colinas for seven months, and was now in her second day of a jury trial. For this reason, Liquida knew that she would be on the bus that morning. Whoever got to her first was to eliminate her with two head shots and drop her photograph on the floor by her seat.

The real target, whose face Liquida's men had all memorized, was to be killed by accident in an apparent cross fire using a gun from one of the dead guards on the bus. While the shooters were doing this, the explosives man was to place three charges connected by det cord along the dash in the front of the bus, from the steering wheel to the passenger door. This would take out the front of the bus and with it the security video recorder, destroying any tape that might have recorded the sequence of events on board.

If all went as planned, they would be off the bus in less than two minutes and on their way to the safe house where they would hide. Once things cooled down, the men could cross the border back into Mexico.

"When do you think we can go?" Katia was talking about the honor farm.

"Maybe as early as next week, maybe sooner," said Daniela.

Today the bus was more than half empty, not enough for a full load, but too many for the smaller vans. The driver and the guard were still shackling two of the women up front to the foot bar that kept them from moving around inside the bus. There were no windows except for small oblong strips of glass up high, near the ceiling, for light.

Katia, who suffered from claustrophobia, didn't like it. She sat next to Daniela on the inside of the bench seat, against the wall where the window should have been. They were two rows from the rear of the bus.

Katia didn't know what she would do if she lost her friend. Before Daniela showed up at the jail, Katia had lived each day in constant fear. Now she faced the prospect of having to deal with it again. Only this time she knew it would be much worse.

This morning she and Daniela were chained together at the waist, each with one ankle also manacled to the metal bar that was welded near the floor to the back of the empty bench seat in front of them.

"You look like this is your first time on the bus," said Daniela.

Katia nodded. "When they brought me out from the courthouse when I was first arrested and saw the judge downtown, they took me to the jail in the back of a sheriff's car."

"We're lucky," said Daniela.

"Why do you say that?"

"Male prisoners normally have their hands cuffed and fastened to the waist chain. Sometimes the women too." Daniela knew this was standard operating procedure. "These two guards are pretty nice. It looks like they're not going to cuff our hands until we get to the courthouse."

"We can talk later today, when we get back," said Katia. "I need to write down everything you need. Maybe you can help me. I'm not good at writing in English. I don't want you to leave the jail for this other place without me."

"I won't." Daniela could see that Katia was both excited and scared.

"I think I can give you everything you need. My mother, my cousin; my father is dead, so he doesn't count, is that right?"

"That's right," said Daniela, "just surviving relatives. But you have to go back as far as your grandparents."

"No problem. And I don't think my lawyers would

mind. I'm sure that if they knew you the way I do, they would tell me to go ahead."

"Yes, but I told you, you can't discuss it with them," said Daniela. "You understand?"

"I won't," said Katia. "I promise you. I would never do anything to get you in trouble. It is our secret, just you and me."

"I know. I'm just a little nervous."

"Are you sure your lawyer can do this? Get us to this honor place, I mean?"

"The honor farm." Daniela nearly cringed as she said it.

"Yes, that's what I meant, the honor farm. You think he can do it?"

"I do." It troubled Daniela to give her such promises. She knew that if Rhytag or Thorpe had Katia alone in a room for ten minutes, they would come to the same realization Daniela had, that Katia Solaz knew nothing about a loose nuke. If you were a terrorist planning an attack you would have to be on drugs to bring her into the loop. Still, it was possible that if her grandfather was alive, Katia might know where he was. "So have you always lived in Costa Rica?" she asked.

"Yes. I was born there."

The driver settled into his seat as the guard closed and locked the steel-and-wire mesh gate that sealed off the prisoners' compartment from the driver's section. The driver pushed a button on the dash and the door up front closed with a hydraulic whoosh. The guard pulled a lever and the four case-hardened steel locking bolts slid into place, securing the heavy steel door.

"And your mother, was she born in Costa Rica as well?"

"Yes."

There was a deep vibration under the seat as the diesel engine stirred and then started. A second later the bus began to roll.

"Well, it should be very easy," said Daniela. "It sounds like your whole family is from Costa Rica." She put out the bait to see if Katia would bite. She didn't. "And your mother's parents, were they born in Costa Rica too?"

"No," said Katia. "*Mi abuela*, how do you say? My grandmother, she was born in Cuba. *Mi abuelo*, my grandfather?"

"That's correct."

"He was born in Russia."

"Really?" Daniela turned toward her and smiled. "That's interesting. Where did they meet?"

"In Cuba."

"Very international," said Daniela. "And romantic."

"Yes, I suppose."

"Are they still alive, your mother's parents?"

"No. Well, actually I'm not sure."

"I don't understand," said Daniela.

"My grandmother is dead. She died many years ago. My grandfather, I'm not sure."

"What do you mean you're not sure?"

"It's a long story," said Katia.

"We have time. It's a long bus ride."

"Well, my grandfather is, how do you say when someone is separated from you for a long time?"

"Estranged."

"Yes, that's it. He is estranged from his family for many years now. When I was little I always thought of my grandfather as the black sheep."

Daniela laughed. "Why is that?"

"Because my mother never talked about him. When

I was little I would ask her, and she would always find something else to talk about. Or she would tell me to go do something. I knew he must have done something bad a long time ago."

"You mean something against the law?" said Daniela.

"No, no, I don't mean that." Katia looked at her anxiously. "I mean, this wouldn't keep me from going to the honor farm right?"

"No, of course not," said Daniela. "As long as you disclose all the details, that's all they care about. They're not going to blame you for what your parents or grandparents did."

"Okay. I mean, sure, it's possible he may have broken the law, but I don't think so. I think it's something else."

"What?"

"I think maybe another woman," said Katia.

"Another woman?" said Daniela.

"Yes, maybe, and maybe more serious than that. My grandfather may have had a child by this woman."

"You think so?"

"Yes, I know it sounds stupid, except that I know my mother. If all he did was break the law, she would have forgiven him long ago."

Daniela had to laugh.

Katia smiled. "You laugh, but I asked her once if he had trouble with the law and that's the reason she wouldn't talk about him and we never saw him. And you know what she said?"

"No, what did she say?"

"She said that for her father, the law was an angry Russian mother, a mistress who had taken his life."

"I see. So you figure the jealous mistress was another woman," said Daniela.

"Of course. What else could it be?"

To Katia this meant a lover. But to Daniela, who seemed to know more about Katia's grandfather than Katia herself, it was obvious. Katia, who was probably a young child at the time, had gotten the words reversed in the translation. The angry mistress who had stolen her grandfather's life was not a Russian mother, but Mother Russia. Nitikin had squandered his life on the run, hiding from the Soviets who wanted to kill him and retrieve the nuclear device, and from the Western powers that wanted to capture him because of what he knew.

"You're probably right," said Daniela. "It must be a woman. Did you ever have a chance to meet him? Your grandfather, I mean?"

"My mother told me once that I did, but I don't remember. I was too small."

"And so you don't know if he's alive or dead?" said Daniela. "That could be a problem."

"Why?"

"Well, because the people my lawyer is working with are going to want to know one way or the other. I mean, most people know whether their grandparents are alive or dead."

There was a long pause as Daniela allowed the anxiety to work its magic on Katia.

"I suppose it's possible he's alive," said Katia. "Let me ask you a question. Just between us."

"Of course."

"Let's say he's alive and I am wrong. Let's suppose it's not another woman but something else that has kept him away from his family all these years."

"Yes?" said Daniela.

"Let's say I make a guess at where he might be; will

they go after him or would they give the information to some other government so they could go after him?"

"Of course not," said Daniela. "The information is only for background, to see if you're telling the truth about your family. It has nothing to do with your grandfather. They probably already know who he is. They would have information on computers."

"I see." Katia had carried the theory of another woman through her entire childhood, only to have it shaken by Emerson Pike and his obsession with the photographs from Colombia. Katia had suspected for some time, even before she met Emerson, that the old man in the photographs might be her grandfather. If she was right, and that was the reason Pike was interested in the pictures, it wasn't because her grandfather had had an affair with another woman. Deep in her soul, though she didn't want to admit it, Katia suspected that her grandfather was hiding something more serious. It was the reason she'd said nothing to her lawyers. If her mother was still with him, and Katia told them where they were, her mother could be in trouble.

"So you think you know where he is?" said Daniela.

Katia looked at her, wondering if she should say anything more. "It's only a guess. It's probably wrong."

"So tell me your best guess," said Daniela.

"If you're sure they won't go after him."

"I'll talk to my lawyer. I'll make sure they won't, and unless he's absolutely certain, I will tell him to forget that part of the information and not give it to anyone else."

"Okay," said Katia. "You see, for a long time now, several years, my mother has been traveling from Costa Rica to your country."

"To the United States?" said Daniela.

"No." Katia looked at her with a puzzled expression. "No. I mean Colombia."

"Ah, Colombia," said Daniela. "Of course."

"That is where you come from, isn't it?"

"Yes. It's just that I've been in the States so much the last few years, it starts to feel as if I live here. You know the feeling?"

"Oh, I know. I hate that," said Katia. "I wish I could go home too. Maybe soon we can both go. Maybe I could visit you in Colombia."

"That would be fun," said Daniela. "So your mother travels to Colombia regularly?"

"Sometimes twice a year. She stays there for a long time. She was gone when I left to come to the United States."

"She was in Colombia at the time?"

"Yes."

"So what does she do down there?"

"She says she visits family."

"You have relatives in Colombia?"

"That's the problem, not that I know of," said Katia. "I have never met them."

"I see," said Daniela.

"My mother tells me that one of her relatives in Colombia is very old and she must go down to provide care."

"Your grandfather?"

"She has never said this, but who else can it be?"

Yakov Nitikin is in Colombia, thought Daniela. "So when she goes down to Colombia, where does she go?" In for a dime, in for a dollar.

"She flies to Medellín."

"Ah, a beautiful city," said Daniela.

"But dangerous," said Katia. "A lot of drugs."

"Not so much anymore," said Daniela. "I've been there recently. The city has changed. I take it you have never been there?"

"No. I would like to go sometime."

"We'll have to do it. And you must tell your mother to take you so you can visit your grandfather."

"If that's who she goes down to see, he doesn't live in Medellín," said Katia.

"But you said that's where she goes?"

"Yes. She flies to Medellín, but she takes a bus from there. I have asked her many times, but she refuses to tell me where she goes. But..." Katia stopped and bit her lower lip a little as she hesitated.

"Yes?"

"Last year I found a bus ticket in her purse for a place called El Chocó. I looked on the Internet, and it is located in the south of Colombia, in a place called Narnio Province."

"You mean Nariño Province," said Daniela.

"Yes, that's it. Do you know it?"

"Yes."

"Have you been there?"

"No," Daniela lied.

"That, plus little things my mother has said over the years. I know she stays in a small village near a river. She has talked about the Indians going up and down the river in dugout canoes. So it must be very rural."

"The Rio Tapaje?" said Daniela.

"Where is that?"

The name sent a chill up Daniela's spine. "It's one of the main rivers in Nariño Province." Daniela had been on the Rio Tapaje five months earlier. The river flowed into the Pacific Ocean in a remote corner of southwest Colombia. The first few miles were controlled by the Colombian army, but only through the use of high-speed boats with .50-caliber machine guns mounted on the front.

The fleet of boats, called Piranhas, was supplied by the U.S. government in an effort to eradicate the coca trade that thrived in the river basin beyond the village of El Chocó. Beyond that point even the Colombian army was reluctant to venture. This was the land of the FARC. And, if Katia was right, it was the place where her grandfather was holed up with a weapon powerful enough to erase half of Manhattan or Washington, D.C.

This morning the bus was late. Liquida steadied his elbows on the edge of the roof as he struggled to focus the big ten-by-fifty-power field glasses. He scanned the surface streets on the other side of the freeway. Liquida was on top of an abandoned commercial building along the side of Highway 67, less than two miles from the women's jail in Santee.

The freeway traffic was bumper-to-bumper during the morning rush hour.

Across the way he could see the Prospect Avenue on-ramp. The big box truck, the one the explosives man had rented, was already in place, parked right at the edge of the on-ramp, halfway down the sharp decline to the freeway. On each side of the paved roadway the ramp fell off steeply, on one side into a shallow ravine, and on the other toward the freeway. A man on foot could cross either slope easily, but a heavy vehicle, a bus or a truck, trying to traverse the steep slope would roll.

A hundred feet beyond the on-ramp, on the other side, across the ravine, Liquida had parked the getaway van. He had rented it the previous morning by using a stolen credit card and stolen driver's license. The van was parked along the side of the road, on North Magnolia Avenue. Liquida had cut a hole in the chain-link fence separating Magnolia from the freeway so the men could quickly pass through in their escape.

A lone figure with a sizable duffel bag at his feet was huddled in the shadows under one of the trees down in the gully of the no-man's-land between the elevated on-ramp and Magnolia.

Liquida watched as a couple of cars turned down the ramp. They passed the box truck without difficulty and drove onto the freeway where they quickly backed up in traffic. He was beginning to get nervous. If the truck remained stalled on the ramp much longer, some pain-in-the-ass commuter would call it in to the highway patrol. It was the one thing he feared. If they were forced to start the fireworks early, the bus driver would see it. Then, instead of turning right onto the on-ramp he would take the bridge straight ahead, over the top of the freeway. The bus would be gone before his men could move.

This nightmare was still rattling around in Liquida's brain when a fuzzy green image crept across the round edge on the lens of the field glasses. He adjusted the focus and watched as the sheriff's bus pulled into the left-hand turn pocket on Magnolia. It nosed to a stop at the traffic light on Prospect.

Liquida grabbed the walkie-talkie from his pocket, pushed the button, and spoke into it. "*Está aquí. Aquí.* It's here."

Before the words were even out of his mouth, the

man in the gully was moving at a run, lugging the heavy duffel bag up the steep slope toward the upper end of the on-ramp. When he reached the top, he lay flat on his stomach against the incline and waited.

"What's the matter?" said Katia.

"Hmm. Oh, nothing," said Daniela.

"You look worried all of a sudden."

"No, it's nothing. I was just wishing the driver would pick up his speed so we could get to the courthouse a little sooner and get off the bus."

"You don't like it," said Katia. "Neither do I, it's too closed in. You can't see nothing. They should put in windows."

Daniela had a different reason for wanting to get off the bus. The minute she was separated from Katia she would fly to a phone and call Thorpe at the bureau headquarters in Washington. She would tell him to gather every resource he could lay his hands on, civilian and military, and throw a wide net over the jungle surrounding the Tapaje River in Colombia. She was praying that it wasn't too late, that Nitikin and the bomb were still there.

TWENTY-NINE

Liquida watched as the bus made the left turn across four lanes of traffic and slipped into the right lane on Prospect. The lumbering bus moved like a snail. Cars were backed up behind it, trying to make their way toward the ramp, but the bus had them blocked.

"Now comes the tricky part," said Liquida under his breath, "traffic control."

As the bus took the tight turn onto the ramp, it nearly came to a complete stop. It eased down the ramp at fifteen miles an hour, and the man with the duffel bag sprang from the grass at the edge of the ramp. With his hand up, he stepped behind the bus as it passed and stopped the line of traffic behind it. Before the driver of the first car realized what was happening, the man with the duffel bag had flung a small satchel. The nylon bag, covered with graphite dust, slid like a hockey puck over the pavement and under the front end of the car. The man with the bag turned and ran in the other direction, down the ramp, toward the bus.

"What the hell?" As the driver started to lift his foot off the brake pedal, the fiery explosion buckled the center of his car and flipped it into the air. The blast ignited the gas in the fuel tank. A half second later the fiery wreck landed on top of the car behind it. A mushroom-shaped bloom of flame leaped thirty feet into the air and engulfed both vehicles.

"Now that's the way to stop traffic," said Liquida.

He shifted the field glasses to look down the ramp toward the bus. Sure enough, human nature had done its part. With the blast, the bus driver had looked in his big side-view mirror. He'd seen the flames and the flying car and instinct took over. He hit the brakes. It was only a few seconds, but it was enough. He was barely rolling, still looking in the mirror, when the box truck pulled out in front of him and blocked the ramp.

"Look out," said the guard.

By the time the driver looked back to the front and realized what was happening, it was too late, the ramp was blocked and he had no momentum to punch his way through.

Five of the button boys came out of the back of the truck, the other two exited from the cab. All of them were wearing dark glasses, their faces covered with scarves. They carried their assault rifles slung from their shoulders and aimed from the hip as they moved swiftly toward the front of the bus.

The guard unlocked the shotgun from its rack as the driver tried to put the bus in reverse. The explosives man with the duffel bag, running down the ramp behind them, slid another satchel charge under the rear of the bus and flung himself facedown on the ground.

The blast lifted the rear wheels of the bus three feet off the pavement. It shredded all eight rear tires on the double dual axles and blew out the transmission. By the time the rear end landed back on the ground, the bus was a stationary death trap.

Several of the women up front on the bus were screaming.

The explosion lifted both Katia and Daniela off the bench seat. It would have sent them to the ceiling except that the ankle chain and the falling weight of the bus jerked them back down, hard, on the thin seat cushion, jamming their backs.

Katia was dazed. She held her head with her hands, looking up first at the ceiling and then turning her head from side to side to make sure her neck wasn't hurt. "A-a-a-ah ... What happened?"

"I don't know." As she said it Daniela heard the hollow ping of metal as the first rounds ripped into the bus, followed half a beat later by the distinctive clatter of Kalashnikovs on full automatic somewhere outside.

"Get down," she told Katia. Daniela reached for the small Walther under her arm. It was wedged into the tight elastic at the side of her sports bra. "Get down on the floor."

"How?" said Katia. She was looking at the chain that joined them around their waists. "Where did you get that?" Katia saw the gun in Daniela's hand.

"Never mind, just get down, as low as you can behind the seat." Chained at the waist, they had to move together if they were going to find cover. With their ankles locked to the metal bar, they were stuck where they were. Their only protection was the thin pad of upholstery on the back of the seat in front of them and the light-gauge sheet-metal backing that supported it.

* * *

The first burst of rounds went high, punching two holes at the top of the windshield and perforating the metal above it. The driver and the guard seemed stunned when they realized that the bulletproof windshield had failed to stop the rounds. The guard punched the button on his shoulder mike and began to call it in.

"Need backup. Shots fired, explosive devices..."

"What's your location?"

The second burst by all seven button boys instantly transformed the entire windshield, from left to right, into what looked like a lacy pattern of frosted glass, a frozen fog of fractured crystals. The glass stayed in place, it didn't shatter, but it was no longer transparent. Every one of the fifty or so armor-piercing rounds passed cleanly through and into the interior of the bus.

One of the assault team with his rifle at the ready cautiously stepped to the passenger side of the bus and glanced through the thick glass in the door. The bloody bundle that had been the guard lay crumpled up against the door, on the stairway inside. The back of the driver's seat looked like Swiss cheese, with tiny strips of foam padding protruding from the back out of each bullet hole. The driver, wet with various shades of crimson, leaned toward the door like a rag doll, his upper body perpendicular to the floor, his arms dangling, as his lower body was held in place by the seat belt.

The button boy slung his weapon over his shoulder and gave the rest of them the all-clear sign. Two of them quickly swapped out clips. They replaced the armor-piercing rounds, to avoid shooting their comrades through the walls of the bus, slapping new clips with hollow points into their rifles. For them, shooting accuracy was no longer an issue. From here on out, everything would be point-blank.

Two of the others quickly took up positions behind the bus, making sure no one came down the ramp behind them. Two others positioned themselves on the freeway side of the bus to watch for any law enforcement that might approach from the highway, while one of them watched Magnolia Avenue from the other side to ensure that their getaway path was clear.

The explosives man took out the shaped charge from his bag. It was a roll of synthetic material that looked and felt like children's Play-Doh. He had worked it into the shape of a rope about an inch thick and twelve feet long. He started at the foot of the bus door and pressed it against the metal. In less than a minute he'd outlined the entire perimeter of the armored door. He pressed a single detonator cap into the soft plastic and pulled the fuse. As it started to smoke, the men on that side of the bus scattered and took cover. A few seconds later there was a loud explosion and the heavy metal door fell from its frame, the strong inside hinges and all four of the locking bolts severed.

The entry team, the two men with rifles loaded with hollow points, whisked some of the smoke away with a sweep of their hands as they swung the muzzles of their rifles into play once more. One of them grabbed the guard in the stairway and rolled his body out onto the pavement. He reached down to retrieve the officer's sidearm.

The explosives man asked him for the key to the wire-mesh cage inside.

The kid with the pistol pulled the guard's keys off his belt. There must have been twenty of them on the ring.

"Forget it," said the explosives man. He reached into his bag and pulled out another small charge and climbed into the bus. He walked toward the steel-and-wire mesh cage and pressed the malleable explosive charge directly over the round steel disk housing the lock for the gate.

He noticed that the mesh of the cage was severed and mangled, with jagged pieces of wire sticking out in several places directly behind the driver's seat, where bullets had passed through the cage. The two women in the first seat inside the cage on that side were already dead, their heads thrown back, their eyes and mouths open as blood ran off the seat and covered the rubber floor mat that ran down the aisle. He looked closely through the wire mesh, but neither woman appeared to be either the one in the picture or the other target whose photograph they had memorized.

He worked to flatten the charge against the lock.

There was a lot of crying and whimpering back in the cage. One woman pleaded with him from behind the wire, her hands pressed together in prayer as she begged him not to hurt her.

He finished shaping, pressed a detonator into the charge, and in a fluid motion pulled the fuse.

He stepped off the bus pushing the two button boys ahead of him until they were a few feet away. The sharp crack of the explosion was followed by more screams inside the bus.

The explosives man gestured toward the bus with a wag of his head as he started to close up his bag while smoke billowed from the bus door. "*Rápido*, huh!"

The two killers waved away the smoke and climbed the bus steps to finish the job. At first they couldn't see.

A gray-white mist filled the front of the bus along with the acrid smell of burnt nitrate. As the smoke began to settle, they could see a large hole in the wire mesh on the gate where the lock had been.

They moved quickly, threw the gate open, and started down the aisle.

The women cowered, some of them down on the floor between the seats, crying.

One of the button boys held the photograph while the other grabbed the women by the hair, one at a time, pulling their heads up so the two men could see their faces. They worked from side to side, first checking seats on the right, then the left, moving toward the rear of the bus.

Halfway down, they stopped. The one holding the photograph held it out right next to the woman's face. The guy holding her by the hair shook his head.

"*Es ella,*" said the one holding the photo.

"No." The other one shook his head.

Before he could say another word, the man holding the photograph raised the guard's pistol and fired a round into the woman's head. Her blood sprayed the prisoner sitting next to her and the wall of the bus behind her.

The sound of the shot and the arbitrary manner in which it happened took Daniela by surprise.

"What's happening?" Katia was glued to Daniela by the waist chain that bound them together.

"Just stay down and be quiet." Daniela pulled the slide back on the Walther and chambered the first round as quietly as she could. The small pistol carried only six shots in the clip. She would have to make them count.

She wanted to try and get the two men closer before she fired. If she could drop them in the aisle a few feet away, she might be able to reach one of the assault rifles slung from their shoulders and fish for extra clips before any of the rest of them could board the bus.

Somewhere off in the distance she could hear the sounds of sirens punctuated by the bleep and blare of their electronics as the police maneuvered through traffic.

After killing the woman, the two button boys continued the process, pulling hair and quickly moving down the aisle. When Daniela peeked around the edge of the seat in front of her, they were just six rows away. Three or four more and she would show them the muzzle of the pistol and take her chances.

Suddenly she heard them talking again. One of them was dressing down the other in street Spanish; "*pendejo,*" calling him a "dumbass."

Daniela peeked around the edge of the seat again. They had another woman by the hair and were holding the picture up to her face.

"I told you the other one wasn't her. *Pero usted tiene que ser el hombre.* But you have to be the man."

"Okay. Enough!" The other guy, who was closest to Daniela, standing sideways in the aisle, started to raise the pistol toward the woman's head. In a fluid motion Daniela leaned into the aisle, dragging Katia with her. She raised the Walther in one hand, braced it with the other, and pulled off a round. It caught the man with the pistol in the left temple. His knees buckled and he went to the floor like a sack of potatoes.

As his buddy fell, the other one still had the woman by her hair. His head and eyes snapped toward Daniela. He let go of the hair. The woman started screaming instantly.

The man tried to swing the AK-47, its muzzle hanging down from the sling over his shoulder, up into firing position. His finger had just reached the trigger guard when Daniela fired the second round.

The sound of the shot was swallowed in the frantic screeches of the woman. A tiny speck of red the size of a pinprick appeared on the man's forehead, above his frozen gaze. An instant later the spot spread to the diameter of a pencil. He toppled over backward, hitting the tubular steel along the top of one of the bench seats. His body spun as he slammed facedown onto the hard steel floor of the aisle.

The woman was still screaming at the top of her lungs, hyperventilating with hysteria and expelling everything.

"Move with me," Daniela told Katia.

She tried. Katia pulled herself out into the aisle as her foot tugged and strained at the end of the ankle chain.

Daniela crawled forward down the aisle. She gained two or three feet, threw her body flat out on the floor dragging Katia with her. She stretched, reaching for the rifle on the first dead man. But the slack on the chain wasn't enough. She needed at least another foot. She yanked frantically on the waist chain as Katia tried desperately to pull herself farther out.

The woman continued to scream.

"Shut up." Daniela looked up at her. "Get the rifle. You can reach it," said Daniela. "Just hand it to me. That's all you have to do."

The woman didn't look at her. She stared out at nothing. Her face was being scratched by the frantic action of her own grasping finger as her frenzied screams reached fever pitch.

"Please!" cried Daniela. "Just lean over and hand me the gun. You'll be fine. I can keep them away from us if I have the gun," she pleaded.

One of the other women ten or twelve rows up crawled out from between the seats, looked back at Daniela, and then reached out and grabbed the assault rifle on the other dead man. She grasped it with one hand.

Daniela looked at her and smiled. "Good! Now pass it to me."

The woman carefully slid the shoulder strap off the dead man.

"See if you can reach the bag on his other shoulder. It should have loaded clips," said Daniela.

The woman reached out and got the bag. She looked inside, reached in and pulled out one of the clips, holding it up for Daniela to see.

"Good," said Daniela. "Toss the bag first. Then the gun."

The woman looked at her as the other one continued to scream. "How does it work? Do I just pull the trigger?"

"No, don't do that," said Daniela. "See the lever on the right, on the side above the trigger? Push it all the way up until it's pointing in the same direction as the barrel. That will put the safety on."

The woman found the lever and pushed it up.

"Good. Now throw the rifle back here."

"No," said the woman. "You're too far back. You can't protect us from there."

"I can," said Daniela.

"*Vamos. Apresurar.* Hurry up. What's all the noise in there?" One of the men pounded on the outside of the bus two or three times. He was running, moving forward toward the open door of the bus.

The woman stopped screaming.

"We don't have all day," said the man.

"Throw it to me," said Daniela.

The woman holding the rifle looked frantically back toward her. As she turned back toward the door, she seemed to freeze.

"The police will be here any minute."

The man bounded up the steps and into the bus. "What's taking so long? Let's move." He looked through the cage door down the aisle. The first thing he saw were the two dead button boys lying on the floor. Next he saw the muzzle of the rifle aimed at his chest.

For an instant she hesitated. Then she pulled the trigger. Nothing happened. She had forgotten to flip the safety lever down.

Daniela reached back on the floor behind her for the Walther, but it was too late. She touched the handle of the gun just as the ear-splitting sound of the man's Kalashnikov and the odor of burnt nitrates from the gunpowder filled the bus.

Daniela got only a glimpse as the opening spray of bullets caught the woman holding the rifle full in the chest. It lifted her off the floor, leaving the rifle in midair, as if it were wired in place, for a full second before it fell. The impact threw her lifeless body across the seat and she collided with the wall of the bus.

Daniela hugged the floor, Katia right behind her, their heads down as the guy emptied the full banana clip into the passenger section of the bus. One of the rounds ricocheted off steel and caromed off the floor.

Katia flinched as she felt something hit Daniela.

It caught her at the top of the shoulder, snapping bone and missing her head by inches. She winced in pain as she heard the quick screams and the dull thud of bullets as they made their marks on others.

When the firing stopped Daniela lifted her head. The woman who had been screaming was sitting straight up in her seat, staring off into the distance. The wall of the bus behind her had more holes than a saltshaker, but the woman hadn't been touched. It is true what they say, thought Daniela, God protects those who are crazy.

The shooter stepped back, away from the cage. Daniela saw him slip down behind the metal partition and into the well of the stairs. Then she heard the click of metal as he changed out clips. He called out to his friends outside and told them to come. There was trouble in the bus.

"If we want to live, we have to move," she told Katia. They crawled on their knees back between the seats, dragging the clinking ankle chains with them. "Whatever you do, stay down," said Daniela, "as close to the floor as you can."

"You're bleeding," said Katia.

"I know." Daniela's right arm hung limp. The right shoulder and chest area of her jail jumpsuit were already soaked with blood.

The sirens were now closer than before. From the direction of the sound, they might be approaching on the freeway.

"We'll be okay," said Katia. "I know we will."

They could hear the muted voices of the men as they talked just outside the door to the bus. They were frenzied, in a hurry. They had to know they were running out of time. Katia and Daniela could hear shooting in the distance, somewhere behind the bus.

"If they come again they will come very quickly,"

said Daniela. "There may be explosions in the bus. It's very important to stay down low, as close to the floor as you can get. In the confusion and smoke they may not see you. If you can survive for the next five minutes, you'll be okay."

Katia looked at her. Her friend's eyes had a distant, glazed look to them. The blood from her shoulder had soaked much of the top of her blue jail jumpsuit. Katia reached down to the bottom of her own pants leg and pulled hard at the stitching on the inseam until the threads holding it together ripped. She quickly opened eight inches of the seam and then was tearing the fabric from around the bottom of her leg until the cloth came free. She folded it into a compress.

"Daniela, we have to stop the bleeding."

"Katia, you need to know. My name is not Daniela. It's Carla Mederios..."

"It doesn't matter," said Katia. "What I know is that you are my friend. The only friend I have."

THIRTY

I don't want excuses," said Liquida. He and the explosives man conversed over the walkie-talkies. "Take the bus and do it now."

Liquida could see the highway patrol units as they closed in along the freeway. They had blocked off the highway in both directions, so the roadway was now empty. Two of the highway patrol cars were already parked under the bridge overpass. The cops were out of their cars, carrying shotguns and rifles, looking for cover and advantageous angles from which to fire.

Sheriff's units from the jail had taken over the intersection of Magnolia and Prospect. They were exchanging gunfire with two of the button boys near the top of the ramp.

Liquida wasn't bothering to inform his people of all the negative details. It would only sap their morale. If they waited much longer, the SWAT unit would arrive.

"How did your men get shot inside the bus?" he asked. "There was only the driver and one guard. You told me you killed them both."

He listened for a second.

"Well, then, who shot your men? What do you mean you don't know? Are your people afraid of a busload of women? Get your ass on board that bus, finish what you came for, and get the hell out of there. Get to the safe house. Otherwise nobody's getting paid. Do you understand?" Liquida threw down the walkie-talkie and looked up at the sky.

They were beginning to breed like mosquitoes. Ten minutes ago there were two, now there were four local news choppers all circling over the action on the ramp.

How the hell did Demo Man think they were going to get to the safe house without being followed from the sky? If Liquida wasn't careful, he would show up on TV. The arrival of the choppers had forced him back from the edge of the roof. He huddled in the shadows between two large air-conditioning units and continued to observe the activity on the ramp through the field glasses.

He watched as the demolition man fired up his soldiers, at least the two of them who were assembled near the bus door. Two others were up near the top of the ramp holding off the cops. The flaming cars were now just smoking rubble with an occasional flicker as fumes from the gas tanks floated past a hot spot.

The last lone soldier from Liquida's army was positioned on this side of the bus, lying prone on the ground and taking occasional shots at the police who were trying to move in from the freeway side of the ramp.

The explosives man finished his pep talk. He reached into his bag of tricks, then walked toward the bus door with something in his hand. A second later he disappeared inside. There were two muted shots, what sounded to Liquida like a small handgun, and a second later the demolition man came off the bus holding his right shoulder. As Liquida watched him, a massive explosion ripped through the bus, blowing out the windshield and ripping a jagged hole in the roof. Smoke billowed from the front of the bus. The soldiers, armed with their AKs, stormed on board while the shock and impact of the blast was still having its effect. Automatic gunfire erupted inside. Liquida tried to zero in with the binoculars.

Suddenly a gun battle broke out at the top of the ramp. A large black SUV raced out from under the bridge on the freeway and drove past the bus, exchanging fire through the windows with the button boy lying on his belly on this side of the bus. Whoever was firing from the car must have hit him, because a second later the button boy dropped his rifle as his head slumped to the ground.

The black vehicle made a beeline for the bottom of the ramp, pulled a U-turn, and drove up the ramp in the wrong direction. It stopped on the other side of the box truck. The doors flew open and six men, all wearing black body armor and carrying short carbines and MP-5s, spilled out of the car. They raced around the truck and moved up the ramp.

Liquida could still hear shots coming from inside the bus.

One of his men at the top of the ramp began to retreat down toward the gully on the other side. Liquida lost sight of him for a moment. When he picked him up again, the button boy had joined up with the explosives expert and both of them were making their way up the embankment toward Magnolia Avenue and the van.

There was another flurry of gunfire at the top of the ramp. Liquida watched as police flanked the remaining lone button boy. Three shots rang out and he went down.

Police started to flood down the ramp on foot, just as the six men from the black SUV reached the door to the bus.

Liquida picked up the walkie-talkie. "Hello. Hello."

A voice crackled back on the other end.

"Are you in contact with them?" He was talking to the explosives man, who was in contact with the button boys on the bus. Through a separate radio. "Is it done?"

"Yes," said the man. "She is dead."

"Are you sure?"

"Yes," came the crackling response.

"Excellent," said Liquida.

He could see the demolition man talking on the handheld unit as he slipped through the hole in the fence, followed closely by the button boy who had left his rifle in the ravine and ditched his dark glasses and face scarf while climbing up the other side.

Liquida watched as three of the armed men from the SUV boarded the bus. A few seconds later gunfire erupted again from inside the bus. This time it didn't last long. He heard several short bursts of pistol rounds from the MP-5s and then silence.

He focused the field glasses back across the ravine. The explosives expert and his young helper had made it to the van. They pulled away from the curb and did a U-turn to avoid all the excitement at the intersection on Prospect. Before they'd gone fifty feet, another shiny black SUV pulled out of a side street and cut them off. The occupants, all dressed like their comrades on the bus, opened the SUV's doors, using them for cover, and trained their assault rifles and pistols on the stopped van through the SUV's open windows.

As he was reaching into his pocket, Liquida had to wonder what the federal government was doing here so heavily armed. No one else used black SUVs like the United States government.

He took out a small metal box from his pocket, flipped the toggle switch on the top, and pressed the small black button. There was a large brilliant flash of light on the other side of the freeway. It was followed a second later by the sound of the blast and the shock wave as it rippled across the rooftop and rattled the metal panels of the air-conditioning unit where Liquida was sitting. Avis would miss one of their rental vans. He would have to remember the next time to use a little less C-4.

THIRTY-ONE

Gil Howser was the lead homicide detective in the Solaz case. This morning he'd buttonholed Templeton while the prosecutor was busy packing his briefcase and getting ready to head to the courthouse.

"Make it quick," said Templeton. "You and I have a meeting with Quinn on Solaz in ten minutes."

"I know, to talk about the deal with her. But there are some problems with the evidence. We have to talk," said Howser.

"Do we need to do it right now?"

"No, but it might be good to have a handle on them in case the judge asks us what kind of an evidentiary basis he has for accepting a plea."

"What kind of problems?" said Templeton.

"The dagger, for example," said Howser. "How do we explain the fact that Solaz's prints are all over it but there's no blood on the handle? If she stabbed him with the other knife first, and according to the post-mortem that's how it went down, she'd have blood on her hands. It would have been transferred to the handle of the dagger. But the handle was clean except for her prints."

"What else?" said Templeton.

"Forensics found tool marks on the coin drawers in Pike's study. Whoever pried them open used a sharp implement of some kind. They think it was a knife. The problem is, the tool marks on the wooden drawers around the locks as well as the scratches on the brass locks themselves don't match either the chef's knife that was used to kill Pike or the point on the dagger that was left in his body. Forensics checked the points on all the other blades in the kitchen. According to their report there would have been some damage to the knife point used to pry open the drawers. There was no evident damage to any of the other knives, and none of them matched the tool marks. So there must have been another knife."

"All right. What else?"

"You do recall that the police in Arizona didn't find a knife on Solaz when they arrested her?"

"I'm aware of that," said Templeton. "What else?"

"The blood around the lock on the front door," said Howser. "The bloody prints, that is, if there ever were any, weren't smeared, they were rubbed, using a cloth, according to forensics. They found patterns in the blood on the door consistent with the fibers on one of the cleaning cloths on the maid's body. And to make it a little more contrived, all the blood was hers, none of it was from Pike."

"There was blood transfer from Pike to the maid's clothing," said Templeton.

"Yes, but it ended there. There was nothing on the front door," said Howser. "If you have blood all over your hands from killing two people and you panic and run out the front door, even if you collect yourself before you go two steps so you can come back and smear the prints on the door, how is it that only the maid's blood shows up there? How do you explain Solaz smearing her prints on the door and taking the time to wash the blood and her prints off the chef's knife and then forgetting her prints on the dagger in Pike's body?"

"Maybe she didn't forget," said Templeton. "Maybe someone else told her he'd take care of it for her. Someone who knew a lot more about crime scene evidence than she did."

"Madriani," said Howser.

"That would explain why the Arizona Highway Patrol didn't find the knife used to jimmy the drawers when they arrested her, or Pike's computer, or the other missing coins, why she went down the front driveway straight into the security camera when whoever helped her went out through the side yard, through the hole in security and over the fence. It would explain a lot of things, wouldn't it? And by the way, I wouldn't put too much faith in the theory that Solaz plunged the dagger into Pike's chest."

"That's the linchpin of your case," said Howser.

"She may have handled the letter opener, but you missed something," said Templeton.

"What's that?"

"A little twist on one of the details that came in late, courtesy of the people in the crime lab. Have you ever read the book entitled *A California Gold Rush History,* by David Bowers?"

"No."

"Neither have I," said Templeton. "I'm told it's a

tome, what you would call a substantial read, one thousand and fifty-five pages in hardcover. Single volume weighs in at more than eleven pounds. It's a big sucker. And according to forensics, whoever left the dagger in Pike used that particular book to pound it into his chest. Now can you see a petite little thing like Katia Solaz holding the dagger in one hand while she swings a big book like that in the other?"

"Now that you mention it," said Howser, "no. When did you find this out?"

"Yesterday morning. Forensics found a strange indentation in the book's cover when they were processing the crime scene. It seems the dimple in the cover matches precisely the shape and contour on the end of the dagger's handle. Just the way you might want to hit it if you wanted to preserve somebody else's prints on the handle."

"So you haven't turned this over to the defense yet?"

"Not yet. Of course I will—sooner or later," said Templeton.

"I have to say, that puts a major focus on the other player," said Howser. He meant the unidentified codefendant. "And you can bet the second we turn it over, Madriani will jump on it and claim that this is solid evidence that some other dude did it."

"And he'll be right," said Templeton. "*He* did it. *He* set her up nine ways from Sunday. She may have invited him in on the party, told him what was in the house, but he took over when he came. Do you have any idea what the value of the gold is that's missing?"

"No," said Howser.

"Just under 146 pounds, it would be a shade under 1.8 million dollars, and that's just by weight. If you could sell the coins at collector's value, who knows, you could probably multiply that by a factor of three or four. That's what they tell me, anyway."

"I'd say that's a pretty good motive for murder," said Howser.

"It could certainly beef up a private pension plan. Anything on that end yet?" said Templeton.

"No. We're not going to know that until we get a subpoena for Madriani's bank records. And we're not going to be able to do that until we go public with the court and open an active investigation on him. Maybe you can get the feds to go online and take a peek at his bank records."

"He's not going to sell the gold and put the cash in a bank account," said Templeton. "Too much money and too many records. He'd have to pay taxes and explain where he got all his sudden wealth on a return. If he melts it down, and I have to assume he probably already has, he's going to put it somewhere safe, where it can't be found or traced, and sit on it until things cool off."

"Still, it's hard to believe that a seasoned lawyer who has seen forensics play out in court a thousand times would miss as many details as we have here," said Howser.

"It's one thing to study it in a courtroom in the cold light of day. It's another to live it," said Templeton. "Can you imagine the frenzied thoughts that crowd the mind after killing someone, in this case two people? And then there's all the glitter from that gold to get in your eyes. That's how he managed to leave the pen behind. A thirty-cent ballpoint pen you can buy by the bushel with your firm name and address printed on them. Madriani wrestles with Pike and the pen ends up on the floor, kicked under the desk. Go figure."

"I still think you should have allowed us to ask him about that," said Howser.

"Why, so he could lie to us again? Make up another story? When you first questioned him, you asked him whether he'd ever been to Pike's house. He said no. You asked him if Solaz had ever been to his office and he said no. You asked him if their meeting at the grocery store was the only time they ever met or talked before she was arrested, and what did he say? He said yes. Now we know they talked by phone at least one other time and had drinks at the restaurant out in front of his office in Coronado on that same day. He had plenty of opportunities to tell us the truth, but he didn't," said Templeton. "Would you like to take bets on what a jury's going to say about how that pen found its way under Pike's desk? I could use the money."

"No, that's all right," said Howser. "They're already taking enough out of my paycheck as it is."

Suddenly Templeton's office door shot open. One of the other prosecutors stuck his head in.

"What is this, no-knock day?" said Templeton.

"Have you guys heard the news?"

"No, but I'm sure you're gonna tell us," Templeton said, glaring at him.

"Somebody just hit the sheriff's bus on its way in from the women's jail out at Santee. Word is, the driver and the guard are dead, smoke and explosions everywhere."

Templeton dropped his briefcase on the floor.

"It's on Fox News and CNN right now, aerial shots."

"What are they saying?" said Templeton.

"Reporters are speculating that it may have been a botched attempt to spring one of the inmates from the bus. The area around the freeway looks like a war zone."

THIRTY-TWO

Much of the inside of the bus was charred. Most of the officers, the sheriff's tactical squad as well as the agents from the FBI's violent crimes task force, had only seen training photographs and films of buses that had been hammered by terrorists in the Middle East.

None of them had ever seen anything like this on American soil. And while they had trained for it, the presumed targets were always soft, inner-city commuter buses and trains, not a locked-down sheriff's transport bus. In a way this was worse. Once the door had been blown, none of the passengers on board had a chance of escape. They were chained to their seats.

A line of ambulances long enough that no one bothered to count them lined up under the freeway overpass, waiting their turn as paramedics and police worked through the bodies on the bus.

The bomb squad gingerly checked the box truck for explosives. Two of the FBI agents had already been badly injured in the blast from the getaway van, and authorities were taking no more chances. The box truck had to be cleared before moving it so that ambulances could pull up on the ramp.

"I don't, sir." One of the FBI agents was on the phone with Thorpe, in Washington. "They're on the bus looking for both of them now. I know. I know. There's nothing the hostage rescue team could have done, believe me. They made no contact with any authorities, no evidence of any interest in negotiating anything. When the sheriff's department tried to communicate with them through the speaker on one of the squad cars up at the top of the ramp, the assailants just opened on them. The minute they blew the door off the bus, they just entered and started shooting people. We had no choice, we had to move in.

"No, from what we can see, there were eight of them. All dead, yes, sir, unfortunately. It's hard to tell. We went through the pockets of the two we killed outside the bus on the ramp. They were carrying nothing. No identification. They were wearing jeans and street clothes. They could have bought them anywhere. But it's pretty clear they're not Islamic. The two outside had gang graffiti tattooed on their bodies. Somebody from the sheriff's gang unit is trying to decipher it now. I have a feeling we're going to find out they're not local, probably from over the border.

"The weapons, yes, sir, Chinese made, AKs, all original military actions, fully automatic. The explosives we don't know yet. We think most of them went up in the van explosion, but we should be able to get residue, trace compounds and markers that should tell us where they originated. I'd say it's pretty clear that it's not ideological. It's either drug related or they were after your woman on the bus."

* * *

"Get them out of here." A big, beefy sergeant from the jail unit at Las Colinas had taken charge on board the bus. He was the same one who had slipped the small Walther pistol to Carla two days earlier.

"Crime scene is gonna want them left where they lay."

"I don't give a shit." The sergeant turned on the officer, still decked out in SWAT gear. He had lost two friends, Jed the driver and the guard, and he was in no mood to debate the issue. "We've got wounded people here and I want this aisle clear. Get some officers to drag those bodies out of here." He gestured toward the dead button boys piled up in the aisle.

"See that they lay 'em outside far enough away so they don't block access to the ambulances. Crime scene can process them there. And tell them to hurry up and get that truck out of there."

"They just cleared it for explosives. They're looking for the keys."

"Let's hope they didn't go up with the van," said the sergeant. "Check their pockets before you take them out of here. The truck keys may be there. Here." The sergeant handed a different set of keys to one of the agents on the FBI assault team. He had found them outside on the ground, near the body of the guard.

The agents and officers were busy trying to get the ankle bracelets off the wounded and remove the waist chains so they could be separated from the dead as paramedics checked the victims and conducted triage. The officers already knew that most of the women up front were dead. Those who hadn't been shot were killed in the blast when the last satchel charge was tossed inside.

It had blown a hole in the roof of the bus and ripped out four of the bench seats, bending them sideways, so that they now rested against the bulging walls of the bus.

"What do you want to do with this?" One of the agents was holding the small Walther pistol.

"Here, give it to me." The sergeant took it, dropped it on the floor, and kicked it under the body of one of the dead button boys. It was clear that one of the women had managed to get the gun away from them. What wasn't clear was how many of them she shot or from what angle or distance. The medical examiner and the forensics team would have to figure that one out, and having moved the bodies, it would be anybody's guess.

The agent worked with the keys, found the one that worked, turned it, and the manacle on her ankle popped open.

"It should be the same key on her waist," said the sergeant.

Two seconds later the agent had it unlocked. "I know her last name, what's her first name?" the agent asked the sergeant.

"Katia. Katia Solaz."

"Katia, listen to me. We have to take you off the bus now. Is she okay to move?" asked the agent.

Katia could see his lips move, but she couldn't hear a word, or any sound for that matter, just a constant ringing in her ears.

One of the paramedics glanced over. "There's a shallow flesh wound, right thigh. I bandaged it. It doesn't look serious. She's got some concussive injury from the overpressure of the blast. May have blown her eardrums, I'm not sure. They'll have to check her at emergency. Make sure they don't give her any depressants in the meantime. But she should be okay to move, if you can get her outside and on a gurney."

"Katia, listen, you have to come with us now. Please." The agent took her hands and tried to pry her arms open.

Katia started to struggle. She tried to fight him off. She wasn't going to let go, no matter what they did. Who were they? If they were here to help, why had they waited so long? Why didn't they come sooner? She buried her head next to Daniela's and clung to her for life, praying that her friend would wake up, that she would stir, open her eyes and offer the reassurance she had given Katia since the moment they'd met—that everything would be okay.

The agent gave up trying to pry her hands from the dead woman. Katia stopped struggling. She looked at them with an expression of fierce determination. Then, with her fingertips, she brushed a few of the bloody and matted hairs from Daniela's face and hugged her, rocking back and forth on the floor between the seats as if in a trance. The last thing Katia remembered was the image of Daniela as she pushed her down and threw herself on top of her an instant before the brilliant white flash engulfed them both. She remembered the French braid of Daniela's shimmering black hair suspended straight out in the flare of superheated air, and then nothing.

She watched as the men talked to one another, but she heard nothing. Two of them nodded. And then the one who had been kneeling down, seeming to talk to her, instead knelt down and leaned in. He worked with a set of keys until he found the one that worked to unlock Daniela's ankle shackle. He removed the manacle from her leg and the chain from her waist. Before Katia realized what was happening he'd lifted Daniela into his arms and suddenly she was gone, being carried down the aisle of the bus, toward the door.

Katia struggled to get to her feet, but her leg hurt. It seemed that it would no longer support her. One of the other men leaned down, put his arm under her shoulder and whisked her up into his arms. They followed Daniela down the aisle and off the bus. It seemed so long, a lifetime since the two of them had climbed on the bus at the jail and talked about the honor farm, Katia's family, and her mother being in Colombia. She knew that Daniela had not told her the truth about who she was or what she wanted. But to Katia it no longer mattered. They had been through so much together that nothing, not even death, could now break the bond she felt.

THIRTY-THREE

By the time Harry and I arrive at the University Medical Center on Hillcrest, Katia had already been admitted. The sheriff's department has a contract with the university for inpatient care of inmates, and this morning the lobby is crawling with law enforcement. There are city police, sheriff's deputies, and federal agents, some of them still wearing tactical gear.

The moment I mention Katia's name at the reception desk, Harry and I are approached by a man in his mid-thirties.

"Excuse me. Who are you?"

He is wearing baggy black tactical pants and is stripped down to his T-shirt up top.

"Who's asking?" says Harry.

"Agent John Swarz." He flashes FBI credentials at us.

"Paul Madriani, my partner, Harry Hinds. We're Ms. Solaz's lawyers."

"Do you have any identification?"

Harry and I show him our driver's licenses and state bar cards. I hand him a business card.

"I don't think she's going to be seeing anybody right now."

"We'd like to know where she is," says Harry.

"Do you know what her condition is?" I ask.

"She's not critical, if that's what you mean. She took a flesh wound in the leg. You can get the details from the doctor. According to the EMT, she suffered some shock, possible concussion, and a chance of some hearing damage from the explosive device."

"Then you saw her?" I say.

"I carried her off the bus. Give me a second," he says.

The agent steps away from us, pulls a cell phone from his pocket, and walks farther away as he presses buttons to dial the number. He stands twenty feet away, glancing at Harry and me as he talks on the phone and looks at my business card. Then he looks at me and motions for me to come over.

"Somebody wants to talk to you," he says, and he hands me his cell phone.

"Hello."

"Mr. Madriani, this is Jim Rhytag. Agent Swarz informs me that you'd like to be able to see your client."

"That's correct."

"That will be up to the doctor, of course. But I want you to know that she will be well protected from here on out. We've made arrangements to have her moved to a private room upstairs in the hospital, outside the jail ward. She will be in the custody of the sheriff's department but there will be two federal marshals assigned at all times while she's there, providing backup, more if we think it's necessary. We have reason to believe that the assault on the bus this morning may have been directed at Ms. Solaz."

"Why don't you tell me what this is about?" I say.

"I've told you all that I can. Just one more thing, we've kept her name off the admissions records at the hospital and my agents covered her with a blanket when they took her off the bus. Law enforcement has agreed not to give her name to the press as a survivor. Whoever tried to kill her may not know she's alive. We'd like to keep it that way, at least for the time being. We've already advised the judge and court personnel. You need to know so you can avoid any questions from the press. It's for your client's own safety."

"I understand. For how long?"

"We're not sure. We'll let you know. The rest you'll have to get from her doctor. Sorry I can't be more helpful." The line went dead.

I hand the phone back to the agent. "Thanks."

Harry and I have cooled our heels, pacing the lobby and sitting on hard wooden benches, for nearly two hours before one of the nurses comes out and tells us that the doctor will see us now. She leads us down a broad corridor and through a pair of wide electrically controlled double doors with the word EMERGENCY blazed across them in red paint.

She tells us to take a seat inside a small room. Before we can sit down, a young intern breezes into the room with a clipboard under his arm.

"Hi. I'm Dr. Johansson. I understand you're here to see Ms. Solaz."

We introduce ourselves.

"The good news is, she's going to be okay. The bad news is, she's undergone a tremendous amount of trauma. There are no broken bones, no internal injuries, the bullet wound in the leg is in soft tissue, some minor muscle damage. It should heal completely. It may take a few weeks. Her hearing loss, we believe, is temporary."

"She can't hear at all?" says Harry.

The doctor shakes his head. "Not at the moment, as far as we can tell. There was some minor bleeding from the nose and ears, the result of a concussion from the explosive pressure wave. Both eardrums were ruptured, but they should heal. That usually takes about two months."

"Will she be able to communicate in the meantime?" I ask.

"That's the real question," says the doctor. "We don't know. She's clearly suffered some concussive brain injury, physical trauma in the form of shock waves to the central nervous system. Coupled with that is the psychological component, all the things she saw, the sheer terror of what happened, and the death of her friend—"

"What friend?" I say.

"She apparently had someone on the bus she was very close to, another woman who, according to the police, may have died in her arms. We don't know. From what I understand, the other woman may have saved her life. Again, we're not sure of all the details. Regardless, you can imagine the stress your client was under, physical and emotional. The problem is, it's hard to separate the two, to determine how much of the damage is physical, resulting from the blast, and how much is psychological.

"The concussive effect of the blast alone on the nervous system can last anywhere from hours or days to weeks. It depends on the individual."

"But she will recover?" I say.

"I think so. The damage usually isn't permanent unless the source of the trauma becomes repetitive, shell shock from long-term combat, for example. In this case, the odds are she'll recover."

"But you can't tell us how long that's going to take?" says Harry.

"Not with any certainty or precision, no. She's going to need a lot of rest and quiet. She won't be going back to the jail anytime soon. I'd say she's either going to be here or in a very quiet semiskilled nursing facility for a minimum of ten days to two weeks, perhaps longer."

"So what you're telling us," I say, "is that Ms. Solaz is not going to be able to give us much help in preparing her defense on criminal charges during that period."

"At the moment she's unable to speak to anyone."

"Because she can't hear?" says Harry.

"No. She's in a stupor, probably as a result of the shock. We'll be doing an MRI and some other tests. There's limited motor response. She doesn't seem to react normally to stimuli. To the extent that anything depends on her participation or cooperation, she may not be able to comply. As I say, it's probably only temporary, but at the moment it's absolute. I can give you a letter if you need it."

"If you don't mind," says Harry, "that would be helpful."

The doctor makes a note on his clipboard. "Right now she's not communicating with anyone. We haven't been able to get a word out of her. The officers who brought her in said they were unable to communicate with her as well."

"Can we see her?" I ask.

"Does she have any family in the area?"

"No," says Harry. "We're it. Her nearest family is in Costa Rica. They don't have U.S. visas or the financial ability to travel up here."

"That's too bad. Sometimes family helps in a situation like this, reaching the patient, I mean. She is sedated, just mildly at the moment. We're going to be moving her upstairs shortly. If you want to see her, you'll have to keep it very quiet and brief. Try to stay fairly still, avoid a lot of movement. Two minutes, that's all. And keep in mind that she's not going to be able to hear you. She may recognize you.

"If you'll come this way." He leads us out of the room, down the hall past a number of curtained-off cubicles with hospital beds, some of them empty, others with patients.

There are three uniformed deputies milling around keeping an eye on the women in blue jail jumpsuits until they can get them upstairs into the jail ward.

"How many of the injured from the bus were delivered here?" says Harry.

"Eight."

"How many did they route to other hospitals?" I ask.

"None. There were only eight survivors, seventeen dead, not counting the driver, the guard, or the gunmen. Absolute insanity," says the doctor.

"Yes, it is," I say.

A few feet farther on he puts his hand out like a traffic cop. "If you'll wait here just a moment." He steps away to confer with a man wearing gray slacks, a dress shirt and tie, and a worn blue blazer with wrinkle marks where it covers the padded holster on his belt.

The man is positioned outside one of the cubicles with the curtains drawn. As the doctor is talking to him, he looks our way and checks us out. He looks like he's crowding fifty, a crew cut with a little moonshine on top, some middle-aged heft around the middle but with shoulders broad enough that you wouldn't want to wrestle him. He is slowly chewing gum as he looks at us.

"Now who do you suppose he is?" says Harry. "Black Rockports resoled with inch-thick rubber soles and Cat's Paw heels. And I thought they stopped making the Cat's Paws years ago."

"No, they just sold the company to the U.S. Marshals Service," I tell him.

"You think he's trying to go undercover?" says Harry.

"No, I'm thinking Rhytag may have already done that number."

"Hmm?" says Harry.

"See if we can get a list of the names of the seventeen inmates killed on the bus, check it against courthouse records, criminal cases pending, or county sentences handed down. My guess is we're either going to find one name from the bus that doesn't have a matching courthouse file, or the coroner is suddenly going to come up one cadaver short in the head count."

"Katia's friend from the bus," says Harry.

"Uh-huh."

The doctor wiggles his finger and motions us to join him. He goes through the opening in the curtain, followed closely by Harry and then me. The marshal comes in behind us.

Harry starts to turn, about to get in his face to assert lawyer-client, but I tap him down low with my hand on his wrist and stop him. "Nothing confidential is happening here today," I whisper as I nod toward the bed.

Katia is flat on her back. The cover sheet is drawn up

to her chest. Her eyes are half open, with a glazed look, a combination of shock and the sedative. Her face is as white as the sheet. It's clear that she will remember none of this in the days that follow.

I move slowly toward the bed and look down at her. She has not even the slightest resemblance to the vivacious, carefree woman I met that morning over the bin of bananas in Del Mar. In just under three months, the state has sucked the life out of her and left this shell in her place.

I touch her hand as it rests on top of the sheet. It is cold as ice. I pick it up and hold it between my hands, trying to warm it.

For an instant her eyelids flicker and her head rolls slightly this way as she struggles to look at me. But the drawn and lifeless expression on her face doesn't change.

"I'm going to have to ask that you not do that," says the marshal.

"Excuse me?" I look at him.

"Nobody but the doctors and hospital staff are allowed to touch her."

"Says who?" says Harry.

"Says me."

"We were told she was under sheriff's custody," I say.

"She is," says the marshal.

"So where are you hiding your sheriff's badge these days?" says Harry.

"We're just helping out," he says.

"If I might ask, on what legal authority? Where is the federal process?" I say. "The documentation for your presence here—"

"Gentlemen, I don't want any arguments in here," the doctor starts to cut me off.

"Doc, I apologize. You're right. And I don't want the marshal to misunderstand. I do not resent his presence. The problem is that neither my partner nor I understand what's happening here, the reason for the federal presence."

"Just doing my job," says the marshal.

"I know. But if there's a reason to believe that our client continues to be in danger, we would like to be informed as to what that danger is. Then by all means we want you here."

"What we don't want is to have you questioning or communicating with her unless one of us is present." Harry glances at the marshal.

"I do my job. Right now that means watching her," he says.

"That's good. That's fine," says Harry. "As long as it doesn't include pumping her full of scopolamine and listening to her dreams, we shouldn't have any problems."

"Harry, please," I tell him.

"Sorry, nothing personal," says Harry.

"It seems the presence of law enforcement makes you foam at the mouth," says the marshal. "I understand. I have the same problem with lawyers."

"Now that that's settled," I say, "Doctor, can I ask you a question?"

"Certainly."

"Would you have any objection if we retain a separate physician, someone to serve as her personal doctor to confer with the staff here at the hospital and keep us apprised of her condition?"

"No. I'd have to check with the sheriff's department. They have custody, but I can't imagine there would be any problem."

"Good. In that case we'll retain a personal physician first thing tomorrow."

"But I think we need to leave for now and let her rest," says the doctor.

"Sure." I slip Katia's cold hand under the sheet. As I release it, her eyelids flicker once more as she looks at me. I take the other hand and place it under the sheet. I touch her forehead with my fingertips and lean down into her ear as I whisper, "Katia, we'll be back. I promise you."

"She can't hear you," said the doctor.

"I know. *Hasta luego*, Katia."

THIRTY-FOUR

At least the news from California was good. Alim read the handwritten translation in Farsi from the original computer e-mail printout. It had been sent in Spanish from San Diego that afternoon. Like all of the communications with the Mexican, the message was cryptic, but the code words were clear. The Russian's granddaughter was dead—mission accomplished.

He lowered the paper and took a deep breath. There would be no trial. The investigations surrounding the American's murder would end, and with them the fear that someone might trip over Katia Solaz's family background.

So far they had managed to stanch the leak from the photographs and the fumbling interference from an aged American, probably one of Satan's agents. Alim knew that without the assistance of the FARC rebels, none of this would have been possible. It was their intelligence source in Costa Rica who had first alerted them to Pike's activities and the fact that he had the photographs as well as Nitikin's granddaughter.

"Do you have any message to send back?" said the Farsi interpreter. They were in one of the small huts used by the FARC for communications. It was situated on a hillside under the dense jungle canopy.

"Yes. Give me a few moments to think."

The interpreter had been sent over by Alim's government, a necessity in the tower of babel that was the jungle hideaway. The man had been pulled from a university post because of his ability to speak Farsi and to teach Spanish. The skills were a combination of increasing importance, not only to Alim's government but to others in the region as they probed for weaknesses in the armor, the southern soft underbelly of the Great Satan.

For the moment, Alim was walking a diplomatic tightrope. He could not afford to alienate the FARC, which had formed a trusting and loyal relationship with Nitikin. The Russian had lived with them in the jungle for decades. Still, each passing day saw Nitikin becoming more and more difficult to deal with. He continued in his refusal to assemble the device until his daughter was returned safely, under the protection of the FARC, to her home in Costa Rica. This was now becoming a problem, threatening to interrupt the time line for Alim's mission. He could wait no longer. Fortunately the Mexican was now free for another assignment.

"Tell him we have another job, this time in San José, Costa Rica."

The translator scribbled with a pencil on a pad.

"Yes, sir."

"One other thing." It was something that had been bothering Alim for some time now, one of those nagging loose ends. "Tell him that the digital camera he sent us from the agent Pike's house was the wrong one. Tell him that according to the Russian's daughter, the real camera may still have the original pictures in it, and the last time she saw it, it was at her house in San José. I want the camera and those pictures. Tell him not to contact us again until he has them. And here, copy this and send it to him."

Alim unfolded a slip of paper from his pocket and handed it to the interpreter. It was the directions to Maricela Solaz's house in San José. Alim had gotten this from Nitikin in preparation for sending her home, so that he could arrange to have the FARC make sure that the place was not under surveillance before she got there.

THIRTY-FIVE

Harry and I hoof it toward the parking lot at the hospital and Harry's car.

"Make sure whoever we hire as Katia's doctor has hospital privileges here," I tell him. "We want a treating physician who has full access to all the facilities. Somebody who can keep an eye on her. Also, call the nurses' registry. Set up a private nurse around the clock, three shifts, so somebody is in the room with her at all times. That way, if the feds try to question her at least we'll know about it."

"That's gonna be expensive," says Harry.

"That's all right. We'll negotiate the bill with Rhytag when we finish with him."

"I'll see if I can get a female physician. Katia might communicate a little better," says Harry, "and a nurse who can speak and write Spanish if I can find one. That way she can talk to her on a pad once she's functioning again."

"Good idea. My biggest regret is that we never had time to press her for information concerning her grandfather. I thought I'd have more time," I tell him.

"Well, at least she's not dead," says Harry.

"True. But she is unavailable, at least for the moment. If she can't help us, we can't help her."

"If she comes to tomorrow, she's going to have one hell of a headache," says Harry.

"Be sure and stop by to see her." I pull the cell phone from the holster on my belt as we walk. I fish the phone's small, flat battery from my suit-coat pocket.

"Where are *you* gonna be?" says Harry.

"Depending on what time the flight arrives, probably in Costa Rica."

"What?"

"Gimme a second."

Harry and I have been forced to pull the batteries from our cell phones. The things you learn from reading cases. We now know that the FBI can use cell phones as a remote bugging device. With a wiretap warrant they can order the service provider to switch on a phone without the owner's knowledge, even if the power is turned off. They can activate the speaker on the phone and record private conversations, anything within earshot of the cell phone, yours or somebody else's. They used the technique to take down the mob. What this means is that every one of us is constantly wearing a wire, whether we know it or not. The only protection is to jerk out the phone's battery. What they say is true: you should always speak as if the world is listening.

"Who are you calling?"

"Herman. He should be home packing for his flight this evening."

"You know you're going to be broadcasting," says Harry.

"I know." I punch the quick dial for Herman's cell.

It rings three times before the voice on the other end says, "Hello."

"Herman. It's Paul."

"I know who it is. You need to talk, we should meet," he says.

"That's all right. Are you packed?"

He hesitates.

"Did you hear me?"

"Yeah, I heard you. I'm almost done," he says.

"Good. Listen, I need some help. First call and book me a ticket on the flight with you to Costa Rica this evening. There'll be two of us going now instead of just you. What time does the flight leave?"

There is silence on the other end. Harry is looking at me, bug-eyed.

"Herman. Did you hear me?"

"Yeah, I heard you." The edge to his voice tells me he's pissed.

"What time?"

"Seven thirty. Is there anything more you need?" he says.

I make him tell me the airline and flight number over the phone. Then I tell him to meet us at the office as soon as possible and to bring his bags because he won't be going back to his apartment. We have one quick errand to run before leaving for the airport. I hang up and pluck the battery from my phone.

"Okay, so what was that all about?" says Harry.

"I wanted to give Rhytag's people the airline and the time so they wouldn't miss the flight," I tell him.

"I don't get it."

"They're going to have to lift the gate so Herman and I can get out of the country, and they're only going to do that if they think I'm gonna lead them to Nitikin. We're only going to get one bite at this. After that, none of us is getting out of the country. You can bet on it," I tell him.

I am assuming that the FBI already knows that Herman works for us. This would mean that they have a check on his passport number in the airline computers. The minute he shows his passport at the airline counter, the feds would get word as to where he's going. They would call ahead and put a tail on him at the other end. Herman and I have already talked about this. He has with him an electronic device so he can locate and remove any tracking devices the government installs in his luggage or on his clothing. Knowing Herman, he will lose any tail in a nanosecond in the hurly-burly of a crowded street or market in downtown San José.

"You think they have a hold on your passport?"

"That's my guess, either the feds, Templeton, or both. For the moment I'm not worried about Templeton. The last time I looked, Homeland Security and passport control belonged to the federal government."

"If Templeton has a hold and finds out you're gone, the Dwarf is gonna go supernova," says Harry.

"Kiss him good-bye for me. You're going to have to stay here and keep an eye on Katia. Make sure the feds don't get to her. Until we know what's going on and what her involvement may be, we've got to hold them at bay."

"What do you mean 'we'?" says Harry. "You're gonna be gone."

"You heard the doctor. There's no sense in both of us sitting here holding her hand while Templeton hones all the rough edges off his case to kill her."

At this point we are invested heavily in Katia's case, both emotionally and financially. We are past the point of no return.

"The answers we need are in Costa Rica on those photographs, and somewhere in Colombia with her mother. One of us needs to go. The other needs to stay here and hold down the fort," I tell him.

"Fine. You stay. I'll go," says Harry.

"You can't."

"Why not?"

"Because if you leave, and Templeton for some stupid reason decides to arrest me, who's going to keep the feds away from Katia?"

I can tell by the look on Harry's face that while he may not like my answer, he has nothing to counter it. "Right!" He fumes.

"Listen, I'll be back in a week, a quick stop in Costa Rica to get the photographs. We'll ditch Rhytag's federal bodyguard and on to Colombia. Depending on what we find out and what I see on those photos, I may be able to leave Herman to finish up alone, in which case I'll be back sooner."

"In the meantime, I'll be dodging pygmy darts from Templeton's blowgun," says Harry. "And I won't even be able to complain to you because you'll be in another hemisphere without a phone."

"Not necessarily. I may have a solution for that."

"What, tin cans and a string?" says Harry.

"Something Herman told me about. It's the errand I mentioned on the phone."

THIRTY-SIX

I t is a sinking feeling leaving Katia like this, alone and in trouble, thousands of miles from her home and family. But there seems to be no other choice. That the federal government now believes Katia to have been the target on the bus and the reason for the assault confirms what Harry and I already suspected. Whatever is playing in the background, the unanswered questions surrounding the Colombian photographs are central to Emerson Pike's murder. Until we know what that is, it is impossible to adequately defend Katia on multiple charges of first-degree murder.

Before leaving San Diego I placed a call to my daughter, Sarah, who is away at college, to tell her I would be gone but without mentioning where, that I might be unreachable for several days, and to stay in touch with Harry. She was filled with questions, but I couldn't answer many of them over the phone. She reminds me so much of Katia, the compelling reason for my involvement in the case. I make a mental note to visit with Sarah when I get back.

Herman snoozes in the seat next to me to the sound

of the jet engines as we wing our way south. We are somewhere over the Gulf, two hours south of Houston, where we spent last night in a hotel before catching the early bird flight to Costa Rica.

If there was a hold on my passport, there was no sign of it either from TSA or the airline at the gate prior to boarding. Herman and I waited for the usual announcement to line up and show passports before they opened the Jetway. Two airline clerks checked the names on our passports against the names on the boarding passes and initialed each boarding pass with a colored felt marker. Herman and I boarded without incident.

We both saw what we believe to be two FBI agents just after getting on at Houston. The flight was full, not a seat to spare. They were closing the door when, at the last minute, two airline employees dressed in civilian clothes and packing scuffed-up black leather flight bags used their credentials to deadhead up front with the flight crew.

Herman nudged me with his elbow as one of them asked the flight attendant for the passenger list. The man took a gander at the list, and then glanced down the aisle. He made eye contact with me just for an instant before he looked away and then handed the passenger list back to the attendant. The two agents waited for the airplane door to be closed and locked before they entered the compartment up front and sealed themselves in with the pilots.

By now their colleagues back at the FBI's San Diego field office should be going crazy. It was the errand we had to run before we left town, the one I mentioned to Herman on the phone. No doubt they followed us, Harry, Herman, and me, to the small electronics shop downtown, a place that Herman had originally told me about.

Inside the shop, Harry and I purchased two new cell phones. These particular phones have a long name. They are called encrypted, unlocked, quad-band GSM cell phones. Along with the phones, I had one of our secretaries purchase two AT&T GSM chips, each programmed for international call coverage. We had the chips installed at the shop.

The phones use encryption algorithms and code keys that are randomly generated. The keys are longer than the human genome and change with each phone call, making them impossible to decode even with the most massive supercomputers. There is no proprietary source key for the government to obtain and no back door that would allow a third party to unscramble a message. We are told that even the National Security Agency has been unable to decode them. It is for this reason that these particular phones are used by the Israeli military.

You do have to wonder what the world is coming to when your own government can't stick a pipe in your brain to suck out your thoughts.

Harry has his phone tied to a shoelace hung around his neck. He says that if he has to, he will shower with it to keep it out of their hands.

For the time being, mine is in my briefcase.

Three hours into the flight, I am just beginning to doze when I notice the door to the flight deck open. A couple of seconds later, both of the deadheading airline employees step out to use the lavatory and close the flight-deck door behind them. One of them uses the restroom up in first class. The other takes the long walk down the aisle.

As he approaches and then passes my seat, he gives me a good once-over, checking my computer, which is still open on the tray table in front of me. As I look up, he's checking things out, looking back over his shoulder at me. I give him a few seconds to get down the aisle, then turn and look as he disappears into one of the vacant restrooms at the rear of the plane.

I waste no time, turn off my computer, release my seat belt, and grab my briefcase from the overhead compartment.

Herman stirs and then wakes to the motion. "Where are we?" he yawns.

"About an hour out," I tell him. I pack my computer back into the briefcase and take out the encrypted cell phone. I slip back into my seat, fasten the seat belt, drop the tray table, and put the phone right in the center of it. It is a little larger than your normal clamshell phone, though it might not catch your attention unless you were looking for it.

By the time the agent makes his way up the aisle, I am dozing again with only half an eye on the phone in front of me. I sense his motion as he stops behind me in the aisle. I stir in my chair and he moves on. A few seconds later he raps on the flight-deck door. It opens and he disappears inside.

I nudge Herman.

"Saw him," he says. Herman can see with his eyes closed.

I hand him the phone. "Make it scarce."

"Hmm?"

"Put it in the bottom of your bag."

The phone disappears into Herman's carry-on under the seat in front of him.

"When we get off the plane, we split up, you grab your bags and get through customs and on through immigration. If they ask you, the reason for the trip is tourism. We'll meet up out in front of the airport. If you get there ahead of me, grab a taxi and wait. And keep an eye out for me."

"You think they're gonna try and stop you here?"

"I doubt it. I just want to be on the safe side."

Fifty minutes later, Herman is jarred awake as the wheels touch down at Juan Santamaria International Airport in San José, Costa Rica. The instant the plane stops at the Jetway and the pilot turns off the seat belt sign, I'm up out of my seat to allow Herman to get into the aisle ahead of me. As the plane starts to empty, I take my time getting my luggage from the overhead compartment as several passengers get between Herman and me.

As we pass the open flight-deck door, there is no sign of the two deadheading airline employees. I continue to hang back so that by the time we get to customs, Herman and I are no longer together. We clear immigration and then spend almost ten minutes standing on opposite sides of the luggage carousel before the bags finally roll in. Herman grabs his and follows the crowd toward the conveyor belt and the two large X-ray machines near the exit.

I let my bag go around three more times as I wait.

I watch the line at the X-ray machine. None of the bags is being opened, and the speed with which they rocket through the machine makes me wonder if the woman operating it is watching cartoons on the screen.

By now, Herman is long gone, out through the door leading outside.

I let my bag go around one more time before I grab it and head toward the machine. I lug both the bag and the briefcase onto the conveyor belt and watch as they roll up the ramp into the machine.

Before I can move, somebody taps me on the shoulder. I turn to a uniformed officer packing a semiautomatic sidearm with a well-worn handle.

"*Señor,* please get your bags and come this way."

"Excuse me?"

"This way." He points toward a door a few feet away. "With your bags, *por favor.*"

I gather my large roll-on and the briefcase and follow him.

Once inside, they close the door behind me and tell me to place the bags on the table in the middle of the room. One of them proceeds to go through my luggage as the other takes my jacket and checks the pockets. Then he has me empty the pockets in my pants and tells me to place everything on the table. I drop a few coins, keys, my billfold, and a money clip.

One of the cops feels around my waist and notices the money belt under my shirt. He tells me to unstrap it and lay it on the table. I lay it down and the other one goes through each pocket on the belt removing the U.S. currency and counting it, nine thousand five hundred dollars exactly.

"*Mucho dinero,*" he says.

"Vacation money," I tell him. It is under the ten-thousand-dollar limit requiring disclosure of cash brought into the country. He folds the currency and carefully places every bill back into the pockets of the belt and leaves it on the table.

By now the two of them are looking at each other

with quizzical glances. What they're looking for isn't here.

"*Señor*, you have a cell phone perhaps?"

"No, I don't think so. Is it illegal to have a cell phone in Costa Rica?"

He doesn't answer me.

"*Un momento.*" One of them disappears outside. The other one waits with me. A minute or so later the other cop comes back. "*Señor*, you may put your things back in your bags," he says. "You are free to go."

"*Gracias.*" I pack it all up, strap the money belt around my waist under my shirt and tuck it in, don my jacket, and head out the door. As I leave I glance toward the mirrored wall behind me knowing that Rhytag's men are back there wondering what happened to the cell phone.

Outside in front of the airport, taxi drivers descend on me like a pack, trying to hustle me to the dispatch ticket booth and from there to their taxi. I have to fight several of them off just to maintain a hold on my bags.

In my best pidgin Spanish I try to tell them that I'm waiting for a friend. Then I see the hulking presence of Herman standing next to a taxi forty feet away.

I make it through the crowd and throw my bags into the open trunk of the taxi. We hop in, Herman up front, me in the back. The driver slips behind the wheel and we pull away.

"Any problems?" says Herman.

"They tried to snag the phone."

He reaches into his bag to make sure it's still there. "You want it back?"

"Hang on to it. We'll find a place to hide it when we get to the hotel."

The romp down the highway is a wild ride, the driver swinging in and out of traffic, past lines of slower-moving trucks and buses, weaving between cars. The right shoulder, it seems, is reserved for underpowered motorbikes.

We pass through an industrial area, new factories with signs and foreign names, European, American, and Asian. All the while, Herman is looking over his shoulder to see if we're being tailed. He shakes his head. "Can't see 'em if they're there."

A half hour later we're jammed up in downtown traffic heading for the center of San José. I notice there are no street signs or address numbers on the buildings. The streets are crowded with pedestrians, and vendors hocking their wares. The taxi takes a sweeping right turn, then a quick left, and we find ourselves on a broad one-way street, five or six lanes, though none of the vehicles seems to stay within them, all jockeying for position as they move uptown. We pass a children's hospital and a large white cathedral on the right. A half mile farther on, we drive past a large plaza on the left. It is flanked by a beautiful colonial building under the patina of a coppered roof. Herman asks the driver and is told that the building is the Teatro Nacional, the national theater.

A few blocks farther on he makes a left and we cut through traffic on a narrow street, stop and go for several lights, then under an old concrete overpass and around another plaza.

Some of the buildings on the side streets are old metal corrugated structures with design features that date them to the end of the nineteenth century when fruit, sugar, and tobacco ruled the region. There are old mansions mixed in, some of them in disrepair, others restored. The driver gestures toward a large yellow colonial house. It is situated behind a high wrought-iron fence. He tells us this is the Casa Amarilla, the yellow house, the offices of the Costa Rican Foreign Ministry.

It takes the driver a few more minutes navigating one-way streets before he makes a turn and pulls to a stop in front of a low-slung building fronted by a low yellow masonry wall and gated entrance covered by a large green awning.

"Your hotel, *señor*. Sportsmens Lodge," he says.

Herman and I have no idea what the rooms are like. Harry and I selected the lodge from a listing of downtown hotels because of its location. Using the directions on the slip of paper from Katia, a map of downtown San José, and satellite images from Google Earth, we determined that from the Sportsmens Lodge, it is less than two blocks to the house where Katia lived with her mother. It is here that we hope to find the camera with the Colombian photographs, assuming they are still there, and if we're lucky, Katia's mother.

A little research informed us that the Sportsmens Lodge is owned by an American and is a hangout for weekenders flying in from the States. Here, Herman and I can mingle with the other guests and blend in until we can lose the FBI and disappear on the next leg of our journey.

We grab our bags out of the back of the taxi, pay the driver, and head into the hotel, down a long corridor, tiled floor flanked by doors leading to some of the rooms. Farther on, the hallway opens onto a large central patio covered by an expansive fiberglass roof that forms a kind of open-air entertainment area. It is part of a sports bar with overhead flat-screen televisions, each one showing a different event, baseball and golf from the States, soccer from Europe and Latin America.

The reception counter is a small kiosk with a pretty girl working inside. She takes our names, finds our reservations, signs us in, and gives us keys to our rooms. I ask her about the exercise area that is supposed to be downstairs. She points toward the bar at the rear of the building and tells me where the stairs are. She has the bellman take our bags, except for the one Herman was carrying with the phone tucked inside.

"How 'bout a beer?" says Herman. He has spied the bar at the other end of the patio.

"Sure."

The guests seem to be mostly Americans in casual dress, shorts and cutoffs, jeans and T-shirts, with a few locals mixed in, Ticos and Ticas, sitting at the tables on the patio. There is a louder crowd inside in the more formal bar area, watching one of the games and downing drinks.

I tip the bellman and ask him to take our bags to my room as Herman and I grab two stools on the patio side of the bar.

The phone rang on Harry's desk. He picked it up.

"Mr. Hinds, a Mr. Rhytag for you on line two," said the receptionist.

"Thanks." Harry punched the button for line two. "Mr. Rhytag, what can I do for you?"

"One of our people is in your neighborhood. He has some information you might be interested in."

"Why don't you just tell me over the phone?" Harry smiled to himself as he asked the question.

"Not something I want to discuss over the phone," said Rhytag.

"I see."

"The man's in the Brigantine right now, the restaurant out in front of your office. He's African-American, he'll be wearing a dark blue suit and a maroon-striped club tie. His name is Agent Sanders. If you go now you can catch him." Before Harry could say another word, the line went dead.

Harry got out from behind his desk and headed out of the office, through the plaza and into the side door of the Brigantine. It was too late for lunch and too early for dinner, so the restaurant was mostly empty. He saw the FBI agent seated at a table by himself out near the front windows. He had his hands folded on top of a large manila envelope resting on the table in front of him.

Harry walked up and introduced himself then sat down.

"You wanted information on one John Waters," said the agent.

"You found something?" said Harry.

"We found six bank accounts in that name all in the greater San Diego area. But only one of them was newly opened under a fresh taxpayer ID number and shows activity in the amount that you described—a near six-figure deposit just after the time Emerson Pike was murdered. Of course, there is no way to know if this is your man, but there was one other thing."

"What's that?" said Harry.

"The depositor, this Mr. Waters, also rented a safe-deposit box at the same bank on the date that he opened the account."

"What's in the box?" said Harry.

"We have no idea."

"What do you mean? Now that you know it's there, you can move on the account, freeze it, and get an order to open the safe-deposit box."

"We have no legal basis," said the agent. "You asked us for information, we got it for you." He slid the envelope across the table to Harry. "The account number, everything you need is in there. Of course, it could be just a coincidence, a perfectly innocent deposit with nothing in the box but a home deed or an insurance policy."

"Great," says Harry.

"Let me make a suggestion," said the agent. "And if you tell anyone where this came from, we'll deny it. You could put together a declaration claiming the account constitutes the proceeds from the sale of the coin in question, and the box contains physical evidence from the crime scene."

"Based on what?" says Harry. "My good looks?"

"Think about it. Who's going to complain? You issue a subpoena based on the declaration seeking to tie up the account and obtain a court order to freeze the assets in the box, pending a hearing before the court. Why would the prosecution complain? They don't own the box or the account. The only interested party is the deposit holder."

"Your boss Rhytag is insidious," said Harry.

"That's how he became the boss," said the agent. "When the depositor receives notice through the bank that the assets are frozen, he can come forward and object at the time of the hearing. If he does you can be sure he's not involved in Pike's death."

"What if he doesn't show up? What if he just sends counsel to object?" says Harry.

"Then the court may want to know who the client is and what's in the box. And if he doesn't show up at all, well..."

Rhytag was using the criminal defense team to smoke out John Waters while the feds hid in the shadows and bugged the lawyers' offices. Harry hated it. If the whole thing blew up and Mr. Waters filed a civil claim for damages because his funds were cut off, the FBI and Rhytag would be nowhere in sight. Still, it was the only avenue available, and it might work.

THIRTY-SEVEN

The black SUV was parked at the curb around the corner, twenty feet up the side street from the Sportsmens Lodge in San José. One of the dead-heading airline employees sat behind the wheel with a pair of binoculars as he watched the two men disappear with their luggage through the gate into the entrance of the hotel. Less than a minute later, two other figures emerged from the shadows between some bushes at the opposite corner of the hotel grounds. They walked quickly toward the car. One of them was carrying a small duffel bag.

A few seconds later, the second FBI agent opened the passenger door and got in. His Costa Rican compatriot climbed into the backseat and closed the door.

"Did you get it done?" asked the driver.

"Both rooms, wired snug as a bug, and the phone's tapped," said the passenger.

"Now if we could only have gotten the cell phone," said the driver.

"If customs didn't find it, where is it?"

"He handed it off to his friend," said the driver. "That's why they split up. Sucker knows we're onto him."

"If he leaves it in the room, we can get it tomorrow. In two seconds I can fry some of the circuitry and he'll think it just quit."

"And what if they take it with them?"

"Perhaps it will be stolen," said the man in the backseat. "Tourists are always being held up at gunpoint and robbed in San José."

"We'll have to talk about that one," said the driver. "Washington may draw the line at shooting a lawyer, even in Costa Rica."

"Turn on the receiver," said the other agent. "Let's see what we get."

"Give it a minute. They haven't had time to get to the rooms yet," said the driver.

Herman and I finish our beers, pay up, and leave the empty bottles on the bar. As we were drinking, I noticed one of the employees carrying a full case of beer up a set of stairs in the bar area on the other side. I know this isn't the way to the exercise area. From what the girl told me at the front desk, those stairs are farther back in the building, through the glass door in the residence area on the way to our rooms.

After making sure the bartender and the waitress are busy with customers, I gesture for Herman to follow me and quickly head from the patio into the formal bar area.

But instead of going through the bar toward the glass door leading to the guest rooms at the back of the building, we quickly veer to the right and slip down the steps into the basement.

They lead to a service and storage area under the bar

upstairs. But at the foot of the steps is a solid wooden door with a heavy metal latch. I turn the latch and open the door. It leads to a small lane, a dogleg in the road that runs behind the lodge. Across the street is a chain-link fence covered in heavy foliage and bounded by old eucalyptus trees. On the other side of the fence is dense jungle undergrowth, where if the images on Google Earth were accurate, a steep incline leads down to the old San José zoo in the canyon below.

For the moment I am more interested in the paved lane and where it leads. If the maps and satellite photographs were accurate, Herman and I should be able to follow the lane past the next intersection. A few hundred feet farther on, we would come to another small street on the right. On the left-hand side of that street, less than two hundred yards from the intersection, is the house that Katia lived in with her mother, and if we are blessed by the gods, the camera with the photographs from Colombia.

"Tonight when it gets dark, we check out the house," I tell Herman. "If her mother's still gone, the place should be dark. Bring your lock picks."

He nods and I close the door. We head back up, and hold it at the top of the steps until the barmaid turns her back to wait on a customer. Herman and I quickly step up and wander casually through the bar toward the glass door and our rooms.

The lodge is a labyrinth of connected buildings and stairways. The front section where the entrance is located is part of an old mansion. It contains twenty-odd rooms on two levels plus a two-room penthouse on a third level.

On the other side in the back is an enclosed ramp

that leads to another three-story mansion on the back street, across from the zoo, and a small condominium complex. According to the online literature, this section was added recently.

Herman and I find our rooms in the new section. I open the door and we both step into mine so Herman can grab his bags. The room is spacious, high ceilinged and ornate, with a king-size bed and exotic hardwood furnishings.

"I hope you didn't get the only good room," says Herman.

"You wanna trade?"

"Not yet. I haven't seen mine."

As we're talking, Herman zips open one of his bags and takes out a small device the size and shape of a folded pocketknife. On one end is a small lens. He holds it up to his eye and peers through it, scanning the room, each wall, all the hanging pictures, the television and bedside clock and phone. He checks the bathroom as well as we discuss the weather and talk about the lack of humidity in San José.

Herman's device is called a SpyFinder Personal. The battery-powered lens will detect any microcamera planted in a room, lighting up the camera's lens with a red dot even if the camera is powered off at the time. It works off the same principle as the camera, using re-fracted light, only instead of using it to capture an image, it shoots beams of concentrated light that are refracted by the camera's lens to reveal its position.

"What time do you want to have breakfast in the morning?" I ask him.

"I don't know. I'm pretty tired," says Herman. "Why don't we sleep in?"

Herman shakes his head regarding any cameras, drops the device back in his bag, and removes the other half of his act, the small electronic bug detector. This is the size of an old transistor radio and has a short telescoping antenna. The entire device would fit inside the breast pocket of your shirt. It has a backup scanner to detect cameras that are transmitting and runs the entire frequency range of electronic bugs. Herman has already turned off the detector's alarm so that it merely vibrates in his hand as the LEDs light up. The room is wired. He points to the phone and nods. Herman is assuming that the phone is tapped as well.

None of this surprises me. We used the firm's credit card to book the hotel rooms, so Rhytag had plenty of time to plan ahead. We will use credit cards as long as we're being observed and go to cash the moment we lose the FBI. Herman is carrying another ninety-five hundred in cash in a belt around his waist.

"Tell you what. Whoever wakes up first in the morning calls the other," I tell him.

"But not before nine," says Herman.

"We can do dinner downstairs. I'm too tired to go out tonight."

"Sounds good to me," says Herman.

I pen a note to him on a pad from the nightstand near the bed. "Sweep the hall and your room for cameras. We meet outside my room tonight at ten—*very quietly!*" I underline the last two words.

"Give me a call when you want to go to dinner." He holds up the cell phone and mouths the words "I'll take care of it."

I nod. "Catch you later."

Herman leaves and closes the door behind him.

I turn on the television, unpack my bags, and take a shower. I am drying myself with a towel as I call the front desk and leave a wake-up call for seven that evening. Then I slip between the covers, lower the television volume a bit, and take a nap to the muted sounds of a soap opera in Spanish playing in the background.

THIRTY-EIGHT

Judgment day had finally arrived. Yakov Nitikin had made his deal with the devil, and now it was time to perform.

Early that morning, Alim Afundi allowed two of the FARC rebels, a man and a woman Nitikin had known for years and whom he trusted, to escort his daughter, Maricela, back to Medellín and from there to her home in Costa Rica.

Nitikin kissed his daughter good-bye. She was crying. She knew she would not see him again. Yakov slipped a folded piece of paper into her hand and made her promise not to open it or read it until she arrived home in San José. After reading it she was to keep the contents to herself. "Do you promise?"

She looked up at him, tears in her eyes. She nodded.

He smiled. "We will see each other again." He told her that he loved her, and kissed her once more, this time on the forehead. Then he watched as she boarded the truck and climbed into the middle of the front seat. Yakov stood in the dust at the side of the road and waved as the truck carrying his daughter to safety pulled away and disappeared in the distance.

But now there was no time for sorrow or tears. Now there was work to be done. In addition to allowing Maricela to leave the compound, Afundi had relented, agreeing to allow one of the other FARC soldiers, a twenty-six-year-old Colombian named Tomas to assist Nitikin in the final assembly of the device, on two conditions: that the work commence immediately, that morning; and that Nitikin verbally communicate each step in the process by using a walkie-talkie and explaining it to an interpreter who would in turn communicate it to Alim.

The Russian agreed to begin immediately, but tried to argue that it was impossible to brief Alim as they proceeded, that it would only serve to distract them and make the process more dangerous. But Alim insisted, and finally Nitikin agreed.

As he had suspected, Alim's own nuclear expert tried to hitch a ride on the early morning truck with Maricela and her two guards. He was plucked off the truck by one of Alim's men. The technician offered some lame excuse about supplies he needed to obtain in Medellín. Alim told him the supplies could wait. He wanted the man close at hand to answer technical questions that Alim might have as the assembly of the device proceeded.

By ten that morning, Nitikin and Tomas, his Colombian assistant, were locked away in the wooden hut with the innards of the gun device spread out before them on a large table in the center of the room.

Against one wall, another table, supported by three sturdy sawhorses, bore the weight of two lead caskets.

These containers shielded the two men from radiation emitted from the uranium projectile in one casket and the four uranium target disks in the other.

The first stage, assembly of the gun itself, involved mere mechanics. Except for the precision of certain measurements involving alignment of the barrel, it was no more complicated than installing minor motor parts in an automobile. The work should have taken less than an hour. It stretched out, consuming more than two hours because of the constant need to communicate with Alim through the walkie-talkie and to answer the endless stream of questions he posed through the interpreter.

Nitikin knew what Afundi was up to. He was having one of his men write it all down, so that if he needed to, he could dispense with the Russian's services whenever he wanted. Except for one thing; Nitikin had no intention of telling him everything. He would let the Iranian know this only when he was finished with the preliminary assembly of the device.

There were certain aspects of the process involving safety features and final arming that only Nitikin would know. Yakov had no intention of allowing them to take the device that he had guarded for decades, and detonate it at some undisclosed location without his express consent and participation. Alim and his men might kill him when they were done, but not before.

Gun-type devices, while being the most rudimentary and reliable of nuclear weapons, were also the most dangerous. The simplicity of design was what made it hazardous. A plutonium implosion device, unlike Nitikin's, while potentially far more destructive, required the intricate and precise alignment of a number of elements before criticality could be achieved. The failure or inhibition of any one of these would neutralize the bomb. But a single subcritical uranium projectile, like Nitikin's, being fired down a tube at high speed by a conventional explosive charge into a larger target of uranium, meant that a simple premature detonation of the firing charge would result in a full-yield nuclear explosion.

Alim had insisted on installing two items himself: the cordite charge, which involved the simple removal of a breech plug from the back end of the gun tube and the insertion of the cordite; and the setting of the timing device that would initiate the firing of the gun. Nitikin had warned Alim not to install the newly acquired cordite charge in the chamber of the gun, behind the uranium projectile, until the last moment. This would be done on-site and could be performed by virtually anyone. In fact, Yakov did not even have possession of the cordite. That was held by Alim.

Apart from a full-yield detonation, the next fear was a high-explosive fizzle. This could occur in the event that the projectile slides down the barrel at a reduced speed. It could happen as a result of gravity if the projectile is not properly installed, or because of kinetic energy following a collision with the vehicle transporting the bomb. In actuality the risk of this happening to Nitikin's device was virtually nonexistent because of its design, though this was not something Yakov shared with Alim.

Nitikin's device incorporated safety features, including compression bands installed around the projectile to secure it firmly in the gun barrel, and a mechanical saving device that blocked the projectile once it was installed in the barrel. This saving mechanism had to be disengaged before firing, and only Nitikin knew the proper sequence for doing so.

Once the safety device was in place, if the gun was fired, the worst that would happen was a fizzle. The device would be blown apart before the two elements of uranium could achieve critical mass and establish a chain reaction. The explosion would kill anyone in close proximity to the device. Depending on the force of the blast, wind velocity, and other factors, it could shower any person within hundreds and up to thousands of feet with a deadly dose of radiation.

The problem was that none of these safety features could be installed until after the uranium target was bolted in place and the projectile was prepared and inserted down the muzzle of the smooth bore tube.

To make things worse, all of this had to be done with precision and speed. During training, in his youth, Yakov had performed the procedure at least eight times and had done so each time in under eight minutes.

While Nitikin and his helper would have the protection of lead-lined suits and gloves, including hoods, face shields, and breathing apparatuses, these garments only provided partial protection. Once they opened the lead coffins containing the uranium, their bodies would begin absorbing radiation.

According to Nitikin's calculations, they had slightly more than twenty minutes to bolt the target in place, prepare and load the projectile, install the saving mechanism, and seal the gun tube assembly inside its lead-shielded case. Anything beyond twenty-five minutes and the burden of radiation their bodies would be absorbing could become lethal.

Nitikin and his helper had practiced the procedure

for four days, using a short section of three-inch pipe for the gun tube and wooden mock-ups of the uranium components.

Yakov liked the young Colombian. Unlike some of the older FARC commanders who had lost sight of the goal of social change and had become warlords presiding over narco empires, Tomas, like most of the young rebels, adhered to revolutionary principles. He would lay down his life in a minute if he believed it would advance the cause of the revolution. In this way he was fearless, but not foolhardy.

Tomas learned quickly and asked questions that made it clear he understood the most critical parts of the procedure and the risks involved. Most of all he understood the time constraints.

After assembling the parts of the tube and the steel anvil that would form the base for the target, Nitikin placed an old alarm clock on the sill of the window directly above the two lead caskets. The clock was set with both hands straight up, twelve o'clock.

Nitikin spoke in Spanish, but his Russian accent destroyed any trill to the Spanish *r*s. "I will set the alarm for twenty minutes. When the alarm goes off, or if it fails for any reason, when the big hand reaches four, Tomas, you are to exit the hut and get as far away from the building as fast as you can, no matter whether we are finished or not. Do you understand?"

"*Sí.*"

"You are not to argue with me, talk to me, or ask any questions, just go. Understood?"

"Yes, *señor.* I understand."

They donned their lead-lined suits, pulled the hoods over their heads, gloved their hands, and began breathing through the respirators. They had only practiced with the suits once before, but they wore the thick gloves each time. The gloves made it difficult to manipulate the tongs that would be used to pick up and carry the sub-critical uranium components and to hold them in place as they were fastened down or fitted with other parts.

Within less than a minute, Tomas and Yakov began to feel the drag of the heavy lead as gravity began to pull on their bodies.

Nitikin used a ratchet-and-socket set to unscrew the four bolts from the lid of the first casket. He reached up with his gloved hand, took the clock from the window-sill, reset the hands to twelve, flipped the alarm lever, and put the clock back on the sill. Then he reached down with his hands and lifted the heavy lid off the casket, setting it on the table.

The target elements of uranium, four of them, rings stacked upside down, forming a V-shaped cup, looked like lead to the naked eye.

Tomas took the tongs and grasped the top ring. Sure-footed and steady, he moved to the table and quickly aligned the first ring. This was the bottom of the cup-shaped target. It fit perfectly in the prepared bed of the high-carbide steel anvil.

Nitikin tried to explain the procedure to Alim through the interpreter, using the walkie-talkie. Because of the hood, the translator was having difficulty understand-ing him. Alim kept coming back, asking for clarifica-tion.

Tomas repeated the process and the second ring of the target was in place.

Nitikin tried to explain this. The question came back, "How many is that now?"

"Two," said Nitikin.

"What did you say? Repeat one more time."

"Two target disks installed."

"How much time remaining?"

"I don't have time to look right now."

"Give us an estimate."

Nitikin ignored them. He could see that the constant static and shouting from the walkie-talkie was making Tomas nervous. If he dropped one of the elements on the floor and deformed it, the device could well be useless.

Without any air-conditioning in the hut, the suits had become stifling. The small glass lens inside Nitikin's hood through which he could see began to fog up.

"What is happening now?"

"Listen to me. You can either have a bomb or a description of how to make one, but you cannot have both. Do you understand? You must decide," said Yakov.

A few seconds passed, then the translator's voice. "Afundi says he wants to come in and see for himself."

"Tell him to come ahead as long as he is prepared to die," said Nitikin. He turned off the walkie-talkie and tossed it on the table.

As Tomas moved back to the casket one more time, Yakov realized there was only one uranium element left in the storage case. The Colombian grabbed it with the metal tongs and quickly placed it on top of the others as Nitikin took up the ratchet and two of the bolts from the lid of the empty casket along with two steel washers. The uranium target disks had been milled with two small holes. These lined up precisely with threaded holes in the base of the anvil. Now that the target disks were stacked and aligned, they were ready to be bolted down.

Avoiding any contact by his gloved hand with the uranium, Yakov put one bolt through a washer and dropped it into the first hole, then did the same with the second bolt. He used the ratchet to carefully tighten them, making certain not to deform the soft uranium.

The moment he was done he turned and looked at the clock. The most critical part of the process was still before them. They had used up seven minutes, including precious time wasted arguing with Alim over the walkie-talkie.

Yakov moved to the second casket and started loosening the bolts. Less than a minute later he had the lid off. The smaller portion of highly enriched uranium, the bullet, lay before them, cradled in a shaped cavity cast in the bottom lead casket.

Tomas moved with the tongs, gripped it, and picked it up. He hadn't cleared the top lip of the casket when the slick cylindrical projectile slipped from the tongs and fell back into its case and settled again in the cavity in the bottom.

Tomas stopped and looked at Nitikin. Yakov could tell he was rattled. He reached over and took the tongs from him. Nitikin delicately reached in and lifted the projectile from the bottom of the case. Gripping the tongs tightly with both hands, he rotated the object up close in front of the thick glass lens of his hood, examining it for any deformation or dents.

"It's all right."

Tomas nodded.

Nitikin set it back down in the case, handed the tongs

back to Tomas, and retrieved another smaller set for himself. Using the smaller tongs, Yakov picked up a brass ring, banded metal, with a fused neoprene seal along the center of the outside of the ring.

Tomas picked up the projectile again, this time using both hands to squeeze the tongs. Holding it firmly, he set the base end on the table so that the bullet rested upright, like a missile on a launch pad. He used the tongs to steady it near the bottom, at its base, as Nitikin carefully slipped the brass ring over the tip of the projectile.

To the naked eye, the bullet looked perfectly cylindrical, but it wasn't. The circumference was imperceptibly larger at the bottom than the top, so that the ring slid down the projectile to the bottom third and stopped. Yakov tested it with the tongs to make sure that it was properly seated. The ring didn't move.

He checked the clock. They were sixteen minutes in. Quickly he picked up the second ring and slipped it over the projectile. This time the slightly smaller ring slid only halfway down before seating itself against the side of the projectile.

Yakov grabbed a can of lubricant, pried open the lid, and with a small brush, dabbed a bit of the viscous clear liquid on the outer neoprene gaskets fused to the two brass rings.

"Ready?" said Yakov. He steadied the projectile with the small tongs while Tomas gained a more secure purchase with the larger tongs.

"You have it?"

"*Sí.*" Tomas picked it up with both hands, turned, and carried it toward the table. He allowed Nitikin to cross in front of him so that he could keep the projectile as far as possible from the uranium target already bolted in place.

Separated, neither of the two portions of uranium-235 possessed sufficient mass to reach criticality. But together, either in close proximity, or, god forbid, should they make contact, the nuclear reaction, and the burst of radiation, would be deadly.

Tomas continued to hold the projectile up, away from his body, as Yakov steadied the tube of the gun's barrel with his gloved hands.

At the moment, the two-foot-long barrel of the gun's tube was swung out on a hinged device of heavy forged steel. Once the projectile was loaded in the tube, the barrel would be swung back and locked into position so that the muzzle was directly aligned with and nearly touching the open cup of the target. The slight gap between the two would be filled with a three-inch disk of uranium-238, a neutron deflector that was nonfissionable and reflected neutrons back to their source. The disk would keep the two portions of highly enriched uranium separated and corral their neutrons even if the projectile accidentally slid down the barrel. It was the final safety mechanism that Yakov would have to remove before the bomb could be detonated. But the safety disk couldn't be inserted until the projectile was properly loaded and the barrel was swung back into position and locked.

Nitikin checked the clock. They were closing in on nineteen minutes.

"Ready?"

Tomas nodded.

"Go ahead."

The Colombian reached over with the tongs and

aligned the base end of the projectile with the muzzle of
the gun's barrel. It passed through the opening until the
neoprene gasket reached the muzzle. Tomas tried to
force it. The tongs slipped on the slick, soft uranium.

"Don't. Stop," said Yakov.

Tomas eased off.

"Do you have it? Can you hold it?"

"*Sí*. I think so."

The neoprene on the brass rings was designed to
compress against the inside of the barrel. But as Yakov
looked at it he realized that the first ring, toward the
base of the projectile, was jammed in the muzzle at a
slight angle.

"Do you think you can ease it out?" said Nitikin. He
took hold of the tube of the barrel with both hands as
Tomas tried to lift the projectile out. The tongs began
to slip.

"Stop." Nitikin was afraid that if Tomas lost his grip
with the tongs, the projectile might come loose from its
own weight and topple onto the anvil and the uranium
target.

"Don't push it, just hold it steady," said Yakov. "Give
me a moment to get the tool."

The tool was a two-foot-long steel ramrod with a
conically shaped concave tip. It was formed precisely to
fit the bullet tip on the projectile.

As soon as Nitikin could grab the ramrod, he would
be able to grasp the uranium bullet by its pointed end.
Then he could use the leverage of the ramrod to line it
up and push it with uniform pressure down the barrel.
After that, he and Tomas could button up in less than
thirty seconds, slip in the safety disk, and close the entire gun assembly inside its lead-lined bomb case. The

case was designed to shield the radiation in the gun from the outer electronic components, including the detonator. Once the lead case was sealed, you could safely approach the bomb without protective gear.

Yakov scanned the hut quickly, turning his head and peering through the fogged lens of his hood searching for the ramrod. He didn't see it. Then he remembered. He had handed it to one of Alim's men that morning when they were setting up. He'd asked the interpreter to tell the man to carry it to the hut. The idiot hadn't done it.

Nitikin looked through the window. He could see Alim down on one knee, the technician, the interpreter, and Alim's cronies all huddled around him under the trees a hundred meters away. He grabbed the walkie-talkie, turned it on, and shouted into the mouthpiece, "The ramrod I handed to your man this morning. Where is it? We need it now!"

He watched through the window as the message was translated for Alim and his men. Afundi got to his feet, turned, and looked at one of them. The man turned up his palms, shrugged his shoulders, and shook his head. Then he suddenly turned his head to the right and pointed. Nitikin followed the trajectory of the man's outstretched arm and finger to a tree perhaps thirty yards away. There against the trunk of the tree, propped up, was the two-foot-long steel ramrod.

"Get it now! Bring it here!" Yakov screamed into the walkie-talkie. He watched as Alim looked at the man and pointed toward the tree. The man shook his head. He took two steps backward, his hands held out, palms open. He was refusing to take the ramrod to the hut, afraid of the radiation.

"Hurry," said Tomas. "I cannot hold it much longer."

Nitikin watched in stark silence as Alim pulled something from his belt. There was a spray of red from the man's head, followed a second later by the report of the shot as the man's legs turned to rubber and he collapsed to the ground. Alim quickly turned the gun on one of his other followers. This time the man ran as fast as his legs could carry him to the tree, grabbed the ramrod, and raced toward the hut as if he were running an Olympic trial.

Yakov turned to Tomas. "Try and hold on. One moment. It's coming."

"Hurry!" cried Tomas.

Nitikin opened the door, struggled to run in the heavy lead suit and meet the man with the ramrod partway. He was maybe thirty feet from the hut when a loud hum and a brilliant cobalt flare enveloped him from behind. The man running toward him tried to shield his eyes from the flash with his free hand, but it was too late. Nitikin knew instantly that both Tomas and the man with the ramrod were dead. It was but a matter of time. He wondered if the lead suit and the distance he had put between himself and the device in the seconds before the dragon whipped its tail might have saved his own life.

THIRTY-NINE

Just after seven in the evening, Herman and I meet for dinner in the covered patio downstairs at the Sportsmens Lodge.

Herman has checked the public hallway outside our rooms. There was nothing emitting a signal, no listening devices or microcams installed, though Herman's room was bugged and his phone tapped.

Herman brought with him the encrypted cellular phone. He's found a place to hide it inside the wall behind an air-conditioning register over the bed in his room.

I spend a few minutes in a crowded section of the bar with one ear covered by my hand, the other pressed to the phone talking to Harry back in San Diego.

Harry tells me that he stopped in to see Katia at the hospital in the early afternoon. The sedation had worn off and, according to Harry, she seemed more alert. But still she did not communicate. Harry has found a local neurologist to examine her and perform the duties as treating physician. According to the doctor, Katia is suffering from severe depression in addition to the physical trauma. He explained that this was not unusual given all that she has been through. Harry tells me the doctor is treating her with antidepressant medication and that the marshal's service is examining every pill and keeping a close eye on her through the hospital staff.

"Considering the fact that Templeton thinks you helped her plunge the knife into Pike, I suppose you can't blame them," says Harry.

"I know the phone is encrypted, but maybe we can find something a little less titillating for the government for you and me to talk about."

"How about the items in question?" says Harry. He means Katia's camera and the pictures from Colombia.

"Give us time. We just got here."

"You said less than a week and you'd be back," says Harry.

"I said I would try."

"Did you call her mother's cell phone?" I ask him.

"I did. I called twice this afternoon. I couldn't understand the Spanish message, but it was the same as all the other times when I called. The message came on after one ring, which I am guessing means the phone is turned off. I'd say she's not there. Where are you? It sounds like a party," says Harry.

"I'm in the bar downstairs at the hotel."

"I thought so. You owe me a vacation when you get back," he says. "By the way, I've run into a snag with the nurse you wanted to hire. The hospital says the doctor's fine, but they're not sure about the nurse. They're worried about liability. They say if she screws up and the patient suffers, they're afraid the hospital may be on the hook."

"What did you tell them?"

"I told them the nurse is just gonna hold Katia's hand, talk to her in Spanish, and maybe slap the marshal once in a while. I promised them that she wouldn't be dishing up any meds or doing any surgery, at least not right away."

"And what did they say?"

"What does any hospital say? They have to check with the administrator who in turn will call the local legal brain trust, which means that by noon tomorrow we'll be told that the nurse is out."

"Stop with the negative brain waves," I tell him. "We could always dress her up in civilian clothes and call her a relative. If the nurse won't do it, we can find a Spanish-speaking female PI. We just want a warm body in the room, somebody to keep an eye on Katia."

"Three shifts a day?" says Harry. "That's a lot of relatives for somebody who's in the country on a visa."

"Yeah, well, it is Southern California, and we are only ten minutes from the border."

"If I listen to you, Rhytag's gonna have half the local nurses' registry on ice with immigration within a week. Let me think about it," says Harry.

"Where are you right now?" I ask.

"If you really want to know, I'm in my backyard standing under a tree in my underwear."

"You're kidding."

"I wish I was. I tried to call you twice. Your phone was turned off. I was on the john when you called. I thought it best that I step outside since half the federal workforce is listening in every time I pass gas or flush the toilet."

I tell him about the rooms being wired and the attempt by the feds to grab the phone at the airport.

"Don't change the subject," says Harry. "You're still the one down there in a bar with all the squealing voices in the background, while I'm standing around my yard in boxer shorts."

"I'm just telling you to keep an eye on your cell phone. They'll snatch it if they can."

"At the moment it's tied to a string around my naked neck," he says. "You know, the thought has crossed my mind that for the moment at least, I don't need your help to send Rhytag up the flagpole. All I have to do is sit in the conference room and let them listen to one half of an encrypted telephone conversation. And I don't need a phone to do it."

"I understand. You're not happy. I owe you big-time when I get back."

"Don't get me wrong," he says. "I'm not trying to put any pressure on you. It's just that if you're not back here by next Tuesday, the FBI's gonna be digging up your backyard with a backhoe looking for Nitikin's bones in the barrel right next to the one holding Jimmy Hoffa. So if you treasure your tulips, you'll be here."

"What you're saying is, don't waste my time talking on the phone."

"Right."

"It's been fun. Let's do it again tomorrow night, same time, same place. Wear clothes," I tell him.

"Leave your phone on," says Harry.

I punch the button and the line goes dead. The last thing we need is a ringing telephone in the air-conditioning duct over Herman's bed.

We finish dinner and trek back toward our rooms.

"Be sure and bring your set of picks."

"Already got 'em," says Herman. "In my pocket."

"Ten o'clock sharp. Let's put the phone back behind the register just in case we run into problems. It'll be safer there."

We split up just outside the door to my room. I kill twenty minutes running an empty shower, then leave the noise from the television on until nine thirty, when I turn off the lights and sit in the dark in the chair against the window, the curtains drawn. Every few minutes I check to see if there are any new vehicles parked on the small lane at the back of the hotel. I can see only part of the road, but there is almost no traffic on the narrow stretch of pavement that flanks the zoo. I hear a faint scratch like fingernails brushing the other side of the door to my room. I check my watch. It's ten o'clock on the dot.

With my running shoes in one hand, I cross the hardwood floor in stocking feet and quietly turn the dead bolt, opening the door. Herman is outside in the hall, his back against the wall, leaning over tying the laces on his shoes.

I silently close the door behind me and join him against the wall, slipping the shoes on my feet.

Neither of us utters a word until we pass through the bar, go down the stairs toward the service area, and are out the door onto the street that borders the zoo.

Herman uses a small piece of duct tape to hold back the spring-loaded bolt on the lock, and then tapes a few thicker pieces onto the edge of the door to wedge it closed. He will have to use a knife to pry it open on the way back. The thick green wooden door has no handle on the outside.

We start to hoof it down the street.

"I hope you know where you're going," said Herman.

"I think I can find it."

The written description given to me by Katia used the name of a local hospital three blocks away, Hospital Calderon Guardia, as the principal point of reference for finding houses or businesses in the area. The directions would lead you to the street where the house was located. Then it would describe the residence with particularity, such as "*casa blanca, segundo a la derecha,*" the white house, second on the right. It made perfectly good sense once you understood the system, though FedEx was out of luck on home delivery unless they could follow the trail of bread crumbs to your front door.

Half a block down, along the fence bordering the zoo, the thick overhead canopy of trees turned the lane into a dark tomb. By now the last streetlight is well behind us, above the green wooden door to the lodge. Ahead is nothing but blackness and the exotic sounds of the bush beyond the fence off to our left. Suddenly there is a guttural, low growl that is unmistakable, and not far off.

"When the woman at the counter said it wasn't safe to walk at night, I thought she was talkin' about the locals." Herman is laughing. "Not some lion who's gonna be pickin' his teeth with my tibia because we took a wrong turn at the zoo."

"Let's hope he's on the other side of the fence."

Herman pulls a Mini Maglite from his pocket, twists the lens, and gives us a narrow beam of light on the pavement so we don't break our necks.

"You think the light's gonna scare him?"

"I hear they're afraid of fire," he says.

"Fire is a match. He'd swallow that like a Twinkie."

"I'm not scared," says Herman. "All I have to do is outrun you."

"You can't fool me. I saw your dinner—two steaks and four eggs. If that poor thing is out on the road, we both know who's gonna get eaten and it won't be me. All I want is the fur for the floor in front of my fireplace," I tell him.

"Here we are arguing and it's the FBI who's in trouble," he says. "How are they gonna explain how the two Americans they were tailing got eaten by a lion behind their hotel, one of them a lawyer, and they didn't even get pictures?"

"You're right. Maybe we should have just stepped out the front and asked them for a lift."

"How do we know they won't be waiting for us when we get to the house?"

"We don't." Herman has a point. Rhytag knows that Katia's mother took the pictures. By now he would have had time to have one of his people, the agent assigned to the U.S. embassy, locate her residence and either place it under surveillance or try to contact her.

"If Harry's information about her cell phone is accurate, Katia's mother is still gone," I tell him.

"Yeah, but they could be watching her house, especially now that they know we're in town. And only two blocks away from where the woman lives," says Herman.

"We'll just have to play it by ear. I don't know what else to do."

In the dark, with only a narrow shaft of light to guide us, it takes almost ten minutes before we figure out our mistake, and then only after passing it three times.

Seen from above through the satellite photos on Google Earth, what appeared to be a normal conjunction of two streets was not an intersection at all.

The street that Katia lived on appears to dead-end at a railing about thirty feet above the level of the road Herman and I are walking on. It can only be reached by a set of uneven concrete steps, cracked in places, quite steep and difficult to navigate, particularly in the dark with only a flashlight to guide us.

As we reach the top of the steps, Herman turns off the Mini Maglite. We stand for a few seconds in the shadows and reconnoiter the houses and cars along the block. They are backlit by overhead lights in the distance, at the far end of the street.

Katia's elaborate address, the written directions for finding the house, were crafted for approach by vehicle from the other end of the block; the white house, second on the right, now on our left. I can see it clearly from where we stand. The entire front of the structure is lit up by a streetlight mounted on a telephone pole directly in front of the house.

All the houses on the block front directly onto a narrow sidewalk on each side of the street, several of them with bushes and vines invading the sidewalk. The roadway itself is wide enough for only a single car, so that several of them are parked partway on the sidewalk.

I point out Katia's house to Herman.

"I see it." At the moment he is more interested in several cars parked on each side, from here to the end of the block. We start to walk.

As we reach the house at the other end of the block, I tell him, "It's the first arched gate."

Herman turns his head and takes a look. By the time

we get to the end of the block, Herman seems satisfied that all of the cars are empty. Still, he keeps walking around the corner to the right as if we are leaving the area. I follow him.

Ten feet around the corner he stops. "I don't like it. Too much light from that pole," he says.

I step back to the corner again so I can see. Herman is right. The entrance is lit up like a spotlight on a stage, with the streetlight directly above the locked gate leading to the front door. A car turning the corner or somebody walking down the street is going to see us in a heartbeat, standing out in front working on the lock.

I step back to where he is standing. "I don't know of any other way in," I tell him.

"I'm just gonna have to work fast," he says. "Can you whistle?"

"What?"

"Can you whistle? You know, like the lady said, put your lips together and blow?"

I try it. My lips are dry and nothing comes out. I lick them and try again. This time I get a weak whistle.

"It'll have to do," says Herman. "I want you to stay here. You see a car comin' or anybody walking this direction you whistle. And make it loud enough so I can hear it." He pulls a small black plastic case from his pocket, opens it, and selects a lock pick and another tiny curved tool of some kind.

"What if somebody comes from the other end of the street, up the steps?" I say.

"You'd have to be crazy to walk there in the dark," says Herman.

"We just did."

"Yeah, but the locals aren't stupid." Herman smiles at

me. "Just remember to whistle, and make it loud so I can hear it."

Before I can wet my lips again, Herman is back around the corner and down the sidewalk. I watch as he crosses the street on a diagonal and walks to the far end of the house and directly up to the arched gate. Hunched over, with his back to me, he starts working with the pick on the lock.

It was the problem with a lot of the countries in Latin America; even if they had access to natural gas they never developed the infrastructure, the pumping stations, and the underground pipes to deliver it, at least not for domestic use.

Fortunately for him, the kitchen Liquida was in this evening had a nice new gas stove. It was hooked up to a large propane tank. He was guessing close to a thousand gallons. The tank was situated in an area that had once been a garage at the back of the place. As far as he was concerned, it was as good as natural gas. In fact, it was probably better. Propane burned faster and hotter than natural gas and was therefore more efficient. It took less time to cook or, for that matter, to do other things.

Tonight it was one of those other things that Liquida was working on. He had easily slid the stove out and turned off the gas valve where the line came out of the wall. He unscrewed the nut holding the compression fitting from the copper line feeding propane into the stove and was busy installing the small unit that was not much bigger than a deck of cards. It had two quarter-inch copper tubes coming out of each end, both with compression fittings. He screwed one end to the propane line coming out of the wall and the other end to the feed line into the stove. He tightened the fittings with a wrench. When he was satisfied that they were snug, he turned the valve and listened for any hissing of gas. It was silent. He sniffed the air close to the unit—nothing.

Then he picked up the small set of controls from the countertop where he had left it. There were all kinds of buttons and switches, along with a tiny joystick toggle. The unit was designed to control model airplanes in flight. But Liquida cared about only two of the buttons. He pressed one of them and listened once more. This time there was the distinctive hiss of gas as propane leaked from a hole in the side of the little box. Some of the vapor turned to liquid dripping from the hole as it continued to run. He pressed the button again and the hissing sound stopped. He reached down, wiped away the liquid, and watched the small hole. There was no more dripping. Liquida smiled; another job well done.

Herman was hunched over the lock cylinder in the gate with the tension wrench, holding back four of the pins. He was working on the last one, feeling for it with the pick, when suddenly there was a loud whistle from the corner behind him, at the end of the block.

"Shit!" Herman whispered under his breath. He looked back over his shoulder while trying not to pull the tiny tools from the lock. Paul was standing at the corner motioning, drawing one hand with his finger out stretched across his throat, a sign to cut and run. A second later the bright beam of headlights lit him up from behind.

Herman pulled the pick and the wrench from the lock, put his hands in his pockets, and started walking casually back toward the corner where Paul was standing.

For an instant the oncoming headlights blinded him as the car turned the corner. It slowed as the driver turned to look, checking Herman out closely. Then the car drove on down the street. It slowed again as the motorized metal doors on a garage in front of a house two doors down from Katia's started to grind and squeak as they opened. Herman continued to walk and watch as the car pulled into the garage and the doors reversed the groaning and closed behind it.

By then Herman had reached Paul, at the corner.

"Damn it. I almost had it."

"You told me to warn you."

"I know. She took a good look when she went by. I doubt they get a lot of walkin' traffic at night on this street. Bein' a dead end and all," says Herman. "We better give it a couple of minutes so she's not peeking through the front window when I go back."

Liquida was sliding the stove back into place when he heard a noise out on the front street. He stopped and listened. A car went by, headlights flashing as they blazed past the window in the dining room. He left the stove where it was and headed for the window, which was about six or eight steps up on a landing where the stairs turned and went up to the bedrooms on the second story. The view out was partially obscured by a thorny bush whose branches wound their way through the wrought-iron metal bars that guarded the window on the outside.

By the time Liquida looked out, the car was gone. But as he looked the other way, to the left, he saw a man walking away, crossing the street. The guy was huge, a black man, bald as a cue ball, with shoulders like a bull. If he was Tico he was on supersteroids.

The man was nearing the walkway on the other side of the street. Liquida was just about to turn from the window when another man stepped from the shadows near the corner. The two of them stopped to talk.

Liquida looked at his watch. Twenty minutes to eleven. It was a strange time for a conversation out on the street, too late to be coming home from work and too early for the bars to have closed. When he looked back the two men were gone.

He thought about it for a moment, then went back to the kitchen and finished sliding the stove back into place. He checked to make sure that everything looked just right. It probably didn't matter. By the time she arrived in the morning, if everything went as planned, she would never have a chance to make it to the kitchen. He would snag her at the front door with the chloroform. He would then arrange her on the floor in front of the stove for her accident. They would find her bones mixed in with all the ashes, probably under the house where the stove would have burned through the floor. And they would never think anything more about it.

After all, this was not the United States where authorities had gadgets to sniff the air and endless money to sift all the debris through screens looking for the reason the gas had exploded. By then, the little plastic box in the back would be vaporized, its metal parts, like everything else that was once part of the house, now just pieces of charred junk to be shoveled into the back of a truck and hauled away.

Liquida was putting away his wrench and closing the lid on his small plastic tool container when he heard a noise again. He glanced back at the window. This time there was no car out on the street. The noise came from out near the front door. He listened. Then he heard it again.

He slid the small toolbox into his left pocket, pulled the knife from the other pocket, and punched the levered button on the side of the handle. The needle-sharp blade snapped open.

Liquida stepped silently through the dining room, then cut through the corner of the living room into the entry, where he pressed himself against the wall next to the entrance to a small powder room near the front door. He stood inches off to the side of the entrance, the knife drawn up in his left hand, close to his ear, ready to be thrust the instant the door opened.

Whoever it was didn't have a key. They were scratching at the lock with a pick, working on the wrought-iron gate outside. The gate formed a barrier leading to a small exterior entry area maybe four or five feet square. Once through the gate, whoever was there would be in the shadows of the entry area, free to work on the lock at the front door.

Liquida glanced at the inside of the door. It was solid enough, thick tropical hardwood of some kind, but the lock and handle assembly was cheap and very old. It wouldn't hold for more than a few seconds. Liquida knew this because it was the same way he had entered.

There was a small rectangular viewing port cut at eye level in the wood of the door. The port was open, uncovered on the inside, and protected only by a small brass grid on the outside.

Liquida took a chance and glanced quickly through the opening. The man outside the gate was bent over, looking down, working on the lock. Liquida couldn't see his face but he could see the bald head and broad shoulders. It was the man he had seen crossing the street. Liquida was sure of it.

He pressed his head back against the wall and thought for a moment. He considered the razor-sharp blade in his hand, and weighed it against the size of the man outside. Even if he could kill him, how would he dispose of the body? Authorities wouldn't think twice about a woman who died in her own house in an accidental fire. But an unidentified male who died with her would raise questions. And what about the other man, up at the corner? Was he still there? If he came down to join his big friend in the house after the locks were picked, Liquida would have his hands full.

He listened as the sharp metal worked the lock in the gate outside. If he was going to do anything, he had to do it now. His eyes scoured the entry area for something, anything he could use to drive the man away. But it was the back of Liquida's right arm and his elbow scratching something on the wall behind him that found the answer. He moved quietly away from the wall, turned, and looked down. There was a plastic cover plate and two light switches mounted on the wall between the front door and the door to the bathroom. He leaned into the bathroom and checked the wall inside with his right hand. There was no switch on the wall. Liquida guessed that the switch on the right, outside the door, was for the light in the bathroom. The other switch had to be an entry light. There was no overhead light in the interior entry itself, just a floor lamp in one corner. It was possible that the switch turned on the lamp.

Liquida eased over and looked through the port in the front door one more time, just as the locked bolt snapped open on the metal gate. There was an overhead light in the ceiling of the entry area outside. Liquida reached over and flipped the switch.

"Oh, shit!"

Liquida heard the tinkle of metal on the concrete walkway out front, and then footsteps as the man retreated from the wrought-iron gate.

Liquida smiled. In his panic the big one had dropped his lock pick. He listened as the loud sound of rubber soles slapping concrete on the street diminished into the distance toward the dark stairs at the dead end of the street.

By the time he turned off the entrance light and opened the front door, the man had disappeared into the darkness. Liquida could still hear the faint sound of the man's heavy footfalls as he ran. He waited several seconds, until the sounds disappeared in the distance. Then he swung open the gate and stepped out onto the sidewalk, under the streetlight. He looked down, then stooped to the cement and pinched the tiny lock pick between his fingers. He stood up and looked in the other direction, toward the corner where he had seen the two men talking earlier. The other guy was gone. Or else he was hiding around the corner. Liquida figured he couldn't have gotten far. If they had a car it would be in the other direction, where the big man ran when the light went on. Instinct would drive him toward safety. And there was no way for his friend to have joined him. Liquida had him cut off.

He moved quickly back into the house. This time he didn't bother to lock or even close the gate behind him. He wouldn't be there that long.

FORTY

As Herman works the lock, I stand at the corner. It's taking longer than I thought it would, and my attention begins to wander.

As I look around, I suddenly realize that if things go bad, there are no yards to hide in or fences that can be jumped easily. As far as I can see, in every direction the buildings all butt up against one another. There are a few gated side yards and two high iron fences, but all of them are guarded by large rolls of razor wire coiled and stretched along the top.

I look away and am thinking that they must have a problem with home security in Costa Rica when suddenly I hear Herman's voice saying something unpleasant.

By the time I look back, Herman is moving away from the gate. The next thing I know, he turns, running in full flight, down the street and away from me, toward the darkness and the stairs at the other end.

I can't tell what has happened. My first instinct is to follow him. Herman must have managed to pick the lock, because the gate at the front of the house is open just slightly. Then I notice the hand gripping one of the wrought-iron bars.

Without even thinking I seem to levitate back around the corner until I find myself on one knee, peeking around the stucco siding. Whoever is coming out of the house is now between Herman and me. There is no way I can follow Herman, and nowhere to hide.

It was, of course, possible that the two men had selected this house under the bright streetlight, and this night, for a random burglary. But Liquida was never one to embrace coincidence. It was the reason he had stayed alive so long.

To Liquida there was only one other person who knew he would be here, his employer. He had taken pains to inform the man that because of previous commitments, he wouldn't be able to make it to the woman's house in San José until the following evening. He remembered because his employer, the man in Colombia, wrote back to confirm this.

By now I am down on my stomach on the sidewalk, peering with one eye around the corner of the building across the street, watching the entrance to Katia's house.

My mind is racing. All I can see is the hand gripping the iron bar on the gate. If it is a woman, it might be Katia's mother. It is possible she has arrived home and Harry was wrong. Perhaps her cell phone is out of order.

If she steps out onto the sidewalk, if I could be sure it's her, I might take a chance and approach her, try to introduce myself in the hope that somehow she might have gotten word that her daughter is in trouble in the States.

I'm hoping that her English might be better than my Spanish when the gate suddenly opens and a man steps out. He is lit from head to toe under the blaring gaze of the streetlight, looking the other way, toward the dark end of the street where Herman has disappeared.

I'm studying him when suddenly and without warning he turns and looks directly at the corner of the building where I am hiding. I pull my head back close to the edge of the house and hold my breath. I can't be sure if he's seen me. If he hasn't, it is only because I am close to the ground and his eyes are searching up higher. Still, I have the feeling, the way he snaps his head in my direction and looks over here, that somehow he knows I am here.

It is possible he might be one of Rhytag's agents, but not likely. If the FBI is camped in the house, perhaps with the assistance of the Costa Rican police, they would have allowed Herman to enter and then bagged him to find out what he was after.

Katia never mentioned any male residents in the house. So who the hell is he? I take a chance. With my chin on the concrete, I edge toward the corner of the building until my right eye clears it. The man is bent over, picking something up off the ground. Then he suddenly disappears, back into the house. But he doesn't close the gate, he leaves it ajar, which means he's coming back.

I stand up and start to collect my thoughts, realizing that if he comes this way, I'm going to be out on the sidewalk all alone, with nowhere to hide. I try to check off in my mind the routes on the map that would take me back to the Sportsmens Lodge.

I could turn and run down the street behind me. It's

well lit. At the next corner, if I turn right and run another block, by the time I got to the end of the street I
should be almost at the front entrance to the lodge.
That's if I read the map correctly. If the FBI was set up
out in front, they couldn't miss me.

Or I could go in the opposite direction, across the
street and up one block. I know with certainty what lies
in that direction: the fence that bounds the zoo and the
winding lane that runs alongside it. It would be dark as
pitch, but if I followed the lane it would loop around
and take me past the stairs at the other end of Katia's
street, where Herman disappeared. Retrace my steps a
few hundred yards farther on and I would come to the
green door at the back of the Sportsmens Lodge.

Without thinking twice I bolt across the street and
dodge behind the corner of the house on the other side.
I stop for a second to catch my breath and try to dismiss
the thought that he might have been watching through
one of the windows when I broke cover.

Liquida moved quickly to straighten up the last few
items in the kitchen as his mind continued to nibble at
the notion that the man who hired him had tried to set
him up.

Of course, this was not necessarily a surprise. Liquida never trusted any of the people he worked for.
After all, they were not saints, or even the distant relatives of saints. They were hiring him to kill others who
had become inconvenient to them. The only saving grace
was that for the most part the victims were no better
than the people who hired Liquida to kill them. Of
course, this was not exactly something to commend you
for membership in the local Rotary Club. And it always

begged the question of whether Liquida himself might be seen as an inconvenience at some point. This had happened only twice. The two wayward employers could now be found residing in the northern desert of Mexico; that is, if you knew where to dig.

But to Liquida this was no sign that he was narrow-minded. He could understand if they were trying to eliminate him for reasons of business, to silence him because he knew too much or perhaps even to avoid payment. Mind you, he would kill in a Mexican minute any employer harboring such notions. Still, he could understand their motives.

But the current customer, the man in Colombia, was a different case. Liquida had good reason to dislike him. The man was arrogant, and it showed. Even though Liquida sensed that the interpreter had tried to dull the sting of insults from his master's words, he could not conceal them. In all of his communications the employer had talked down to Liquida. He had accused him of incompetence for missing the woman at the house that night and for compounding this error by having her arrested for the murder of the man Pike. It was not Liquida's fault that the woman had picked that night to run. And still the employer had never forgiven him, even after he had fixed the problem during the ambush of the sheriff's bus.

He finished cleaning up and snatched the two items he had left behind on the countertop, the remote control and the woman's camera with the photographs. Another task done for which Liquida was certain there would be no appreciation.

He'd had to turn the house upside down looking for the camera. But he had found it. Who the hell leaves a camera on a shelf in the laundry room? He had already checked the images in the camera's view screen. The pictures were still there inside, the same ones Liquida had seen on the computer screen the night he killed the man at the photo lab in Virginia. He had done everything he was asked to do and he had done it well. And in the morning, when the woman's mother arrived home, she would be greeted by Liquida and his carefully prepared accident. What more could the man in Colombia ask?

This man had no appreciation of the work Liquida had done. Now he had sent two of his minions to set him up. Liquida would teach him a lesson he would not soon forget. He hurried toward the front door and the open gate while there was still time.

I am still at the corner catching my breath, trying to guess the distance to the lodge from here, perhaps a mile, maybe more, when I hear the slam of the metal gate.

I sneak a look. The guy is back outside, down on one knee at the gate. On the sidewalk next to him are some items. At this distance I can't make out what they are.

He doesn't have a key. He is working the lock the same way Herman had, and seems to be talking to himself as he does it. I can almost hear his voice. It is as if he's arguing with someone. He was no FBI agent, that was certain. And his chances of being a social guest diminish considerably as I watch him pick the lock on the gate to close up. I don't know if he is more skilled than Herman, but I have to admit he is faster, which probably means that he's had more practice.

He is finishing up, putting the pick back in a container. I start to look around for places to hide. If he walks this way, I am in trouble. There is a car parked at the curb, maybe forty feet behind me; some thin, straggly bushes; and a long-abandoned, rusted set of railroad tracks across the street.

I stand up, and when I peer around the corner again he has finished and is on his feet. He gathers the objects from the sidewalk and, just when I think I might have to run, he turns away and walks in the opposite direction, down the street and away from me. I step away from the corner, take a deep breath, and hold my chest. Harry was right. I should have stayed home.

Then it strikes me that maybe he is going after Herman. If he is, he is taking his time. Just when I think I have it knocked, I hear a car door slam and then an engine start, and before I look around the corner, the screech of tires. The beam of the headlights nearly catches me looking around the edge of the building. He is screaming up the street directly at me.

I turn and run as fast as I can for the car at the curb. I know I have no chance.

When I turn back and look, he is stopped at the corner, gunning the engine and hitting the brake, inching forward in jumps, looking the other way. I glimpse the back of his head as I dive for the gutter behind the parked car.

The few seconds as he looked the wrong way were the difference. By the time he turned to look toward me, I was already in the deep gully where the paved road dipped down to meet the high curb of the sidewalk. As I lie hiding in the shadows, looking through the slight gap between the rear tire and the curb, I see his face. He scans the sidewalk in my direction as far as he can, and then turns his eyes on the car I am hiding behind. He studies the windshield for a long moment, takes out a small flashlight, and shoots the beam toward the front of the car. I duck down as best I can, trying to make myself smaller to hide behind the rear wheel.

I can't see him any longer, but I can see the tires of his car as they move out into the intersection and turn this way. The wheels inch forward as pieces of loose gravel pop under the weight and the friction of his tires. I can hear the muted sounds of salsa as it plays on the radio inside his car. I slide forward on my stomach under the car as his wheels roll slowly this way. He edges in close, along the side of the car.

I glance back. My feet have just passed under the rear bumper as I continue to wiggle forward. I hear the slight hum of the electric motor and whish of the glass as the driver's side window rolls down. The brassy sound and beat of salsa spills out all over the street. The music drowns out any noise I might make as I inch forward under the car.

I know what he is doing. He is peering through the side windows with his flashlight, checking the car's interior, making sure there is no one inside. If I could only get him to move a few blocks away and try it again, he might be greeted by the flash of nine-millimeter muzzles and the FBI. Something tells me there is a connection here if I could only figure it out.

He rolls forward a few inches. A second later the sound of the music diminishes as the window closes. If he keeps going forward and looks in his mirror, or drives to the corner and turns around, I am dead. He would see me silhouetted under the car, backlit by the overhead lights down the street.

As this thought enters my brain, he guns the engine. His rear wheels squeal. My nostrils fill with the acrid odor of burnt rubber as his car chatters sideways for half a beat before it shoots back down the street in reverse. He throws the rear end into the opening at Katia's street and in a single fluid motion makes a three-point turn and speeds off in the other direction. I watch as his brake lights flare at the next intersection. He slows for a few seconds and looks in both directions, down to the right toward the Sportsmens Lodge, and up to the left toward the hospital.

The brake lights dim and he shoots straight ahead, down the hill. The road curves to the right and he disappears around the bend.

I crawl out from under the car. I don't stop to brush off my clothes. Instead I begin to run faster and faster into the darkness under the trees near the fence at the zoo. My heart is pounding. I turn and fall against the chain link, leaning with all of my weight as I catch my breath. Then I make my way slowly in the dark along the twisting lane. I can't run, though I want to. In the pitch-black under the shadows of the trees, I would break my neck.

I am passing the first intersection when suddenly I see the lights of a vehicle winding its way along the lane, coming toward me. I look for somewhere to hide. There are some scrub bushes along the fence near the gnarled trunk of a eucalyptus tree. I make my way to the tree and position myself between the trunk and the fence and watch the headlights, trying to keep the tree between myself and the twin beams of light as the car approaches.

It isn't until the flare of the bright light is past me that I can see the windows of the taxi and Herman in the backseat with the window down and looking out the other side.

"Herman! Here." I step out into the street.

"*Alto. Aquí*," says Herman.

The taxi driver throws on the brakes.

I run up along the right side of the car and get in the front seat. "Go," I tell him. A second later we are moving.

"I waited for ya at the top of the stairs," says Herman. "I saw the guy come outside. Then when he went in I saw you run across the street. But I wasn't sure how to get to you. I figured the best way was to get a cab. Is he still at the house?"

"No."

"Who was he?"

"I don't know."

"What did you see?"

"A visitation from the angel of death," I tell him.

"What do you mean?"

"I saw him up close for only an instant. He was behind a car window. But it was a face I won't forget. It was pockmarked, one side of it, not the usual adolescent acne. It was something more sinister. Maybe smallpox or fire scarred, I couldn't tell."

"Funny you should say that. When I was at the gate working on the lock, I had a real edgy feeling, like somebody or something was lookin' at me, and not just lookin', if you know what I mean."

"I know what you mean." I don't tell Herman, but the reason I couldn't look more closely at his face was because my focus was drawn to something in the eyes. It is hard to explain, something you have to see to understand, a kind of reflection of evil.

I have seen that look before. As a young prosecutor in Capitol City, I had sent someone with those same haunted eyes to prison. He was a man who had killed many times, and according to the doctors, he liked to do it, and given the chance would do it again. I remember some years later I stood on the riser and looked through the blinds, through the plate-glass window of a green metal room. I watched as the demons were drawn and exorcised from the eyes of Brian Danley, in the fog of the San Quentin gas chamber.

FORTY-ONE

The uranium projectile suddenly toppled from the muzzle of the gun. Instinctively Tomas reached out with his gloved right hand and caught it in midflight. But at arm's length, reaching across the table, he couldn't hold the weight.

The projectile's leverage and the momentum of its fall forced his hand down until his fingers were suddenly pinched between the heavy, falling uranium slug and its fissile target.

Tomas pulled the projectile back toward his chest as the air in the room ignited in a brilliant violet light. It rippled in waves and hues of blue that Tomas had never before seen. The heat was intense. It burned his fingers right through the gloves, but Tomas was so dazzled by the radiance that he didn't notice. As the glow from the agitated molecules of air evaporated, the heat sapped the energy from his body.

He looked down and realized he was holding the enriched uranium against his chest. He carefully laid the projectile on the table, as far from the target as he could.

Then he turned and walked out the door to where Nitikin and the other man were standing.

When Yakov turned and saw him, Tomas had already lifted the protective hood from his head. His face was running with a river of sweat. Other than that, he looked fine. He was animated, smiling and laughing, like a soccer goalie who has just blocked a free kick.

He assured Nitikin that the projectile had not struck the uranium target. He had saved it, but his fingers had been pinched in the process.

Tomas did not seem to comprehend the flash of blue light and the intense heat that was still sending rising vapors of smoke off of his suit. He told Yakov that everything was all right, then lifted his right arm to pull off his glove.

Tomas stopped in midstride and looked at his hand. There was nothing left of the first three fingers but charred stumps.

Yakov reached him the instant before he collapsed. He laid him on the ground and helped him take off his suit. He hollered at Alim's man, the one holding the ramrod, to help him. But the man just stood there shaking his head.

Alim and the rest of his cadre remained off in the trees, at least a hundred meters away. Yakov told the man with the ramrod to put on Tomas's suit, that he would need his assistance. When the man didn't understand, Nitikin gestured with his hands, sign language, to put it on.

The man looked at him and slowly shook his head as he backed away. Yakov yelled into the trees and a couple of seconds later he heard Alim's commanding voice speaking in Farsi. The man looked to the trees, then back at Nitikin with a kind of trapped expression on his face. Reluctantly he stepped forward and began to put on the suit.

Nitikin hollered assurances to the translator off in the jungle, asking him to tell the man that there was no longer anything to fear. With the proper tools, Nitikin could now complete the assembly quickly and safely. They would be finished in a matter of minutes. The translation came back and the man nodded. What the Russian didn't tell them was that Alim's man, who was now donning the suit, was already dead. The lifetime body burden of radiation was far exceeded by his naked exposure to the wicked tail of the dragon.

Together they entered the hut. The radiation had elevated the temperature inside the room to the point that they could not remain more than two or three minutes.

Yakov had the man steady the barrel of the cannon, his bare fingers projecting through the holes burned into the right-hand glove. Nitikin retrieved the projectile with the tongs. In less than a minute, using the ramrod, Yakov seated the uranium bullet securely down the barrel of the gun.

It took another thirty seconds to insert the safety disk of uranium-238, the neutron deflector, into the slot between the end of the gun barrel and the target. Once in place, the disk of uranium-238 began doing its job. It bounced the wandering neutrons from the two elements of highly enriched uranium, the projectile and the target, back to their respective sources, instantly reducing the gain in radiation. Nitikin heard the rapid clicking from the Geiger counter on the table suddenly fall off sharply.

The safety disk of U-238 was attached to a rigid piece of steel wire. The wire protruded through a tiny hole in the side of the bomb case. A quarter-twist of the wire in a clockwise direction locked the safety disk in place. Anyone trying to remove the disk without first twisting the wire in a counterclockwise direction would snap the brittle connection between the safety disk and the wire, rendering the bomb useless. The gun would fire. The cordite explosion would destroy the barrel and bomb housing, but there would be no nuclear chain reaction. Even radioactive fallout would be minimal and generally contained to any structure the device was in.

Properly turned and pulled, the wire would slide the disk from its slot, leaving the pathway clear for the projectile to be fired into the uranium target.

The only procedure more delicate than removing the safety disk was replacing it if the need ever arose. With the bomb housing closed, it would be impossible to see the disk or the slot into which it should slide. With only the rigid wire to manipulate the disk, replacing it in the slot was a matter of trial and error. It required the deft fingers and touch of a surgeon. Even Nitikin was not sure if he could do this any longer, though in his youth, in training, he had accomplished it twice on dummy mockups of the warhead.

Having locked the safety disk in place, it took less than a minute to seal the lead-lined bomb case and render the device safe.

As the two men stepped from the building, Alim's man lifted the hood from his head and smiled with a toothy grin as the expression of relief flooded his sweaty face.

Nitikin had no way of measuring the dose of radiation emitted by the ionizing blue flare. But he knew that Tomas and the smiling lad he was now looking at were both dead.

The old Russian hovered over Tomas's bed for four days and five nights. During this entire period, neither Yakov nor the FARC physicians could do much to comfort the young Colombian.

An ocean of water could not satisfy his thirst, even if he could keep it down. He was wretched with nausea, vomited constantly, and passed bloody diarrhea as the radiation began to kill his body from within.

After three days, Tomas's fingernails turned black. His thick, dark hair fell from his head in patches so that a nurse had to brush it from his pillow every few hours, into a box that was to be buried somewhere in a deep hole. Open sores developed around his mouth and eyes. When the doctor lifted the sheet, he realized that these bloody sores covered Tomas's entire body.

Nitikin could not even touch him for fear of further infecting his wounds, though the Russian knew there was no hope. The end was near. A high fever set in on the fourth day as infection began to take its toll. Tomas struggled for every breath as his airway swelled and his lungs filled with fluid. Just after midnight on the fifth day, Tomas suddenly went into convulsions. He arched his back as if a steel spring had snapped in his body. He shook the entire bed for almost a minute and then went limp.

Yakov noticed that in his stillness, Tomas was no longer struggling for breath. He didn't have to wait for the doctor to check his pulse or put the stethoscope to

Tomas's ulcerated chest to know he was dead. He stood and slowly covered Tomas's face with the bedsheet.

Tomas may not have understood entirely what he was doing, but Nitikin knew that his quick reactions and nimble fingers had averted a nuclear disaster that could have lit up the jungle and killed them all.

"Excuse me, but Mr. Hinds is on the phone with a client. If you'll wait a moment—"

"Officer, if she gets in the way again, arrest her."

Harry was on the phone, but he recognized the voice outside his office door. A second later it opened.

"Listen, I'm going to have to get back to you," said Harry.

Before Harry could hang up the phone, Templeton was standing on the other side of his desk, backed up by a hefty sheriff's deputy, muscle in a uniform, and one of the homicide detectives in Katia's case. The detective had his arm in the air, holding a sheaf of folded papers as if it was a cocked pistol and the Dwarf was about to level the muzzle on Harry.

"We're going to have to continue this later. I'll call you. Yeah, yeah…call you this afternoon." Harry hung up the phone.

The detective slapped the papers on the desk in front of him. "Consider yourself served."

"What's this about?"

"Search warrant," said Templeton. "Bring some of those boxes in here!" he hollered to whoever was outside the door. Harry's secretary, standing in the doorway, nearly got run over by the hand truck being pushed by one of the deputies, followed by another cop. The dolly was loaded with flattened cardboard boxes. They began unfolding and assembling the boxes on the floor, using packing tape and a tape gun to bind the bottoms.

"Why don't you tell me what this is about?" By now Harry was standing behind the desk fumbling with the papers.

"Read the warrant," said Templeton. "Sergeant, anything with the name Solaz on it, box it and seal it for review. If you have questions about anything, ask me. You!" He pointed to one of the other deputies. "Get some of those boxes and follow me." Templeton headed out of the office.

Harry, who was still trying to read the documents, followed him out of the office and joined the parade headed down the hall. There were three more deputies outside in the reception area already boxing up files from the filing cabinets.

"Wait, wait wait. What are they doing?" said Harry. "They can't reach in and take the files out of the cabinets."

"You want us to roll the cabinets out and put them on the truck, that's fine by me," said Templeton, still walking.

"I'm going to have to ask you to have your staff leave the office until we're done collecting everything. Then they can come back," said Templeton.

"Why don't you stop for a second so we can talk about this?" said Harry.

"Time for talk is over." Templeton breezed through the open door of Paul's office, reached up on the wall, and flipped the light switch. "You can start with the desk," he told one of the cops. "No. No. On second thought I think I'd rather have Detective Howser do that. Gil, get every drawer. Clean it out. You guys can work on the file cabinets, here and the ones outside by the secretaries. And don't forget the bookshelves. Those binders all contain documents. Box 'em up," said Templeton. "Take 'em all."

By now, Harry had devoured the few pages accompanying the search warrant. It had been signed by another judge, not Quinn.

"Wait a minute." Harry saw one of the cops starting to grab binders off the shelves. "Those files have nothing to do with the Solaz case. The warrant is limited to Solaz."

"In that event you'll get 'em back," said Templeton. "Procedure's been set up for a review by a non-taint team and it's been approved by the judge."

"What the hell's a non-taint team?" said Harry.

"You don't know?"

"I've never had my office ransacked before."

"Get those up there. The high ones." Templeton had ignored him and had instead started directing one of the taller deputies, pointing to the top shelf, up near the ceiling, as if he was having the man sweep for cobwebs.

"A non-taint team involves another prosecutor from my office and a detective from homicide, not Detective Howser here, somebody else. They will make up the non-taint team. Neither of them is involved in any way in the Solaz case. They'll look at everything we take and decide whether it's within the scope of the warrant. If it's not, you'll get it back. I can't say exactly when you'll get it back." Templeton quickly looked at Harry over his shoulder and winked at him.

"Those files contain privileged information, lawyer-client," said Harry. "And the clients have nothing to do with Solaz."

"The other prosecutor will decide if any privilege attaches to any of it, lawyer-client or otherwise. If it does, you'll get that back too."

"When, after your office copies it all?" said Harry.

"We represent law enforcement," said Templeton. "I'm shocked."

"Yeah, well you're going to be spreading your shocked little body pretty thin when I drag you in front of half the judges downtown, demanding continuances and dismissals because you're sitting on our files and peeking at our work product in their cases. And while you're at it, you might wanna call the attorney general and tell him to expect an appeal on any case out of our office ending in a conviction in the next four or five years. If he's lucky, there'll simply be a blanket order of reversal on all of them. Save him time," said Harry.

"Guess we'll have to cross that bridge when we get to it. Officer, get . . . yeah, that's it, grab that one up there." Templeton continued to ignore him.

"So that's your procedure? That's it?" said Harry.

"You don't like it, you can always go to court," said Templeton.

"You bet I will."

"But I'd have to warn you, the judge seemed very satisfied with the process."

"I'm sure he was. After all, he used to work for the DA's office," said Harry. "Back then he could only dream about such things."

"I didn't know that." Templeton smiled. "Anyway, the team will look at it and decide what is evidence and what is not."

"Evidence of what?" There was a tone of hesitance as Harry said it.

"That's right, I forgot. You don't know. I'm sorry." For the first time since entering the room, Templeton turned to look at him. "You might want to get on the phone and check with your partner to see if he wants to get outside counsel or whether maybe he wants you to represent him. I wouldn't want to give you any advice on that. But if he wants you to represent him, we can save time and serve you with the other papers right now."

Harry was almost afraid to ask. "What other papers?"

"Let's see, there are warrants for arrest on two counts of first-degree murder, aiding and abetting, breaking and entering, grand larceny, and conspiracy to commit all of the above. Let me think. I don't want to forget anything. We're still weighing the issue of witness tampering, seeing as he was sitting on top of his codefendant and telling her what to say and what not to say."

"He is her lawyer," said Harry.

"Was," said Templeton. "And I'm sure he wasn't going to let that get in his way. And, of course, there is the bus thing."

"What are you talking about?"

"Word on the street is, it was your client who was the target. They're still counting bodies, but if it turns out that your partner was involved, you might want to tell him the stuff on the bus isn't going to be covered by lawyer-client privilege. He can try to argue attorney work product, but I doubt if the judge will buy it."

"You're out of your mind," said Harry.

"All the same, if we tag him on that one, you can expect a lot more paper. Figure a ticker-tape parade," said Templeton.

Harry was getting grim looks from the deputies standing around the desk.

"Oh, yeah! And we'll be adding a fugitive arrest warrant later today, just to add a little international spice."

Harry stood there looking at him.

"Well, do you want to call him and give him the news?" said Templeton. "He'd probably rather hear it from you than read it in the newspaper. Or maybe he doesn't read Spanish? You do know where he is?" Templeton looked at him and waited to see if Harry was going to fess up. When he didn't, the Dwarf said, "You might try Costa Rica. At least according to the airline, that's where his plane landed. You did know he was down there?"

"So what? There were no warrants outstanding when he left," said Harry.

"You might remind him of that and see if you can coax him back. By the way, you wouldn't know how he got out of the country, seeing as the state had placed restrictions on his passport, would you?"

Harry looked at him and just swallowed a little saliva.

"Well?"

"No."

Templeton knew he was lying. He also knew that the federal government had been pushing buttons and pulling levers. The Dwarf had been given the shaft. It didn't take a mind meld to know what was up. Let the horse out of the barn and follow him.

By morning Templeton would have the FBI in a legal headlock. If they were tailing Madriani, once a fugitive warrant was issued for the lawyer's arrest and the FBI received notice, they would be compelled by law to arrest him immediately. The state would then have to arrange extradition. If the FBI failed to take Madriani into custody and he slipped through their fingers, the federal government would have to answer for its conduct in a courtroom and explain to a judge the reason for their actions. In a case of multiple murder, Templeton would be all over them, national security or no national security. The Dwarf would climb on a stump and start pumping out headlines ending in question marks—what was the federal government up to, and why did they allow a multiple murderer to leave the country and then run free?

"Larry." Howser was trying to catch Templeton's attention from the other side of the desk.

"Well, are you going to call him or not?" Templeton's gaze was locked on Harry.

"If I do, I'll let you know," said Harry.

"Larry!" Howser was standing there looking down at the open drawer on the other side of the desk.

"What?" Templeton was aggravated by the interruption.

"I think you better look at this."

He walked around to the other side of the desk. "What is it?"

Howser pointed. "Right there."

At first Templeton didn't say anything, at least not with his lips. Instead the Dwarf stood there looking as if he had just found the original gold nugget at Sutter's Mill.

"Okay. Okay. I want everybody outta here," he said. "Clear the offices. I want everybody outside now. And call the crime lab, tell them to send a van over here right away. I want two CS technicians, and tell them we're gonna need photos."

"What are you talking about?" said Harry.

"Maybe you can tell us how you're gonna explain that?" said Templeton.

"What?" Harry edged his way around the desk.

"That." Templeton was pointing toward a lot of clutter, pens and paper clips, some loose change, rubber bands, and a roll of Scotch tape in a center section of the top drawer of Paul's desk. "Right there."

The second Harry saw it, all the blood seemed to drain from his head. He began to sway. For a moment he thought he might actually fall.

Templeton grabbed his arm as if he could hold him up. "Are you all right?"

"I'm okay. I'm fine," Harry lied.

"I know. I know," said Templeton.

In that moment Harry and the Dwarf seemed to communicate on a level that transcended language. With the evidence he had and the charges he'd brought, it was clear that even Templeton, deep down, harbored nagging doubts that another lawyer could have done this.

But there in front of them in the drawer was one of the bags of catnip. It looked identical to the bags found by the police and photographed, the catnip used to take down the motion sensors in the side yard, the path used by the killer to enter Emerson Pike's house.

FORTY-TWO

had just finished shaving when I stepped from the bathroom and noticed that someone had slipped an envelope under the door to my room at the Sportsmens Lodge. I reached down, grabbed the envelope, and opened it. It was from the front desk, "a message from a Mr. Hinds. You are to call him in San Diego." I knew that Harry wouldn't call the hotel unless it was important. He must have called the cell phone and realized it was turned off.

A few minutes later Herman and I descend into the basement of the Sportsmens Lodge, near the exercise area. The place is deserted except for some of the hotel staff taking care of laundry. Herman watches the stairs while I make the call.

Harry answers the phone on the first ring and doesn't even say hello. "I hope you're sitting down. Let me get outside."

I give him a few seconds to get out of the office so that federal bugs can't pick up the conversation.

"What's wrong?"

"Templeton dropped the world on us early this

morning," says Harry. "He raided the office, seized all the files in Katia's case. There's a warrant out for your arrest."

Even though Harry and I have talked about this, the possibility that Templeton might charge me, the actual news that he has now done it knocks the breath out of me.

"Where are you now?" says Harry.

When I don't answer he says, "Are you there?"

"I'm here." I am swallowing hard.

"Are you still in the hotel?"

"Ye...Ah, yeah. Down, we're, Herman and I, are down in the basement."

"Get your stuff together and get outta there," says Harry. "Do it now."

"First tell me what's happened."

"Trust me. You don't have time to talk," says Harry. "Gather your bags, check out, and don't leave by the front door. Is there another way out?"

"Yeah. Tell me what's going on."

"Templeton knows you're in Costa Rica. He's working on a fugitive warrant. The minute he gets it, he'll bring fire down on the FBI to pick you up. You can bet on it. You were right; he had a hold on your passport, so he's hopping mad. He knows the feds had it lifted. He's already leaking information to the press to turn the heat on Rhytag. I got a phone call from a friend. It's already been on Fox News. San Diego lawyer charged with murder, and the report is that you're hiding out in Costa Rica with federal authorities close on your heels. You've got to move."

"He still has a pretty thin case," I tell him.

"Not after he found the bag of catnip in your desk drawer."

"Oh, shit."

"You might want to think about where it came from," says Harry, "and we can talk about it later."

"I forgot all about it. I found it the day we were out at Pike's house."

"I'm not the one you have to convince," says Harry.

"It was cumulative evidence. The cops already had their own collection of the little white bags, all of them the same. I couldn't see how one, more or less, was going to change anything," I tell him.

"Yeah, well, the Dwarf must have feline DNA in his blood then, because he looked like he wanted to roll in your drawer and have an orgasm when they found the bag there," says Harry. "And one other thing; it seems the cops have been holding back another piece of evidence."

"What evidence?"

"You remember the promotional pens we had made up last year, the plastic ballpoints? We did a batch of them for New Year's, along with the calendars, to give to clients."

"I remember."

"Forensics found one of the pens in the study, underneath Emerson Pike's desk, when they processed the crime scene."

There is a pause on the phone as Harry allows this to sink in. "Are you there?" he says.

"Yes."

"According to their investigative notes, you told the police you'd never been to Pike's house and that neither Pike nor Katia had ever been to our office. So Templeton is dying to know how the pen got there."

My mind is racing with all of this.

"We don't have time to talk about it now. Just get your stuff and get outta there. If the FBI doesn't pick you up, the Costa Rican police will. Get back to Katia's house, find the camera, get the pictures, and scoot. Lose the federal tail and get out of Costa Rica as fast as you can. It's the only chance you've got."

"Herman and I were going to wait until tonight, try one more time after dark."

"You no longer have that luxury," says Harry. He's right.

"I understand. Listen, I'm sorry about the item in the desk drawer."

"Save it for later," says Harry. "Just don't come back here unless you have something solid by way of evidence. Otherwise you and Katia are going down for the count. Do you understand?"

"Yes."

"They'll nail you the second you enter the country. That is if they don't catch up with you down there first. So get moving," says Harry.

"How is she doing?"

"Katia?"

"Yes."

"Don't ask," says Harry. "Just get moving. I don't care what you did, or why you did it, just find whatever you need. And call me tomorrow."

"Harry, listen to me."

"Just keep me posted. Let me know where you are." With that the line goes dead on the other end as Harry hangs up.

Having watched Tomas die, Nitikin decided that he could at least use the lethal dragon's breath to his own advantage. This, as he maneuvered for final leverage with Alim.

Alim Afundi's man, who had retrieved the ramrod against the tree, paid for his effort in agony. He lingered for two more days after Tomas died. He was more distant than Tomas from the source of radiation, but unlike Yakov, he was without the protection of a lead-lined suit. It was the reason Yakov had selected him to help finish the job. Nitikin knew the man was dead the moment he felt the heat of the ionizing flash.

Alim wanted to use the expedience of a quick bullet to end the man's pain, but he was facing a small rebellion. The dying man's brother was part of Afundi's group, and Alim had resorted to his pistol as the tool of command once too often. To shoot another of his followers, even under the guise of putting the man out of his misery, might inspire thoughts of mutiny among his dwindling band.

Now that the bomb was assembled, Afundi needed to move the device and do it quickly. Instead they were forced to sit and watch as his follower died on his own clock, bleeding from every orifice.

Nitikin could read the anxiety in Alim's eyes. Yakov had never been informed as to the final target, but he knew that Alim was running out of time. During the weeks of preparation the Russian had picked up bits of information from friends in the FARC and subtle signals from Alim himself. He knew that the device was to be shipped, at least partway, by sea inside a container that had been specially lined with lead. Yakov had seen the container. It was ready to go.

He also knew that the container was to be transferred from a small coastal freighter to a larger ocean-going ship at the port of Panama City. Nitikin had been told by one of his FARC comrades that a fax had been received from a shipping company in Panama and that the transfer was to take place in three days. This did not leave Afundi much time. If his man did not die today, Yakov knew that Alim would have to find some excuse to clear the hospital room by nightfall so that he could smother the man with a pillow.

Nitikin picked this moment to enter the sweaty death room where Alim's man lay dying. He caught the eye of the interpreter and motioned him with a finger. Alim got up and followed the interpreter as they both approached the Russian.

"I want you to give them a message," said Nitikin. He gestured toward Alim's men. "Tell them that the device now contains a safety mechanism and that it will not be armed and cannot be detonated until this mechanism is removed. You can tell them that the device is now completely safe."

The interpreter whispered the message to Alim, who nodded and smiled. This was good news, something to quell the fear of his men as they watched their comrade die.

In a forceful voice the interpreter delivered the message to Alim's men. The four remaining men nodded, and three of them offered up reassured smiles.

Nitikin now finished the message. "They must understand that only I can remove the safety mechanism, and that can only be done after the device is transported to its final target. It would not be safe to move the device otherwise." He waited and watched.

This time when the interpreter whispered in Farsi to Alim, Afundi did not smile. Instead he said something to the interpreter and gestured that he wanted to step outside, presumably to discuss the matter with Nitikin there.

Yakov refused to budge from the door. "Tell them." His voice was raised a full octave and several decibels in volume.

Alim glanced over his shoulder and realized the men were watching. He could tell by the looks on their faces, they knew something was wrong. Afundi looked at the interpreter, his lips drawn and tight. There was nothing he could do. The Russian had boxed him in. He nodded. Then he studied his men as they listened to the translation, the rasping breath of their dying comrade as background. They looked at each other for a moment and then began to whisper among themselves. Alim walked over and joined them. They talked for a few more seconds. Alim patted one of them on the shoulder as he smiled and spoke to them. He was doing PR. He needed them to move the bomb, and Yakov knew it.

After a few more words with his men, Alim looked at Nitikin and said something in Farsi. "They understand. What you say is acceptable to them," said the translator.

The words did not square with the livid expression that flashed in Afundi's eyes at this moment. But the Russian didn't care. He had gambled on the superstition of Alim's men. They wanted someone between themselves and the demon that belched blue fire from the hut in the jungle. Of the three men in close proximity, only Nitikin had survived to tame the beast. Surely they had to wonder whether the dragon's egg he had hidden all these years returned the favor by declining to take the life of its sentinel and guardian.

FORTY-THREE

So what do I tell them?" Thorpe was already on the phone from FBI headquarters to Rhytag at Justice. A reporter from the Associated Press had already called wanting to know if it was true that a San Diego lawyer wanted for murder was on the lam in Costa Rica and the FBI was about to make an arrest.

"What did you tell them so far?" said Rhytag.

"I didn't take the call. I had my secretary tell them I was busy."

"Tell them no comment," said Rhytag. "Tell them it's a matter under investigation and that we don't discuss active investigations."

"That'll hold 'em for a while," said Thorpe. "But we have to make a decision. Do we pick him up or do we continue to tail him?"

Rhytag had to think about this for a few seconds. "Damn it. We should have handled the state's prosecutor with a little more diplomacy."

"We could let him in on it, tell him about Nitikin and the device," said Thorpe.

"It's too late for that. Templeton's already gone to the

press. They're not going to let it go now. If Templeton suddenly backs off, the media is going to want to know why. You don't allow someone under a fugitive arrest warrant for two murders to wander free unless there's a reason," said Rhytag.

"We can tell them we're still looking," said Thorpe.

"Except for one thing; the Costa Rican authorities already know we have Madriani under surveillance. They don't know why, but sooner or later word is going to get out that we had him on a string. Then all hell is gonna break loose. And what if he slips the tail?"

"You've got a point there," said Thorpe.

"You do know where he is?"

"We're in contact with our agents down there now. He's still in his hotel room. No one has seen them yet this morning. We posted one of our agents inside in the restaurant just a few minutes ago."

"I take it there was no word from your people on where he might be headed or what he's doing down there?"

"Not yet," said Thorpe. "We did get a line on the other defendant's house, Solaz. One of our resident agents called in the location. It's only a few blocks from the hotel where Madriani is staying."

"Then that's a definite possibility," said Rhytag.

"We had one of the agents go by the place just after nine this morning. He rang the doorbell but nobody answered. We've had it checked out before and the place is deserted. The mother's not there. We had the local authorities run a background check on her. She has no record."

There were a few moments of silence. "Your call," said Thorpe. "What do we do?"

Rhytag thought about it, fumed, and then said, "Pick him up."

"What about the other guy?"

"There's no warrant out on him," said Rhytag. "Let him go, but keep a tail on him. But we can't afford to take any more chances with Madriani."

"We can try and hold him down there for a few days, sweat him for information in a Costa Rican jail," said Thorpe. "If we're lucky, his lawyer may refuse to waive extradition, turn him into a legal piñata."

"I don't want to know about it," said Rhytag. "Just do what you have to."

Liquida was so angry this morning that he would have to restrain himself to keep from cutting the woman's throat when she arrived home. The previous afternoon he had tried to transfer funds from his savings account in San Diego to his ATM account under the name of John Waters, only to find out that the account was frozen. Somehow Katia Solaz's lawyers had found Liquida's bank account. How they had done this he didn't know. He should never have sold the coin. The old man must have talked. What was worse, the lawyers had placed a hold on the gold ingots Liquida had stored in the safe-deposit box. The woman at the bank assured him that no one had opened the box, but they had scheduled a hearing and invited Mr. Waters to attend. There was no chance of that happening. The critics were right. The U.S. banking system was a mess. What the hell good was a bank if you couldn't get at your own money without robbing it?

For the moment he tried to put it out of his mind as he planned the last details for the woman's arrival home. He had covered all the bases. But he still didn't trust his employer in Colombia. He had double-checked to make sure that the woman would arrive home alone. Her companions, the two FARC attendants who were to escort her, would be delayed in Medellín until Liquida had finished the job in San José.

When the front doorbell rang, it scared the hell out of him. Liquida had been sitting quietly in the living room reading a newspaper, waiting, like the spider for the fly.

He knew it couldn't be the owner of the house. She would have used her key and let herself in. He glanced at his watch. Her flight from Medellín, through Panama City and then to San José, wasn't scheduled to land at the airport for another forty minutes.

Liquida set the newspaper aside and silently slipped across the living room toward the front door.

Whoever was there was impatient. They rang the bell once more before he could even get to the door.

The bright morning sunlight outside and the darkness of the entry allowed Liquida to steal a glance through the peephole in the door without being seen. There was a man standing outside the wrought-iron gate. He was wearing a dark blue suit and striped tie. Fair skinned, he was tall, with brown hair. The fingers of his right hand played with the closed button on his suit coat as he stood there looking down at his shoes.

The man had a look of impatience about him. He punched the bell one more time, silently chafing because no one was answering. To Liquida, he smacked of authority, but not Costa Rican. If he was *policía*, he was *norteamericano*, thought Liquida. What was he doing here?

The Mexican stood silently off to the side of the door as the bell rang two more times. "Come on, answer!"

He could hear the man whispering to himself.

"Looks like nobody's home." This time the voice came from somewhere farther off.

"Looks like it," the man at the gate shouted back.

"Come on, let's go."

The guy at the gate turned and walked away.

Liquida quickly tiptoed into the dining room and climbed the stairs to the first landing, where he watched from the window as the stranger crossed the street and leaned into the open passenger-side window of a large dark Town Car parked at the curb on the other side. The man talked to whoever was behind the wheel for several seconds.

Liquida was sure he was not one of the men he had seen the other night, certainly not the man at the gate with the pick, and the build was wrong for his friend, who Liquida had seen standing at the corner.

Suddenly the man lifted his head out of the car and looked back at the house.

Liquida leaned away from the window wondering if somehow the guy had sensed that there was someone inside. His mind quickly turned to alternatives, finding some other way out and postponing his meeting with the woman, when he heard the engine start and the car door slam.

By the time Liquida looked out, the big black sedan was backing up the street at full speed, toward the corner. It backed into the intersection taking the turn. The car shifted into forward and a second later it was gone.

Liquida stood at the window looking in both directions along the street. There were cars parked at the curb, mostly on the other side. All of them appeared to be empty. Liquida had entered the house quickly, standing at the gate as if he had a key, using his pick. He was certain the house was not being watched. Still, for a place that was supposedly deserted, there were entirely too many visitors to make it feel comfortable.

He glanced at his watch again. Then he headed down the steps, through the dining room and into the kitchen. He picked up a small brown glass bottle from the counter where it rested on top of a thick piece of folded cotton cloth. Liquida held the bottle to the light. He had already checked it twice. He wanted to be sure there was enough ether left inside to do the job. He satisfied himself once more, then put the bottle back down on top of the cloth and began pacing the floor. He was hoping the plane wasn't late, or God forbid, that she had missed her connecting flight in Panama.

FORTY-FOUR

"Two minutes, *señor*, to get my men into position at the back of the hotel." The Costa Rican lieutenant was in uniform, talking in English to the FBI agent standing on the street next to him, and then in Spanish into the microphone clipped to the shoulder loop of his shirt as he gave instructions to his officers strung out around the Sportsmens Lodge.

"Take your time. They're not going anywhere." One of the FBI agents was assembling some forms from a briefcase in the backseat of the black SUV parked across the street from the front entrance to the lodge.

His partner checked the clip in his .357 Sig Sauer, then slid it back into the handle of the pistol, slapped it home, and pulled the slide back, chambering the first round.

"¿Señor?"

"Yes?"

"Are you expecting them to be armed? My men will need to know."

"Not as far as we know. Oh, you mean the gun?" said the agent. "That's just force of habit. I doubt that they're armed. Can't give you any guarantees, of course, but the suspect is a lawyer."

"¿*Abogado*?"

"*Sí.*"

"He's charged with murder," said the agent in the car. "Tell your people not to take any chances."

"What about the other man? The big one."

"The other man is an employee. We believe he's a private investigator. We simply want to detain him to keep him out of the way. We have no warrant on him. Just make sure he doesn't get in the way. We'll let him go when we're done."

"He is very big," said the lieutenant.

"Yes."

The Costa Rican slowly moved away with his hand pressed to the microphone clipped on his shoulder. He turned his head and spoke into it again.

A few seconds later one of the cops near the gate at the hotel's front entrance lifted his twelve-gauge shotgun and worked the pump, loading the first round of double-ought shot. The weapon was an ugly thing with a pistol grip where the shoulder stock should have been.

Following my conversation with Harry, Herman and I packed quickly. We wait just inside the glass door leading to the bar until the help goes into the kitchen. Then we hustle through the bar and down the steps to the green wooden door at the back of the Sportsmens Lodge.

We don't stop to pay the bill. Everything was on the credit card. We were booked through that night. So as far as we are concerned, they can charge it.

We are out the door and down the street, hauling our

luggage less than five minutes after I hung up with Harry. At least in daylight it would be easy to find the steps leading up to Katia's street. We will have one more shot to get the camera and the pictures, then either way I would have to run. Off to Colombia without a lead. The way we planned it, Herman would stick around, maybe wait for Katia's mother and make another attempt to find the camera if he thought it would do any good.

This morning the lion at the zoo isn't growling. He is probably asleep, something I hadn't had much of the night before. Thoughts of the man with the pockmarked face kept me awake.

"I'm missin' one of my picks," says Herman. "Think I dropped it last night."

We were walking quickly, both of us breathing hard.

"Can you open the gate without it?"

"Think so. I'm gonna have to," said Herman. "Just hoping there's not too many people out on the street. If neighbors see what we're doin', they're gonna call the cops. Where do you wanna stash the stuff?" Herman is talking about the luggage.

"I was thinking we might put it behind that tree, near the fence where I was hiding last night when you pulled up in the taxi."

"Good," says Herman. "Let's hope nobody sees it."

Just like clockwork the woman showed up, right on time.

As she walked through the front door carrying her suitcase and purse, Liquida stepped out of the dark bathroom just off the entry. He cupped the ether-soaked cloth over her mouth and nose as he wrapped his other arm around her and lifted her off the floor. She struggled for maybe ten seconds before she went limp.

He kept the cloth over her face for about ten more seconds to make sure she was out cold. Then he carried her to the kitchen and laid her body on the floor in front of the stove before returning to the entry. He glanced at the gate. She hadn't had a chance to lock it. Liquida left it that way. He simply closed the front door. He left her suitcase where it was, just inside the entry. This way it would look as if she'd returned home, smelled the fumes, gone into the kitchen to investigate, and been overcome by the propane before the explosion and fire killed her.

He went back into the kitchen and arranged her body on the floor with just enough artistry to make it look natural. He would have picked her up and dropped her but Liquida was afraid that the neighbors might hear the noise through the common wall next door and come to see what had happened.

He unscrewed the cap from the small brown bottle, turned his head away, and soaked the cloth in more ether. He emptied the bottle. The odor was making Liquida light-headed. He quickly threaded the cap back on the bottle and laid the dripping cloth over the woman's mouth and nose. This way there was no chance that the anesthetic would wear off. He used ether instead of chloroform because ether was highly flammable. By the time the fire department found the body, there would be nothing left of the cloth.

He put the brown bottle in his pocket, stepped back a few feet, and checked the body positioning one last time. Liquida wanted to make sure she would get the full effect of the fiery blast. Then he picked up the model airplane remote control from the countertop and pressed the button.

This turned the tiny servomotor opening the valve. Propane began to leak from the stove. He had already extinguished all the pilot lights on the burners to guard against any accident, a premature fire that might only smoke up the place. He listened for several seconds. After he was satisfied that the propane was flowing nicely, he pressed the other button setting the electronic timer. As the propane fumes spilled out into the lower level of the house, the clock was now running. In twenty minutes the tiny electronic chip operating the timer would trigger the spark emitter and the blast would rattle the entire block.

Herman is right. In the bright morning sunshine, leaning against the gate and picking the lock, we may as well take our clothes off and do it naked. Anyone who sees us is going to call the cops. We aren't even up the block to Katia's house yet and I am beginning to sweat.

"Jeez, I don't know," says Herman. "I don't like it. We're just begging to get nailed."

This morning there are a lot more cars parked out on the street. What is worse is that the building directly across the street from the house appears to be a business and this morning it's busy.

"I didn't see that last night," says Herman. We are walking slowly up the sidewalk on the same side as Katia's house. We are now just one house away.

"That's because it was closed last night."

"Looks like a beauty salon," says Herman. "We're gonna have to make a decision pretty quick whether we keep walking or stop."

We are thirty feet from the gate at the front of the house when two young women come out of the building across the street. They are wearing blue smocks, talking and laughing as they walk across the street toward Katia's house. They stop in the middle of the street for a second. One of them lights a cigarette, then offers the flame to her friend, who lights up. Before they can take a second puff, three more women come out of the building and join them. They are all dressed in the same blue smocks.

"It's a beauty school." Herman says it under his breath. He is right. They're on a break. Before we reach the gate, three of the women plant themselves on the curb directly in front of Katia's house and sit. They are laughing and talking a mile a minute in Spanish.

"Any ideas?" I say.

"Yeah, ask 'em if we can borrow a bobby pin to pick the lock," says Herman.

Without saying another word, we keep walking until we are opposite the gate to Katia's house; suddenly Herman slows down. "What the hell is that?" He lifts his nose and sniffs the air a little. This takes him in the direction of the gate.

"I don't smell anything."

"Put your nose over here," he says.

I do. The second I get near the wrought-iron bars I pick up the odor.

"It's stronger down here," says Herman.

He is right. Down near the tile floor in the entry behind the gate the heavy vapor is actually visible.

"It's propane," says Herman.

By now several of the women on the sidewalk are looking at us, wondering what's happening.

Herman turns to them. *"¡Apaguen sus cigarrillos! Hay gas. Es peligroso."*

They stand there looking at him.

"Peligroso. It's dangerous. Put out your cigarettes. Go! *Ir. ¡Corren—Escapen!"* Herman starts waving his arms at them. They begin backing away, more frightened by Herman than what he is saying.

Herman is trying to dig his pick set out of his pocket.

I reach through the bars and try the little lever on the inside knowing it will be locked. Instead the lever snaps down and the gate swings open.

"It wasn't locked," I say.

I charge through the open gate and try the front door. The same result. Whoever left last didn't lock up.

As the door swings open, we get the full effect as vapors of propane wash out through the open portal like a wave. I wade into the house trying to hold my breath, Herman right behind me. I trip over something, knock it over, and then kick it against the wall in trying to keep my balance. It's a suitcase.

With my hand over my mouth and nose, eyes watering, I feel my way past the entry to the living room. I glance to my right. I see the dining room and the kitchen beyond. There is a set of stairs going up just inside the dining room.

"You check down. I'll go up," says Herman. He is coughing as he bounds up the steps two at a time.

Just inside the kitchen door I see the body on the floor, something over her face. I reach the stove. I can tell that this is the point of the emission. The vapors here are overpowering.

As if in a dream state I hear the pounding of heavy footfalls on the wooden floor overhead. Herman is either wrestling with someone or checking the rooms. I can't tell.

I try turning the knobs on the stove, thinking she must have left one of them open. But even with my eyes watering I can see that they are all turned off.

I reach down and pull the cloth from her face, grip her under the arms, and lift her until she is vertical, like a limp rag held out in front of me. I get a glimpse of her face. I don't have to ask to know who she is. The resemblance to Katia is uncanny. Holding her steady, I sweep one arm under her legs at the knees and lift her into my arms.

She is not heavy. Still, I am staggering, unable to stand, fighting for breath. It is all I can do to hold her up. Putting one foot in front of the other, retracing my steps toward the door is impossible.

I take one step, then another. Like a dark night it envelops me. I have only the slightest sensation, the feeling that I am weightless as my head hits the edge of the countertop on the way down, and then nothing.

"So how the hell did they get out without being seen?" The lead agent, the one packing the papers is angry.

"I don't know," said the other agent.

Madriani's room was empty. No clothes in the closet, no luggage, and nothing in the bathroom. Now they find the same thing in his friend's room.

"These are the right rooms?"

"*Sí, señor.*" One of the hotel employees is still holding the passkey in his hand after letting them in.

The beds had been slept in, but it was as if they had checked out. However, the girl at the front desk told the Costa Rican police that the two men were still registered.

"So who tipped them off?" said the lead agent.

"You got me," said the other one.

"Have your men search every room. They've got to be in the hotel somewhere. They couldn't have gotten out." The lead agent was now giving orders to the police. The lieutenant in charge wasn't sure about this.

"*Un momento.*" He stopped one of his subordinates before the man could get out of the room. "I am not sure that we have the authority to disturb the other guests. I am going to have to check with my superiors. You are certain that they were here in the hotel this morning, and that they stayed here last night?"

"Yes, I'm sure!" The agent was now turning his venom on the Costa Rican cop. Unless Madriani and his man were hiding out in a supply closet in the hotel, he was going to have to explain to Thorpe in Washington how the two men, one of them the size of a small mountain, had slipped through the net unseen.

"Lieutenant, can you call the airport? Make sure that he doesn't catch a flight out of the country?"

"If you can supply me with his passport number, I will see what I can do."

"It's in the file, in the car," said the other agent.

"Why don't you go get it?" said the lead agent.

"What's this?" said the other agent. He was holding a small brass grid in his hand, a metal cover for a heat or air-conditioning register.

"Where did you get that?" said the lead agent.

"It was under the sheet on top of the bed."

The FBI agent started searching the floor with his eyes, looking for an open heat register.

"*Señor.*" The lieutenant gestured toward an area high on the wall above the polished hardwood headboard and the pillows. There was an open rectangular air duct about six feet above the bed.

The lieutenant reached over and drew his fingers across the polished dark wood of the headboard, leaving a clear track in the dusting of white plaster left from the screw holes drilled by whoever had removed the grill from the register. "It looks as if they were hiding something. Perhaps they knew you were here."

As he said it there was just the slightest motion, as if someone gently rocked the room. It was almost imperceptible. You might not have noticed except that when it stopped, the small chandelier overhead was swaying. A second later the shock wave jingled the dangling glass crystals of the fixture.

FORTY-FIVE

hey had it all wrong. Colombian coffee was all right, but the best-flavored coffee in the world came from Costa Rica. For Liquida's money, compared with fresh-roasted Costa Rican consumed on the spot, the stuff at Starbucks sucked.

He was savoring a cup and nibbling on a pastry, what the girl behind the counter of the little coffee shop called *"Fruitas,"* when the mushrooming fireball reflected off the windows of the Hospital Calderon Guardia across the street.

Even three blocks away the shock wave of the blast rattled the glass all around him. It sent everyone from the open-air café out onto the street to look. The only one who didn't have to was Liquida. He knew that no one could possibly survive that.

"What do you mean, you lost them?" Thorpe almost crawled through the phone line, all the way to Costa Rica. "How the hell could they get away? You had the entire building surrounded. That's what you told me.

"Give me a minute." Thorpe took the phone away

from his ear and thought for a moment, then quickly brought it back up. "Do you have the airports covered?

"Well, at least that's something. I'll call Justice and see if they can get hold of somebody at State to turn the screws on the Costa Rican government so they pull out all the stops. Without their help we can't possibly cover all the exits. In the meantime, get off your ass and look for them." Thorpe slammed down the receiver.

Getting international assistance was not going to be easy. The Costa Rican government was already asking questions; why should they be expected to expend so many resources chasing a single American fugitive? True, it was a capital crime, but there was a limit to how many police officers they could spare. After all, it was not their fault that the Americans had allowed the man to leave the U.S.

Thorpe knew that the administration was still unwilling to share information concerning the other half of the story, the possibility of a nuclear device loose in Latin America. While some in the White House believed the information to be credible, skeptics were demanding hard evidence.

The bigger problem was the politics of Guantanamo. Powerful people were covering their asses because of wild-eyed intelligence rumors that escaped prisoners from Guantanamo had somehow become attached to the device. As with every paranoid delusion, there was just enough truth to this one that it caused policy makers to throw a blanket over the entire Nitikin affair. While there was no evidence that Middle East radicals had become involved, it was known in high government circles that seven prisoners had escaped from Guantanamo some months earlier. Whether they were still in

Cuba or had been shuttled back to their homeland was unknown. Either way, the administration wasn't anxious to have the story on CNN.

Thorpe thought about it for a couple of minutes and then picked up the phone again. He dialed a number for one of the offices in the intelligence directorate downstairs and then waited while it rang.

"Bob, Zeb Thorpe here. You know, I was trying to recall last week when we had that briefing on the Madriani surveillance. You guys had run up a dead end on the encrypted phone they were using.

"Yeah, that's what I remember you saying. I don't imagine you've had any luck since?

"I didn't think so. Let me ask you a question; forget for the moment cracking the encryption code. I assume the phone puts out and receives a signal to and from the nearest cell tower, just like any other cell phone.

"It does.

"So is there any way we can identify the signal that these phones are putting out when they're being used?"

According to the techno wizard on the other end, the answer was yes. Every cell phone, as long as the phone was powered up, must maintain contact with the nearest satellite tower. It does this by emitting a roaming signal, a periodic electronic handshake so that the cell system can determine which is the best tower for the phone to use in the event of an incoming or outgoing call. The roaming signal is traceable and its signal strength will identify the general location of the person carrying the phone. Using equipment that can zero in and triangulate on the signal, the precise location can be fixed. It is the reason world leaders are usually not allowed to carry cell phones on their persons, and their protection details use only secure radio frequencies for communications.

"So you can track him if the phone is powered up. You're sure about that?

"Okay, good. One last question. After you find the location, can you jam the frequency so they won't be able to communicate? You can? If I asked you to set that up in San José, Costa Rica, how long would it take?

"Do it," said Thorpe, "and call me the minute your people pinpoint the signal. Tell them to jam the line so they can't talk, and call me immediately." He hung up the phone, leaned back in his chair, and smiled.

All I can feel is the hard concrete under my behind as some great weight pushes on my back, pressing my head between my knees. I begin sucking in large quantities of air as the weight is suddenly removed from my shoulders and back.

"Stay there." The sound of Herman's voice, and the feeling that it is snowing, light flakes dusting my forearms and the ground all around my feet.

As I lift my head I realize that what is falling is not snow. It is ash. There are pieces of burning wood, broken glass, and bits of plaster all over the street.

I am sitting on the curb at the other side, fifty yards down the block from Katia's house. As I look up I see flames and black smoke billowing from a gaping hole where the roof and the front of the house used to be. The white exterior, what is left of it, is scorched, turned black in places by flames and soot. The front door is blown off its hinges and still burning as it leans up against the iron gate at the entry.

I sense motion on the sidewalk behind me. I am still

dazed. I look, and Herman is working on Katia's mother. She is stretched out on the cement sidewalk next to her purse. Herman is giving her mouth-to-mouth resuscitation, punctuated by compressions to her chest with his powerful hands. He is pushing hard enough to break ribs.

I start to struggle to my feet.

"Stay down before you fall! I got my hands full right now." Herman struggles between bellows of breath and pressure on her chest to tell me what to do.

"I'm all right," I tell him.

"Right."

Neighbors from the other houses are milling around on the street, some of them looking at the burning house. A small group gathers around us, watching Herman as he works on the woman.

"*¿Ella está muerta?*" Some woman asks if she is dead.

"*No sé,*" whispers another voice. He doesn't know.

One lady, a neighbor, wants to help, but isn't sure what to do. Herman doesn't have time to show her.

"I'll do it," I say. I give up on the idea of getting to my feet and instead I roll to my side and crawl on my hands and knees. I kneel over her torso and start doing the compressions on her chest so that Herman can concentrate on filling her lungs with air. Within a few seconds we get a rhythm going. A minute or so later her legs kick, she coughs up fluids, turns her head to the side, and vomits.

Several of the women clap and smile.

Herman holds her on her side with her head down as she retches several times. He gently pats her on the back. "*¡Bueno!*" Then he says something else in Spanish up close to her ear that I cannot hear.

"Here, hold her on her side," he tells me. "Don't want her breathing fluid into her lungs."

I hold her while he heads across the street. I watch as he kicks the flaming front door away from the iron gate, then uses the bottom of his shirt to grab the metal gate and opens it. He disappears into the house.

The woman takes a couple of deep breaths. Finally, she turns her head, looks at me, and says, "Who are you?" in perfect English.

"You are Katia's mother?" I say.

"Yes. Who are you?"

"We are friends of Katia from the United States. She is in a great deal of trouble. We need your help."

She is breathing heavily now, making up for the deficit of oxygen. "What kind of trouble?"

"We must find a place where we can talk," I tell her. "Not here."

When I look back, Herman is out of the house, coming this way.

Katia's mother has now boosted herself up so that she is sitting on the sidewalk. She is talking to one of the other women in Spanish, then turns to me. "She is a friend. She lives down the street. We can go to her house."

"I don't think that's a good idea." Herman overhears the conversation as he approaches. He gestures with his head to the left, up the street.

When I turn and look, I see people in white hospital smocks. Apparently they have wandered down from the hospital up the hill. Next to one of them is a motorcycle cop. He has parked his bike and is propping his helmet on the seat. Then we hear the sound of sirens in the distance.

"We need to talk somewhere else," I tell her. "Do you have any friends outside the neighborhood?"

She thinks for a moment. "Yes. There is someone else."

"How are you feeling?" says Herman.

"My head hurts," she says.

"That's the fumes from the gas," he tells her. "You're going to have a headache."

"What about you?" He looks at me.

"I'm fine."

He reaches in his pocket and pulls out a handkerchief. "Here."

"What's that for?"

"Your head's bleeding."

I reach up and sure enough there is blood on the side of my face, dripping onto the shoulder of my shirt. I remember hitting the countertop just before I blacked out in the kitchen.

I press the handkerchief to my head and hold it there.

"Why did you go back in the house?"

"Wanted to see if I could grab her luggage," says Herman. "But it's flamed. I snagged her purse on the way out, but that was all because I had my hands full with the two of you."

"Could have left me and gotten the suitcase," I tell him.

"Thought about it," he says. "But then who's gonna pay my bill?" He winks at me. "If we help you up, do you think you can stand?" he asks her.

"I will try."

He hands her purse to her. We each get under one arm and help her to her feet. The blare of a siren suddenly fills the air. The bright red of the first fire truck turns the corner at the other end of the block, followed by two more cops riding Suzuki dirt bikes.

The cops quickly busy themselves directing traffic. The crowd around us suddenly disperses as their attention is drawn to the truck. With their backs to us, they watch the firemen as they come off and start hauling hoses.

Katia's mother takes a few steps and says something to the lady who offered to allow us to use her house.

"What did she say?" Herman didn't hear it.

"I don't know."

"Let's get out of here," he says.

Within seconds the three of us are hobbling down the street in the other direction, away from the crowd. As we reach the stairs at the end of the block, Herman takes the lead, helping Katia's mother down the steps.

I stand above them on one of the steps, my eyes just at street level for a few seconds, making sure that no one is following us.

Looking back I see a cop in a dark blue uniform talking to some of the people who had gathered around us on the sidewalk. He is taking notes. A woman who is talking to him gestures toward the sidewalk behind her without bothering to turn to look.

He says something to her.

She turns and starts to point at the curb where I had been sitting, and then suddenly stops. She looks around as if she is confused. She knows we were there. She turns back to the officer and they continue to talk. Just as the cop begins to lift his eyes from his notebook to glance down the block in my direction, I drop down one more step and disappear below the level of the street.

FORTY-SIX

Nitikin went to bed at his usual time, eight o'clock, but he didn't sleep. He tossed and turned for hours, troubled by the thought that what he had been told was wrong. Ten days earlier, he had been shown a copy of a fax by one of his friends in the FARC. It was a bill of lading from a Panamanian shipping company. It had arrived at the FARC communications hut earlier that day.

The bill of lading was a contract for the shipment of a single cargo container by sea from the Port of Tumaco on the Pacific coast of Colombia to the container terminal at Balboa, Panama, at the western approach to the Panama Canal.

As Nitikin lay tossing on his bed he was troubled by the fact that according to the bill of lading, the shipment was scheduled for the following morning, with the deadline for loading containers set for two A.M., sailing by four.

The distance between the FARC encampment in the Tapaje River valley and the Port of Tumaco was more than sixty miles as the crow flies, an hour by car on a fast highway. But there was no highway, only dirt roads that wound through the deep river gorges and over the mountains. Because one had to dodge Colombian military patrols, the trip could take more than a day; that is, if none of the bridges over the rivers was washed out.

By early afternoon, when no truck had arrived to transport the container with the device, Nitikin was forced to conclude that the information he had seen on the fax was wrong; either that or Alim was playing games with him.

Yakov had set everything up premised on the one assumption that thirty-six hours after departing the harbor at Tumaco, he and the device would be in Panama. Whether this was their final destination he had no way of knowing. But through some FARC friends he had managed to obtain a cell phone with a Panamanian GSM chip. It was useless in the jungles of Colombia, but at the Port of Balboa, near Panama City, he would be able to get a cellular signal. The chip contained just enough minutes for a brief long-distance call to his daughter's cell phone in Costa Rica. Nitikin was desperate to be sure that she was safe, and to tell her one last time that he loved her.

It was a three-story concrete building just two blocks south of the Sportsmens Lodge. But it took us the better part of an hour to get there hauling our luggage and helping Katia's mother, Maricela Solaz, along the way. She introduced herself as we walked. I filled her in as much as I could concerning Katia, the fact that she was charged with serious crimes and in the hospital following an attempt on her life.

She said she had never heard the name Emerson

Pike, but after what had happened she was not surprised that an attempt had been made on Katia's life. It was the photographs she had taken in Colombia. Though her father had told her almost nothing, she was certain that the people she had accidentally caught in the pictures were dangerous. "Whoever tried to kill my daughter also tried to kill me."

"Did you see him? Could you identify him?" I ask.

"No. But I can identify the man in Colombia," she says. "And I am certain that he is the one who ordered it."

"What man?"

"I will tell you when we get there."

We took a wide berth around the lodge, walking several blocks out of our way, up the hill and around the hospital to avoid the police and any FBI who might be lingering around our hotel.

She pointed out the apartment building as we approached. It looked as if it dated to the thirties. The gray concrete structure curved with the street and incorporated elements of Art Deco, concrete columns with molded threads in the form of a winepress set into the facade.

"The yellow house across the street behind the fence is the Casa Amarilla, it is the *ministerio* of exterior relations. How do you say?"

"The foreign ministry?"

"Yes. That's it. My friend lives on the second floor in the apartments across the street." She leads the way. When we arrive in front of the curving iron gate at the door, she takes hold of the bars with one hand and rattles it, then steps back a few feet to the curb and hollers up to the window overhead, "Lorenzo. It's Maricela. Open the door."

For a few seconds there is nothing. She rattles the gate again. Then a voice overhead. "Who is it?"

"*Es Maricela y sus amigos.* Let us in."

The man who sticks his head out the window a couple of seconds later looks no more Costa Rican than I do. "Where have you been? I have been trying to reach you for the last six weeks," he says. "Katia is in trouble."

"I know," she tells him. "Lemme in, please."

"Give me a minute to find my key." He disappears from the window.

"Your friend is an American," I say.

"Yes. His name is Larry Goudaz. He calls himself Lorenzo. He is from California. The Silicon Valley," she says.

"I see." I remember the name Lorenzo Goudaz from one of our meetings with Katia at the jail. "I think Katia mentioned him as a friend."

"Yes, I'm sure she would have told you about him."

Lorenzo Goudaz was on Harry's short list of people in San José as possible contacts, names given to him by Katia, who might be able to reach her mother. According to Katia she had introduced Goudaz to Emerson Pike before she and Pike left for California. Goudaz didn't particularly like Pike. If Katia had listened to him and stayed home, none of this would have happened.

As I listen to her, Maricela describes a man who is a professional networker. He has situated himself between the local Costa Ricans and the Americans, some who live here and some who trek to the city periodically from up north, and has made himself useful to all.

"Lorenzo has been here twenty years at least," says Maricela. "He has been a friend and from time to time has helped people in the neighborhood. All the *norte-americanos*, what you call expatriates..."

"Yes."

"They all know him. When they come to town they visit him. They call him the mayor of Gringo Gulch. Katia calls him 'the MOGG.'" She explains that this is short for mayor of Gringo Gulch. "But don't say it in front of him. Katia jokes, but I don't think he likes it." She looks at me and smiles, the same intriguing smile as her daughter's.

We hear him coming down the stairs.

"Why do they call him the mayor?" says Herman.

"Because he has been here so long and knows so many people. If you are in trouble, you go see Lorenzo and he will fix it, or knows somebody who can."

A second later the front door opens. We are greeted with a broad grin under a shiny bald head. His stocky, round white body is naked to the waist, and there are only a few wisps of gray hair on the chest.

The second he looks at Maricela he loses the smile. "You look as if you're sick. What's happened?"

"There's been a fire at my house. Please let us in."

"Of course." He fumbles with a large brass ring of keys trying to find the one that works the gate.

"How did it happen?"

"I'll tell you when we get inside."

He struggles with the ring, then drops it on the ground. "Fucking keys," he says as he bends over to pick them up. When he stands up he's staring straight at Maricela. "Excuse my French," he says. He gives Herman and me a cockeyed, impish grin through the bars.

"Please hurry," she says. "I need to use your bathroom."

He finds the right key, turns it in the lock, and opens the gate.

Maricela shoots through the door and up the cement spiral staircase ahead of us.

"What can I say? Any friend of Maricela's is a friend of mine." He smiles a little, as if to acknowledge that this is a mantra in which Maricela's name is interchangeable with the name of every other person he knows. "Excuse my appearance. It's laundry day and I've run out of shirts. So you get to see the washboard abs and the rugged me."

Herman and I laugh. Goudaz has the natural charm of a glad-hander. He does it easily and with a certain grace, even naked from the waist up.

"Sorry to barge in on you like this. My name's Paul, this is Herman."

"That's what I like, people on a first-name basis." He shakes our hands while he's looking at our duffel bags.

"I hope it doesn't look like we're planning on staying," says Herman.

"Don't worry about it. Come on in. I'm sure Maricela has told you about me. I'm the local curiosity." He locks the gate behind us and closes the door.

"Everything except how you got the name Lorenzo," I say.

"It's because Ms. Blind Costa Rica loves to toy with this single hair on my chest, so she calls me Lorenzo the Magnificent. If you have any other questions, just ask, 'cause I've got lots of lies," he says.

Herman and I laugh as we trudge up the stairs hauling our luggage.

"So tell me what happened."

*   *   *

Shortly after midnight the demons stopped dancing in his head and Yakov fell asleep. It was deep and restful, though he couldn't be sure how long it lasted.

He wakened suddenly to a sound overhead unlike anything he had ever heard before. A deep whomping percussion that became louder and shook the entire hut as it drew near. It was a helicopter. The Colombian military had found the base.

Nitikin rolled over and was suddenly blinded by a flashlight beam directed into his eyes. "Get up. We are leaving."

Yakov held up a hand to shade his eyes. It was Alim's interpreter. The man lowered the flashlight. "Put on your clothes. Leave everything else. Take nothing. Everything you need will be provided. Come. Hurry." The man stepped just outside the door of the hut and waited. "Quickly!"

Yakov began to put on his pants as the deafening sound of the helicopter moved overhead. He glanced at his watch and realized it was just after three in the morning.

Nitikin put on his shirt and buttoned it. He looked for his watch and couldn't find it.

"Hurry up!"

He grabbed his boots and his field jacket, then reached under the bed into a bag he had already packed. He felt around inside the bag for the shape of the small clamshell cell phone. He disconnected the wire that had been charging it, and then slipped the phone into his pants pocket. He reached for the charger, plugged into the wall on the other side of the bed.

"Hurry! What are you doing?" The interpreter came back into the hut.

"I am looking for some socks."

"You don't need socks. We don't have time. Put your boots on now. Let's go."

The man stood there and watched him as Nitikin laced up his boots over his naked feet. Yakov hadn't worn socks in years. But he needed time to get the charger for the cell phone. Now he would have to leave it and pray that he had enough battery power to make the call to Maricela.

He followed the interpreter out the door and through the maze of huts. By now several of the FARC commandos had taken up their Kalashnikov rifles and were headed in the same direction. Helicopters overhead always charged the entire camp with fear. They were employed against the FARC both for attacks as well as subterfuge. Recently they had been used to trick the FARC into releasing hostages the rebels believed were merely being transported from one camp to another.

By now the bird was on the ground. Yakov could hear the gentle woofing of the blades as they idled quietly, whipping the air in the clearing beyond the huts. As he came around the corner of the last building, he suddenly realized why Alim had waited so long to transport the container.

This was no ordinary helicopter. Yakov had seen it before, but it was always in the distance, miles away, where you couldn't gain a true appreciation of its size. The huge Sikorsky Skycrane was used for logging in remote areas, in particular for hauling high-end exotic hardwoods from inaccessible river valleys. Yakov had heard stories of logs hollowed out to carry even more valuable crops, thousands of pounds of cocaine whisked through the air to unknown destinations.

On the ground close-up, the Skycrane looked like a giant dragonfly. Its seventy-two-foot-diameter rotor blades and giant twin turboshaft engines could lift a fully armed battle tank to nearly ten thousand feet. It could carry it two hundred miles in less than two hours and gently set it back on the ground. Yakov noticed there was something different about this particular Skycrane from the ones he had seen before. There were two large exterior tanks fitted into the normally vacant area under what looked like the rigid backbone of the craft.

Nitikin saw Alim in the distance, standing next to the chopper, gesturing with his arms and pointing in the direction of the cargo container a hundred meters away just at the edge of the clearing near the trees.

Two crew members in orange jumpsuits were arranging the lift cables under the helicopter's belly tanks. The cable lines looked as if they were at least a hundred feet long. From these the container would dangle like a pendulum beneath the belly of the huge chopper.

"This way." The interpreter tapped Yakov on the shoulder, directing him away from the helicopter and toward the cargo container where the four surviving members of Afundi's group were waiting. As they approached, one of them opened the cargo container door, swinging it wide. He gestured for Nitikin to get inside.

The wooden crate containing the device was already bolted in place, fastened to the floor in the center of the container. The bomb was not heavy. It was a fraction of the weight of the atomic device dubbed Little Boy that had been dropped on Hiroshima in Japan at the end of World War II, though its yield would be equal to or perhaps even more destructive. Both the Soviets and the U.S. had made strides in reducing the size and weight of warheads in the years immediately following the war.

The real weight of the load was in the lead lining of the cargo container itself, a precaution not so much for safety as against detection. Nitikin had told Alim that this was unnecessary, but Afundi refused to believe him. A warhead using highly enriched uranium, while more primitive and less powerful, was more difficult to detect than an implosion device using plutonium. The gamma rays and neutrons emitted by a shielded uranium device allowed for detection only at very short distances, no more than two to four feet. More important was the time required to count a sufficient number of particle emissions from a uranium bomb in order to set off an alarm. This could take anywhere from several minutes to hours. By then, any vehicle carrying the device through a border check or control point would be long gone.

Yakov just stood in the open doorway looking at the crate. One of Alim's men tossed three large duffel bags into the container. Then he nudged Yakov toward the door. As Nitikin stepped inside the man gestured for him to sit on the floor. He sat with his back against the container wall and his feet against the wooden crate. When he looked up he saw Alim at the doorway, looking down at him with a simpering smile.

Afundi had packed a few personal items. He knew he would not be coming back to the camp. In a light day pack he carried the newspaper given to him by Fidel that morning in Havana and Emerson Pike's small laptop. He figured, why not? He didn't own a computer and the dead American no longer needed it.

Within seconds, Alim, his four men, and the interpreter joined Nitikin inside the cargo container. The interpreter handed Yakov two small white pills. "Here, take these."

"What is it?"

"Dramamine, for motion sickness. Trust me, you will need it."

Nitikin swallowed the two pills.

Someone outside closed the door. Yakov heard the screech of metal as the steel bar was dropped into position, sealing them behind the heavy metal door. The interpreter turned on his flashlight as they sat and waited.

FORTY-SEVEN

Liquida read the brief account of the fire in the local newspaper the next morning. One fatality, a woman, her identity withheld until they could notify the next of kin.

Later that afternoon, after packing his luggage for the return to Mexico, he took a detour on his way to the airport. He parked the car and took a stroll down the dead-end street. Everything was back to normal, except for the burned-out house two doors from the corner. Someone had swept the glass and debris from the street. The front gate on the house was padlocked, probably to prevent looters from falling into the charred pit that was inside.

Liquida could see all the way up to the sky through the broken windows on the front. All that was left standing were the exterior masonry walls. From what he could see, the interior was totally gutted. The old wood had burned well.

Wearing oversize sunglasses and a baseball cap with the New York Yankees' logo on it, he walked slowly down the sidewalk on the other side of the street. With his hands in his pockets, he surveyed his handiwork. If he had a camera, he would have taken pictures to send to his employer. The camel jockey was never satisfied.

Liquida walked past the house and ended up three doors down where a woman was dragging a hose and watering some plants in her front yard.

He smiled, then spoke to her in Spanish. "Good afternoon."

"Hello." She nodded and smiled back.

"What a shame." He stood there looking back at the house across the street.

"Yes. It was a very bad fire. And the explosion shook the entire block."

"Really?" said Liquida.

"Oh, yes. *Propano,*" she said. "That's why I don't have it in my house. It's too dangerous. Only electricity," she said. "The fire got so hot it burned the telephone wires." She pointed to the cables running between the poles across the street.

"I hope no one was hurt."

"Well, a woman had a heart attack," she said.

"You mean the woman who lived in the house?" Liquida was surprised there was enough of her left that they could find her heart.

"No, no, not Maricela, the lady next door to her. She was in her eighties. It was probably all the excitement from the explosion. No, the woman who lived in the house was very lucky. She got out."

Liquida nearly got whiplash turning to look at her.

"Some students up at the beauty school said that two men who were walking up the sidewalk smelled fumes coming from the house. They managed to get inside and one of them carried her out, just before the house blew up."

Liquida didn't say anything. He just stood there looking at her as she continued watering her plants.

"Was she hurt?"

"Oh, yes. She was unconscious when they brought her out."

"So I assume she's in the hospital?"

"No. One of the men, the one who carried her out, a very big *hombre*, managed to revive her. Right up there on the sidewalk." She pointed up the street. "I would say it was a miracle. I was sure she was dead when he brought her out. And his friend, the other man, he didn't look too good either."

"What did this man look like?" said Liquida.

"As I said he was very big. A black man."

Liquida immediately understood. "So what happened to Maricela?"

"Do you know her?"

"No, I just heard you say her name."

"Oh. I think she left with the two men."

"So they must have been friends of hers?"

"I don't think so. They were not locals. I have never seen them before. *Americanos*, I think."

"The black man, you say he was big," said Liquida.

"*Mucho grande*," she said.

"Was he bald? Did he have a shiny head?"

"Do you know him?"

"No, but I think I may have seen him around the neighborhood."

"Then perhaps I am wrong. Maybe they are local. I offered them my house to rest, but Maricela said she wanted to go stay with the mayor."

"She knows the mayor of San José?" A cold chill ran down Liquida's spine.

"No." The woman laughed. "It is a joke. He is a friend. His name is Lorenzo. In the neighborhood some people call him the mayor of Gringo Gulch because he knows everybody and everything. He lives a few blocks down that way." She gestured with one hand in a general direction toward downtown.

Liquida would have asked her for Lorenzo's last name, better yet, a map to his house and whether it was hooked up to propane. But to ask more questions was to invite suspicion.

Yesterday afternoon after arriving safely at Lorenzo's apartment, the trauma of the event finally caught up with Maricela. She collapsed on a couch in his back room and slept all night. By the time she wakes up this morning, it is almost noon.

"I have to tell you, Maricela, I didn't trust him," says Goudaz. "And I tried to warn Katia. She wouldn't listen to me." He is talking about Emerson Pike. "He was asking too many personal questions. Anybody want a beer?"

Herman raises his hand. "Yeah, I'll have one."

"How about you?"

"Not for me," I say. We are seated around the dining table grabbing a bite, something Goudaz has whipped up, rice and chicken and some black beans. He seems to like to cook. After being under his roof for one night, it is hard to size him up completely. There is a bit of roguish charisma to the man. You get the sense that he survives in the gap between the two cultures. It is difficult to say what Maricela thinks of him.

For the moment he has his head in the refrigerator. He comes out with two bottles of Imperial, knocks the caps off, and hands one of them to Herman as he takes a swig from the other.

Lorenzo doesn't move fast, but he seems to get things done. The minute we arrived he found accommodations for us. One of the other tenants in the building is out of town. The mayor has the key and says the man won't mind. Last night Herman and I sacked out on a bed and a rollaway in the other apartment.

It's a little tight but it'll work, at least for a few days, until we can figure out where we're going. That will depend in large part on what we can find out from Maricela.

This morning I brief her on Katia's predicament in California. We talk about the photographs from Colombia, Emerson Pike's obsession with them, and his murder. She wants to know what Pike's involvement in all of this was. I tell her we're not sure. I don't tell her about the FBI or the fact that I am now charged as a codefendant along with her daughter, only that we were interested in recovering the photographs from the camera at her house. But, of course they are now gone, destroyed in the fire.

She tells us that it was, in fact, her father who was in the photographs along with a man she calls Alim and several of his followers, who she believes were responsible for the attack at her house and the fire.

When I ask her where the photographs were taken, she becomes vague. She tells us she was always picked up at a rural bus stop by men in a small truck. It was a very long ride to the village in the jungle where her father was. It took most of a day and sometimes longer depending on the route they took and the condition of the mountain roads. According to Maricela she would often fall asleep and never paid much attention to where they were or their direction of travel.

"What makes you believe this man, Alim, is responsible for what happened at your house?" says Goudaz.

"I'm sure of it," says Maricela. "He was very threatening. My father was certain he would never allow me to leave, to come home. So he made special arrangements for a man and a woman whom he trusted to accompany me to San José. When we arrived at the airport in Medellín, there was a message waiting for them, some emergency back home and they both had to return."

"And so you figure Alim was responsible?" says Goudaz.

"Who else?"

"What is your father doing down there?" says the mayor.

"Excuse me, some of this information may be confidential," I tell him. "Because it may have to do with a pending case. I know we've barged in on you without warning and I apologize for that, but I wonder if we could have just a few minutes alone."

"Sure, I'm sorry," says Goudaz. "I didn't realize. Listen, you take all the time you need. I've got work to do in the study. Call me if you need me."

"Thanks."

He disappears down the hall and closes the door to the study.

"Thank you," she says. "Lorenzo is a good friend, but he has a habit of making other people's business his own."

"I noticed," I tell her. "You said Alim and his followers didn't speak Spanish."

"That's correct."

"Do you have any idea where they were from?"

"The country, no. The area, I believe, is the Middle East. Several times each day they would get down on their knees and pray, always with their heads toward the east."

"So they were Muslim?" I say.

"I think so."

Maricela tells Herman and me that her father has always been very secretive. He was absent for large periods of her life when she was a child, and he refused to tell her anything about what he was doing in Colombia. She doesn't believe he is involved in any way with drugs, so she has dismissed this from the range of possibilities. All she knows is that whatever the project is, it is nearing completion. This was the reason he sent her home. He told her that he would be leaving Colombia shortly and would not be back. She got the very clear sense that it was to be their last visit.

The thought of never seeing him again, followed by the events at her house, has left her emotionally fragile. Trying to probe for details is difficult.

We talk for a while about what she saw when she was there in the encampment. There were a large number of men, most of them young, some of them children, along with young women in uniforms, many of them carrying rifles. She doesn't believe they were part of the Colombian army and therefore were probably rebels. She knows that Colombia has for many years been involved in a revolution. Her father seemed to know many of these people and none of them seemed to be a threat to him, only Alim and his followers.

Suddenly she sits bolt upright in the chair. "Oh, my God, I forgot." She stands and starts feeling in the pockets of her pants as if maybe she's lost her keys or something.

"What is it?"

"It's ah, something…someone gave me. I hope I didn't lose it. With the fire and everything, I forgot." She's riffling through each pocket.

"What was it?" says Herman.

"Just a note." She feels something in her right-front pocket. She reaches in, and when her hand comes out, she is holding a small folded piece of paper. "Thank God." She takes a deep breath, turns her back for a moment, and walks a few steps from the table as she unfolds the note. It appears to be about the size of a single half sheet of paper, and I see what looks like handwriting in pencil on the page. As she reads Maricela keeps her back to us.

Herman and I look at each other.

"If it's something that would help Katia, we need to know about it," I tell her.

When she finishes she drops her hand to her side, still clutching the paper tightly. When she turns and looks at us, there are tears running down her cheeks. "What is today?"

"Wednesday," says Herman. "Why?"

"No, I mean the date."

He looks at his watch. "It's the twelfth," he says.

She takes a deep breath and lets it out. "That means we still have time."

"Time for what?" I say.

She looks at me. "My father made me promise not to tell anyone. But none of us knew what was happening then. I cannot think of anyone who would want to kill me other than Alim. And if he tried to kill me, then he probably also tried to kill Katia and killed her friend. What was his name?"

"Emerson Pike."

"I believe if my father knew all of this, he would want me to tell you. It may be the last chance we have to talk to him. The note says he is going to try and call me."

"When?" says Herman.

She hands him the note. "He says he is going to be in Panama. But he doesn't say why." Suddenly a dark expression blankets her face.

"What's wrong?" I ask.

"He won't be able to reach me."

"Why not?"

"The only number he has for me is my cell phone. It was at the house."

FORTY-EIGHT

Within minutes, three of Alim's men were overcome by motion sickness. Swaying and twisting in the dimly lit container under the flapping rotor of the huge blades, Nitikin could hear them retching in alternate waves on the other side of the wooden crate.

Alim hollered at them, but it seemed to have little effect. The men could not control themselves. The air in the metal coffin was stifling, and the constant motion in the enclosed container disoriented the inner ear even with the Dramamine.

Yakov closed his eyes, propped his elbows on his knees, and steadied his head in his hands to control himself. In less than five minutes, he was unconscious.

Alim had had enough of the weaklings who followed him. The one he shot through the head the day of the dragon's breath had tried twice to abandon his comrades and escape from the camp. He looked at the two on the floor by the crate as they soiled themselves. He jammed a fully loaded thirty-round banana clip into the receiver of his rifle. He would have shot them on the spot except he knew he would need them, at least for a few more days.

On the other side of the crate he could see shadowed faces in the dim light, the interpreter and two brothers, who struggled to their feet. The two young men looked almost ashen, and were breathing heavily. But at least they were trying. Alim grabbed one of the other rifles from the duffel, jammed a clip into the receiver, then tossed it to one of them. He grabbed one more weapon and a clip, and then glanced down at the Russian who by now had toppled over and was laid out flat on the floor. Alim kicked him with one foot to make sure he was out before stepping away from the unguarded weapons still in the duffel bag. He loaded the other rifle and handed the Kalashnikov to the other brother. He told them to sit and relax and to keep an eye on the Russian.

It would be a long ride. Alim knew that the extra fuel tanks on the Skycrane would extend the usual three-hundred-mile range of the helicopter out to nearly two thousand miles, almost all of it over the ocean. It would take them ten hours to rendezvous, and then from there just under four days to their destination. Before anyone knew what was happening, they would be there.

Afundi tapped the interpreter on the shoulder and the two men slipped between the wooden crate and the wall to where Nitikin was lying on the floor.

The interpreter lifted the Russian's eyelids, first one and then the other. He checked the pupils in both eyes with the flashlight and checked Nitikin's pulse.

"He's okay," said the interpreter.

The last thing they wanted was an overdose. The cartel's doctor in Tijuana was very precise regarding the amount to use. They wanted to know the weight of the victim, the age, and whether the pills would be administered with alcohol.

The tablets were known in some circles as "Mexican Valium." In the U.S. it fell under the rubric of one of the more popular date-rape drugs. In the right amount, it would knock the victim out for hours. Properly managed and administered it could keep them in a haze for days. And when they finally woke up, they would remember nothing.

This evening Maricela, Herman, and I go over Nitikin's note line by line looking for any information we might glean. She had promised her father that she would maintain the note in confidence. But because Katia is now in trouble, she is certain that her father would want her to do everything in her power to help.

Goudaz is in the other room working at his computer with the door closed. We talk in hushed tones as we sit at the dining table.

"He doesn't mention a ship by name," says Herman. "But somehow he knows that he is going to be at the Port of Balboa in Panama in two days. He doesn't give us a certain time, but he says he's gonna call."

Most of the message is personal. For Maricela this is painful. All indications are that Nitikin's phone call from Panama is intended as a final good-bye. While he doesn't say it in so many words, the message has an ominous tone. Reading the note carefully conveys the definite sense that whatever is happening, the Russian does not expect to survive.

"Why would he be working with these people?" she says. "He detested Alim. I could tell."

"Maybe he has no choice," I tell her.

"What I don't get is this part right here," says Herman. "Who is the contender?" He points to the word in Spanish on the note. The Russian's handwriting is a scrawl. "He says, 'The contender is ready.' Do you know what that means?" He looks at Maricela.

She shakes her head.

"How is the word used in Spanish?" I ask. "What is a 'contender'? Is it an enemy? It could be a reference to Alim."

"No," she says. "'Contender' in Spanish is spelled the same as English. It means the same thing. It's not an enemy. It's like a competitor." She squints and looks more closely at the note. "Ah. The word he uses is *contenedor*. How do you say?" She looks around as if her eyes are scanning the floor and the walls for the English translation, and then says, "Container. He is saying that the container is ready."

"What kind of container?" says Herman.

"If he's going by ship to Panama, it could be a cargo container," I say.

"That would make sense," says Herman. "When you were down there with your father, did you see any cargo containers? You know, a large metal box, about the size of a small truck trailer."

She shakes her head. "My father would not permit me to move around the camp. He didn't want me to see what was happening."

"Assuming that's what it is, then all we need to know is what's in the container," I say.

"That seems to be the sixty-four-thousand-dollar question." The voice comes from behind me. When I turn in the chair, the mayor is standing in the hallway holding some papers in one hand and a pen in the other. He seems to have been listening for some time.

"I couldn't help but overhear. I know that the Port at Balboa, in Panama, is a major transshipment point. There is a large international container facility there. The reason I know this is one of my sidelines. I install electronic sound systems in small boutique hotels and my supplier runs the stuff across the border around customs for me from the port in Panama. I don't know if you remember, but a few years ago there was a big flap because the Chinese government was in negotiations with Panama to purchase the container terminal. It became a very touchy subject because of the canal."

"I remember," says Herman. "Did the sale ever go through?"

"To tell you the truth, I'm not sure," said Goudaz. "I take it you're trying to track a container?"

"It's possible," I tell him. "We're not sure."

"From Colombia to Balboa?"

"Maybe."

"I don't want to butt in, but I know somebody who works at Puntarenas, the Pacific port facilities here in Costa Rica. If you want I'll give him a call and see what I can find out." Goudaz seems to know everybody everywhere. It's the nature of his chosen line of work. I am hoping that he doesn't trip over the news that there's a warrant out for my arrest floating around Costa Rica.

"It could be a waste of time," I say.

"That's what I'm here for," says Goudaz.

"You are so good," says Maricela.

"Give me a few minutes." He disappears back down the hall and into his study.

"How long do you think he was listening?" Maricela says it under her breath.

"I don't know," I tell her. "Long enough to know we were talking about a cargo container." There are limits to the degree of trust Maricela places in Goudaz. It is one thing to seek shelter in his apartment in an emergency, another to tell him where her father is. Clearly they are both using each other to some degree. The price of friendship for Goudaz is information. The question is, what does he do with it all? The problem Herman and I have is that we cannot check into a hotel without being arrested. So all we can do is make the best of it, and thank Goudaz for his hospitality.

We look down the hall to make sure the door to his study is now closed.

"I don't want to sound too optimistic," Herman whispers, "but it is possible that your father's part in whatever they're doing down in Colombia is done. Maybe they're just gonna let him go. It could be that's the reason he's going to Panama."

"Why would they try to kill me and let my father go?" says Maricela.

"Yeah, well, you got a point," says Herman.

"No. When my father is no longer necessary, they will kill him. If he is going to Panama it is because they are taking him there, and if they are taking him there, it is because they need him. It is how he forced them to let me go. He didn't tell me, but I knew. If he finds out what they did to Katia and that they tried to kill me, I guarantee you he will no longer help them."

"We can hold that in reserve," says Herman. "In the meantime, what do you think it is?" He looks at me.

"What?"

"What it is that's in the container."

"All the pieces fit. The special National Security Court, a small group of no names from somewhere in the Middle East, a container that's ready to move, the FBI throwing open the gate so they could track us through Central America; most of all, the look on Rhytag's face when I mentioned the name Nitikin. I think we've known for a while, we just didn't want to say it out loud."

"Yes, but is it chemical, nuclear, or biological?" says Herman. "And is it for real or is it something some amateur cooked up in his kitchen last night?"

"It is painful," says Maricela, "but still I am grateful, to both of you."

"For what?" I ask.

"That finally someone else has said what I have been thinking for so long. What I have been afraid to say for so many years. It is like waking up from a nightmare. Do you understand?"

"So you knew?" I say.

"No. But I suspected. How do you share such thoughts with someone else, especially when they involve someone you love? As you have done, I went through all of the other possibilities. I thought maybe he stole a large amount of money. Maybe he killed someone. I thought about drugs. But none of them fit. When he started to work on this thing, when Alim and his men showed up, I think I knew. And to answer your question," she looks at Herman, "I don't think it is something, as you say, cooked up in a kitchen last night. I believe it is real, and that my father has had possession of it for many years. I believe it is the reason he has been hiding all this time."

"What is it?" I say.

"I would only be guessing."

"So give us your best guess," says Herman.

"My mother has been dead for many years. She lived much of her life in Costa Rica. But she was born in Cuba. My father, as you know, is Russian."

The second she says it, I realize that Harry and I had spent our time with Katia asking the wrong questions. We had concentrated our entire focus on her grandfather. We never asked about her grandmother, where she was from.

"When they were married he was already in trouble with his own government, hiding from them. That much I know," she says.

"Where did they meet?" I ask.

"In Cuba."

"Your father was with the Soviet military in Cuba?" I say.

"Yes."

"When was this?"

"The early 1960s."

The look on Herman's face says it all. "We can cross off chemical and biological," he says.

"Did Katia know this?" I ask.

"She doesn't even know her grandfather is alive. I told her many years ago that he was dead. He wanted it that way."

We sit there for several seconds in silence. Herman is looking at me. "You're thinking about calling Rhytag, aren't you, filling him in? Let's you and me step outside for a second." Herman tells Maricela to excuse us for a moment and he and I step out of the apartment to talk in the stairwell outside.

"We're out of our league," I tell him. "We're not equipped to deal with this."

"Fact is, nothing's changed," says Herman. "I'm bet-tin' this is the part Rhytag already knows about. It's what he's holding back from us, Maricela's pictures of her father. Give you three guesses as to why."

"Because the government probably has a history on Nitikin. And you can bet it's classified. They want to keep it under wraps, find him, find whatever it is he has, and make it all disappear."

"Right," says Herman. "That way people never find out how close they came to gettin' their asses flamed."

"And you're thinking that if I call Rhytag and tell him what it is we think we know, he's only going to be bored. Because all he wants to know is where it is."

"That's my guess. And when he finds out you don't know where it is, he's gonna arrest your ass and turn you over to Templeton. And if you try and tell a jury about any of this, the Dwarf's gonna tell the judge it's a fairy tale, that without hard evidence you can't be al-lowed to even mention it. And he's gonna be right, be-cause that's the way the screwed-up rules of evidence work." This is coming out of Herman's mouth, but he has been in court enough times to know that this is how the system works.

"Still, I can't ask you to get involved in this," I tell him.

"I shoulda' left you in the smokehouse yesterday," says Herman. "I'm already involved. Hear me out. You try to call Rhytag until we know more, I'll beat you to death with the phone."

"Right now I'm charged with only two counts of murder. We get in the way and a mushroom cloud goes up and they could end up adding a few more counts."

"Yeah, but right now we got nothing," says Herman.

"Think about this. If the feds bag Nitikin, Alim, and his followers, say they catch 'em with the goods, unless we're standing right there to witness it all, we still have nothing. They'll stamp 'classified' on the bomb and throw the national security blanket over everything they find. They'll cart it all up in boxes and bury it in some vault.

"That means if you and Katia end up getting strapped to gurneys for a ride to the death house, I wouldn't be holdin' my breath waiting for somebody in the federal government to step up and raise his hand just 'cause they got a Dumpster full of evidence showing somebody else did it. As far as the government's concerned, their only downside is one less sheep to shear come tax time. Katia's a foreign national. The prisons are full of people who didn't do the crimes. Every time they do a new DNA test, they empty another cell block. It's the problem we got, the justice system has absolutely nothin' to do with justice."

Herman takes a deep breath.

"Don't sugarcoat it," I say. "Tell me how you really feel."

"Okay, I shot my wad." He laughs.

"I thought African-Americans were supposed to like government?"

"That's why you never wanna get hooked on stereotypes," he says. "We better get back inside."

"Who is this Rhytag?" As soon as we sit down again, Maricela wants to know.

"Later," says Herman.

So far we have avoided telling her anything about the FBI or the fact that I am charged as a codefendant in Pike's murder. Herman and I haven't talked about this, but we seem to have come to a mutual understanding. Neither of us can be sure whether her cooperation will continue once she realizes I've been charged along with her daughter.

"Problem is, we're missing the same piece to the puzzle he is, the location, where it is. So where do we go from here?"

"It sounds to me like we're going to Panama," says Herman.

"I wouldn't if I were you." Goudaz comes in behind us holding a notepad in one hand, twirling a pen in the other. He's picked up only the last bit of the conversation.

It turns out his friend at the docks at Puntarenas is a storehouse of information.

"He has a line on containerized shipping from all over the world," says Goudaz. "According to him, any container cargo coming out of that area, southwest Colombia on the Pacific side, would ship from a place called Tumaco. His computer shows only one vessel leaving Tumaco bound for Balboa within the next four days, a ship called the *Mariah*. It left Tumaco this morning and is scheduled to make port in Balboa day after tomorrow."

"Then that's it," says Herman. "That's gotta be it."

"There's one problem," says the mayor. "The *Mariah* left Tumaco empty. No cargo. It's supposed to be taking on cargo in Balboa. It's not showing any ports of call between Tumaco and Balboa. But here's the interesting part. The records at the other end in Balboa show preliminary arrangements for transshipment of one cargo container from the *Mariah* to another vessel. So far, the other vessel is unidentified."

Maricela is shaking her head, a perplexed look on her face. "I don't understand."

"You're wondering how the *Mariah* could leave Tumaco empty and arrive in Panama with a container?" says Goudaz.

"Yes."

"Colombian magic," he says. "According to the man in Puntarenas, anything is possible in Colombia. A mystery container gets put on at sea, or they make an uncharted stop in some cove along the coast. He tells me it's also possible the *Mariah* may never show up in Balboa at all."

"How is that?" I say.

"He says smugglers often fog the shipping records. They'll show one destination and sail to another, create false bills of lading for cargo. Sometimes they'll even change the name of the ship en route. They identify a registered container ship, same size as the one they're sailing. The other ship could be in dry dock somewhere or in another port halfway around the world. They borrow the ship's name for a few days. If they plan ahead and create a paper trail and a new destination for the new ship, nobody is going to ask any questions when it arrives on time. And if the paperwork shows the port of origin as a place that's not known for smuggling, officials at the port of destination probably won't check the cargo that closely. Customs will collect any duty, and before you know it the container is on the back of a truck headed someplace else."

"So what you're tellin' us," says Herman, "is we don't know where Nitikin is or the container?"

"If I had to guess, I'd say somewhere out on the big blue. That's the bad news," says Goudaz. "The good news is, we may know more by tomorrow. If by then the computer shows the name of the other ship, the one that's supposed to receive the container, and the *Mariah* actually shows up at Balboa the next day, then the transfer is likely to take place, in which case we should get a final destination."

"What do we do in the meantime?" says Herman.

"I'd sit tight, have another beer if I were you," says Goudaz.

"A man after my own heart." Herman laughs and gets up out of the chair, the whole hulking six foot four of him. He puts his arm around Goudaz's shoulder, dwarfing the man.

"Just one more thing. I hate to even ask, but we don't know who else to turn to. And you're such a helpful guy." This is Herman in full bullshit mode.

Goudaz laughs. "What do you want?"

"Paul and I are afraid the prosecutor in Katia's case may have attached a couple of investigators to us when we traveled down here. If we're going to find information we can use at trial, we need to lose them. We're not going to be able to do that traveling under our own passports. I'm betting you might know someone in town who could produce a couple of good passports on short notice."

"U.S. or foreign?" Goudaz doesn't even miss a beat.

"Too many holograms and threads running through the paper on U.S.," says Herman. "Let's say Canadian."

"When do you need them?"

"Yesterday," says Herman.

"It's gonna cost you."

Herman looks my way for approval.

"Sounds like a business expense to me."

FORTY-NINE

Alim felt the steel sides of the cargo container shudder as the unremitting chop of the rotors suddenly changed. The noise woke him as his stomach told him they were descending. He checked his watch and then jumped to his feet, grabbed his rifle, and reached into the duffel bag where he found a pocket pouch containing four more loaded clips.

He strapped the pouch over his shoulder and glanced at the bag of grenades in the bottom of the duffel. Alim decided to leave them. He took one last look at Nitikin, on the floor. The Russian hadn't stirred since they'd checked his eyeballs earlier that day.

Moving quickly around the wooden crate, he stepped over one of his subordinates who was fast asleep, and kicked the other one who was cowering like a whipped dog.

He got down in his face and told the man, "Get a rifle and load it. You are to guard the container and the Russian. If anything happens to either one, I will cut off your head and feed your body to the sharks. Do you understand?"

The man nodded.

"Move," said Alim.

The man scurried on his hands and knees, around him and toward the duffel bag on the floor.

Alim moved to the two brothers, tapping one of them on the shoulder with the butt of his rifle to wake him. The movement woke the other as well. Afundi gestured for them to stand and join him as he unfolded a sheet of paper and laid it out on top of the wooden crate. He pointed to an area on the drawing and then to one of the two brothers.

The man nodded. He understood what he was supposed to do.

Alim gestured to the other one and pointed to another area on the drawing. The man nodded.

"According to the information there should only be seven targets. But we must get them all. If one of them gets away, there are too many places to hide. If they're wearing red shirts, don't shoot. Do you understand?"

Both men nodded.

They had spent two days practicing, but now they were shorthanded. They would simply have to move faster to make up the difference. He reached into the pocket pouch and gave each of the brothers an extra thirty-round clip.

"Use short bursts, and make them count."

The descent seemed to take forever. At one point they hovered for several minutes, then climbed again, swung out, and circled. Centrifugal force sent the container in a wide arc as the three men grabbed the sides of the wooden crate and struggled to maintain their footing on the steel floor. It was the reason they were confined in the container. The chopper couldn't land on board, but the container could be settled on the deck. And once there, their confederates would open the steel door and they could surge out and take control.

They felt the helicopter move forward slowly and then hover as the heavy cargo container swung back and forth like a pendulum from the steel cables.

When they finally touched down, it came with a jarring blow. It knocked one of the brothers off his feet and threw Alim, shoulder first, into the thin lead shield bolted to the side wall of the container. The men quickly recovered and moved toward the door.

They heard the rotors descending as the giant chopper came down close to the roof of the container, men's voices outside yelling. This was followed by the rasp of metal cables against the outside of the steel container, and a few seconds later the ebbing noise of the rotors as the helicopter pulled skyward.

Alim pulled the bolt back on the assault rifle and let it slam forward, seating the first round in the chamber. The grinding click of metal was followed two more times as the brothers did the same.

They listened as the steel bar on the door was lifted. A second later a blast of cool, damp air rushed into the container.

Alim clicked off the safety and moved the lever down to the middle position, for full automatic fire.

As he did so, a swarthy thin man in a red T-shirt and ragged worn chinos pulled open the heavy steel door, put his shoulder to it, and pushed it wide and out of the way.

For a second the ship's bright deck lights blinded Alim and his followers as they stood in the darkened cave of the container. Then peripheral movement caught the attention of one of the brothers.

Off to the right a short, stocky man in ragged clothes came running out of the darkness. He was swinging a long-bladed machete high over his head and closing in on the man in the red T-shirt.

Afundi's follower swung the muzzle of his rifle and fired from the hip. The first burst went high, sending sparks off a steel railing above the target's head and twenty feet behind him.

The man changed his path, charging the open door. Alim lowered the muzzle of his AK and pulled the trigger. The steel-jacketed rounds spun the man like a Raggedy Ann doll. One of them sparked off the blade of the machete, ripping it from his hand as he collapsed on the deck.

One down, six left.

"Go," said Alim.

The two brothers raced from the open container and out onto the deck.

Afundi turned to his interpreter. The man was shielding himself behind the device and its wooden crate. Alim pointed to the man in the red T-shirt. "Ask him if they have the bridge under control."

The interpreter said something in Spanish, waited for the reply, and translated for Alim. "He says they hold the bridge and the captain. They have temporarily disabled the antenna array." That meant the ship had no radio or satellite capability, at least until Alim's confederates reconnected the antennas.

"Good." Alim headed out into the night air, running toward the bow of the ship. He felt the sway of the open sea under his feet. Even though everything beyond the railing was black, lost in darkness, Afundi could feel the heavy chop as the vessel bucked a stiff headwind.

As he glanced over his shoulder he caught a glimpse

of the open container, perched no more than two feet from the ship's starboard gunwale. One slip and the chopper pilot would have dropped them over the side. They would have gone down, crushed by the pressures of the deep sea, never knowing what happened.

Alim heard shots coming from the other side of the wheelhouse, short bursts of automatic fire. He ducked through one of the steel doorways leading from the cargo deck into the ship's superstructure. He moved slowly down the passageway toward the center of the ship, opening the doors, flipping on overhead lights, and checking each compartment.

He was almost through a large storage area when a sudden burst of shots from the deck above caused something to move in the far corner. Alim aimed the muzzle of his rifle in the general direction of the movement. He flipped the safety lever down one notch to semiauto and fired two single rounds into the steel bulkhead.

The ear-piercing explosions caused the two men to pop up like jacks-in-the-box from behind a row of fifty-gallon drums, their hands stretched high in the air. The two were slight of build, diminutive, and dark skinned. One of them couldn't have been five feet tall. He was wearing an oil-stained tank top and had short shocks of black hair that seemed to shoot in every direction from his small round head. The only thing about him that was big was his eyes as they focused on the muzzle of Afundi's assault rifle. Alim figured the two men were probably Filipino or Southeast Asian. The ship was of Panamanian registry, but the crew came from wherever wages were cheap.

Alim considered dropping them where they were until he saw the lettering on the fifty-gallon drums the two men were standing behind. He couldn't read the words, but he knew the international symbol for flammability.

He gestured with his head and the barrel of his gun for the men to walk toward the door.

They did as he ordered with their hands in the air. Once out of the compartment, Alim marched them down the passageway toward the cargo deck. As they reached the deck, the taller of the two men looked back to get direction as to which way to go, forward or aft.

Alim nodded with his head toward the railing as he lifted the safety lever to the middle position.

The second he heard the click, the man bolted. Afundi pulled the trigger. The burst of bullets caught the Asian before he could take a second step. They ripped through his back and chest before his shocked dead body could hit the deck.

The little one stood frozen in place with his hands up, his back to Alim. His head was turned and his eyes cast down on the bloody mass that an instant earlier had been his crewmate.

With all the thought he might employ in reaching for a cup of coffee, Alim swept the muzzle of his rifle back thirty degrees and emptied the clip.

The man's knees buckled as his body disintegrated in bits of spattered tissue and sprayed blood.

With the casual air of a hunter who has just shot a duck, Afundi turned from the riddled corpse before it could even stop moving. He went through the ritual of reloading, scrupulously depositing the empty clip into his pocket pouch. Then he headed back into the interior of the ship looking to bag another bird.

FIFTY

This morning as Herman and I step out of the cab downtown, I have donned a floppy canvas jungle hat packed from home, and a pair of dark glasses. I have the brim on my hat pulled low over my eyes.

It has taken the mayor the better part of a day to find someone who could produce the passports within the time frame we have.

Just before we left Goudaz's apartment, I tried to reach Harry at the office using the encrypted cell phone. Harry answered; we got a few words in, but a couple of seconds later the call was dropped. I redialed three more times and each time the same thing happened. Herman thinks it's the thick concrete walls in the mayor's apartment building. He calls it the bat cave. I got enough of the message to Harry that he knows we're all right. I'll try again later.

We walk two blocks to Avenida Central, a pedestrians-only avenue that runs half a mile or so through the heart of downtown San José. The mayor has put us on to a small shop where they make document copies and do photographic work. He has called the owner and the man is expecting us.

As we shoulder our way through the crowds walking in the center of the street, I feel as though I'm naked. Templeton has a warrant out for my arrest, but I'm worried that the FBI may have identified Herman, in which case they may have circulated his photograph to the local authorities. Even in a crowd he is big enough that walking next to him is like carrying a signpost.

Half a block down we find the shop. Herman and I quickly get off the street. We give the girl at the counter Lorenzo Goudaz's name, and a few seconds later a tall, slender man with a pencil mustache and drooping eyelids motions us to follow him behind the counter. He takes us to a back room where he quickly closes the door the moment we're inside.

He turns and looks at me. "What is your name, *señor*?"

"We're Lorenzo's friends," I tell him.

"I need to see some identification."

"Is that necessary?" I ask.

"Yes."

I show him my driver's license.

He takes a piece of paper from his pocket, unfolds it, and checks something written on the paper against the information on my license. "Okay. And you, *señor*?"

Herman does the same.

"Okay. Mr. Goudaz says you need them today."

"Correct," says Herman.

"Did he tell you how much?"

"No."

The man smiles a little. "It must be cash. I only take cash."

"How much?" says Herman.

"Twenty-five hundred dollars, each," he says.

"Five grand, that's pretty steep," says Herman.

"You need them in a hurry. Of course, you are free to find someone else who will do them for less," says the man.

"No, we'll have them done here," I say. "But they'll have to be good."

"My work is always good. I have never had any complaints; the pages are all properly stitched; the covers, you cannot tell the difference between the real passport and mine; and the printing and documentation you will see for yourself are excellent."

"How long will it take?" I ask.

"Give me a few moments." He starts for the door, then stops. "You wanted Canadian, correct?"

"That's right," says Herman.

"You know, for ten thousand I could give you two French passports, official paper, real covers, the genuine article."

"Do I sound French to you?" says Herman.

The guy looks at him, doesn't say a word. He steps out of the room, leaving Herman and me alone with the door closed.

"This is probably where the Costa Rican police come in and bust our ass for passport fraud," says Herman.

"In which case the Dwarf will probably give them foreign aid," I tell him. "How much of the money here is going into Larry's pocket?"

"I don't know, but you gotta figure the DSG fee down here is probably pretty high. I know it was in Mexico when I lived there."

"What's the DSG fee?" I ask.

"Delivering stupid gringos," says Herman. "You notice

the mayor couldn't wait to step up and swallow my lie about the prosecutor having us followed as the reason we need new passports."

"That wasn't a lie."

"The way I told it, it was."

"You don't think he believed you?" I ask.

"I don't think he heard me," says Herman. "Calculator in his head was making too much noise trying to figure out the freight on the passports. Mind you, his beer's not bad. But I can't recommend the overnight accommodations."

"Compared to the local jail, I'm thinking I'd probably give it four stars," I tell him. "The real question is whether his Urban Information Exchange is spitting out accurate poop."

"You mean the *Mariah*?" says Herman.

"For starters."

The ship *Mariah* never arrived at the port of Balboa in Panama. According to Goudaz, it should have been there by now. That means that either Nitikin is traveling by other means, or the information in his handwritten note to Maricela is wrong, in which case he may not be in Panama at all.

"Like Goudaz said, it's possible the *Mariah* went somewhere else," says Herman.

Our first hope was to find Katia's camera with the photos from Colombia. We could prop them up in court, identify whatever was in them, and explain the significance to the jury as the reason Pike was murdered. Failing that, our backup was to locate Katia's mother in hopes that she could either provide leads to solid evidence or testify as to what her father was doing in Colombia. The fact that she doesn't know anything means we're batting zero for two.

"I'm troubled by one thing," I say.

"Only one? That's not bad," says Herman.

"How did Goudaz know the container would be shipping out of southwest Colombia?"

"Huh?" Herman looks at me.

"Remember when he came into the room after the phone call to his man in Puntarenas? He showered us with all kinds of information. But the first thing he said was, any container coming out of southwest Colombia would most likely ship from the place he called Tumaco. How did he know the container would be coming out of southwest Colombia?"

Herman thinks about it for a second. "Easy. He knew Maricela flew in and out of Medellín."

"That's what I thought, until I looked at a Google map of Colombia on Goudaz's computer. Medellín's not in southwest Colombia. It's more or less in the center of the country. Maricela said she took a bus from Medellín to some small village where they picked her up in a truck and drove her to where her father was. She didn't say how long the bus ride took, but she said the ride in the truck took most of a day and that she couldn't remember much of it, which I don't buy."

"You think she's lying?" says Herman.

"Let's just say she's protecting her dad. Which still leaves us with the question, how did Goudaz know?"

"If he's wrong," says Herman, "then everything he's told us is out the window."

"I'm not saying he's wrong. Maricela didn't correct him when he said it. And you can bet she didn't tell him."

"Good question," says Herman. "Maybe we should ask him when we get back."

I nod. "Which reminds me. Where is Maricela?"

"She took off early this morning," says Herman. "She went up to the house to see if she could salvage anything. She was hoping to find her phone. She came back an hour later, said there was nothing but ashes. So she took a taxi over to the phone company—I think she said it was called EESAY. Said she was gonna try to buy a new phone and see if she could get her old cell number back. She's still hoping to snag her father's phone call."

"She's a good daughter."

"According to Goudaz, she's wasting her time. Her old phone was GSM. It ran off a chip. Larry told her there's no way they can assign the old number to a new chip. Apparently he's tried it before. He says the assigned phone numbers are already embedded in the chips when the local phone company buys them from the manufacturer. So if you lose the chip, the number's gone."

"We better keep an eye on her. She's wandering all over town alone. Remember what Rhytag said about Katia in the hospital after the bloodbath on the bus? It was better if whoever had tried to kill her thought she was dead."

"So what's Maricela gonna do when we leave?"

"Fortunately you saved her passport when you snatched her purse from the fire. She doesn't know it yet, but depending on where we go, she may be coming with us."

As I say it, the door in this little back office opens. I turn, half expecting to see the police. Instead the man with the mustache is carrying a shoe box with the lid on and a label on the side that reads CANADA.

He puts the box on the table and lifts the lid. It is filled with passports, each one with a black cover, the word CANADA printed above the coat of arms, with the word PASSPORT in both English and French printed below it. All of the lettering and design is in gold ink.

"First you pay, then you pick out a name, any name you want as long as it's in the box," says the mustache. "We will take your pictures, put in the necessary descriptions, and provide the entry stamp for Costa Rica and the temporary entry document. That's the base package.

"For five hundred dollars more you get the professional upgrade. That includes entry and exit stamps for four other countries of your own choosing, assorted artistic stains, and a press job."

"What the hell's a press job?" says Herman.

"We put the passport through a steam press. That bends the binding so it looks like it's had many trips in your hip pocket. I would recommend that you get the professional package since it makes the passport look much more authentic."

"Lemme see if I got this straight," says Herman. "We can pay twenty-five hundred dollars and get your base unit, which is probably good for a stint in a Costa Rican jail, or we can pay three thousand and get a passport that might get us out of Costa Rica and into another country. Is that pretty much it?"

"Up to you."

As Herman is haggling with the man, I turn my back and start fishing in the cash in the money belt under my shirt. When I turn around I'm holding fifty one-hundred-dollar bills. I lay them all out on the counter. He looks at them, the green reality being much better than talk.

In my other hand I'm holding three more one-hundred-dollar bills. "You can keep the press job and the stains. You give us the four extra entry and exit stamps on each passport, you get three hundred more. Otherwise we're walking."

Ordinarily I might not have pressed him. But given the fact that we can no longer use credit or debit cards without leaving a trail like bread crumbs, cash is now king.

"The stains and the bending are very important," he tells us.

"I can spill my own coffee," says Herman. "And I bet you if I sit on it, my ass will bend the binding. You want me to try one and see?"

"Take it or leave it," I tell him. "You can always tell the mayor we went for the base package. He'll never know, in which case you just made three hundred bucks."

He looks me in the eyes, tries to read my resolve. When he can't be sure, he glances back down at the money.

I start to pick up the bills from the counter.

"Okay. You got a deal," he says.

FIFTY-ONE

Liquida spent almost forty minutes trolling the San
José neighborhood in his car, never drifting more
than three or four blocks from the burned-out
house. He wore the oversize shades and the baseball cap.

He pulled up in front of a boutique hotel, rolled down
the passenger window, and told the guard out front he
was looking for a man named Lorenzo who lived in the
area. Perhaps he knew him as the mayor of Gringo
Gulch.

The guard laughed, shook his head. "Never heard of
him."

"Thank you." Liquida drove down the street. He
talked to a pedestrian on the sidewalk a block down and
got the same reply. The lady with the hose was wrong.
The mayor of Gringo Gulch did not know everybody.

He passed a large old colonial house with the words
HOTEL VESUVIO painted on the front wall, above the awning. He drove to the end of the block and had started
to turn left when he saw two gray-haired gringos in
sandals and shorts crossing the street just ahead of him.

He hesitated for a moment. What if one of them was the *alcalde* himself?

Liquida's mind quickly came up with a cover story. He pulled up next to them, rolled down his window, and said, "Excuse me. I am looking for a man who lives near here. His name is Lorenzo. I don't know his last name, but his friends sometimes call him the mayor of Gringo Gulch."

"You mean Larry Goudaz," said one of them.

"You know him?"

"Yeah, he lives down the street." The guy leaned down toward the car window. "Just go straight down, through the next intersection. Go one more block and you have to turn right. If you park at the curb after you make the turn, you'll be right in front of the Casa Amarilla, big yellow house, can't miss it. Larry's place is in the apartment building right across the street, on your left. Second floor."

"Thank you," said Liquida. *"Muchas gracias."*

"Or you could wait until four and catch him at the bar inside the Sportsmens. Larry's got a stool there with his name engraved on it." The gringo laughed.

Liquida smiled, rolled up his window, and drove on. But instead of following the directions he turned at the next intersection and went halfway up the block until he found a space to park.

He took his time inching into the space. The streets in San José were layered with so many pours of asphalt that the roadways arched like rainbows. Drive too close to the edge, your car might roll on its side and disappear into the canyon at the curb. To be safe Liquida left the rental car three feet out from the sidewalk.

He locked it up and crossed the street on foot. He

had walked one more block, passing under some trees and overhanging bushes that arched above the sidewalk, when he saw the big yellow house off to the right. It was an old colonial from the plantation period. Behind it, on the same grounds, was a modern high-rise office building that looked as if it had wandered into the wrong century. The entire compound was sealed off from the street by a high, spiked iron fence that surrounded the L-shaped block.

As he moved farther along the fence toward the yellow house, Liquida noticed a gate with a guard kiosk. There were a dozen or more expensive cars, Mercedeses and Lexuses, parked inside the grounds. Men in dark suits with briefcases and women in tight power outfits, some of them carrying file folders, walked with an air of consequence between the yellow house and the high-rise. To Liquida, the uniformed security, power people, and expensive cars meant one thing—high-level government offices.

The guard kiosk was directly across the street from the apartment building the two gringos had told him about, the place where Lorenzo lived.

Liquida slowed his stride for a moment as he studied the situation. There was no heavy traffic. The quiet lane that separated the gray-masonry apartment house from the government compound made a dogleg, turning to the left almost directly in front of the entrance to the apartments. Liquida figured he had nothing to lose by walking along the sidewalk and checking it out.

When he came to the end of the block, he crossed the street and ended up directly in front of the apartment building. Turning to his right he strolled along the narrow sidewalk as it curved toward the dogleg in front of the building. It was possible there was another entrance into the building, either around the corner or in the back, where he could pick the lock and not be seen entering by a guard in the kiosk across the street.

He was approaching the entrance to the apartments when he heard the clang of metal. The steel gate at the front door suddenly opened. It blocked the sidewalk directly in front of him. The man stepping out didn't see him. He nearly collided with Liquida.

"*Perdón!* Excuse me." He stood there confused for a moment, hanging on to the gate and blocking the way.

Liquida smiled, said, "Excuse me," and stepped through the open gate and into the building as if he belonged there. "*Gracias.*"

"*De nada,*" said the man. He locked the gate from the outside as the Mexican closed the front door. Why look a gift horse in the mouth?

The entrance area was small, a kind of tower with concrete stairs that spiraled up around a central core to the next level. Liquida quickly climbed to the second floor. Finding the right apartment wasn't going to be difficult. The stairs continued up, but on the second level there appeared to be only one apartment with a single door.

Liquida carefully approached it and put his ear gently to the small pane of translucent glass in the top section of the door. If no one was home, he would take a few minutes to check the place out, make sure he had the right apartment, and look for any trace of the woman. He listened for voices and movement inside as he felt for the small box of picks in his pocket.

The ship *Amora* was a coastal cargo carrier but with sufficient fuel capacity for long-range travel. Because it had been traveling empty-handed to Guatemala to pick up a load of lumber, it was operating with a skeleton crew. Its tanks had been topped off with cheap Venezuelan diesel for ballast. It had been designed originally as a Great Lakes freighter, with the wheelhouse and superstructure forward, near the bow.

It was less than three hundred tons in gross weight. This meant that it was exempt from the international automatic identification system, otherwise known as AIS. The system tracked the location and identity of large cargo ships around the world by using satellites. It broadcast information as to their identity and location every two minutes over VHF radio frequencies. Originally designed for collision avoidance, the AIS system was now being used increasingly to guard against terrorism and escalating acts of piracy.

Alim had coordinated with the Tijuana cartel. Two of the cartel members had joined the *Amora*'s crew in Colombia. Armed with handguns, they had disabled the radio and seized the bridge just moments before the container was delivered on board.

Alim and two of his gunmen cornered the last crew member shortly before midnight. By one in the morning, the bodies of the dead were weighted with chain, pitched over the side, and the decks washed clean with high-pressure hoses.

Only the captain remained alive, up on the bridge where Afundi held him at gunpoint until he could rendezvous with the other boat. He would be replaced by a skipper provided by the cartel, along with a new crew, and the *Amora*'s captain would join his men in the eternal chain locker at the bottom of the sea.

* * *

"The Costa Rican government is getting nervous. They're asking a lot of questions. They want to know why the FBI is making such a big deal out of a case involving a single fugitive." James Rhytag sat behind his desk in his Washington office and talked into the telephone as he looked at the report from Thorpe's agents in San José.

"Listen, Jim, give us another day and my people will have him. We're that close." Thorpe was on the other end of the line, trying to buy more time.

"The State Department and the White House are getting nervous," said Rhytag. "There's a complaint from Costa Rican law enforcement that U.S. agents are conducting electronic surveillance on Costa Rican soil without their government's knowledge or approval. The Ticos are threatening to file a formal diplomatic note with our ambassador, in which the government is going to start asking questions in the international press. The White House wants a lid on it."

"My men have locked in on a weak signal from Madriani's cell phone twice in the last two days. They're telling me one more time and they'll have him. Have you seen the report?"

"I'm looking at it now," said Rhytag.

"The house belonged to Nitikin's daughter. According to the neighbors, two men got her out just before the place went up. The two men fit the description of Madriani and the guy he's traveling with. The three of them, the daughter, Madriani, and his friend, all disappeared off the street after the fire. That means if we nab Madriani we may get the daughter as well. And if she took the pictures, she knows where Nitikin is."

"Who the hell blew up the house?" said Rhytag.

"That's the point," said Thorpe. "I can smell it. Something is happening. This thing's going down. Get somebody to tell the people in the White House that if they shut us down now, they may end up having to answer some very painful questions later."

FIFTY-TWO

Y akov woke to the sound of a train, the diesel engine switching gears somewhere off in the distance. He was lying facedown, spittle running from the corner of his mouth. What looked like a gray linen sheet and the open end of a matching pillowcase inches from his face transformed itself to soiled white as it slowly came into focus. There were stains that looked and smelled like motor oil or grease.

For some reason he was famished. The rumbling in his stomach competed for attention with the noise of the diesel engine. He tried to recall when he had eaten last. It was at dinner in the common dining area. Since he never ate much, the meal, some chicken, potatoes, a healthy portion of salad, and bread, should have been plenty.

He began to roll over, then covered his eyes with his hand. Nitikin's head felt as if it were a melon about to split. He could tell by the bright sunlight that it was morning, but he had no idea where he was.

He remembered waking up on the cot in his hut, the piercing beam of the flashlight in his eyes, and the helicopter with its giant rotors whipping the air in the clearing. In his mind he could see the large steel container with its open door yawning wide, waiting to swallow him.

Yakov lay there for what must have been several minutes. But try as he might he could remember almost nothing after entering the cargo container. He recalled seeing the wooden crate, the pressure of his back against the hard metal wall. He had a foggy image of Alim, his cold, evil eyes looking down, his lips moving, saying something. Nitikin couldn't be sure if the image was real or imagined.

He touched his naked wrist and realized that his watch wasn't there. He remembered trying to find it in the bag under his bed but being stopped by the interpreter. Then suddenly he reached down and felt for the shape and the hard plastic of the cell phone in his pants pocket. It was still there. Yakov took a deep breath, brought his hands up, and pressed his fingers to his temples. He closed his eyes and tried to stop the spinning motion.

As the fog in his head began to clear, his eyes focused farther out, on the room and his surroundings. He was dizzy with the constant sensation of motion. The shaft of light piercing the room through the small round window in the wall was also in motion, as were the thin gauze drapes that seemed to dance from the rod above the window. Slowly it settled on him, he remembered the Port of Tumaco, and realized he was on board a ship, but for how long?

Yakov struggled to sit up. He lifted his leaden legs and dropped his feet onto the floor. No wonder they were so heavy, he was still wearing his boots. He crunched with his abdominals as he pushed with his arms, lifting his upper body until he was sitting upright at the edge of the bed. The blood raced to his stomach as his head pounded.

He sat there for two or three minutes unable to move as he collected his strength and looked at the door. The nausea rising in his stomach suddenly curbed his appetite.

Yakov stood up and then stumbled over to the washbasin in the small bathroom. He doused his face with water, then checked the phone in his pocket for any sign of a cell signal. The little screen read NO SERVICE. The time on the screen read 11:22. It was almost noon. He couldn't remember if there was a change in time zones between the encampment in Colombia and Panama City.

When Nitikin tried to open the door to the cabin he found it was locked. He tried releasing the four steel-handled levers that sealed the door tight. Yakov couldn't budge them. Somehow they'd been jammed from the outside. He went back into the bathroom, grabbed a tin cup, and started banging on the steel door until, a few seconds later, the door swung open, revealing one of Alim's minions standing there with an assault rifle pointed at him.

As he was escorted along the deck at the point of a rifle, Yakov looked to see if he could find any sight of land off to his right. He saw nothing but open ocean. He wondered how long before they would get to Panama. His mind began to search for methods to slip away, to make his phone call to Maricela, and perhaps to escape. But first he had to know that his daughter was safe. He would tell her to run, to get away from her house. She had relatives in Limón, on the Caribbean coast. He would tell her to go there and hide out. If he survived, he would try to find her.

He passed crewmen going about their chores but Nitikin didn't recognize any of them. The men glanced at him. None of them seemed particularly concerned by the fact that the man walking behind Yakov was carrying an automatic weapon. Since the crewmen weren't being guarded themselves, Nitikin had to assume that somehow the ship's company had been bought off or co-opted by Alim.

As they approached the superstructure at the front of the ship, the guard pushed Yakov with his rifle toward a set of stairs. They climbed up four decks and arrived on the wing of the bridge, where the guard pushed him toward an open door and the wheelhouse.

Inside, Alim and his interpreter were talking to another man. They were studying the screen of a small monitor mounted on the console next to the ship's wheel. Another crew member was steering the ship.

Nitikin couldn't understand what Alim was saying. But as the translator repeated it in Spanish, Yakov realized that the men were trying to fix the precise position of the ship on the vessel's GPS navigational system.

The captain was a Latino, but from the Spanish vernacular he used, Yakov could tell he was not Colombian or Costa Rican. He couldn't quite place the accent, but he might be Mexican.

The answer to Nitikin's burning question, the distance from Panama, came a second later when the captain looked at the screen and told the interpreter that they were less than twenty-four hours from their destination.

When he heard it, this seemed to please Alim. Afundi then turned his attention to Yakov. He asked him how he was feeling. Yakov said he would feel much better if his men stopped pointing their guns at him. Except for that, he was fine, although he was hungry.

Alim said something to the interpreter, who told the captain to contact the galley to prepare some food and something to drink for Yakov.

Afundi turned back to the Russian, said something to the interpreter, who asked Nitikin whether he'd had a chance to check the bomb. Though Yakov had no recollection of it, according to Alim the container had been handled very roughly as it was loaded onto the ship. The fact that Alim was willing to talk openly about the cargo in front of the captain and the other crew member told Yakov all he needed to know about the ship's company. No doubt they had been well paid.

"How could I possibly check the device? I've been locked up all night."

Alim told him to check it and to report back if there was any problem.

"How long before we arrive in Panama?" asked Nitikin.

As soon as it was translated, Alim looked at him through snake eyes, then offered a sinister smile and spoke.

"He wants to know why you think we're going to Panama."

"Tell him I am informed by intuition because of my Gypsy blood," said Yakov.

Alim laughed.

Apparently the Russian still had a sense of humor.

But that wasn't why Afundi was laughing. Nitikin

didn't know it but thanks to the extended fuel tanks on the helicopter and the fact that Yakov had been maintained in an unconscious state in his cabin for almost four days, they were now nearly three thousand miles north of Panama City, a few hundred miles beyond Cabo San Lucas and just forty-two miles off the coast of Mexico's Baja peninsula. By midafternoon tomorrow they would be tied up at the dock of the international cargo terminal at Ensenada, Mexico, just sixty miles south of the U.S. border.

"Tell him to check the bomb. If there is no damage, I want him to arm the device now, everything except the cordite charge, which I will load, and timer, which I will set myself. The device should be safe from here on out." He wanted Yakov to remove the safety.

Nitikin waited for the interpretation and then replied, "Not until I know the target."

"The target is not your concern." Alim was getting angry.

"It is if you wish to deliver the bomb in one piece. Tell me, do you intend to transport it beyond the ship?"

Following the translation, Alim looked at him with a stern expression, but didn't answer.

"Tell him I will not arm it until I know how it is being transported and where," Yakov said.

Afundi ignored him for the moment and talked to the interpreter in Farsi. "What time do we expect the phone call?"

The interpreter checked his watch. "Any minute now. In fact, he is late."

"I don't want him on the bridge." Alim dismissed Yakov with his eyes. "Tell him to go check the device to make sure there is no damage. And I want a report

back." Alim turned to his man with the assault rifle.
"Watch him closely. And when he's finished, lock him
back in his cabin. I am holding you personally responsible."

As he said it the satellite phone lying on top of the
console rang. "Get him out of here."

Larry Goudaz huddled over the desktop computer in
his apartment as he cradled the phone against his
shoulder and spoke into the mouthpiece.

"That's right, he failed both times. If I were you, I'd
get my money back, unless you haven't paid him yet."

Goudaz waited for the reply.

"Ah, your man is smarter than I thought," Goudaz
said. "How do I know? Because I had lunch yesterday
afternoon with the mother, Maricela, the one who blew
up and burned in her house the day before. She was
here with the lawyer for her daughter—that would be
Katia, Nitikin's granddaughter, the woman he missed at
Pike's house and killed on the bus. She's in the hospital
in San Diego and recovering nicely, thank you. Listen,
when this is all over, tell him I'll send him a DVD. It's a
Road Runner cartoon. There's a character in it you'll
recognize, he's called Wile E. Coyote. I think he's related to the Mexican you hired.

"Yeah, never mind, you'd have to see it to appreci-
ate it.

"Listen, don't...no, don't worry, you can tell him
that I took care of everything. Right now I have them
running errands. And when they come back, I'm going
to give them some urgent news and send them off on a
vacation to Panama for a few days. How much time do
you need?"

He waited and listened.

"No problem. I can give you more if you need it. Yeah, let me get paper and a pencil. I don't want to put that kind of stuff in my computer. Just a second."

FIFTY-THREE

H e stepped away for a moment." The interpreter looked at Alim as he held the satellite phone away from his ear.

"Are you still in contact with the Mexican?" said Alim, talking about Liquida.

"Yes, by e-mail, to different addresses each time."

"Good. Then send him an e-mail and tell him that if he wants his money, he's going to have to meet us in Tijuana, just south of the American border. That's his home. He should feel safe there. Tell him we are going to pay him in gold and narcotics, which will explain why we are not wiring the funds. Because it is not in cash, we will be giving him a significant increase over the market value of these commodities. Tell him you are surprised because we have never offered this to anyone before. Give him the location of the warehouse and say the meeting will be tomorrow afternoon. We are scheduled to arrive in the port about noon, so tell him we will meet at four o'clock sharp. Tell him not to be late."

"He's back." The interpreter put the phone to his ear again. "Okay, here's the deal," he said to the person at the other end. "We are sending a fax from the bridge in just a few minutes. We have the fax number for your cargo-container broker at Puntarenas. You have arranged everything with him, correct?" The interpreter waited.

"Good. Then in our fax we will give him the name of the ship, the registered number on the cargo container, and our estimated time of arrival at Ensenada. The contents of the container will be listed as machine parts. The broker will prepare the necessary customs documents and transmit them to Mexican customs at Ensenada. Here's the information. Write it down. We want you to have it so you can follow up. And make sure he does it today. Immediately. It is critical." The interpreter read the information over the phone and waited while it was read back to him.

"That's correct."

Alim whispered to the interpreter, "Tell him we are going to send him a separate copy of the fax, that way he will have a reminder. We can afford to take no chances on this."

If the documents did not arrive on time, Mexican customs would throw a blanket over the cargo and do a thorough search of the container, including the shielded warhead case inside. If that happened, Alim's mission would be over, and the gamma radiation shriveling the testicles of the customs officers would assure that they would have no more children.

"Listen, the extra service at this end, cleaning up your Mexican's mess, is going to cost quite a bit more," said Goudaz. He had already figured in the thirty-thousand-dollar kickback he would be getting from the cargo broker at Puntarenas.

"Since you're stopping payment on his services, you should have no difficulty paying the surcharge on mine." He quoted them an additional seventy-five thousand dollars. After all it was only money, and who knew when an opportunity like this would come again. What he got was silence on the other end of the phone.

"Tell you what, let's round up and make it an even hundred thousand," said Goudaz. "By the way, I thought you'd like to know, I heard the lawyer and his friend talking. They were wondering just how big your bomb is, how much radioactive fallout something like that might produce. Given that I'm going to have to keep the lid on this until you're done, I would think my fee is worth it."

Ordinarily the nature of the cargo would be beyond the purview of the mayor. His business was simply providing municipal services. But in this case, Maricela and the lawyer had given him some extra leverage, and Goudaz was never one to ignore a gift.

"I knew you'd understand," said Goudaz. "Yes, yes, you can send it by wire transfer to the same numbered account. I wouldn't wait. I'd do it now, this afternoon. That will give me something to think about so I don't forget to follow up with the broker. Good. Excellent. Well, listen, good luck. And take care now." He hung up the phone, clapped his hands, and laughed as he did a little jig around his desk chair.

He carried the dance into the kitchen where he punched the button on the electric hot water kettle on the countertop and got out the French press for a cup of coffee. Goudaz was turning toward the small pantry to grab the bottle of amaretto from the top shelf when he came face-to-face with a man he didn't know.

Before the mayor could even think, Liquida went in through the stomach, piercing the diaphragm. He wiggled the needle-sharp point of the dagger up inside the right-lower chamber of Larry's heart.

"So you cleaned up the Mexican's mess," whispered Liquida.

Goudaz stared back through bulging eyes.

"Wile E. Coyote, huh? Well, beep beep, asshole!" Liquida pushed hard on the handle of the knife and moved it around until he found what he wanted. Blood gushed from the severed aorta as the mayor flopped to the ground.

"The only mess I see is the one on your kitchen floor." Liquida's brain bristled with thoughts of revenge, a growing list that started with the Arab for his arrogance and ended with the lawyer who had interfered to save the woman from the fiery house. He remembered the black man, the big one at the door to the house, and the other one, the shadowy figure at the corner, the one he had tried to find on the street that night.

"So that's who it was." Liquida spoke out loud to himself.

He remembered sitting on the broad avenue outside the lawyer's office and seeing his name in the papers— Madriani. He remembered it as something almost musical. But now emotions of fury consumed him, especially the thought that perhaps he had also meddled in the bus ambush to save the woman's daughter.

Liquida leaned over and picked through Goudaz's pockets until he found his apartment key. Then he stepped around the body, quickly washed the blood off his hands, and cleaned the dagger at the sink. He dried his hands before he picked up the note with the shipping information that the mayor had laid by the kettle on the countertop. Liquida was still reading the note when he heard the metal gate rattle downstairs.

Herman uses Goudaz's spare key to let us in. We have decided to pack up, grab Maricela, and find other accommodations until we can decide where we're going. With the new passports we can start staying in hotels again as long as we use cash. We climb the steps to the apartment. Herman uses the other key to open Goudaz's door.

"It's just us," Herman shouts as I close the door behind us.

"We need to go up and get our stuff together," I tell him.

"You think we ought to tell Maricela so she can get ready?" Herman and I are whispering in the entry area.

"We'll tell her just before we go. I don't want her talking to Goudaz about it. He may try and convince her not to go with us."

Herman nods. "Where is he?"

"I don't know. Probably in his study." I head down the hall to tell the mayor that everything went well with the passports, but nobody is there.

"Paul! Get out here." Herman's voice from the other room tells me something is wrong.

By the time I get to the kitchen, all I see is Herman's hulking frame standing there looking down at something on the floor. I don't see the blood or Goudaz's body until I come through the door.

"Ain't no sense checking for a pulse," says Herman. "Look at his eyes." Herman slowly backs away from the body and edges over toward one of the drawers near the sink. He slides the drawer open and reaches in, his eyes constantly scanning the two doors leading into the kitchen. He takes a quick glance down at the open drawer and grabs a large butcher knife. He hands me another sharp blade.

"Let's check the rooms," he says. "Stay together. If he jumps me, use the knife, put it in him deep, as many times as you can—and don't hesitate. Can you do it?"

I nod.

It takes us several minutes, moving cautiously from room to room, to clear the apartment. Whoever killed Goudaz is gone, and so is Maricela. There is no sign of her, and no note.

"You think he might have taken her?" says Herman.

"Why would he take her now if he tried to kill her before? It doesn't make sense. He could have dumped her body someplace else."

The thought hits us both at the same moment. We break for the door.

I stop to grab the key from the hook as Herman runs ahead of me up the steps to the other apartment. With blood and a dead body on the floor, I lock the door from the outside so no neighbors wander in.

I am hoping that Maricela is hiding upstairs in the other apartment, praying that whoever killed Goudaz didn't find her and dump her body there.

By the time I get up the steps to the open apartment door, Herman has already used the key in his pocket and raced through the rooms. He is standing in the living room shaking his head. "She ain't here," he says.

"You checked every room?"

"I looked. She's not here."

We check again, this time carefully, opening every

closet, looking under the bed. We even check the refrigerator, a thing macabre movies make you do. Nothing.

We close the door, lock up, and head back down.

"What time did she leave to go to the phone company?" I ask.

"I don't know. I think it was probably a little after nine," says Herman.

"She can't still be there."

Without a phone to reach her, there is no way of knowing.

"What do we do now?" he says. "We can't stay here."

"No. We need to pack up. But first we have to make sure we have everything out downstairs."

"You think we oughta wipe the place down?" says Herman.

"You mean the body?"

"No. I mean our prints, anything we mighta' touched."

I think about this for a second. "No. If we do and the killer left any trace evidence, we're likely to destroy it. Besides, two days in a confined area like the apartment and trace evidence of our presence would be everywhere. We'd never get it all."

"Sure." Still, Herman takes the knife out of my hand, wipes the handle and the blade with the tail of his shirt as I use the key to open Goudaz's apartment door.

As I do, I hear the phone in the study ring. Herman and I look at each other, then I break and run toward the sound. I can't tell how long it's been ringing. Before I get there the automatic answering device picks up the call.

I wait and listen, hoping at least that I might hear the message. Instead there is a long beep as the fax machine on the desk kicks in. I wait a few seconds. The machine spits out a single sheet and then quits.

"Who was it?" Herman has put the knives back in the drawer and is now standing behind me.

"I don't know, it's a fax." I grab the page and start to read, but it's in Spanish. Herman studies it over my shoulder.

"Son of a bitch!" he says. "That answers your question, how Goudaz knew where the container was comin' from. Look," he says. Herman points with his finger. "The name of the ship, and it ain't the *Mariah*. Vessel's called the *Amora*. Its ETA, where it's headed, even the container number. And the name at the bottom, 'A. Afundi.' First name Alim," says Herman.

"But why? It doesn't make any sense."

"It's a copy of a fax sent to a cargo broker. They wanted Goudaz to follow up on it. From what I'm readin' he gave 'em the lead on the broker. Like you said, he was selling information."

"So that's how they knew about Pike and the fact that he had the pictures. It still doesn't make any sense. If they needed his help, why did they kill him?"

"Who knows," says Herman. "At least we know where we're going."

I look at my watch. "What's the time difference between here and Ensenada?"

"Same as at home," says Herman. "It's one hour later here, I believe."

I hear the gate clatter downstairs and a shrill voice. "Lorenzo! Lemme in." It's Maricela. I run to the little French windows leading to the tiny balcony, step out, and stick my head over the railing. "Stay there, we'll be down in a minute."

"Lorenzo was right. They couldn't gimme my old phone number. So I don't know what we do now," she says.

"Just wait there."

I don't even bother to close the window. "Let's grab our bags." I see a phone book on a shelf in the kitchen. "Hold on a second. How do you say 'charter air' in Spanish?"

Herman thinks for a moment.

"Never mind." I grab the book and take it. "Make sure Maricela's got her purse."

"Why?"

"Because her passport is in it."

FIFTY-FOUR

As he marched toward his car, Liquida knew the Arab would be sending him an e-mail any minute telling him he wanted to meet him to pay him. Liquida would meet him all right, on his own timetable and perhaps at a place of his own choosing.

He no longer cared about killing the woman. As far as he was concerned, at least for the moment, he was working for himself, and there were only two people on his current hit parade: the man called Afundi who owed him a bundle, and the lawyer who had interfered for the last time.

In his present state of agitation, Liquida was a good fit for the Tico traffic of San José. He whipped out of the parking space without bothering to look in his mirror, cutting off a woman who hit her brakes and laid on the horn.

Liquida gave her the finger out his open window as he laid rubber on the rainbow road, streaking for the airport. He was already calculating in his mind which terminal in northern Mexico to parachute into that would put him closest to the port of Ensenada.

* * *

They say that with enough money you can buy anything. At the moment Herman and I are testing the concept. Sitting in the backseat of one of the little red taxi sedans, we are rumbling down Highway 1 just beyond the broad avenue known as Paseo Colón. The shocks are gone on the car's rear end, so we feel every bump and groove in the road as it vibrates from the tailbone up the spine.

Herman and I are silently counting the currency from our money belts as Maricela sits, watching us from over the front-passenger seat. We have not told her that Lorenzo is dead, only that we have information regarding her father, where we think he will be, that there is no time to talk, and that we will fill her in later.

"I don't think it's enough," says Herman. "You gotta figure it's at least twenty-five hundred miles, maybe more."

Herman and I left the States with a total of nineteen thousand dollars between us in the two money belts. Less the fifty-three hundred we paid for the two passports leaves us thirteen thousand seven hundred. Even if I wanted to use it, the feds have probably put a stop on my credit card. Herman could use his, but it has a twenty-five-hundred-dollar limit and there's no question they would trace it.

"I booked a charter flight out of Mexico a few years ago for a client and it cost us twelve grand back then. And we didn't go nearly that far," he says.

"We won't know unless we try," I tell him.

"*Señor*, we are coming up to the turnoff, I need to know if you want me to take it or keep going."

"Give us a minute," says Herman.

"This time of the day the only commercial flights north are gonna take us to the States. Maricela can't get in without a visa even to transfer flights. And then there's the question, do you really want to try and run the U.S. border on these things?" I tap the phony Canadian passport next to me on the seat.

"Take the turnoff," says Herman.

The driver cuts across three lanes of traffic, setting off horns all across the city. He hangs a quick right on the short off-ramp, rolls through the stop sign, and starts winding through the back streets. I ask Herman for the cell phone and call Harry. I have tried to reach him repeatedly over the last several days. I am wondering if perhaps the carrier simply doesn't have good coverage in this area.

I am holding the fax from Goudaz's apartment in my hand as Harry answers.

"Where the hell have you been? I've been trying to reach you for two days," he says.

I tell him to get a piece of paper and write down what I'm about to tell him. With what we now know from the fax, Herman and I have decided that we can no longer withhold the information from the federal authorities.

"Wait till I get outside," says Harry.

"You're in the office?"

"Where the hell else would I be?" he says.

"Then stay there, you won't need a pencil. Just repeat everything as I give it to you out loud. As I say it."

"You know what you're doing?"

"Yes, we're talking to the world," I tell him. "I want you to contact Rhytag and give him the following information. Go ahead. Say it out loud."

"You want me to contact Rhytag and give him the following information."

"The weapon is in transit on board a ship."

"What weapon?" says Harry.

"Never mind, just say it."

He repeats it out loud.

"The name of the ship is…" Before I can say the word *Amora*, the line goes dead. "Hello. Hello. Damn it!"

Just as I push the button to dial again, the driver starts goosing the taxi, bumping aross the deep swales at blind intersections as if this were the national sport. Herman and I bounce all over the backseat.

The phone rang on his desk and Thorpe picked it up.

"Hello."

"Director Thorpe, Bob Mendez."

"Yes, Bob, have you got something for me?"

"We think so. We've zeroed in on the cell phone signal. It's clear as a bell. At a place called Pavas."

"Where's that?"

"It's a suburb just a few miles north of San José. It seems that Madriani and the other man are on the move. We were having trouble honing in on the signal downtown. We were getting interference from someplace. Then we realized the Costa Rican Foreign Ministry had an antenna array on top of their building. We were picking up their transmission signals and jamming them by mistake."

"The ministry?"

"Unfortunately, yes."

Thorpe winced.

"Don't worry, we won't put it in any reports," said Mendez. "The good news is, the cell phone is now in the clear. He keeps powering down, so we lose the signal every once in a while. He was moving, but he appears to be stationary now. We're triangulating the position. We have agents closing in on the area, along with the Costa Rican police. I thought you'd want to know."

"Excellent. Are you in communication with your agents?"

"I am."

"Good. Then tell them the following. There is a chance that a woman is traveling with Madriani and the other man." Thorpe pawed through some papers on the top of his desk until he found the one he wanted. "Her name is Maricela Nitikin-Osa de Solaz." Agents in Costa Rica had found the name in official records after they realized Maricela had survived the blast at her house and has been seen with Madriani and Herman.

"Tell your agents that it is absolutely essential that the Costa Rican authorities hold her for questioning. Also tell them to make sure she's given adequate security. We think there's already been one attempt made on her life. And tell the agents that Justice and State are working on some kind of documentation to get permission from the Costa Ricans so that we can question her. It's going to be dicey. She's a Costa Rican national. Tell your agents that if the local authorities let her go, I want a tail put on her twenty-four–seven. Understood?"

"Yes, sir."

"And if she tries to leave the country, stay with her."

"Hold on a second," said Mendez, "something's coming in now." He went off the line for a second. Thorpe could hear voices in the background. Then Mendez was back. "They're less than a mile from the signal, do you want to hold?"

"Yeah, I'll stay on the line."

FIFTY-FIVE

As Realtors will tell you, location is everything. For us, the good news is that Costa Rica sits dead center, right on the spine of the Americas.

The airport in Pavas is smaller than San José International, known as Juan Santamaría. The Pavas airport caters to domestic flights and eco tours to the coasts. It offers occasional international charters, from small prop jobs to jets, the occasional Citation, and even a Gulfstream or two as we learn today.

Ordinarily you couldn't touch a charter flight from San José to northern Mexico for anything close to thirteen grand. But the bad economy and the good location have conspired to make things possible. These days, flights coming from the south are often snagged in the air by radio if the passengers are willing to allow a few more on board in return for a good discount.

Today we get lucky. A Gulfstream is already on the ground, sitting on the runway. It is headed from Panama City to Los Angeles and will stop in Mexico City for the couple who are now getting ready to board.

A phone call from the charter desk out to the plane,

followed by a quick vote by the other two people already on board, and for a little over eleven thousand dollars all three of us have a ride north.

"Do we get any hors d'oeuvres on board?" asks Herman.

I give him a look to kill.

"Just wondering." He gives me a moping face. "Been a while since we had breakfast."

"There is food on board." The man behind the counter is working the computer, not even looking at us when he says it, so he doesn't see the broad smile on Herman's face.

"See, it pays to ask," says Herman. "Bet you they got beer too," he whispers in my ear.

The man at the counter barely looks at our passports, just long enough to take the names and put them in the computer, then hand them off to the resident immigration officer a few feet away who punches them with an exit stamp and hands them back to us. We allow Maricela to take the lead on this as she speaks impeccable Spanish and makes Herman and I appear almost civil.

If I'd known, I could have saved us five grand, though I may be happy to be a Canadian citizen on the Mexican end. There are no boarding passes. We just haul our luggage out onto the tarmac. When the three of us climb the steps and get inside, we see the luxury of the deep leather chairs, all of which seem to swivel and recline. The four other passengers are standing next to a center table, munching and clinking their iced glasses.

They turn with broad smiles and introductions to welcome the rest of the partygoers. *Hi, my name's Paul. I'm an international fugitive. Please excuse the blood on my hands. There simply wasn't time to wash up.*

Instead I shake hands and use my Canadian name to make new friends. I haven't figured out what I do for a living yet, but I'm sure they'll ask. I take the cell phone from Herman, move to the back of the plane, and make one last attempt to reach Harry.

"We got 'em," said Mendez.

"Did you get the woman?" said Thorpe.

"If she's with him, they'll have her in just a few seconds."

"What do you mean? Either you have him or you don't," said Thorpe.

"The agents are turning onto the street right now. They're less than a hundred feet from the signal. They're right on top of them, could reach out and touch them," said Mendez.

"Can you hear what's going on?" said Thorpe.

"What do you mean it's a different tower?" Mendez was talking to someone else. Thorpe could hear more voices, a lot of excitement at the other end. "What?"

"What's happening?" said Thorpe.

"Sir, there's a little confusion here. We're getting some signals we don't understand. There's got to be a tower malfunction. The signal's been handed off to three separate towers. What? How fast?"

"What's going on?" said Thorpe. "Talk to me."

"According to our technicians the signal is moving again. Whoever has the phone is doing about a hundred and forty knots."

"What?"

"That's about a hundred and sixty miles an hour."

"I know what a goddamn knot is," said Thorpe.

"He appears to be on an airplane."

"Do we have any military assets in the area? WACs, anything that can track it on radar?"

"I don't know."

"Well, find out. And see if you can get the tower at the airport to call the plane back. Costa Rican police ought to be able to do something. And call me when you know." Thorpe slammed the receiver down so hard it bounced off the cradle on the phone and onto the floor, where he got up and kicked it.

Nitikin had spent most of his life shielding the bomb and harboring it for a purpose. In his youth, the device was an instrument of the revolution. That Khrushchev would not use it for that purpose and share the power with their comrades in Cuba had angered Nitikin. The revolution was an ideal, pure and pristine. Yakov had never abandoned his country. On the contrary, its leaders had abandoned the revolution. Despite all the years he spent in hiding, Yakov Nitikin was still a soldier.

But now that he was old, he was confused. He longed only to spend time with his daughter, to see her again, to talk to her, to hold her. He wanted to see his granddaughter, Katia, whom he had seen only once as an infant, but whom he talked about endlessly with Maricela, asking questions and looking at photographs. All of these were now lost, left behind in his hut at the encampment. He had cried himself to sleep, bellowing like a baby the night Maricela left the camp. Something had snapped in him. He feared for her and could not wait to call her on the phone.

He now hovered anxiously on the edge, caught between duty and the desire to escape.

Nitikin knew that there was no way to bargain with

Alim. To attempt it was to invite a quick death. How does one bargain with the devil? The moment Afundi knew that the bomb was armed, he would pull out his pistol and Yakov would be dead. There were times he thought he hated the man enough that he could kill him, but the thought of sabotaging the bomb never entered his mind.

To fail now was to betray everything he believed in, all that he had worked for all those years. He had traded a life with his family for the mission of the bomb. It was not his child, though there were times when he felt as if it throbbed with life, the embryo of revolution.

He searched for some way out, some method by which he could satisfy duty and still see his daughter. What he needed was time.

Yakov was working through an open side panel of the wooden crate, inside the container, presumably checking the device for any damage, as instructed by Alim.

Nitikin had lied to him. The bomb was entirely safe to transport. The safety device was redundant. After all, the warhead had been designed for delivery in the belly of an unmanned MiG jet, a cruise missile launched from a ramp, not unlike the V-1 rocket. The gravitational and kinetic forces applied to the warhead at launch were probably three or four times greater than those experienced in the most violent vehicle collision or other accident.

True, the safety device would prevent the bomb from achieving a chain reaction if the gun was fired accidentally, but there was no chance of that unless the cordite charge was loaded under the breech plug, which only a fool would do except immediately prior to deployment.

For Nitikin the safety device had but a single purpose: it made him indispensable and kept him alive. It had one other advantage—only he knew whether the safety device was engaged or not.

"He wants to know if there is any damage."

Nitikin was startled by the voice coming from behind him. He looked out and saw the brooding face of the interpreter standing in the bright sunlight just outside the open door of the container.

"No, it looks fine. I'm just checking the last few items."

"Then I can tell him the device is in working order? You're sure?"

"Yes, I'm sure." Yakov spoke from inside the box, without looking. When he didn't hear any further comment, he stuck his head out and saw the larded backside of the interpreter twenty feet away, walking in the other direction along the deck, toward the bridge.

Nitikin turned back to the bomb. He used the flashlight he'd borrowed from the interpreter to check and make sure that the minute groove cut into the safety wire was properly aligned, a quarter turn, ninety degrees, in a clockwise direction. Once satisfied, he took hold of the wire and turned it counterclockwise until the groove in the wire was facing straight up.

Very gently, so as not to break the delicate bond holding the wire to the safety disk, Yakov eased the wire toward himself until he saw the fine red line painted on it at the outer edge of the bomb case. The safety disk was now clear of the gun barrel. It was housed in a separate supporting container welded to the inside of the bomb case. Reinserting the safety in the barrel would take knowledge of the settings as well as fine hand skills that even Nitikin doubted he possessed any longer.

Yakov crawled from the crate, closed the wooden side panel, and screwed it down tight.

Arming the bomb had fulfilled his duty as a soldier even though he had no intention of informing Alim until the last moment, and then hopefully through a note or a message delivered by another. Now Yakov was free to escape and join his family, if he could only find the means.

FIFTY-SIX

Unfortunately the Gulfstream had everything on board but an in-flight phone system. The copilot who saw me trying to talk to Harry on takeoff told me to shut it down. The cell phone might interfere with their avionics.

An hour into the flight and the passengers seemed to settle down. The other two couples paired off to seats and settled in for the ride. Herman and I spent the time in the rear of the plane trying to explain to Maricela what we'd found when we returned to Lorenzo's apartment.

At first she couldn't believe that he was dead, and when she finally came to accept it, she blamed herself for leading the killer to his front door.

"You don't understand," I say. "Lorenzo was selling them information." I showed her the fax from his machine.

As she read it her eyes gravitated to the name at the bottom of the page. "That's it. I remember. I heard only once, but his last name was Afundi. I knew that I'd heard it. I just couldn't remember. But why? Why would Lorenzo be working with them?"

"The oldest reason in the world," says Herman, "money."

"You mean he sold Katia's life for a few dollars?"

"He may not have known that they would try to kill her, but I doubt if there's any question that he fingered Pike."

"How did he meet such people?" she says.

"He was dealing with the same people your father is," I tell her.

"Yes, but my father has no choice."

"Regardless, the result may be the same. We need your help."

"How?"

"We can't identify either Alim or your father. We need to find them and track the container until we can get the authorities to stop it. If we don't, a great many people are going to die. Do you understand?"

She doesn't say anything. She just looks at me. "I cannot believe my father would do something like that."

"Perhaps, as you say, he has no choice. If that's the case, we're going to have to do what we can to help him get free."

She looks at me, then nods. "Then I will help you," she says.

"Good."

Three hours later we land in Mexico City to off-load the first passengers. I tell the pilot that my cell phone is on the fritz and ask him if there is any way he can send a message over the plane's VHF radio to a friend in San

Diego. I can't very well tell him about the bomb without raising eyebrows and being arrested.

Instead the man lets me use his cell phone. I take it to the back of the plane for privacy.

It is after hours. The office will be closed, so I call in the open to Harry's unguarded cell line. I don't have Rhytag's phone number or I would make the call myself.

Harry doesn't answer. I can't be sure if he is even carrying his regular cell phone any longer. Harry hates cops. With the federal government now listening in, he has probably flushed the phone down the toilet.

Nonetheless I leave the message to have Harry call Rhytag and tell him about the bomb. I give him the name of the ship, *Amora,* and its estimated time of arrival in Ensenada. I am hoping that the feds are listening in.

Then I call Harry's house. Again he doesn't answer, so I leave the same message on his home phone. For the moment, at least, it's all I can do.

Liquida got bounced like a Ping-Pong ball all over the hemisphere trying to get back to northern Mexico. From San José he shuttled to Houston and from there caught a connecting flight to San Diego. He didn't even try to fly south from there. Instead he rented a car and stopped for coffee at one of his haunts, a twenty-four-hour Internet java shop just outside National City.

Inside he ordered a latte and sat down at a computer to check his e-mail. He was anxious to snag the Arab's message and read his lies. Liquida knew that between the coffee and the raghead's brazen deceit, it should be enough to get his blood going again, to keep him awake at least until he could get across the border.

He was feeling pretty good. He had spent several hours snoozing on the planes, dreaming of ways to entertain his employer. He wondered if the man had family, and if so whether they had any money, and how much an ear or part of a nose might go for among relatives in the Middle East. He could give them a discount and sell him by the pound, a piece at a time. Liquida dreamed that maybe he could take the Arab alive, and get him alone somewhere, in which case the one thing he could promise the man was that he wouldn't die fast.

At least Liquida could now relax. According to the note he took from the dead cartoon critic at the apartment in San José, he had plenty of time to meet the boat at Ensenada. It wasn't due in until sometime around noon tomorrow.

He punched up the screen on the computer and waited a second to enter the floating ether of his endless e-mail domains. Then he slipped down through the junk mail and found what he wanted.

Liquida opened the message and sure enough there was text on the screen, so he knew that the Arab was lying again. The e-mail was filled with irritating false praise for the fine job he had done. Because of this, his employer wished to reward him with valuable commodities— gold and fully marketable narcotics and hints that they might even throw in the moon and the stars. But Liquida would have to stop by to pick it all up personally since FedEx was balking at delivering the heroin and the springs on their van couldn't seem to take the weight from the mountain of gold they had for him. They apologized for the inconvenience and said they hoped he'd understand.

Liquida was angry with today's e-mail provider. If

their bullshit checker had been working properly, every word in the message should have been underlined, flashing and depositing little drips of brown down the screen by now.

The Arab translator even gave him an address in Tijuana where Liquida could hook up his trailer to haul this treasure trove home, and told him tomorrow, four o'clock sharp, not to be late. The Arab's other assassins must charge overtime, thought Liquida.

He wrote down the address, signed off on the computer, finished his coffee, then looked at his watch. He wondered if it was too late to drop by one of his suppliers and pick up some stuff, or whether the guy would still be awake. Then he dismissed the thought; after all, that's what doorbells were for.

And if he didn't answer, there was always the fire alarm.

FIFTY-SEVEN

It was edging up toward ten o'clock at night by the time the sleek Gulfstream dropped us at the airport just a few miles south of the port at Ensenada. In less than ten minutes we had our luggage, and had cleared customs as well as immigration. A single sleepy-eyed officer took one look at our bags, then searched for a blank page on our passports, hit them with the stamp, and welcomed us to Mexico.

We took a taxi and laid up overnight in a small hotel on the waterfront near the pleasure-boat docks on the harbor. We booked a separate room for Maricela, while Herman and I bunked together to save cash. We were now down to a little under seven hundred dollars. As a last resort I could always try my ATM card, though by now I am certain that Templeton will have it blocked.

The following morning we get up early and grab breakfast at a small restaurant on the waterfront. Most of the stores and shops aren't open yet. We find an outdoor market that has what we need.

I open our piggy bank and we use a little over a hundred dollars of the cash we have left to buy a beach bag, some items of clothing for Maricela, and a few snacks. Since the fire, except for a few sundries and necessities she purchased yesterday morning on her way to the phone company in San José, Maricela has nothing.

Back in our room I stand at the window and look out at the small boats in the slips that line the floating docks in front of the hotel. Off to the left is the cruise terminal with its long concrete dock that, at the moment, is empty.

About a mile away on the other side, I can see the international cargo terminal. It lies along a jetty that forms the breakwater between the harbor and the Pacific Ocean. My best guess is that we are now roughly eighty miles south of San Diego.

There is a large container ship the size of a small city tied up to the dock across the harbor and being off-loaded. It is riding high in the water and appears to be almost empty. Four enormous container cranes silhouetted against the open sky stand like steel giraffes. One of them is digging deep into the hold of the ship. It lifts out two containers at a time and stacks them on the dock. Smaller portable gantries roll up and down the wharf lifting cargo onto trucks that are lined up waiting to carry materials to the factories up north.

"What time do you have?" My watch has stopped.

"Ten forty," says Herman.

By now Harry should have gotten my messages, and Rhytag should be mustering his forces, contacting the Mexican Federal Judicial Police and making arrangements to send agents south from the border.

"If the fax is accurate and the ship's on time," says Herman, "that gives us less than ninety minutes. Any ideas how you want to do this?"

"Do you have your binoculars?"

"In my bag," he says.

"Can I borrow them?"

"Sure." Herman fishes through the bag, finds the small Zeiss four-power glasses, and hands them to me.

From where I am standing, even with the field glasses I can barely make out the name on the bow of the container ship. Just enough to know that it's not the *Amora*.

"One thing's for sure, we need to find a place where we can see better. Why don't we pack up and leave the bags by the door? Then let's get Maricela and take a walk."

We go two blocks away from the water, then head along a main drag until we come to a bridge that crosses the canal. We turn right and follow the path along the canal out to where the cruise ships dock. By the time we get there, the container ship is buttoned up and two tugs have moved in to ease it away from the dock across the harbor.

We find a bench and the three of us sit like bumps on a log to wait.

Maricela watches through the field glasses as the tugs, with meticulous care, nudge the huge ship out into the center of the channel. They assist the empty cargo container as she turns in her own length. Ten minutes later the ship gets her bow pointed out to the open sea, and the massive screws begin to churn the water under her stern. In less than five minutes she is out beyond the jetty with the two tugs trailing alongside.

I am wondering if I should try and call Harry again, though I'm not sure how.

The two tugs have peeled away from the larger ship, but they aren't coming back to port. Instead they are sitting there. They appear to be dead in the water, maybe a couple of miles out. If I strain my eyes I can see what appears to be a dot just this side of the horizon.

"Somethin' out there," says Herman.

"Yeah, I see it."

"Can I see the glasses?"

Maricela hands them to Herman.

He peers through the binoculars for ten seconds, maybe longer, trying to fine-tune the focus. "It's a cargo ship. Looks like it might be empty, but I can't tell."

"Why wasn't I informed?" said Rhytag. He was standing at his desk barking into the phone. "So I was in a meeting. So you should have interrupted me.

"I don't care if the agents thought it was a hoax.

"I know. I know. I'm aware that Madriani and his partner know we've been monitoring them. So what if they're playing games. I still want to know. Has anyone checked out the information?

"What I'm saying"—his voice went up a whole octave—"is do we know if there's a ship named the *Amora* scheduled to dock at Ensenada?

"Well, then find out! And call me back," Rhytag shouted into the phone. He didn't even bother to hang up. He just pushed the button for the other line and dialed a new number. He waited a few seconds and the instant the phone on the other end was picked up he said, "Zeb. Jim here, have you heard? Last night a phone call came in on the wiretap at Madriani's partner's house. There was no answer, so the caller left a message. He identified himself as Paul. The agents say the voice sounded like Madriani. He told his partner to call me and tell me that the bomb was on board a ship. According to the message, the ship is named the *Amora* and it's scheduled to dock at Ensenada, Mexico, sometime today. They didn't bother to report it because it's clear that Madriani and his partner know the offices are bugged and the phones are tapped. The agents are certain it was a hoax.

"Why? Because yesterday afternoon there was another phone call. Presumably it came in over the lawyer's encrypted cell phone, so the agents couldn't hear the actual conversation. But according to what they heard over the bug in the office, the partner appeared to be using our wire to jerk the agents around. He was taking them right to the cusp of something important, apparently pretending to repeat information he was getting over the phone and then pretending the phone went dead...Zeb, Zeb, are you there? I thought I lost you," said Rhytag.

"What's that?"

Rhytag listened to the long explanation about triangulation and jamming as the blood seemed to drain from his head. He was getting the details when his secretary came through the door with a handwritten note and handed it to him.

He read the note as he was listening to the litany of excuses from Thorpe: "Confirmed. Panamanian-registered ship *Amora,* currently docked container port Ensenada, Mex. Agent M. Trufold."

"Zeb, never mind that. Shut up and listen..."

We sit quietly on the bench and watch as the *Amora* clears the jetty and heads into the channel. She's much smaller than the other container ship that left port almost an hour earlier, and she's riding high in the water. As she swings her stern to clear the breakwater, I see a single cargo container resting on the deck, near the stern.

"You think that's it?" says Herman.

"It's gotta be, unless there are more containers belowdecks," I say.

I scan with the glasses back in the other direction hoping to see a train of police vehicles streaming into the port. Instead all I see are trucks hauling cargo containers in the other direction, up the coast highway toward Tijuana and the border.

"Can I see?" said Maricela. Apparently she sees something on the ship she wants to look at.

I hand her the field glasses.

She puts them to her eyes and adjusts the focus, looks for a moment, and then says, "That's him!"

"Your father?" I ask.

"No. Alim," she says. "On the stairs." She hands the glasses back to me. "Up at the top."

I adjust them and look. A slender man with dark hair, wearing white coveralls, is standing on the wing of the bridge and just starting to make his way down the steps. I get a good look at him as he climbs to the main deck and disappears through a door in the tower section of the ship.

"Are you sure it's him?" I ask.

"Yes. I would know that face anywhere. But where's my father?" She wants the glasses back.

I hand them to her.

I turn to Herman. "If that's the container on the deck, it's not going to take them long to off-load. If they get it on the back of a truck and clear customs, they'll be out along the jetty and up on the highway before we can move. Do you see a road coming in here anywhere?"

Herman turns, scans the parking area behind us. "It's all fenced off. But back along the path by the canal, there was a street that came in."

"Listen, see if you can get out on the road and flag down a taxi. Take it to the street by the canal and wait for us. I'll stay here with Maricela, see if we can catch a glimpse of her father and keep an eye on the container. Just wait for us out there."

Herman heads out on the run.

By the time I look back, the tugs have the *Amora* pressed up against the cargo dock across the way. It appears as if they aren't even waiting to tie her up. One of the huge cargo cranes is lining up to lift the container from the aft deck.

Maricela is frantically scanning the deck from bow to stern looking for any sign of her father.

In no time at all the container is in the air and lifted free of the vessel. The mammoth arm of the crane swivels as the container swings over the side and disappears from sight down onto the dock on the other side of the ship.

"We're gonna have to go," I tell her.

"But where is my father?" she says.

"He could be on the other side of the ship, behind the superstructure, or in one of the cabins. Or possibly he's already down on the dock."

She looks at me with a certain anxiety in her eyes. *Or he could be dead*, she must be thinking. But she doesn't say it.

"We can't wait any longer," I tell her. "We need to get

to the taxi, grab our stuff at the room, and get out there." I point to the end of the road that runs along the top of the breakwater where it merges with the coast highway heading north. "If we lose them now, we'll never find them again."

We head off running as fast as we can along the path toward the canal.

FIFTY-EIGHT

L isten, thank him for us. How many units are they sending?" Thorpe listened as he penciled notes on a pad on the table.

Rhytag looked on. They were closeted in the operations center in the bowels of the FBI building with communications at their fingertips and a small army of agents and technicians working computers and handling phones.

"Any idea how long it'll be before they get there?" Thorpe flashed all five fingers of one hand at Rhytag twice in quick succession. Ten minutes.

"Did you offer them the NEST team?"

NEST was the Nuclear Emergency Support Team, a group of scientists, technicians, and engineers operating under the U.S. Department of Energy. The teams were trained and prepared to respond to nuclear accidents or incidents anywhere in the world.

Thorpe shook his head slowly and made a face. It was apparent that the Mexican government, at least for the moment, had declined the assistance of the specialists.

"So they understand they may be getting in over their heads?

"Okay, keep me posted." He hung up the phone.

"They've got thirty police units going in. The Mexican government is also bringing in some military forces to cordon off the area around the port. The problem is, the container may have already left the facility. They won't know for at least fifteen, maybe twenty minutes. Until then there's nothing we can do but wait."

"No. You're wrong," said Rhytag. "Contact the director at Homeland Security. Tell him what we've got and that our recommendation is that they close the border immediately. Every crossing from San Ysidro east to the Arizona border. Tell them to shut 'em down now. Nothing gets through. No cars, no trucks until we can figure out where this thing is and how to stop it. And tell them to be sure and warn our people at the border as to what they're dealing with."

"The second we shut the border the media's gonna know. It'll be all over the news. If the device is still at the port and the Mexicans stop it, the White House will hand you your head when the public finds out how close they came to another nine-eleven or worse," said Thorpe.

He was right. Too many law enforcement officials would have to be told what they were looking for to keep it under wraps.

"Then the White House spinmeisters can make up a story to feed the media. We can't stick our head in the sand any longer. I'll take full responsibility. Besides, what if the Mexicans don't stop it?"

Thorpe didn't have an answer.

* * *

By the time we get to the canal, Herman has a taxi waiting. Maricela and I bundle into the backseat as Herman gives directions to the driver in Spanish.

From the backseat of the taxi I am straining my eyes through the binoculars to see if I can pick up any sight of the container. From here it is a long distance across the water, and the *Amora* is in the way. But I can see part of the road leading out of the port, and there is a train of trucks on it, heading for the highway.

"It was a strange shade of green," says Maricela. She is talking about the container. "It had some lettering sprayed on one side."

She is right. I see the container on the back of a truck just as the taxi passes a building on the left that cuts off my view.

"You wanna stop and pick up the bags at the hotel?" says Herman.

"Leave them. We can't take the time." I can once again see the truck with the container, across the harbor. It is only a few hundred feet from the exit gate at the port where a uniformed guard is checking vehicles and paperwork. If we could only get there, we could stop it.

"Herman, tell him to pick it up, otherwise we're gonna lose him going through town. If he gets out on that highway and takes a turnoff, we'll never see him again."

Herman says something to the driver, and the man says something back.

"He says his foot's on the floor," says Herman.

"Great! Let's hope there are a lot of hills between here and wherever that truck's going, because we're never going to catch him at the gate."

We make the wide swing to the left around the port, headed for where the port facility joins the highway.

When I look once more with the field glasses, the truck with the container is gone. It's already cleared the gate. As the road curves to the right and heads up the hill, I see it chugging up the grade about a quarter of a mile ahead of us. It's just ahead of a U-Haul truck struggling up the hill, unable to pass it.

Herman points with his finger and says something to the taxi driver who slides into the right lane and slows down. The highway is first world, two lanes in each direction with a center divider and cross traffic only where the divider is broken.

There are several vehicles between us and the cargo carrier. The driver wants to know if he should pass them. Herman tells him no, to keep a few of the vehicles between us, but not to lose the container truck.

As we continue to climb the hill, the few cars ahead of us begin to pull out. Within ten minutes we find ourselves directly behind the U-Haul, trying to stay shielded behind the big box truck and not appear too obvious.

Herman tells the driver to back off a little and the guy says something back to him. "He wants to know how far we're going," says Herman.

"Tell him we'll know when we get there."

This doesn't seem to satisfy him. He has a longer conversation with Herman.

"He says he stops at Rosarita," says Herman. "He won't go any farther north than that. He says the traffic up around Tijuana coming back this way in the afternoon is too much. He'll lose too many fares."

"Tell him we'll pay him for his time."

"You're getting pretty extravagant," says Herman. "Maybe we should count up our cash again, see what we've got left."

"We've got close to six hundred," I tell him. "For that he ought to take us to San Francisco."

"I can tell you one thing, if they cross the border he won't go beyond there. He can't unless he's got a visa and insurance. Maricela's gonna have the same problem, and if you try and cross you'll get your ass arrested." The minute he says it Herman looks at me and bites his lip.

We both glance at Maricela. She is looking so intently out the side window, her face pressed up close to the glass, that she didn't even hear him.

"If they try to cross the border, at least one of us has to make it to the kiosk to get the border patrol to stop them," I tell him.

"That means me, since you can't run for squat," he says.

A half hour past the turnoff to El Descanso the road becomes a freeway and the driver tells us we're approaching Rosarita. Just as he says it the U-Haul hits its turn signal to make a right on the next off-ramp.

Herman tells the taxi driver to slow down, and as we fall back I nearly panic when I realize the container truck is no longer out in front on the highway. Then I see it on the off-ramp in front of the U-Haul.

"¡A la derecha! ¡A la derecha!" says Herman.

The taxi driver swings to the right and falls in line behind the U-Haul, nearly plowing into the back of the truck. The driver is angry, saying something in Spanish to Herman, both of his hands off the wheel for a moment as we lumber into the outskirts of Rosarita. We drive off of pavement and onto dirt streets.

I can't tell what the driver is saying, only that he is getting short with Herman.

"You know, I'm getting the sense those two are together." Herman is ignoring the driver, talking about the cargo carrier and the U-Haul.

I'm hoping that we're coming to the end of the trip. Maybe they'll stop for the night. "Herman, you got the cell phone?"

"Yeah."

"Check it and see if we have a signal."

He pulls it out, powers it up and waits, then shakes his head. "Nothing."

We're hanging back, rolling slowly along the dusty, unpaved street when half a block up the two trucks pull into a Pemex station. The driver of the U-Haul climbs down out of the truck and starts to gas up. The container truck pulls on through and stops in a wide area next to the little mini-mart in the gas station. It looks like a bladder break, all of them suddenly jumping out of the trucks.

"My father!" says Maricela. "That's him!" Her face lights up as she points.

"Where?"

"There's my father." Maricela reaches for the door, and before I can stop her she's out, running along the edge of the road.

Herman is out before I can move.

I try to go and the driver grabs my arm. "*¡Señor! ¡Mi tarifa, por favor!*"

He wants his money.

By the time I look up, Herman has caught up to Maricela and pulled her into some bushes off the road.

I pay the driver and tell him in my best pidgin Spanish and sign language to wait. A few seconds later I join Herman and Maricela in the bushes.

"What's wrong with you?" Herman is giving her a piece of his mind. "You want to get us all killed? To say nothing of a few thousand bystanders. Think, woman!"

Maricela looks as if she's about to cry.

"She'll be all right. Calm down. She got excited, that's all. She didn't know if he was alive or dead. When she saw him," I shrug a shoulder, "she snapped. Cut her some slack," I tell him.

Herman shakes his head slowly and takes a deep breath. He apologizes and removes his huge hands from her shoulders.

As we're talking I hear the engine start behind us. Before I can even turn to look, the taxi driver pulls a U-turn from his parking position and heads the other way down the dusty street.

"Great!" says Herman. "That cuts it. What do we do now?"

There is no time to think or talk. "Stay here and keep an eye on her." I step out of the bushes and walk as fast as I can along the side of the road toward the gas station at the end of the block. If we lose the truck now, we'll never find it again. We could get ourselves killed, but what choice do we have? I've never done anything like this before, but then I've never been in a situation like this. Sometimes we surprise ourselves—what adrenaline can do.

When I reach the corner, only one of the men is outside, keeping an eye on the trucks as the pump continues to fill the empty tank on the U-Haul. The guy is moving around over by the container. He is checking it out, making sure it's fastened down tight on the rails that form the bed on the back of the cargo carrier.

The others are still inside the mini-mart. When I look back, the guy at the container truck has moved to the other side.

I notice that the back of the U-Haul is not locked. I swing the handle on the catch out of the way and gently lift the roll-up gate just enough to crawl inside. Once in, I lift the gate a little farther so Herman, down the street, can see me. Holding the gate in one hand, I'm motioning with the other for them to join me, and to make it fast.

Before they can move very far, I hear voices coming out of the mini-mart. A foreign tongue that isn't Spanish. I put my hand out and Herman steps off the road and into the bushes with Maricela once more.

As I quietly lower the gate, I see a small piece of wood on the bed of the truck, just inside the door. I slip it under the edge at the bottom of the door just enough to keep the outside hand lever from sliding into the lock and sealing me in.

A few seconds later the voices get louder as they approach. I hear someone pull the fuel nozzle from the tank and hook it back to the pump, and a few seconds later the doors as they open and slam closed. Off in the distance I hear the diesel engine on the container truck as it turns over and starts, and a second later the U-Haul ignition as it kicks in, then the deep rumble of the engine.

I stand and lift the gate high over my head and look for Herman. He sees me from the bushes. I point with my thumb, like a hitchhiker, to the other side of the street.

Quickly Herman grabs Maricela by the hand and the

two of them scoot across the street and end up behind an old pickup truck off its wheels on blocks at the side of the road.

It's a gamble, but I'm assuming these guys have pulled off the highway for gas, which means they may be heading back to the highway. I hear the container truck as it swings in front of the U-Haul to make the turn back down the dusty street to the freeway. The U-Haul starts to make the turn to fall in behind it. I am holding on to the gate to steady myself, hanging on to it over my head as the truck rocks back and forth leaving the pavement and going onto the dirt.

The driver misses a shift and grinds the gears just as Herman steps out from behind the parked pickup. He is carrying Maricela on his shoulders and before the truck can get up to ten miles an hour he tosses her up to me. All I can do is break her fall with one hand and part of my body as I hold the gate for Herman. A second later he is on board.

I look down at Maricela. She's smiling back at me. She's fine. Herman and I carefully lower the gate and I stick the piece of wood underneath it again.

We can barely see each other in the dark, but there is no chance they're going to hear us up front, not with the rumble of the engine and the road noise.

"May as well make ourselves comfortable," says Herman. He grabs a heavy packing blanket off the top of a wooden crate up front, brings it back, and spreads it in a double thickness on the floor, for us to sit on.

I catch my breath, but still can't believe we've just done this. That we are so close to risking it all.

FIFTY-NINE

o they have no idea where the truck is headed?"
said Rhytag.

Thorpe shook his head. "According to our agents
the Mexican police are pushing them pretty hard.
They got the captain and two of the others down
belowdecks right now teaching them about the inquisition." Thorpe was talking about the ship's crew, the
captain and the others brought on board the *Amora* to
replace the original crew members, who have all disappeared except for two who signed on in Colombia.

"All we know right now is that the current crew
members appear to be connected to the Tijuana cartel.
Most of them are seamen or have some sea experience.
They were contacted by people they knew in the cartel
to bring in the ship. They're telling the Mexican authorities that's all they know. When they were shown the
photos taken by Nitikin's daughter, they IDed Nitikin
as being on board as well as at least three and possibly
four other individuals in the photographs. According to
the cartel crew members, they have no idea what Nitikin was doing or what was in the container. We did get

a good description of the container, color and size. It's a twenty-footer, lime green, and one of the crew members gave us a partial plate number off the truck. It was a Mexican commercial plate. Mexican government is checking it now as to the owner and possible destination. Also, there was another vehicle, a box truck. One of the crew members said he thought it was a rental truck of some kind but he couldn't remember the name of the company or the license number. There was one thing that was curious though."

"What's that?" said Rhytag.

"Some of the crew members said it looked as if the Russian was being held captive. According to them he was being guarded pretty heavily and was locked in a cabin on the ship most of the time."

"You think he's acting under duress?" said Rhytag.

"Who knows?"

"What about the others, the people with him?"

"All foreigners. One of them spoke Spanish and some other language. He seemed to be doing all the interpreting. The crew members said they didn't know what the other language was, and they claim they didn't overhear any of the translated conversations. The Mexican authorities don't believe them. According to them somebody had to overhear something. It's why they've got the captain and the others belowdecks having discussions."

Rhytag took a deep breath and thought for a moment. When he spoke again his voice was a near whisper so that none of the others in the room working the computers or the telephones could hear. "For the record, I didn't ask this question," he said, "but have the Mexicans taken them surfing?"

"Surfing" was a euphemism for waterboarding. ACLU types condemned it as torture, but experience had proved that when time was of the essence, it was the one sure way to extract information and to do it quickly. Oftentimes less than two minutes.

"That may be a touch too subtle for the Mexicans," said Thorpe. "According to our agent on the scene, they got the captain hooked up to a car battery with a coil and alligator clips, charging up his nipples and various other body parts every minute or so. They let him rest just long enough to stop glowing. If he knows anything, he's not talking. Seems the Mexicans are willing to keep at it all night. If they have to, they'll bring the crew down in shifts and get some more batteries."

"The problem is that if the crew doesn't know where the truck is headed, all that pain is likely to extract is false information. Which means we could find ourselves sent on some wild-goose chase," said Rhytag. "What do we have by way of assets up along the border?"

"You mean besides the world's biggest traffic jam?" said Thorpe. "At last count we had two hundred highway patrol men, another hundred on the way. The NEST team is already deployed to San Ysidro. We're assuming that's the nearest border crossing, so that's likely to be where they try to come in. We've pulled in border patrol from as far east as Yuma. We have two FBI SWAT teams, and Delta Force is sending us two of their cracker-jack sniper teams, but we're told that's not for public consumption. We're also bringing in one of our own hostage-rescue teams."

"Why hostage rescue?" said Rhytag.

"It was a suggestion from one of our tactical commanders. He says that hostage rescue has expertise and training in vehicle breeches, mostly buses. It's the same team that went in to try and extract Agent Mederios and the others from the bus. If we can locate the cargo truck, we'll use the HR team as the spear to gain access to the container, followed closely by the NEST team, to try and defuse the thing.

"So all we need now is to find it," said Rhytag. He asked what kind of equipment was set up along the border in terms of detection.

"That's the problem," said Thorpe. "None of our detection equipment does us any good if nothing's moving. According to the people on the NEST team, it probably wouldn't do any good anyway. I talked with Llewellyn, he agrees. He says the fissionable material in the bomb is highly enriched uranium, and since it's probably shielded, the equipment we have is next to useless. It could read plutonium fairly easily. But with uranium we'd have to be right up against the carrier, no more than three or four feet away, to read anything. And we'd probably have to be there for an extended period of time before we got a sufficient reading."

"In other words, Nitikin and his friends are in a position to sit us out and wait," said Rhytag.

"We could use thermal imaging," said Thorpe. "We'd be looking for high-density anomalies, lead in the shield, for example. We could reduce the number of vehicles to be searched. The problem is, the bomb, from everything we know, is on the other side of the border. The Mexican government is not willing to allow us to use imaging."

"Why not?"

"They're afraid if we find it, Nitikin and his cohorts will detonate the damn thing and turn Tijuana into a crater."

"That would get rid of the cartel for them," said Rhytag.

"No, that would get rid of the cartel for us. They don't seem to mind. Especially now. With oil down that's the only growth sector in their economy. Half of those factories on the other side of the border are shut down. What did they call those things?" said Thorpe.

"*Maquiladoras*," said Rhytag.

SIXTY

In the late nineties, politicians eager to pocket million-dollar speaking fees from foreign trade groups embraced the concept of a global economy. They teamed up with Chinese businessmen and Mexican manufacturers and carved out a zone along the U.S. southern border where trade restrictions were virtually eliminated.

American politicians sold the country on the concept of our being an information economy, that we no longer needed manufacturing or heavy industry, as if you could drive words and eat sentences. They shipped entire job sectors abroad and then railed at the demise of the middle class.

Places like Ensenada with its sleepy port suddenly boomed. In less than two years, vast amounts of commercial cargo moved off docks in Los Angeles and San Diego and landed instead in northern Mexico. China began shipping oceans of cheap component parts to ports along the Mexican coast, most of which were delivered to factories known as *maquiladoras* on the northern border. There the parts were assembled into finished products that flowed into the American market on trucks owned and operated by Mexican trucking companies.

It was a win-win situation if you were looking to buy a cheap television, or a politician collecting on IOUs from foreign constituents. But for those who once worked in the shuttered factories or drove trucks for a living, it was the end of the road.

For more than a decade, the *maquiladoras* flourished, until they fell on hard times, in a way a victim of their own success. It's difficult to sell televisions, even if they're cheap, to millions of Americans who are out of work.

Liquida smiled at the thought as he wandered through the empty building, wondering why the raghead would want to meet him here. He got in by picking a small lock on a door at the rear of the building. The place was huge, cavernous, all under a single roof with overhead doors large enough to accommodate Noah's ark.

Like all of the *maquiladora* facilities, it was situated in the trade zone nestled right up against the U.S. border. While the Americans controlled their side with vast areas of vacant land and highly trained dogs, the Mexicans punched right up against the fence in many places. Both sides of the border were arid desert with rugged ravines and hills. The American side was only sparsely developed, mostly commercial warehouses and trucking facilities with a vast array of border checkpoints. With the downturn in the economy, some of the warehouses on both sides were now empty, chained-up facilities waiting for better days.

Liquida was sweating because of the long coat he was wearing. It was necessary to conceal the heavy item underneath. He checked his watch. He was two hours early. He had parked his car several blocks away and walked so that his early visit would come as a surprise to his employer.

He had gone to the port at Ensenada earlier that day. From the overview on the knoll above the highway, overlooking the harbor, Liquida could see police crawling all over the ship, so many uniforms he was afraid it would sink.

He had watched with heavy-duty binoculars for some time and was pretty sure that Afundi had gotten away. Because of all the ongoing interrogations the police were still looking for someone or something. There were enough squad cars parked along the dock with hoods up and batteries missing that the chief in Tijuana would have to call Delco to get them all home.

He was musing over the events at the harbor when suddenly he heard a noise from outside the warehouse. It was the sound of a heavy truck coming from the direction of the large fenced-in parking area.

Liquida sprinted over to the door and peeked through a crack. A man was unlocking the gate out on the street. There was a large container truck and another smaller box truck that looked like a rental vehicle behind it.

Liquida watched for a few seconds as the man unlocked the chain and pulled the double gates open. The two trucks started to roll through the gate, toward the warehouse.

Liquida retreated to a ladder in the far corner of the building and climbed to an overhead loft area, a kind of industrial catwalk where he could perch and take in the show without being seen. He made himself comfortable, took off his long coat, and set it and the object strapped under it on the catwalk next to him.

A couple of minutes later the large overhead garage door was lifted by someone outside. For the first time Liquida realized it hadn't been locked. The mammoth door was so delicately balanced that the man was able to hoist it with one arm and send it sailing along the track until it settled almost against the roof of the building.

Liquida wondered if anyone had been inside watching him. He was fairly confident there were no cameras. Those he had looked for. But the unlocked overhead door surprised him.

A minute later both trucks were inside the building. Liquida could smell the odor of diesel exhaust as it wafted up to the balcony where he lay. The engines shut off and four men climbed down from the two trucks. Three from the rental vehicle and the driver of the cargo-container truck. The fifth waited by the huge open door with one hand on the rope, as if he were going to pull it and close the overhead door. But he didn't. He waited for several minutes, looking out the open door as if expecting someone else, while three of the other men talked. Liquida couldn't understand a thing they said. They were speaking in a foreign tongue of some kind. The other man, the fifth one, stood not far from the rental truck and seemed to be off somewhere in his own world. He didn't look like the others either. He was older, fair haired, and though Liquida couldn't get a good look at him from up high, he appeared to be taller as well.

A few minutes later another vehicle, this one a small, dark sedan, came rocketing through the open door and hit its brakes inside the building.

The man pulled the rope and the large door came screeching down along the track until it hit the concrete floor with a bang. This time the man pushed the locking bolt into the slot, sealing it tight from the inside.

Two more men got out of the car, and the six of them, the three who were originally talking, the man by the door, and the two from the car, huddled together some distance away from the seventh man, who was now wandering all alone near the rear of the rental truck.

Liquida watched as the five cohorts stood in a small circle near the container truck. One of them who seemed to be the leader was doing most of the talking while the others listened. The language was not something Liquida had ever heard before. He knew it must be Arabic and that the man talking had to be the boss man from Colombia. Language barrier or not, Liquida could clearly see that he was barking the orders and the others were listening. He got a good look at the man.

Liquida reached over on the platform next to where he was lying, opened the coat, and pulled apart the two snaps inside. Having freed it from the inside of the coat, he picked up the weapon. It looked like something from a space movie, with a silencer the size of an exhaust pipe on the muzzle end, and a box clip for the 5.56-millimeter rounds at the other end where it slipped into the receiver up inside the shoulder stock under the shooter's armpit. The weapon had a strange-looking device mounted underneath the barrel and a small scope on top.

The modified bull pup had the advantage of a full-length rifle barrel in a gun that, without the silencer, was little more than twenty inches long.

He held the gun close as he continued to watch the conference down below.

The lone wolf wandering near the rear of the rental truck apparently saw something out of place. He approached the lift gate and played with the heavy latch for a moment. Apparently it wasn't closed. He lifted the gate a little, and then seemed to stand there for a moment as if he were frozen in place.

Afundi said something and one of the others hollered out in perfect Spanish, telling the man at the rear of the rental truck to leave it alone and come out where they could see him. The one who spoke Spanish separated himself from the others and walked toward the rear of the rental vehicle.

Before he could get there, the other man lowered the lift gate and quickly moved around the truck where he rapidly closed the distance between the two of them with his hands out, turning the other, fatter man around. "It was nothing. A piece of wood caught under the door. I took care of it. It's fine."

The other man stood there for a second looking at him, and then pushed past him, walked to the back of the truck, and checked it out. The other, taller man was close behind him.

Liquida heard the metal of the hooked lever lock on the back of the truck as the fat man tested it to make sure that the catch was working and the door was sealed.

While the two of them were still standing at the back of the truck, the leader stopped talking, stepped away from the others, and started walking over to join them. By then the fat man was satisfied that everything was fine. He headed back the other way, said something to his leader, and the two of them joined their comrades in discussion once again.

Liquida thought about popping Afundi as he stood

there talking, but that would be too easy. Besides, he'd probably end up in a gunfight with the others, and taking rounds through the bottom of the catwalk was not something he wanted to think about. Liquida would wait them out. He'd whittle them down with the silencer a shot at a time, so they wouldn't know where it was coming from.

The conversation went on for a couple more minutes, until Afundi handed two of the men a piece of paper and began talking to them. He pointed to the sheet as if he was giving them directions of some kind.

They nodded, one of them took the sheet of paper, and the two men headed toward the car. But they didn't get in, instead they grabbed two assault rifles out of the backseat.

Afundi said something to one of them and pointed toward the back wall of the building. As he watched the man walk in that direction, suddenly the diesel engine on the container truck started up. Liquida turned to look back at the trucks as another of the men climbed up into the container truck. He closed the truck's doors and waited with the engine running. The other three men, including the tall one who didn't seem to fit, got into the rental truck and started its engine.

Liquida wondered where they were going. No one had opened the large overhead door. The fumes were beginning to build up. Suddenly an overhead door on the other side of the building opened up. It was being opened by a heavy electrical motor. Liquida looked at it and realized that the door was surrounded not by metal, but heavy concrete. The opening was cut into a retaining wall where the building backed up to an incline in the earth outside.

Once the door was fully up, Liquida could see that the concrete floor beyond the opening dropped off in a steep decline. It was ramped down. Within seconds the two trucks drove through the opening and down the ramp, disappearing in a blue haze of exhaust as the noise of their engines slowly receded into the distance.

SIXTY-ONE

After spending millions of dollars of his government's money, Alim was gratified by the results. It had taken seven months for the cartel to acquire the two buildings, one on each side of the border, to engineer and dig the tunnel, and to shore it up with concrete and steel rebar.

It had been a seamless operation. The cartel knew that the U.S. border patrol and customs watched the Mexican side of the border for unusual traffic volume and patterns. So the cartel purchased the trucks from the original *maquiladora* operator just as the manufacturer folded. They used the trucks to remove the earth from the excavation of the tunnel as well as to deliver the building materials. To anyone watching, the volume of truck traffic coming and going from the building never changed, as if the manufacturing concern was just humming along. The cartel greased some palms in the city government and no one ever looked.

The joint venture between Afundi and the cartel meant that a good portion of the cash Alim received from his government went to finance the tunnel's construction. The cartel oversaw construction and built the tunnel. Alim then had an option for its exclusive use for thirty days, after which time the entire project would revert to the cartel, which could then continue to use it as a narco highway for as long as they could maintain the secret.

The tunnel was only a few hundred meters east of the Tijuana airport and less than three hundred yards long. The building on the Mexican side was less than a hundred feet from the border fence. The tunnel, sixty feet underground where thermal imaging and motion and vibration detectors sealed off by the heavy concrete walls would never be able to detect a thing from the surface, spanned the distance between the two buildings. Alim smiled at the thought that the cartel had employed a retired engineer from the California Department of Transportation to design the whole thing, though the man never had a clue as to where it would be located or what it would be used for.

In a little more than a minute the trucks were on the surface once more, inside the building on the U.S. side of the border. They wasted no time opening the doors and exiting from the building to merge with the surrounding California traffic.

Alim looked at his watch. Amazingly, they were still on schedule. It was just after three in the afternoon. According to the news reports, festivities were not scheduled to get under way until just before five.

Though Nitikin didn't know it, Afundi had already installed the cordite and set the timer for five o'clock, maximum effect. The Russian had been in the jungle for so long that he didn't know about the high-tech gadgets the world had invented in his absence. This included the tiny pencil-lens camera Alim had installed inside the wooden crate, through which he watched as Yakov pulled the safety device, arming the bomb. Alim now no longer needed him. He could have killed the Russian at any time, but he was saving that pleasure for later.

The haze of the exhaust hadn't even settled inside the building before Liquida centered the red dot on the first of the two men left behind in the building. As he squeezed the trigger, a crimson halo exploded around the first man's head as the mercury-tipped bullet did its job.

The second man never saw or heard a thing. With his back turned, he was smiling. He pointed toward the open tunnel and turned to share the wonder of the thing with his friend just as the next round transited the top of his head. The exploding bullet blew out a sizable hunk of skull bone, now bouncing off the concrete floor behind him.

In seconds Liquida was down the ladder. He retrieved the sheet of paper Afundi had left for his men. It was a printed map of San Diego, with a route traced along the freeways. It had a dark pen mark at one location. Liquida didn't need the map. He knew the location well. He had been there only a few months earlier. But as he looked at the detail at the north end, near the end of the route, he had to wonder what the hell was going on.

He thought about his rental car half a mile away and decided Avis could probably find the vehicle by itself. The man whose wallet, credit card, and driver's license Liquida had stolen on his flight from Houston would probably get a whopping surprise on his credit card bill. He fished through the dead men's pockets until he found the keys to the small blue sedan. He jumped in the car and two seconds later disappeared down Alice's rabbit hole to see where it went.

We have no idea where we are. Herman is flat on his belly on the bed of the truck, trying to release the catch on the lock outside with a pocketknife. He is using the light from the screen on my worthless encrypted cell phone to guide his probing with the blade under the crack of the door.

For the first several minutes the vehicle seems to bounce all over the place, first a steep decline and then back up. For ten minutes a lot of stop and go and then finally the constant hum and steady movement of a highway.

Herman finally gives up with the knife.

"No use," he says. "Blade's too short. But the good news is, you were right about your father." He is looking at Maricela in earnest as he says it. "He's gotta be acting under duress. The way he closed the gate and protected us, kept his mouth shut. Otherwise, I don't know about you, but Paul and I would be dead right now."

Maricela seemed stunned and still in shock after the sudden appearance of her father at the back of the truck. The only one more surprised was Nitikin himself. From the look on his face when he saw her, I thought he would die. One thing is certain, we now have his attention, though none of us has a clue as to where we are or where the truck is headed.

"They picked up a signal from Madriani's cell phone," said Thorpe. He came rushing into the command center.

"Where?" said Rhytag.

"San Diego."

"What?"

"Intelligence picked it up two minutes ago. They're not sure, but it looks as if the signal's coming from somewhere along I-5, just south of San Diego."

"How the hell did he get there?"

"We don't know."

"He can't be with Nitikin," said Rhytag.

Thorpe shrugged his shoulders. "Your guess is as good as mine."

Rhytag thought for a moment. "Pull the tactical squads back from the border," he said.

"Should we open up the border crossings?"

"No. Just get the SWAT teams, some highway patrol if you can, the NEST team, and the snipers you got from Delta. Alert the hostage-rescue team and tell them we may need them on short notice. Get a precise location on the signal. Give the highway patrol the description of the cargo container and partial plate off the truck and tell them to put out an all-points on it. If they find it, tell them to track it from a distance, but not to stop it. To monitor its location and call it in."

SIXTY-TWO

From the middle of the bench seat in the U-Haul truck, Nitikin kept seeing signs as they passed them, Chula Vista, National City. He had never seen so much traffic. His mind raced with thoughts of how to free Maricela from the back of the truck, and who the two men were who were with her. But he was trapped in the middle, between the translator who was driving and Alim.

His brain was so occupied with these thoughts that he didn't even notice when the rental truck slipped into the right lane of the freeway. When he looked up he suddenly realized that they were driving at high speed on some kind of long off-ramp paralleling the freeway but separated from it by a low retaining wall. The cargo truck with the container on the back was still out on the highway, going straight ahead.

Yakov nudged the interpreter.

"Don't worry about it," said the interpreter.

"You're going to trust the two men on the truck to arm the bomb?" said Nitikin.

The interpreter said something in Farsi. Alim responded, and the interpreter told Yakov, "The cordite charge is already loaded and the timer is set."

Nitikin was stunned. "The safety device is still on," he told them.

"Do yourself a favor and save your lies," said the interpreter. "We saw you remove it."

Yakov knew this was not possible. He knew they could not possibly have seen inside the crate tucked away in the dark container when he pulled the wire.

"Where is the truck going? What is the target?" said Nitikin.

The interpreter said something to Alim, who smiled and said nothing.

The off-ramp suddenly veered to the left and passed over the top of the freeway. Yakov looked out the right window and watched as the cargo container, surrounded by traffic, streamed down the freeway. Soon it was out of sight.

Nitikin now knew that Alim no longer needed him. Yakov was running out of time. If Afundi found Maricela in the back of the truck, he would kill her in a heartbeat. Yakov was her only hope. Desperate to free his daughter, he knew he would have to do it before he took his last breath.

By now Thorpe and Rhytag were taking their orders from a higher authority. The director of Homeland Security, now at the command center, watched the screen on the computer as well as the streaming video, on the huge monitor, being fed to them by a military helicopter. The chopper was flying at four thousand feet, high above the cargo container on the freeway below.

The highway patrol had picked up the truck just north of San Diego and tracked it from a distance for more than twenty miles, until the interstate entered the area of Camp Pendleton, the sprawling marine base on the Pacific Coast. There tens of thousands of acres of barren hillsides replaced the endless housing tracts and subdivisions of Southern California.

CHP units had slowed traffic several miles out in front where they could not be seen by Alim's two men in the container truck. Over the course of several miles, driving a pattern of long, slow S curves, they finally brought the traffic to a halt. Other units cut off traffic in a southerly direction as two Delta Force sniper teams were deployed from helicopters on each side of the highway, three hundred yards out from the truck.

Alim's men were frustrated by the stalled traffic. Busy talking to each other they never saw a thing before the glass on the truck's side windows shattered. A separate .308 round nailed each of them in the head at the same instant as their bloodied bodies piled up in the center of the seat.

Most of the motorists around them never noticed a thing, even when the distant muted crack of gunfire reached them a second or so later.

Within seconds the highway patrol started traffic moving again, everything except the truck. They emptied the interstate of vehicles for a distance of five miles and landed the NEST team and the FBI hostage unit on the highway a short distance from the truck.

"Like clockwork." Thorpe smiled, and slapped the table.

They watched on the large screen as two of the FBI officers, in full black body armor, approached the rear of the container. Two more approached from the other side. They checked the two occupants in the truck. Both were dead. Still, they searched for any detonator or triggering mechanism that might be attached to the device in the back. They didn't see anything.

The two agents at the back of the truck didn't open the container door. Instead one of them probed for a crack around the hinge of the door, then inserted what on the screen, from a distance, looked like a wire but was in fact a small pinhole camera with its own light source mounted on the end of a thin, flexible tube.

The agent manipulated the tube to move the lens around inside.

"Appears there's a wooden crate in the center of the container." The voice crackled over the tactical radio system where it was piped into the speakers at the command center in Washington. "Looks like lead shielding on the inner walls of the container. Can't tell for sure."

"Hold on a second. Let me take a look." One of the NEST team specialists came in for a closer look at the monitor on the Panasonic Toughbook laptop where the video from the pinhole camera was being viewed. "Move it around a little more." He lifted his face mask and looked more closely at the computer screen. "That is lead shielding," said the tech. "Hold on a second, you wanna make sure there's no trip wires or detonating devices running from the door."

The agent kept moving the lens around.

The agent kneeling behind him at the computer looked at the screen closely as the tiny eye of the camera lens scoured the sealed interior of the container. "I don't see any wires. Just some kind of large wooden crate in the center of the floor. I can't see any wires or anything running to it. What else am I looking for?" asked the agent. He was seeking guidance from the NEST team.

One of the NEST team members came up behind them carrying a Geiger counter, searching for evidence of radiation emissions.

"Not getting much. Slightly more elevated than normal background radiation is all."

"What am I looking for in terms of initiators for detonation?" said the agent at the computer.

"Probably a timing device," said one of the NEST team.

"What would it look like?" said the agent.

"Most likely it would be inside the crate," said the technician. "You wouldn't be able to see it."

"Well, what do we do?" said the agent.

Thorpe and Rhytag sat anxiously watching the big screen listening to the chatter over the speakers in the command center.

Three members of the NEST team huddled a few feet from the agents. "Do you wanna try and move it? Bring in a heavy-lift helo. We could haul it out to sea, dump it in deep water."

"Plutonium, I'd say yes. But not uranium. The salt water could complete the chemical bond between the two elements of HEU in the gun and start a chain reaction. We'd get a partial or full-yield nuclear blast, and the onshore winds could carry the fallout across half of Southern California."

One of the other team members agreed with him. "Besides, they could have a barometric trigger on it. Either that or if there's a timed detonator and it goes off as we're lifting it, we'll end up getting an airburst."

They all knew what that meant. Little Boy had been designed specifically for an airburst over Hiroshima at the end of the war. The bomb had achieved maximum devastation over the widest possible area from an altitude of less than two thousand feet.

"That means we take it apart here," said one of them.

"I'd say that looks like the best alternative among a bad lot."

They all agreed. "Let's get the tools," said one of them.

They had already taken steps to move everyone back along the highway a distance of at least two miles in either direction, including all of the highway patrol units. All that lingered now was the single helicopter for support that mounted the camera through which Thorpe, Rhytag, the head of Homeland Security, and the rest in the room watched on the big screen. The chopper hovered about a quarter mile off and zeroed in with a powerful telescopic video lens.

"Why don't you guys go back to the safety point?" said one of the agents. "There's no sense in all of us staying up here. I can pull the doors by myself."

"Two miles out and two miles back, we don't have time," said the head of NEST. He was already donning a radiation suit from their equipment bags, dropped from the helicopters when they landed. "Besides, if we get a full-yield detonation it won't make much difference. On the other hand, if we get a fizzle I want you and all of your agents as well as the rest of my team to take cover over there behind that concrete divider."

None of them argued with him. Thorpe and Rhytag watched on the screen as two more members of NEST put on radiation suits. Then the two men joined the agents behind the concrete divider.

There were two doors on the rear of the container, each with two sets of heavy locking pins, one at the top and one at the bottom. Each locking pin was controlled by a levered handle. Pull up or push down on the handle and the pin would be released.

The head of NEST gripped one of the levered handles on the container door. "Are you ready?" he called out.

"Go ahead. Do it."

He pulled the handle up, sliding the heavy steel pin from the latch at the top of the container. "Got it. That one's out. One down, one to go," he said.

He took the second lever at the bottom of the door. "For some reason this one doesn't want to come," he said. He let go of it, straightened his back, and took a deep breath.

He pushed again. "Damn thing's stuck..."

"Be careful, don't force it," said one of them.

"The container's got some dents. It's just bent." This time he put his full weight on the lever. The pin started to slide from the hole. "Got it," he said.

Several hundred pounds of steel plate backed by a liner of lead shielding hit the leader of the NEST team like a rocket sled. The heat from the blast radiated in ripples from the back of the container, tearing the door from its hinges. It tossed the man's limp body fifty yards down the highway as the steel door, sliding along beside him on the pavement, threw up sparks.

An instant later the shock wave rattled the camera on the helicopter a quarter of a mile away and broke up the picture for a few seconds.

"Oh, no!" said Rhytag.

When the images flickered back into focus, they could

see sheets of flame and smoke billowing from the open end of the cargo container. The side nearest them was bulged out by the blast. It flattened the rear tires of the truck, and one of them caught fire.

"Bring in fire suppression. Foam...And get an ambulance in here now." There was chaos at the scene as two of the agents jumped the divider and ran toward the downed man. The two NEST team members, hampered by the bulky radiation suits, moved more slowly. They cleared the divider and approached the back end of the twisted container. One of them was holding a Geiger counter.

"What are you reading on the meter?"

"Nothing. A few rads above background."

"Doesn't make sense. The shielding's been blasted out." The two men disappeared into the smoke at the rear of the container.

Everyone in the command center sat silently, their eyes riveted on the huge screen as they listened for voices over the tactical communication system.

A few seconds later the two men emerged from the smoke. "Conventional explosives," said one of them. He pulled off his hood, sweat pouring down his face as the camera zeroed in on him.

"It could be Semtex or C-four, or some other synthetic, I can't be sure."

They could hear the electronic wail of sirens in the background as the ambulance made its way up the highway. "There are traces of elevated radiation around what's left of the wooden crate inside, but the device is not there."

SIXTY-THREE

After separating from the cargo carrier, the rental truck continued west for almost a mile until it approached a high-arching bridge over what appeared to be a big harbor dotted with yachts and large ships. The truck moved along at full speed, staying with the traffic as it climbed onto the bridge, two lanes in each direction separated by a concrete divider.

Yakov could see what appeared to be a kind of fairyland through the mist ahead of them. Below the bridge on the left were white sand beaches and a nestled cove harboring luxury boats, brigantines, and other exotic sailing craft.

Straight ahead there was what looked like an island except for the endless strip of sand that disappeared into the haze along the ocean to the south. The area directly across the bridge was awash in lush vegetation, a green oasis of palms and billowing eucalyptus. Though he didn't know it, Nitikin was looking at a golf course. In the distance he could see the broad blue expanse of the Pacific. And laid right at its sandy shore, the fantasy touch of a layered wedding cake, an immense wooden structure with red roofs in various shapes, its round one topped by a cupola itself capped by a large American flag. It was the Hotel del Coronado. The place where the film *Some Like It Hot* had been shot back in the sixties.

None of this meant a thing to Alim. He was seated next to the Russian on the front seat with only one thing on his mind.

Off to the right, a little over two miles away, Alim could see the immense flat expanse of the ship tied up to the dock as four fireboats out in the channel shot arcs of colored water, red, white, and blue, high into the air in celebration. It was the moment Afundi had worked for since that morning in Havana at Fidel's linen-covered dining table, when through sleepy eyes he first saw the photograph of the aircraft carrier the Americans called the USS *Ronald Reagan*, the viper that had nursed the warplanes that killed Alim's mother and father.

For months, information had come from comrades-in-arms around the world tracking the progress of the ship as it moved from one ocean to the next. Reports were sent to Havana from newspapers and online blog sites reporting the current location of the carrier and its strike force.

From his camp in Colombia, Alim devoured the news, like Ahab chasing the great white whale. At one point he was nearly sick with stress when he read reports that the carrier was expected to proceed to its home base, restock its stores of supplies, and return to sea before the bomb could be ready.

But as Castro had told him that morning, this was

destiny. A typhoon swept across the far Pacific and the great carrier, which was on its way home, was diverted to the Philippines. According to American propaganda the ship and its devil fleet were assigned to fly aid missions carrying food, water, and medicine to stricken islanders. Despite all of the Americans' lies, Afundi didn't care as long as the ship was delayed.

Then ten days ago he'd received the final piece of information that the *Reagan* had weighed anchor in the Philippines. Two sailors on leave the night before had told some girls in Cebu that they would call them from San Diego the minute they reached port, and gave them the date the carrier would arrive back home.

After more than six months at sea, the crew of fifty-five hundred, more than were killed in the World Trade Center on 9/11, now lined her decks for the arrival. Thousands of family members and friends were gathered along the pier in the shadow of the ship. This did not include the entire carrier strike group now in the harbor, missile cruisers and destroyers, frigates and supply ships, along with part of the carrier's air wing, now down on the field at North Island Naval Air Station.

The destruction from the single atomic blast would dwarf the events at Pearl Harbor. Worse for the Americans, who seemed to suck their strength from their vanquished enemies, there would be no identifiable foe to whom they could attach blame, no place where they could scratch their itch for vengeance. They would have to lick their wounds and complain of injustice to a world that no longer cared.

As the truck rumbled across the bridge and down past the open ticket kiosk on Coronado, Alim saw the promise of the future, the destruction of the great powers at the hands of single individuals such as himself. With a single weapon in the back of a truck, they could now deliver death and destruction on a level never before dreamed of in history. If the gun was the great equalizer of men, then the infliction of nuclear terror was the ultimate counterweight for oppressed people everywhere. It was the dawning of a new age and Alim Afundi was about to give it birth.

SIXTY-FOUR

I look at Herman as the truck begins to slow. Perhaps it's tied up in traffic or is pausing for a stop sign. It comes to a complete stop, then begins to back up. We feel the rear end of the heavy vehicle maneuver to the right.

"He's parking," says Herman. He gets on his feet and moves toward the rear of the truck's bed.

The driver finishes the maneuver. The truck suddenly lurches to a stop and Herman stumbles a bit, then catches himself, and the driver turns off the engine.

"I don't like it," Herman whispers.

I can hear the hum of voices up front in the truck's cab, though I can't make out what they're saying.

Maricela looks at me, big, oval, dark eyes. Then she starts to say something. I put my finger to my lips to silence her. Without the engine and road noise to cover our sounds, the men up front can hear us as well as we can hear them.

Herman flips open the encrypted cell phone and punches the power button for light, then gets down on his stomach and goes to work with the pocketknife once more, quietly, but with an urgent desperation this time.

"What do we have on the other truck, the one the cartel crew said they thought was a rental?" said Rhytag.

"Nothing. Not enough to track it," said Thorpe.

"So where the hell did the damn thing go?"

"The drivers of the cargo truck had more than three hours from the time they left the ship in Ensenada to the time the CHP picked them up on the highway, up by Pendleton. They could have dropped the device off anywhere along the way," said Thorpe.

"It still begs the question, how did they get across the border?" said Rhytag.

"It's too late for that now." The director of Homeland Security hustled through the door. He was followed by three high-ranking military officers. "The problem now is how to get as many people as possible out of the greater metropolitan San Diego area. The president's been on a conference call with the governor and the city's mayor, and it's agreed that in"—he looked at his watch—"exactly twenty-two minutes, the president is going live on national television to make the announcement. Local authorities are implementing an emergency evacuation plan. We're diverting all planes away from the San Diego airports. We're shutting down all incoming highway traffic and making all lanes outbound. We're using buses, trains, anything that rolls to get people out of the area. We're telling them to take absolutely nothing, only themselves and their children."

"You'll have a traffic jam to choke a horse," said Rhytag. "Besides, how do we know they didn't transfer the bomb to another vehicle? For all we know it could be eastbound right now, headed here."

"We have to exercise our best judgment based on what we do know. And the last information we had was that the device was in the San Diego area."

As they argued, one of Thorpe's minions stuck his head in the door. "Sir, line two is for you."

Thorpe swung around in his chair and grabbed the phone behind him on the credenza. He punched the line button. "Thorpe here.

"Yes. Yeah.

"Where?"

Suddenly all the conversations in the room stopped.

"Have you pinpointed the location?

"Can you shoot it down here and put it on the screen?

"Do it!"

Thorpe hung up the phone and swung around to face them again.

"What is it?" said the director.

"Madriani's back in town. They've picked up a signal from his cell phone again. This time in Coronado."

"Isn't that where you said his office was located?" said the director.

"It is," said Thorpe.

"So maybe he's just going home."

"No," said Rhytag. "If he's there it's for a reason and it's not because he's going home. The border was closed, right? Shut down tight. We can't explain how the cargo container got across?"

"Agreed," said the director.

"Madriani calls his partner on his home phone, which he knows we have tapped, and tells his partner to call my office with the information on the ship in Ensenada.

So he's tracking the device. Somehow he has information. He's trying to get it to us."

"Unless he's feeding us false leads," said Thorpe. "The container didn't have the bomb, remember?"

"No. It's in the other truck," said Rhytag, "and Madriani knows it. If he's shooting signals from that phone, it's for a reason. There's a fugitive warrant out for his arrest, the police are watching the airports, and the border is closed. So ask yourself, how did he get into the country?"

Thorpe was busy making a note on a legal pad. But as he stopped and lifted his eyes, the look of revelation on his face said it all.

"That's right," said Rhytag, "the same way the truck with the cargo container did. Madriani is either following, or else he's on that other truck, and so is the bomb."

A second later the large screen on the wall in the outer room flickered, as did the smaller monitor in the conference room. All eyes were on it as the satellite image honed in on a quiet street along the waterfront in Coronado.

"There it is," said one of the military officers.

Sure enough, the orange-and-yellow top and cab of a box truck came into view.

The phone rang through this time, and Thorpe picked it up. "Yeah. We see it. Do you have an address?" Thorpe jotted it down on his pad. "Forward the information to the away team up on I-5. Tell them to get NEST, the two Delta snipers, and as many of our hostage-rescue people as possible. Pile them into choppers and dispatch them ASAP to that location. Give them the description of the truck and see if you can forward the satellite imagery so they can see it."

One of the military officers tried to get Thorpe's attention. "Ask them if they can zoom out on the image," he said. "I'd like to see a larger area so we can assess what's involved."

Thorpe relayed the message, and a few seconds later the satellite image pulled back, offering a smaller-scale image and less detail of a much larger area including parts of the bay. The second it came into focus the officer, his eyes glued to the screen, said, "Oh, God! No!"

SIXTY-FIVE

Alim opened the passenger-side door to the truck and climbed down onto the curb at the side of the road. He motioned for Nitikin to follow him.

The street was in a quiet residential area on what had once been an island many years before. It was still called North Island, but the narrow strip of water that had once separated the island from the town of Coronado had been filled in by the military when the island had been taken over as a naval base before World War II.

The street itself was one lane in each direction, with little traffic due to the fact that it dead-ended at a gate to the naval base. On each side of the street were expensive homes. On the east side where the truck was parked, they were more in the nature of estates, each one fronting on San Diego Bay, some with large boats docked on the water behind them. The sidewalks were virtually abandoned except for the occasional jogger or a resident walking a dog. The commercial and shopping areas of town were three miles away, to the south, along Orange Boulevard, near the Hotel del Coronado.

All the traffic for the homecoming of the USS *Ronald Reagan* had been routed through the main entrance to the base several blocks to the west, leaving this area almost deserted.

Afundi was wearing white overalls with a zipper down the front, the kind a painter or furniture mover might wear. There were two large pockets in the pants that passed directly through to the pockets in his slacks underneath the overalls. He carried a small Walther PPK pistol in the right pocket of his pants and made a point of showing it to Nitikin as the Russian stepped down out of the truck.

Alim said something to the interpreter, who told Nitikin to go and stand by the back of the truck.

The Russian immediately did as he was told, while Afundi and the interpreter continued to talk up front.

As he reached the back of the truck, Yakov's eyes were riveted on the latch sealing the truck's rear lift gate. He glanced at Alim and saw that he was deep in a discussion with the interpreter over something. Nitikin realized he would never have another chance. It was now or never. Casually he stepped off the curb and behind the truck, then silently opened the latch and without a sound lifted the door just enough to look inside.

Before his eyes could adjust to the darkness, Herman's pocketknife was at his throat.

I cup my hand over Maricela's mouth before she can cry out or say anything as I hold her quietly in place. Then I turn her head so she can see me and put the forefinger of my other hand to my lips.

She nods, and I let go of her.

Silently she crawls forward toward her father until she is right in his face as he whispers something to her in Spanish. She eases Herman's knife away from his throat, then turns and motions that I should follow her and does the same to Herman. I crawl quickly forward.

By then Maricela has slipped through the two-foot opening under the lift gate. Herman holds the gate up as Nitikin helps his daughter to the ground where he directs her under the back of the truck. I follow her, and Herman takes up the rear.

A second later, without a word being spoken, the three of us are flat on our stomachs on the pavement under the truck. An inch at a time we ease slowly forward so that our feet won't be seen by anyone standing up close next to the lift gate at the back of the vehicle.

I can feel the heat of the exhaust from the manifold and hear the engine tick and tack, issuing all the noises of contracting metal as it cools.

Herman is on the driver's side, I'm on the right, with Maricela between us, each of us with the sides of our faces pressed to the pavement. I can see the shoes of the other man standing at the curb next to the passenger door. His left foot is so close that if I tried I could reach out and touch it with my right hand as we continue to inch forward toward the center of the truck.

Suddenly I feel someone touch my left hand. I lift my head and turn as Maricela is looking directly at me. She mouths something, but I don't understand what she's saying. Then she points up toward the bottom of the truck. I look at the undercarriage but I don't see anything. She taps my hand again and shakes her head. She mouths the words "my father." This I understand. Then she squeezes my hand and forms the word "bomb" with her lips as she points up toward the bed of the truck. Her father has told her the bomb is on the truck. The wooden crate!

*   *   *

Yakov had gently lowered the lift gate and was just about to latch it when he heard Alim's raspy voice hollering by the side of the truck.

Afundi suddenly realized that Yakov had disappeared. An instant later the driver's door opened and both men converged on the Russian from opposite sides of the vehicle.

The translator was twirling a closed padlock around his finger, shaking his head and smiling as he looked at the Russian.

Afundi had his pistol in his hand, looking at Nitikin through slit eyes until his gaze fell on the open latch at the back of the truck. Seeing it, he pushed Yakov out of the way and threw open the lift gate. He pointed the pistol inside as he scanned the interior and the large box. His focus finally centered on the area around the wooden crate up near the front wall, directly behind the cab.

Alim was about to climb onto the bed of the truck when his fingers touched something tucked just inside the corner behind the metal track that guided the lift gate up and down. He stopped and reached into the recess behind the railing. There his fingers found a small clamshell cell phone. He looked at it for a second and then turned to Yakov. He held the phone up and said something.

"He wants to know where it came from," said the interpreter.

Nitikin locked eyes with Alim for a moment, then glanced back at the phone in his hand. "Tell him it's mine. I have two of them," he said. Then Yakov touched the front pocket of his pants with one hand as if to show them where the other phone was.

An instant later the interpreter was searching his pockets. Alim exploded and struck the Russian across the side of his face, full force with the back of his hand, the one holding the pistol. The front sight on the Walther's short barrel caught Yakov's cheek and ripped a jagged inch-long wound just under his left eye. The force of the blow sent the Russian to the ground.

Before the interpreter could pick him back up, Nitikin had sprung to his feet. His quickness surprised the two men as he spit a string of Russian invective at Afundi, blood dripping down his face.

Alim dropped both phones onto the pavement and stomped them into tiny bits of plastic and metal. He said something in Farsi.

"He wants to know who you called," said the interpreter.

"Tell him I wanted to talk to my daughter, to make sure that she was all right, but he never went to Panama, so I couldn't get a signal."

As he listened to the translation, Alim eyed Yakov for a moment and then he smiled. "Tell him that his daughter is dead. Tell him I had her killed in San José and that she died slowly and screaming in pain."

"There is no need," said the interpreter. "We don't have time for this."

"Tell him!" Afundi yelled. He pointed the little pistol at the translator and then directed the barrel back into the Russian's face before the translator could finish delivering the message.

Nitikin's eyes showed his fury but it rolled off Alim like water. He motioned Yakov up into the back of the truck and the interpreter followed him while Afundi covered the Russian with the pistol.

Alim checked his watch as the interpreter slipped the closed padlock into his back pocket, pulled a set of handcuffs from his left front pocket, and pushed Nitikin toward the front of the truck and into the shadows where anyone driving by or walking down the sidewalk was less likely to see him. Then the interpreter clasped one of the handcuffs around the Russian's wrists.

Alim kept checking his watch, then looking over his shoulder for the blue sedan. The two brothers who were supposed to take care of the Mexican should have been here by now.

From his pocket the interpreter pulled several pieces of cotton cloth, balled them up, and stuffed them into the Russian's mouth. Then he retrieved a roll of duct tape and placed pieces over the Russian's mouth and eyes.

With his mouth closed tight, Nitikin had to struggle to avoid choking on the cloth while he breathed through his nose. Blinded by the tape over his eyes, he was forced to hang on to the tie-down rail for fear of becoming disoriented, losing his balance, and falling.

Only then did Alim climb into the back of the truck. He pulled a screwdriver from his inside pants pocket, removed the side panel from the wooden crate, and checked the electronic timing circuit.

The timing device had been procured from a manufacturer in Switzerland and modified by technicians in Alim's homeland before being trekked across the ocean in a Cuban diplomatic pouch. It was designed for industrial use and employed a handheld time setter about the size of a cell phone. This plugged into the small electronic circuit board that contained the digital timing chip. The circuit board was connected by two wires to the electronic detonator, which in turn was embedded in the cordite charge in the breech of the nuclear gun barrel.

The timing circuit had been modified to include an antitamper loop. Anyone trying to sever the connection to the detonator, or damage or alter the circuit board, would trigger an immediate detonation.

Alim checked the time setting, then looked at his watch. In seventeen minutes, unless someone reset the electronic clock with the handheld setter, the circuit would fire, setting off the cordite charge in the bomb's gun barrel. In the blink of an eye, a fireball hotter than the surface of the sun would incinerate everything within the radius of a mile, including the aircraft carrier and thousands of sailors and military families on the dock. It would leave at the epicenter a crater into which the ocean would flow.

He held the small timing tool in his hand and looked out the open end of the truck searching for the two idiot brothers in the blue sedan. They were late.

Alim and the interpreter had plenty of time to put enough distance between themselves and the blast if only the car would get here. Otherwise Afundi would have to reset the clock. He looked at his watch one more time, checked it against the digital countdown clock on the time setter, and watched the seconds tick down.

"Where are you?" Thorpe was now at a computer console with a headset and mike talking to one of the pilots on the incoming choppers.

"We're about six minutes out," said the pilot. "I can see Mission Bay up ahead."

There were four helicopters, one each for the two

sniper teams, with the NEST team and hostage rescue loaded onto the other two. It took longer than Thorpe had hoped to gather their equipment, muster the choppers, and get everyone on board.

The game plan was the same as for the cargo truck: bring in the snipers, take out anyone in or around the vehicle, hope that they got them all and that none of them had access to a triggering mechanism. Hostage rescue would move in to breech the truck and provide security, and NEST would deal with the bomb. They would now have to do it without their leader. The head of the NEST team had been pronounced dead moments before while on the medivac flight to the hospital.

Rhytag moved up behind Thorpe, at the console, looking over Thorpe's shoulder at the monitor. The camera showed the ground streaming beneath one of the low-flying helicopters as it screamed south toward Coronado.

"Tell them to keep an eye out for Madriani," said Rhytag.

"Sorry," said Thorpe, "but we don't have time to pick and choose or identify targets. If Madriani is around that truck, he's dead. At most, we'll have ten or fifteen seconds of tactical surprise. After that, all hell's gonna break loose. We have got to isolate that truck. Gimme a second."

"Can you patch me in to the NEST team leader?" he asked.

A few seconds later a voice came over the tactical frequency.

"Stop me if you don't have time. But I have a question," said Thorpe.

"Go ahead."

"If the detonator is electronic, is there any chance of jamming it?" asked Thorpe.

"We have it covered," said the man. "The answer is affirmative if the electronic detonator is wireless remote. We scrambled two EA-Six Prowlers for the container earlier. They jammed frequencies up and down the line, any radio or microwave signal, including cell phones. They'll do it again over Coronado. But chances are the detonator is probably hardwired, with an analog backup or antitamper device. Which means if we try to fry their electronics, we run the risk of setting it off."

"Understood," said Thorpe. So much for second-guessing the experts. "Good luck!"

A few minutes ago, coming out of the truck with my back to Nitikin, I had no idea where I was. But for now my universe was the concrete curb a few feet from my face. It was the strangest sensation. Lying on the pavement under the truck, I thought about life and how short it might be as I heard muffled voices in the truck above me. I lifted my head and looked out between the two front tires. And there in front of me, like déjà vu, was the familiar image of a gate I had driven by a thousand times. Suddenly I realized I was home.

The open chain-link gate and the small guardhouse a hundred yards beyond is one of the entrances to North Island, the naval base. It is less than a mile from my house. I can easily walk there. A little over a mile to the office. I look at my watch and realize that Harry is probably there now. Oh, God. The only saving grace is that Sarah, my daughter, is away at school.

No doubt we all wonder from time to time what random thoughts will stream through our brains at the moment of death, but for me I have always known deep down that they would be memories of Sarah.

"There!" said Alim. He nearly dropped the timing device as he pointed from the back of the open truck.

Down the street, two blocks away, he saw the blue sedan coming this way.

Alim looked down at the timing device and checked the clock. Still enough time, if they moved. They could get across the bridge and head south toward the border. He had already mapped out a surface street that would take them on a direct line to the building on this side of the border and the tunnel beneath. Even if they got only halfway, they would be well beyond the blast zone. Once inside the building and into the tunnel, nothing could touch them. Within days, Alim would be back in the Zagros Mountains of his homeland, a hero to his people.

Alim turned once more expecting to see the blue sedan pulling up to the truck, but it wasn't there. Now he could see it again, up the street. The idiots were backing the sedan into a parking space at the curb two blocks away. Were they blind? Couldn't they see the truck? Afundi cursed out loud.

"Jamal!" he hollered at the translator, who was standing guard outside the truck. The interpreter stuck his head in the open door.

"Go get them. Tell them to drive the car down here, and hurry."

The translator took off running, all the speed he could muster with his stodgy middle-aged body.

Alim checked the clock and his watch, then disconnected the lead wires. He didn't bother to close up the wooden panel. Instead he quickly made his way to the door, jumped from the truck, and pulled the lift door down behind him. He sealed the latch and looked for the padlock, checked his pockets, and suddenly realized Jamal had been twirling it on his finger.

By the time Alim turned to look, the translator was already a block away. He shook his head and raced up toward the cab. He opened the passenger door and grabbed his day pack. He pulled from behind the seat another larger sports bag that held an assault rifle, three clips of ammunition, and two bottles of water.

He took a drink as he walked toward the rear of the truck with the two bags. The blue sedan hadn't moved. And he could no longer see Jamal, either on the street or the sidewalk.

Afundi shook his head, glanced at the unlocked latch on the back of the truck, and started moving as fast as he could down the sidewalk and toward the car.

SIXTY-SIX

I am sliding sideways under the truck so I can see down the sidewalk behind us when I realize we are alone. I can see him in the distance walking the other way, toting two bags over his shoulders.

"Herman."

"Yeah."

"Slide out on your side. There's nobody here. I think they've gone."

The three of us make our way out from under the truck on the left side. We stay low, moving toward the front of the truck so that if someone on the sidewalk looked back they wouldn't see us.

We wait until he is a block away and then race for the lift gate in the back. Herman throws the gate up as Maricela and I clamber aboard. Herman comes in behind us and lowers the gate, but not all the way.

He holds it up a few inches, just enough for light to come in so Maricela and I can try and get her father free. He is shackled to a metal rail along the inside of the fiberglass box.

Maricela removes the tape from his mouth and eyes

as I try to figure out some way to release his hand from the metal rail.

As soon as the gag is out of his mouth, he starts spitting instructions at his daughter in Spanish.

"What's he saying?" I ask Herman.

She is arguing with him.

"He wants her to go. He wants us all to leave now. He says to run as fast as we can."

I look down and see the open panel on the side of the wooden crate, get on my knees, and look inside. There is a green metal container, just a little smaller than the crate itself.

"Ask him"—I look up at Maricela—"ask him if there's any way to stop it."

Herman is looking around desperately for something to prop up the door with so he can help me.

She says something to him and Nitikin responds with an answer that seems to take forever.

"He says there's a safety. A wire on the side of the metal box inside the crate. But he says it won't do us any good. It will stop the big bomb, but the little explosion will kill us all anyway. He says we must leave now."

"There must be a way to stop it," I tell her. "Ask him again. Tell him we're not leaving until we stop it."

She speaks to him and they argue. He yells at her. She reaches up and pulls on his arms, trying to free his hands as tears run down her face. Suddenly he says something, a quieter and calmer voice this time as he looks over his shoulder at the crate behind him.

"He says there's a pipe sticking out of the metal box inside, near the top, in the front. It should have two wires coming out of it. Do you see it?"

I look, but I can't see a thing. It's too dark inside the crate, especially with the lift gate down.

"I need more light."

"Screw it," says Herman. He throws the lift gate all the way up. Light streams in through the back of the truck. I see the two wires and then the black metal pipe. Dangling from the end of the wires is a small green circuit board not much bigger than a playing card.

Alim wondered what was going on. He was halfway between the truck and the car and he still couldn't see the two brothers anywhere. But Jamal was in the passenger seat looking down at something in his lap. Alim could see him even with the late-afternoon sun glinting off the car's windshield.

With the straps from the two heavy bags over his shoulders Afundi waved his arms in the air and signaled for the car to pick him up. But Jamal wasn't looking. His attention was drawn to something else.

At this rate, by the time Alim made it to the car, they would have to drive back to the truck to reset the timer in order to gain enough of a cushion to get away. As he thought about it, Afundi turned and glanced back over his shoulder at the truck, then turned back toward the waiting car. He was walking toward the sedan before the image in his brain registered. When it did, he stopped dead, turned around, and studied the back of the truck. The lift gate was up!

Alim dropped both bags on the sidewalk, unzipped one, and pulled out the Kalashnikov along with two of the loaded clips. He pushed a clip up into the receiver, slapped it home, then cycled the bolt to chamber the first round. He left the folded stock closed knowing the gun would be easier to conceal.

He tried to signal Jamal, who was still sitting in the passenger seat. It looked as if he was reading something. In his mind, Alim made a pledge to shoot the bastard and to take the heads of the two brothers with a sword at the first opportunity.

"I think I see it." I follow the wires with my eyes until they disappear beyond the end of the pipe.

Nitikin tells his daughter something.

"He says that's the breech of the gun barrel. There is a cork . . . ¿cómo se dice?" She says something in Spanish to her father. He corrects her.

"He says it's a plug," she says. "The plug screws into the end of the barrel where the wires go in. Do you see it?"

Herman comes over to the crate and moves around behind me to stay out of the light. He pulls on the tie-down rail holding Nitikin's wrists to the wall, hoping to free him so the Russian can help me.

I feel with my hand along the two thin wires until I find where they disappear into what feels like tiny holes in the threaded plug. The plug is screwed into the end of the barrel. The metal is warm to the touch. I don't even want to ask what is causing the heat. With my fingernail I can feel about a quarter inch of exposed thread along the edge where the plug sits above the closed end of the barrel of the gun.

"Yes. I can feel it," I tell her.

She relays this to her father, who is looking anxiously over his shoulder as Herman jerks on the steel rail, trying to free him.

He says something else to her.

"If you can unscrew the plug, he says you will be able to pull the wires, they will be attached to something... I don't understand the word he is using," she says.

"It's a detonator." Herman is jerking hard on the metal rail tie-down as he speaks. Then he stops for a second to catch his breath. "He says it's an electronic detonator attached to a cordite charge. Which means it's probably enough to take your hand off up to the elbow. 'Course if it goes off in the gun, you won't have to worry about that."

"My father says that once the small explosive charge is removed the gun will no longer work. If we throw the small explosive out the door, no one will be hurt when it blows up."

I trace the wires back up to the end of the gun and feel the plug with my fingers once more. I touch the sharp edges of a hex head, like the hexagonal head on a bolt, only larger. If I had an expandable wrench I might be able to get a purchase on the plug and unscrew it. I try turning it with my fingers, but it won't budge.

The two small MH-6 Night Stalkers came in at two thousand feet with their blades running on whisper mode so that the sniper teams could reconnoiter the area around the truck.

Using forward-looking infrared (FLIR), the "little birds" searched for warm bodies out in the clear and then zeroed in on the windows of the truck's cab.

They circled for two or three minutes, but the only heat signatures they picked up came from the box in the back where the thin fiberglass shell revealed four separate figures as well as a larger square inanimate object that seemed to be emitting heat. The object rested on the forward center section of the bed, up near the cab.

As the snipers hovered in place, the larger Blackhawk put the NEST team down in the middle of an intersection cleared by the police. They dropped their duffel bags with their gear and asked one of the officers to load them into patrol cars and to follow them to the site. They took only their tool belts with the basic implements needed to get at the bomb. As soon as the empty bird lifted off, the next chopper, carrying the hostage rescue team, used the same controlled intersection and deposited the agents.

Together the two teams jogged east down the street toward San Diego Bay and the box truck parked two blocks away.

The snipers circling in the air overhead asked the NEST team about the wisdom of firing through the fiberglass shell of the truck's back half.

The answer came back in a flash, negative. Depending on the source of detonation and whether the people inside could trigger it, a loose round in the wrong place or a ricochet and they could set off the device.

Alim folded the stock back on the Kalashnikov, unzipped the front of his overalls, and slipped the assault rifle inside to conceal it. He held it with his right hand by the pistol grip with one finger on the lever between safety and full automatic.

Afundi moved to the other side of the street, into the shadows, and slowly walked back toward the truck. Halfway down the block he stopped and set up under some trees, behind a parked car.

Because of the deep shadows inside the truck he

couldn't see far enough into the open back end to make out what was happening.

Alim checked his watch and knew he was now at the point of no return. He either had to break and run for the car to get across the bridge at near-light speed, or take his chances on entering the truck to reset the timer. It was one or the other. The single certainty was that he couldn't wait any longer.

SIXTY-SEVEN

Herman finally realizes that what he needs is leverage. He grabs the wooden panel from the side of the crate and looks at it. It is heavy, made of South American junk wood, something called Ipe, hard as iron and almost as strong.

He slides the wooden panel up under the tie-down rail a few inches from where Nitikin's hands are chained, puts his foot against the inside wall of the truck's box, and lifts with all of his might. The washer and bolt holding the section of rail in place from the outside of the box pops through the fiberglass. Herman grabs the loose section of railing and bends it back. A second later Yakov is free.

Maricela tries to grab her father to hug him. She wants to wipe the blood from the side of his face but instead the old man goes down on his knees and moves toward the opening in the crate.

I get out of his way, figuring if anyone can do it, he can. I watch him as he stretches his arm to the end of the barrel and strains with his fingers to turn the breech plug. I can see the pain on his face as his fingers are rubbed raw by the metal.

Herman drops from the back of the truck and runs around to see if there are any tools in the cab of the truck, but I hear him pulling on the doors. Both of them are locked. Next he starts pounding on the window trying to break it, but he can't, at least not with his fists. A few seconds later he's back in the truck shaking his head.

"Lemme try," he says.

I tap Nitikin on the shoulder and point to Herman. We want to get the man with the brawn in there. The Russian backs out of the opening in the crate and Herman squeezes into it. He tries to turn the plug, but it's frozen tight. None of us can get a grip on it or sufficient leverage to turn it.

"Ask him what happens if we pull wires?" I say.

Maricela puts the question to her father, who quickly shakes his head. I don't have to wait for the translation. I can tell by the look on his face that this is not a good idea.

"Be careful of wires," I tell Herman.

Just as Alim started to break cover to head for the truck, the ear-splitting rush of noise overhead sent him ducking back into the shadows under the trees. The helicopter streaked through the sky, cut an arc directly over the truck, and proceeded on a direct course toward the naval carrier.

For a second Afundi thought it was probably just part of the festivities in the harbor, but a moment later a man in black combat gear with a rifle rushed from in front of a house a few doors down. Another broke cover farther on. They both approached the truck from the same side. Suddenly another helicopter moved in and hovered overhead no more than fifty yards in front of Afundi's position. The sound of the rotors and whine of the turbine engine drowned out every other noise. It also gave Alim just the opening he needed.

He pulled the rifle from his overalls, unfolded the stock, and pushed the safety lever all the way down, setting up for single shots. Alim took careful aim and squeezed off a round. He watched as one of the men in black fell to the ground ten feet out from the truck. Quickly he moved the muzzle and acquired another target and faster than he could think he dropped it.

The noise of the helicopter and the beat of its rotors lay like a blanket over the sound of Alim's shots as he picked off two more. By now the pavement behind the truck was littered with bodies.

"Where is it coming from?" one of the snipers asked.

"I don't know." They were baffled. "It could be coming from the back of the truck." The element of surprise was gone and so was the initiative. The order was given to pull back and a few seconds later the helicopter dipped its rotors and disappeared out over the bay.

As I watch a guy in military gear go down just beyond the open door to the truck, I think he has tripped. But as I stand and look, I notice that he isn't moving. When I see the other two go down, I know someone is shooting but we can't hear them because of the noise of the helicopter.

Maricela sees what is happening and starts toward the door. I grab her and pull her back.

Behind me Nitikin is shaking his head. Then Herman comes out from inside the crate.

"No use," he hollers. "We need something to turn it."

I put Maricela's back against the inside wall and tell her to stay there, not to move. Her dad comes up to take care of her, and I join Herman by the open crate.

"Any ideas?" I say.

"No." I can see the fear in Herman's eyes. The only saving aspect is that when it happens, it is likely to be so quick that none of us will even feel a thing. If I had a phone at this moment, I would call Sarah and say good-bye.

Suddenly the roar of the helicopter is gone and all I hear is the plaintive cry of Maricela as she calls my name. By the time I turn and look she is pointing out the back of the truck toward her father, who is outside on the ground running.

I scurry across the bed of the truck on my hands and knees until I land flat on my stomach at the open door. Trying to present the smallest target possible, I watch as the Russian reaches one of the bodies prostrate on the pavement behind the truck. He bends over, fumbling with something on the man's belt.

"Target acquired. Do I have a green light?"

"Take him out," said Thorpe.

The sniper squeezed the trigger. The recoil rocked his shoulder as the bullet sliced through the air.

When he rises back up and turns to face me, I can finally see what it is that he has in his hand. Nitikin starts to run back toward us. He takes two long strides. His eyes connect with his daughter as his upthrust hand releases the heavy item, tossing it toward the bed of the truck. Just as he does it, the bullet rips through his upper body, sending a cloud of crimson mist out the front of his chest.

The wrench clatters across the smooth metal bed of the truck. I hear the shriek from Maricela as she tries to get past me and out the back. She is desperate to reach her father, sprawled on the pavement. From my knees I smother her in my arms and drive her back against the fiberglass wall of the truck.

As the helicopter peeled away out over the bay, Alim threw the assault rifle and the extra clip into some bushes, and ran toward Jamal, in the car down the street.

Afundi abandoned the two bags he'd left on the sidewalk across the street. There was no time. Pike's computer and the newspaper from Castro were not worth dying for.

He closed the distance on the blue sedan. Breathless, he reached the driver's side and climbed in. "Why didn't you pick me up?" Alim looked at the ignition. "Where are the keys?" He saw a patch of blood on Jamal's shirt and the fixed gaze of death in his eyes.

Liquida reached for Alim from the backseat and had the ether-soaked rag over his face before he could move. Alim fumbled for the pistol in his pocket, but it was too late.

With the sound of the shot that kills Nitikin, Herman jumps out from the opening in the side of the crate. He sees for the first time what has happened and within seconds he is over to help me with Maricela. He lifts her and carries her back into the darker interior of the sheltering truck.

I scramble across the floor to retrieve the six-inch

crescent wrench that Maricela's father purchased with his life. Two seconds later, my head is in the opening at the side of the wooden crate. I feel for the metal plug at the breech of the gun, adjust the spanner wheel until the wrench fits snugly over the hex head on the plug. Then I pull. It won't budge. I pull again, this time harder. Then I realize I'm turning it in the wrong direction. I push on the handle. It doesn't move. I jar the handle with my hand, giving it more muscle.

"You want me to try?" says Herman.

"Nooo," I groan. But then the plug begins to move. A slow quarter turn at first, and then it loosens. I pull off the wrench and turn it with my fingers, twisting the two wires as I go. Suddenly the plug comes free in my hand.

Carefully I lift it straight out, away from the closed end of the barrel. I feel the heat from the radiation inside and quickly draw my hand with the plug away from the gun. The entire assembly comes free, the metal plug with the wires running through it. On one end of the wires is the electronic detonator. On the other is the small green circuit board with the timer.

I hold it gingerly in my hand as I get to my feet and walk toward the open door. I get down from the truck and throw the assembly as far as I can, out onto the street.

I yell at the top of my lungs, "The detonator is out. The bomb is safe." Less than a minute later an explosion the size of an MD-80, a large cherry bomb some say is a quarter stick of dynamite, goes off in the street.

Within seconds a federal agent on a squad car PA system tells us to come out of the truck with our hands in the air. Men in tactical gear surround us with rifles as officers throw us to the ground.

Agents in black Kevlar storm the truck and huddle around the crate inside.

Police stand over us holding rifles as others search our pockets, pat us down, and cuff our hands.

Maricela struggles to get to her father. One of the cops kneels on her back, jamming her face into the pavement as two of his burly brethren grab her hands and manacle them behind her back.

"Leave her alone," I say.

"Shut up." I get the muzzle of a rifle jammed into my back.

Liquida turned the key in the ignition and started the car. With all the confusion around the truck two blocks away, who could blame them for not noticing the small blue sedan as it pulled away from the curb, did a U-turn, and headed south toward the Coronado bridge.

SIXTY-EIGHT

It took a few days for the dust to settle. By then federal authorities had hauled the device to a safe location where they could study it and dispose of the fissile materials when they were finished. The press and the media never got wind of exactly what had happened.

The president had delayed his televised warning by an additional half hour to provide more time for logistical planning. In the meantime, the device had been defused and the need for a warning evaporated. None of the more than ten thousand people on the naval base that day ever learned just how close they had come to Armageddon. Nor did the thousands who lived in Coronado or those in San Diego, across the bay.

Within days of the event, government analysts, physicists, and weapons-design experts assessed the potential yield of Nitikin's device and crunched the numbers. They determined that the distance between the giant aircraft carrier moored at the dock and the epicenter of the blast where the truck was parked was just over half a mile, which placed the carrier squarely within the zone of total destruction.

Structures within a mile of the epicenter would have been totally destroyed, either by the blast effect or by heat from the fireball. Within that one-mile radius, virtually no living thing above the surface of the sea would have survived. Those who were not instantly incinerated would have suffocated as a result of oxygen deprivation, all oxygen having been consumed in the blast, or from the lethal dose of radiation poisoning.

Within a two-mile zone the vast majority of those in the open, without shelter, would have been killed. Any wooden structures would have been, for the most part, ignited by the superheated air from the blast and destroyed by fire.

Beyond that, radiation poisoning would have devastated those who survived the initial blast, some of whom would die within days, others over longer periods.

Much of the city of Coronado would lie in ruins. The blast effect, unimpeded by any structures on the water, would reach across the bay to wreak havoc on buildings along the waterfront in San Diego, and the effects of radiation would drift across the harbor and contaminate large portions of the city as well as the suburbs beyond. To those with visions of the California dream—balmy beaches and bikinied blue-eyed blondes—Southern California would never look the same again.

But for Paul Madriani and Katia Solaz, the most important item may not have been the bomb. Their salvation was found farther down the street.

In some brush near a house a half block from the location of the rental truck, police found an abandoned weapon, a Chinese Kalashnikov rifle along with an extra clip of ammunition. Ballistics tests showed that the rifle in question was the weapon used to kill three federal agents and to wound two others, all of whom were hit from behind as they approached the truck.

Fingerprints lifted from the rifle were run through federal computers and a positive match identified. The prints belonged to a man named Alim Afundi, the same name given to the authorities by Maricela Solaz. Military records showed that Afundi was a noncombatant detainee who'd been captured in Afghanistan and transported to the U.S. detention facility at Guantanamo Bay, Cuba. He and several followers had escaped, disappeared, and were presumed dead somewhere in the swamps or sea surrounding the base.

Of more immediate importance were the contents of a small day pack found on the sidewalk across the street from where the rifle had been found. Inside the backpack was a laptop computer belonging to Emerson Pike, one of the victims in the double murder at Del Mar months earlier. Fingerprints on the computer also matched Afundi's, as did digital images in photographs found on the computer's hard drive when matched with mug shots taken at Guantanamo.

With Yakov Nitikin now dead and his device safely disposed of, federal authorities no longer had reason to withhold the coveted photographs. Faced with the fact that the laptop computer was known to be in the victim's residence on the night of the murders, and the unassailable evidence of Afundi's prints all over it, plus the fact that he had clearly committed further acts of violence, state prosecutors had no choice.

Ten days after the events in Coronado, Deputy District Attorney Lawrence Templeton unceremoniously slipped into the courtroom of Judge Plato Quinn and, without notice to the press or public, filed motions for dismissal with prejudice regarding all charges against Katia Solaz and Paul Madriani in the double murders at Emerson Pike's house.

Katia and Maricela went back to Costa Rica to begin their lives anew. Katia continued to mend and was released from the hospital to be cared for by her mother. The reunion between the two was the perfect medicine for the woman who'd lost her best friend in the carnage on the sheriff's bus. The chief regret was that Yakov Nitikin would never have the chance to know his granddaughter, nor she him. Though now at least she would have the chance to learn about him from the woman who loved him most, his daughter, Maricela.

As for Harry, he finally forgave me for some of the more stupid things I'd done, including the failure to tell him about the catnip in my desk drawer or my second meeting with Katia at the Brigantine. As always, Harry was there to pick up the pieces, and I'll never forget that.

The case of Katia Solaz changed my life. The practice of law no longer held the same fascination or urgency it once did. It is difficult to know why. They say that those who have a near-death experience often use their second chance at life to redeem their earlier mistakes; some pursue the spiritual, and others search for meaning in what remains of their existence on this earth. Discovering what this is for me has now become a quest.

SIXTY-NINE

Tonight Liquida was back at the auto-body shop where he had melted the gold, the dingy chop shop owned by his friend. While he wasn't making gold bricks this time, to Liquida this task was something almost as enjoyable.

Like in an Aztec ceremony he had the Arab chained to the steel rafter on the ceiling, his feet dangling just off the floor. Except for his boxers Alim was naked, with his ankles taped together and strapped to an eighty-pound anvil. Liquida moved around him with a pair of pliers testing the flesh for thickness and durability as he poked and prodded for pockets of pain, those special little places that only intimacy with iron tongs can reveal.

With his mouth taped shut and his eyes wide open, Alim watched in horror as the Mexican flipped a switch and powered up the arc welder.

Liquida stepped over and sparked him a couple of times, then smiled as he watched him dance on the end of the chain. It was going to be a long night, and Liquida was determined to enjoy every minute of it. The only thing that could have made it better was if the lawyer and his partner were chained over the rafter as counterweights.

Madriani had saved the woman in San José and was probably responsible for the mess on the sheriff's bus. But most of all Liquida's anger at Madriani was reserved for the loss of the gold, a small fortune that could have seen Liquida through his retirement years. When John Waters didn't show up for the court hearing, the authorities had drilled into the safe-deposit box and found the gold ingots. It was in all the newspapers.

It took them a while, but after the shootout in Coronado they finally got around to weighing the gold bars. According to the news reports, the weight of the bricks matched almost precisely the records maintained by Emerson Pike showing the weight of the missing coins from his study. The authorities now had a lead on the identity of Pike's killer, one John Waters. Fortunately, they would have no film from the bank's security cameras, as too much time had elapsed since the date he had opened the account, no thanks to the lawyers. Besides, Liquida had worn a good disguise, gray hair and makeup to age him considerably and Cuban heels to make him four inches taller than he actually was on the day he rented the safe-deposit box.

Still, he was having difficulty sleeping at night. He kept hearing the infernal "beep-beep" of the Road Runner cartoon. In his mind he kept seeing the big African-American outside the house in San José that night, and the lawyer up at the corner, the man he couldn't find when he went looking.

As far as Liquida was concerned, all of them, Madriani; his partner, Harry Hinds; and the investigator,

Herman Diggs, were now among the walking dead. He was already busy doing research on their habits and routines. He would have to squeeze them in between paying jobs since he was now a poor man once more. But it would be a labor of love. They were now on Liquida's short list, and the man known in Tijuana as the Mexecutioner had a very long memory.

AUTHOR'S NOTE

The Nuclear Warhead and the Cuban Backstory

The foundation of this story is constructed on historic fact.

The warhead used in this story is a fourteen-kiloton device for an obsolete Soviet FKR cruise missile. It possessed roughly the same destructive force as Little Boy, the bomb the United States dropped on Hiroshima, Japan, in August 1945.

During the Cuban Missile Crisis, President John F. Kennedy knew about the existence in Cuba of other warheads for the R-14 and R-12, intermediate and long-range ballistic missiles (1- and 2-megaton devices). However these remained on board the ship *Aleksandrovsk* and were never off-loaded or deployed in Cuba.

However, the deadly secret—one that could easily have resulted in a global nuclear holocaust—was that there were also approximately one hundred battlefield nuclear weapons on the island, each one capable of destroying a good-size city. For thirty years the United

States had not even the slightest clue that there were a large number of tactical nuclear weapons on the island in 1962. This was not made public until the early nineties following the collapse of the Soviet Union.

In October 1962, Kennedy placed U.S. troops on alert, including marines at Camp Pendleton in California, for possible invasion of Cuba. Many of these troops had already been deployed to Florida for possible use in an invasion of the island. If he had ordered that invasion, we now know that because of limited intelligence regarding the lethal potential of Russian battlefield weapons on Cuba, any amphibious landing would have resulted in a nuclear nightmare.

Forty-four of the FKR warheads arrived at the port of La Isabela, Cuba, on the morning of October 25, 1962, shortly after President Kennedy declared a naval blockade of the island.

The FKRs were short-range battlefield tactical weapons. They were designed to be delivered by a type of cruise missile, a scaled-down version of the old Russian MiG with an effective range of about a hundred miles. Under the heightened tension of the time, the U.S. naval blockade, and the possibility of an invasion, the FKRs and their warheads were deployed immediately to Oriente Province for possible use against the U.S. naval base at Guantanamo Bay and to protect the Cuban coastline from any U.S. invasion.

After the crisis, the world was told that all of the Russian nuclear weapons were removed from Cuba by Christmas Day, December 25, 1962. But we now know that that was not true because many of the tactical nuclear weapons remained, at least for a while. We also now know that these battlefield weapons were a major point of contention between Fidel Castro, the Cuban dictator, and Nikita Khrushchev, the Soviet premier. Castro wanted the tactical nuclear weapons to remain on the island in hopes that they might ultimately be placed under Cuban control. Castro saw these as the ultimate guarantee that there would be no further attempts by the United States to invade Cuba. However, Khrushchev was concerned because during the missile crisis, Castro had urged the Russians to launch a preemptive nuclear strike against the United States, believing the winner would be the one who struck first. The Soviet premier was terrified that if Castro got his hands on the weapons and attacked the United States, Russia would be drawn into a full-scale nuclear war. At some point it is reported that Khrushchev removed all of the tactical nuclear weapons from the island, though the date of action is unclear.

At the conclusion of the crisis, Kennedy argued for on-site verification, a tour of the Russian nuclear storage facilities on Cuba by U.S. and international officials to assure themselves that the missiles and the warheads were gone. But because of continuing friction in U.S.-Soviet relations, this never happened. Instead the United States was forced to rely on aerial surveillance and reconnaissance photos to track the removal and return of the missiles and warheads to Russia.

However, U.S. officials never knew about the tactical battlefield weapons. So when the large long-range missiles and their warheads, packed into nuclear storage vans, were identified on board ships on their way back to the Soviet Union, they assumed that all weapons of mass destruction were removed from the island. We know now that this was not true.

In November 1963, Kennedy was assassinated amid rumors that Soviet and Cuban intrigue may have played a role in his death. In 1964, Nikita Khrushchev was deposed and forced to step down as Soviet premier in large part because of his loss of face in the international community as a result of the missile crisis.

Tickling the Dragon's Tail

The term "tickling the dragon's tail" was in fact coined by physicist Richard Feynman at Los Alamos in the early days of experimentation following development of the first successful nuclear devices. At the time, physicists were involved in "criticality testing" to determine the precise mass of fissile materials (highly enriched uranium) required to reach near-critical levels in order to trigger a chain reaction. These tests (that were somewhat crude and later determined to be far too dangerous to continue in the same manner) involved the movement of two elements of highly enriched uranium in close proximity to each other to test the emission of radiation. Dr. Feynman referred to these experiments as "tickling the tail of a sleeping dragon" because of the risk that any slip of the hand could be fatal.

In fact during two incidents, one in August 1945 and the other in May 1946, two scientists, Harry Daghlian Jr. and Louis Slotin, were irradiated with lethal doses of radiation poisoning. In each of those cases the same core of 6.2 kilograms (roughly 14 pounds) of plutonium, later dubbed the "demon core," was used in the experiments. All further testing of this kind was scrubbed as a result of these accidents.

The Slotin accident reports state that Slotin was engaged in testing the commencement of a fission reaction by bringing two metal hemispheres of highly reactive, beryllium-coated plutonium into close proximity without allowing them to touch. On the date in question, May 21, 1946, after successfully conducting the experiment on numerous occasions, the metal screwdriver used to separate the two hemispheres slipped and allowed contact. Observers reported "a blue glow and a wave of heat that swept through the room" as the air itself became ionized. The heat was unbearable, and the brilliant flash of blue was reported to be brighter than the sunshine of a spring day. A prickling metallic taste was experienced on the tongue of those in the room. Slotin is reputed to have shielded others with his own body. He died nine days later and was buried in Winnipeg, Canada.

The blue glow is known as cerenkov radiation and is the result of highly charged particles, such as electrons, traveling through transparent material at a speed greater than the local speed of light. There is some debate among scientists as to whether the blue flash actually occurs or is merely the result of ionization of the moisture in the eyeballs of those witnessing the chain reaction.

The Threat of the Drug Cartels

Today the dangers emanating from the Mexican drug cartels, chiefly in Tijuana, Juárez, and Sinaloa, cannot be overstated. In the eighties and early nineties, the U.S. government launched a war against the narcotic drug lords of Colombia. At that time Mexico was a part of the transportation network for the movement of illicit narcotics from Colombia into the United States.

Since then, with the death of the Colombian drug lord Pablo Escobar and the disruption of the Cali and Medellín cartels, the organized violence of the drug underworld has only moved closer to the southern border of the United States. In recent years it has intensified and is reputed to have corrupted large segments of Mexico's government and law enforcement in the same way that it did in Colombia two decades earlier. To believe that we in this country are immune to such corrupting influences is foolishness.

The cartels are now centered in cities such as Tijuana, Nuevo Laredo, and Juárez, where scores of people are murdered daily in ongoing turf wars over who will control the drug trade. That these cartels have links to Middle Eastern terror groups should come as no surprise, since Al Qaeda and others generate much of their revenue for terrorist operations from poppy fields in Afghanistan and elsewhere and are believed to be well connected within the drug underworld.

It is also well known that the cartels and those smuggling illicit drugs into the United States have in the past used tunnels as the preferred method for shipping large quantities of "product" under the U.S.-Mexican border. As the American economy declines and revenue from illegal narcotics escalates, the cartels that already employ their own private forces armed with automatic weapons, including grenade launchers, become an even greater threat. The commander of the U.S. marine base at Camp Pendleton, California, recently posted Tijuana, Mexico, as off-limits to all marine personnel because it was judged to be too dangerous a venue for rest and tourism. U.S. marines can travel to Baghdad and Afghanistan, but they can no longer cross the border into Mexico without special permission. This should tell us something about the emerging dangers along our southern border.

If you enjoyed
Guardian of Lies,
don't miss
The Rule of Nine,
the next Paul Madriani thriller
from Steve Martini

Available in hardcover June 2010
from William Morrow
An Imprint of HarperCollins Publishers

J immie Snyder was twenty-three, tall and lanky. He had been in his current job less than two months, and he was scared. He knew he had screwed up. Like Chinese water torture, he laid awake at nights worrying about it, waiting for the next drip to hit him in the forehead. It was all about expectations, mostly his father's.

Snyder's dad was the managing partner in a large law firm in Chicago. Jimmie had graduated prelaw from Stanford a year earlier, and his father wanted him to go to law school. But Jimmie wanted to go into film production. His father would have none of it. As far as the old man was concerned, Jimmie needed credentials to round out his law school application and beef up his less than stellar undergraduate grades and middling LSAT score.

Toward that end his father pulled every string within reach to land the boy a job in Washington. The best he could do on short notice was a temporary position as a part-time guide. The job was a holding pattern until dad could yank more levers and land something better.

It took him three months and a hefty contribution to a congressman in Alabama, but he found a spot for Jimmie as a staff gofer with one of the many House sub-committees. This particular panel was charged with overseeing Capitol security. As it turned out, the nature of the assignment now made the situation even worse for his son.

It might take a while for the details to trickle back, to filter from one branch to the other, but sooner or later Jimmie knew he would be called on the carpet and asked to explain how he could have done something so stupid. How could he allow some middle-aged lawyer from California wearing a polo shirt and shorts to talk his way backstage, past all the locked doors and the phalanx of security, into the private sanctum off-limits to all but the gods of government? In an earlier decade, what might have been a minor transgression became grounds for job termination and possible criminal prosecution in the age of terror.

Jimmie had spent a week of sleepless nights trying to conjure some plausible explanation for why he had done it. Call it bad judgment. Maybe it was because he was angry and bored. He hated the job and the fact that his father manipulated him into taking it. It was that, but also the fact that the man he met that day was so easy to talk to. Unlike Snyder's father, the guy was affable, approachable, and interested. He listened to everything Jimmie had to say. When Jimmie told him he really didn't want to pursue a career in law, the lawyer, a perfect stranger, gave him absolution. He told Jimmie that the first rule of success in life was to follow your dreams. And then to find out that the guy was a Stanford law alum on vacation, how could Jimmie say no? All the man wanted was to see a few of the rooms off-limits to the public. Jimmie had already finished his tour of duty for the day. What was the harm? It wasn't as if they had done anything wrong. Other than take a few pictures, chat, and look around, you would have never known the man was there. Jimmie still had the guy's business card in his wallet—WARREN HUMPHREYS, ATTORNEY AT LAW—an address in Santa Rosa, California.

Now one of the other house staffers told Jimmie that inquiries were being made. Nothing formal as yet, but it was likely to cause waves because the incident could not be contained on the legislative side. Sooner or later, Jimmie would probably be visited by investigators.

Like a bad dream, all the little details tripped through his brain as he walked down the steps of the Rayburn House Office Building. Even now, a few minutes after six, with the sun sailing toward the horizon, the heat of early summer was oppressive. Most of the members of Congress had returned to their districts for the recess, leaving staff to wither in the sultry heat of the national swamp. Beads of sweat ran down the back of his shirt collar as he thought about what could happen. He didn't dare tell his father.

Every little aspect of what seemed an innocent

adventure, a courtesy to a friendly tourist, now appeared much more ominous.

The man's camera was something that hadn't even occurred to Jimmie until later, when he realized he was in trouble. Cameras where prohibited except in the public areas. He wondered how the little point-and-shoot job got through the metal detector without setting off the alarm.

Maybe the man had posted some of his pictures on the Internet. That would explain how they found out. He scoured his brain trying to remember whether he might have absently slipped into one or more of the shots. There was no way to be sure, but he didn't think so. All the man wanted was a few snapshots of some of the interiors. He seemed most interested in the walnut-paneled library, which was elegant, and the gymnasium upstairs. The gym was nothing special, just one of those conversational curiosities inside the beltway.

Jimmie strode onto the sidewalk and headed for the Metro rail and home. It was a short ride. He lived alone in a small sublet apartment in Alexandria. Rent was high in the area, but he was lucky. He had gotten a deal on the place for the summer. When the members of Congress returned, so would the tenant, a lobbyist for the drug industry, and Jimmie would have to find another place to live. If there was a silver lining to any of this, it was the fact that if they fired him he would not have to find new digs come fall. He would be gone.

A few blocks later, Jimmie ventured onto the long,

steep escalator and down into the immense cavern of the Metro rail. He slipped his card into the slot at the turnstile, slid through, and ran for the train. He caught it just before the doors closed.

The thought of escaping Washington, even at the cost of failure, left Jimmie to wonder if it would be enough for his father to finally give up on him. This and the deep sense of disappointment he would have to endure occupied him as he sat listening to the wheels skim over the steel rails.

Twelve minutes later, he emerged from the King Street Station in Alexandria. The setting sun had finally dipped behind the buildings by the time he reached the entrance to the three-story brick apartment house. There were only fourteen units. They ranged from studios to three bedrooms, all of them equipped with updated fixtures and hardwood floors. There was no elevator or front desk, and no twenty-four-hour security. The lobbyist who held the lease to Jimmie's unit was looking for a summer tenant to watch the place. As long as Jimmie didn't throw parties and didn't smoke, the single-bedroom apartment was his for two hundred dollars a month until fall. It was a steal.

He climbed the five steps, fishing in his pocket for his key to the front entrance. By the time he got there, he realized that the heavy oak door wasn't locked. Something was wrong with the door's overhead closing arm that caused it to stay open just a crack. He had noticed it a couple of days earlier.

He pushed the door and it opened. Once inside, he waited for the door to close, then gave it a shove until he heard the lock snap into place. He made a mental note to tell the building manager.

He used his apartment key to check his mail in the locked boxes in the lobby. There was nothing but a few pieces of junk mail and one business envelope from his father's law firm. Probably more suggestions for his law school resume. He headed for the stairs.

Using his key as a letter opener, he tore a jagged opening in the envelope. He was looking down at the single folded page inside when peripheral vision caught a dark image in front of him on the stairs. Jimmie glanced up.

There, sprawled across the steps from the banister to the wall, was the hunched-up body of an indigent. Some beggar had wandered into the building. Unshaven, wearing a soiled dark trench coat and scuffed-up black shoes with no socks. The guy looked like a dropped sack of potatoes. For a moment Jimmie wondered if he was dead. But as he studied the motionless figure in front of him, he detected the subtle rise of respiration under the wrinkled, dirty coat.

"Excuse me."

The guy didn't move.

"Mister." Jimmie nudged him with his foot.

The body didn't budge.

"If you don't get out of here, I'm going to have to call the cops."

Still, there was no movement. A faint odor of alcohol lingered over the slumped form. He had wandered into the building, probably looking for a cool place to sleep, and passed out on the stairs.

Jimmie nudged him again, but the guy didn't move. He couldn't get around him so he lifted one long leg, took a giant stride, and tried to navigate three steps going over the top of the guy. As he straddled the man, a gloved hand suddenly reached out from the trench coat and grabbed Jimmie's ankle.

Jimmie smiled. "Excuse me!" The man's grip was amazingly powerful for a semi-conscious drunk.

"What are you doing?" Jimmie reached down to grab the hand that was on his ankle. As he did, he felt a sharp sting on the back of his hand, as if a snake had bitten him.

He tried to jerk his hand back, but just as quickly, it was held fast by the gloved hand that held his ankle.

"What the hell!" A burning sensation spread like fire through the vein on the back of his right hand between the first two fingers. "What are you doing?"

The ripped envelope fluttered down the stairs like a fallen leaf. It was followed by the jangle of keys onto the stairs. Before the envelope settled at the foot of the steps, Jimmie's vision began to blur. An amazing sensation of euphoria swept through his body carried by the heat that flushed his veins. He stood there weaving in a broad circle as if floating on a cloud. Sprawl-legged over the man lying on the stairs, a sensation of uncaring bliss flooded his body.

As if in a dream, Jimmie watched as the bum left the syringe still buried deep in his right hand. The leather glove reached up and grabbed him by the shoulder. In a rapture, Jimmie settled onto the stairs, his delirious gaze focused at the fuzzy edge of the carpeted runner where his cheek landed. His vision clouded. He blinked twice. There was a fleeting sensation of drool as it ran from the corner of his paralyzed mouth, then nothing as the filament of existence dissolved.

The bum shifted his body and pulled himself out from beneath his fallen victim. He was slightly built, the kind of spindly character who could cross a crowded street and never garner more than a fleeting glance by those who passed him. He had a pockmarked face from an adolescence of acne. But even this did not distinguish him, unless you happened to engage his eyes. If the iris was the window into the soul, Muerte Liquida's glassy stare offered a view of hell. To a growing list of victims, it was the last thing they ever saw.

He glanced quickly at the plunger on the syringe to make sure it was all the way in. He didn't remove it, but instead grabbed a roll of surgical tape from the pocket of his trench coat. He wrapped three rounds of the tape around the syringe and the dead man's hand to hold the hypodermic in place.

Then, as if in a single motion, he grabbed the keys and slipped down the stairs to retrieve the envelope. Like a jack-in-the-box, he came back up and lifted the body from under the arms and around the chest. For someone slight of build he was deceptively strong. Liquida carried the body up the few steps to the second floor. Down the corridor a short distance he found Room 204.

He leaned the body against the wall and held it there with his shoulder as he opened the door with the key. Within seconds he and the lifeless body were inside with the door closed. He tossed the keys and placed the envelope on the chair next to the door.

Now he moved with lightning speed. Liquida lifted the kid in his arms, so as not to leave drag marks, and carried him into the bedroom. He laid him on the bed, then removed his coat, tie, and shoes, opening his shirt collar and rolling up his sleeves.

Liquida then reached into the oversized pockets within his trench coat and started pulling out the paraphernalia. This included a short length of elastic surgical tubing, a box of fresh syringes, a tablespoon properly burned and scoured with a residue of heroin, and a small jar with a charred wick—an alcohol burner. To this he added several cotton balls, all of which had been soaked in a solution of heroin and left to dry.

After impressing a thumb and fingerprint from the victim onto the working end of the spoon and burner, Liquida lit the burner and allowed some of the residue from the hot spoon to permeate up to the lampshade on the nightstand next to the bed. He put the hot spoon on the wooden surface of the nightstand, where it left a burn mark. He arranged everything on the nightstand next to the bed, except for the tubing, which he stretched out under the kid's right forearm, a few inches above the taped syringe that was still embedded in the large vein at the back of the victim's hand. He removed the surgical tape and carefully impressed a single left thumbprint from the victim on the plunger of the hypodermic. Then he ran a few carefully smudged prints with the dead man's fingers down the barrel of the syringe.

Finally Liquida retrieved six small packets of silvery aluminum foil from the pocket of his trench coat. Four of these contained two small chips each of black tar heroin, heavily cut and stepped on, any one of which would be unlikely to cause an overdose. The fifth sealed packet contained two deadly doses of pure heroin. He placed these in the top drawer of the nightstand. Then he unfolded the foil on the sixth packet and left it on the nightstand next to the spoon. It contained one small chip of black tar, almost five hundred milligrams of pure heroin. The second chip from the packet Liquida had processed using the spoon and burner before loading it into the syringe.

When the crime unit processed the scene, they would find an inexperienced recreational user who had gotten a mixed bag of product and overshot his tolerance by not realizing the potency of his purchase.

The job was nearly done. There was only one more item. Liquida grabbed the kid's suit coat from the floor, reached inside, and found Jimmie Snyder's wallet. He opened it and started looking. Sure enough, behind one of the credit cards, he found it, just like the man said. He plucked the business card from the wallet and put it in his pocket.

He was finished, except for one final touch, something special, a personal perk. It was something for himself that the client hadn't asked for but was going to get anyway. It would give Liquida immense pleasure. Time to draw the fly into the web. Fumbling with his gloved fingers, he pulled a small plastic bag from his pocket. Inside was a single business card. He lifted the card from the bag.

Paul Madriani
Attorney at Law
Madriani & Hinds

He slipped it behind the credit card in the kid's wallet. Then he replaced the wallet in the coat pocket and laid the coat at the foot of the bed next to the body.

In less than a minute, Liquida was out the door and down the stairs. He stopped only briefly to remove the duct tape he had put on the overhead closing arm at the front door two days earlier to keep it from locking.

Out on the street he mixed in with a few pedestrians. By the time they reached the corner, the disheveled vagrant in the dirty, dark trench coat had disappeared like a lethal wisp of smoke.

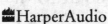